THE WORLD TURNED UPSIDE DOWN

23/5/24

Chin,
To the struggle
which is ours!
Leo

The World Turned Upside Down

LEO ZEILIG

BFP

BOOKS FARM HOUSE & PUBLISHERS

The World Turned Upside Down
Leo Zeilig

First Published in 2021
By Books Farm House & Publishers
Signs & Wonders Shopping Complex
Ekotedo Iyalobe (Opp Central Hotel)
Dugbe, Ibadan
+2348175109802

ISBN: 978 1 5136 8508 3

Typeset in Berkeley Oldstyle by Oxford Publishing Services.

To Ray Bush and Mette Wiggen

'The only great ~~men~~ women among the unfree and the oppressed are those who struggle to destroy the oppressor.'

Walter Rodney (1972)

Prologue

'I'm here to tell you about destruction'

Present Day

EVEN AS A 12-year-old, the King dreamed of wealth.

Charles King came from a middle-class family and was brought up in a red-stone house in the town, semi-detached, set back from the road up a short driveway. As a schoolboy at the state boarding school eight miles away, he would return on the weekend, stand in front of his house, put his hands on either side of his temples so he couldn't see the road or the others houses and pretend that his family lived in a large house, in a field, out of town, owning everything around them.

Thirty-five years later the only people he really understood were other bankers, and the only people he respected were other *richer* bankers.

No one, including his parents, children and ex-wife, were worth anything to him because in the final instance they'd all failed. His ex-wife had always been a leach on his talent and money. The King held his father in special contempt, for never achieving anything in his life except a large house in Bridgewater, and a pension from the high-street bank he'd run. Failure was everywhere in his life – his wife, his children, his siblings, his parents. Most people disgusted him.

* * *

Jogging on the spot, Charles waited for the lift in the carpeted hallway, and then in the five-second descent from the eleventh-floor apartment, he completed ten squats. He ran to his office, three miles away. Running in the roads, which were normally empty at this time of day – pretending he was the sole survivor of a nuclear holocaust that had killed off the rest of his species, leaving only the buildings, and that he had been charged with clearing the city of human vermin and filth, so each person he saw in his morning exercise routine he would secretly target and kill.

Arriving at the Citigroup Centre, he showered in his private bathroom adjoining the office, put on his towelling dressing gown, then changed into his suit and made a coffee. Finally, he stood at his window, overlooking the city, from his godlike height he felt the immensity of life. Today, as every morning, he thought, looking out of his thirtieth-floor window from the huge pane of glass, and before he started to work, that he *wanted* what he saw.

King – long before it had been fashionable – conducted most of his day standing, pacing the length of the room, barking orders and making jokes during hands-free calls. Today, he was tidying up a mess for a client from Primebrand, a big client but by no means his biggest. A sweatshop in Bangladesh had collapsed in April 2013 and crushed some workers as they had stitched, sown, and laboured.

'Charles, there were just over 1,100 dead and about 2,500 injured. There is pressure on us, the government are complaining about demonstrations and there are some NGOs and journalists sniffing around. We promised to work out some sort of pay-out arrangement.'

The King bristled. 'I have managed to knock $10m from our last offer,' he bellowed at the jumpy investor. He knew how the banks, companies and financial houses he worked for functioned. In pay-outs to injured parties they were thorough, careful with their cash flow; compensating as little as possible – and it was his job to make this happen. Take care of those few tens of millions, those dollars and cents, that a lesser banker would think too small to deserve his attention, and the real money, the hundreds of millions, and billions, will add up. 'Our liability is not as great as first thought, therefore, the total cost of compensation revised down is now close to $30 million. This is Primebrand's costs.' King paused for this information to take effect. 'We do this under a sourcing company named New Wave Boston so the compensation comes from NWB – Primebrand is clear, clean of any involvement. NWB takes 100 per cent responsibility for directly compensating NWB victims. There can be no further claim, no liability and no fucking mess. I have put this in the paperwork.'

The King enjoyed the investor's stunned silence.

* * *

At the end of the evening, the King jogged back to his apartment. As he approached the building, he slowed and entered the lobby. He felt more breathless than normal, so he took the lift and not the stairs. As he walked slowly along the carpeted corridor to his flat, he removed his T-shirt, kicked off his trainers and hooked them on two fingers. He dropped his clothes in the bedroom and kneed open the door to the bathroom. The shower felt good.

He pulled two towels away from the heated rail; one he threw on the floor and the other he draped over his shoulder. There was a sudden slight change in the temperature of the room, a movement that he couldn't exactly see, but could feel. His heart quickened, powered up again, he tensed, turned slightly, looked around the room – there was nothing.

Then, before he could turn, before he could grasp what was happening, a darkness crossed the room and the lights flickered off – there was a sudden and sharp, hard sensation at the base of his spine and for a moment it was not even a pain; it was like nothing he'd ever felt, yet with instantaneous, sickening clarity, he knew that it was not a sensation that would go away or could be repaired.

Involuntarily his knees folded and before he could crumble completely to the floor, he was gripped from behind, a clothed body held him and took his weight, lowered him, an arm coiled around his neck. For a second, perversely he felt reassured, grateful and wanted to speak.

Charles was held a foot from the floor, there was a rush of sensation, fear like he had never felt, his pulse thumping hard in his mouth, his temples, wrists, under his arms and then that terrible certain unfixable thud in the base of his back – this is where he felt, not an excoriating pain, but a horror, and with it the certainty that life was pulsing out of him.

A voice spoke to him, calm, almost gentle, incongruous, and again his fear dissipated, he was going to be helped.

'Just let go Charles, there is nothing you can do any more. I have waited for this, to meet you. I know you intimately, the work of course, that's the easy bit, though now here, I realise I know who you have really been, what your life has meant, the routines, the runs, the food you eat, the hours you keep – there is much we share. Yet, through it all …' Charles couldn't move, worse he couldn't feel his legs and with each beat of his heart, he felt an inexorable ebbing and with the fear that accompanied the pulse of his blood out of his back, he tried to clench, to fight back, though cradled on the floor he kept jerking, spasming as he tried to regain control.

The voice continued, '… through the months I've been following you, I became overwhelmed by boredom. You see, you bankers, the rich, are only interested in each other. Each of you thinks you're unique, yet you are all identical.'

Charles was now propped up on the towels, a dark pool of blood around his folded legs and a small tablet set-up on the edge of the sink, a short video playing on repeat – badly filmed clips, recorded on a telephone, of rubble and bodies, figures staggering out of a collapsed building, screams, confusion, death. Further slabs of concrete falling, twisting on the steel frame, then snapping like string; rising clouds of dust over the people trying to escape.

'You are dead, Charles, and you are just the start. How lucky you are, to be remembered always as the first.'

Charles tried to keep his eyes open, to focus on the images on the small screen, to maintain his grip. Then he felt a foot press down on his chest, comforting at first. He tried desperately to move, as he was flattened onto the floor, his breath cut off; he heard his ribs cracking, forced out by the pressure on his sternum, several of them breaking together so shards of bone burst through the skin. Still, the pressure came, heavier now until he felt the weight press down on his heart.

PART 1

'You know you got to clean your brain'

1

Present Day

THE BEACH was a slum. The sand was knotted with rubbish – plastic bottles, bags, clothes, glass, which had been discarded, swallowed by the sea and then regurgitated and finally ploughed into the beach, like a crop. The effect was beautiful and grotesque. Rivulets of sewage ran down the cliffs, over the dunes and into the water. On these dunes, which fell dramatically to the shore, there were shacks – not the sturdy, patiently built wood-boarded lean-tos I had seen in South Africa, but metre-high cardboard huts, some cut into the sand, held together by string, weighed down by stones.

As I started to walk along the beach, children zigzagged in front of me. I passed a torn parasol, a woman selling plastic half-litre bags of water, then on the stretch of sand a group of women, one in a long, tight dress with a fringe of lace and tassels, sat on a white horse, the animal's shoulders, hips, back protruding. The group walked slowly along the shore. They were laughing, the woman on the animal smiled at me, the horse was being led by a hollow-eyed man, and running in front of them was a photographer.

The beach was beggared – human misery thrown at its mercy. The planet's unwanted, the continent's human jetsam. Above the beach, not far from this scene, were shacks dug into the cliff wall, and several huge gated houses. Perimeter fences three metres high – satellite dishes, the blue water of the swimming pool reflected on the white walls of the building. Only the sweet, rancid odour of the beach, when the wind changed direction, a reminder to the rich of the poor dying on their threshold.

* * *

I was in Accra, Ghana, for a conference, a talk, part of my global tour. I knew the country, hated its poverty, its capital's class of NGO liberals who adored the heat, the cafés, food and nightlife. I had spoken the night before, answered questions from the audience, raged – as I do – and then argued with the organisers, the righteous Lords and Ladies of Poverty who had invited me to speak.

'If you think I am going to address any member of the government then you are deluded, and I couldn't give a damn if they are recently elected and promise a fresh start – they are charlatans, who offer us nothing. So, to make it absolutely clear, I do not speak to politicians, ambassadors, business groups, NGO officials, entrepreneurs – unless you mean the unemployed, which seems to be the term for the jobless in Ghana – or wannabe business leaders, politicians, diplomats or United Nations disciples. None of the above. Understand? Each of these groups, in its unique and special way, has cast this landmass to hell, and its people into the grave. To summarise, I do not speak to the advocates of genocide, mass murderers and their hangers on ...' And here I stuttered, partly for effect – I was irritated, the day had been long, the talks useless, and I was standing in the lobby of a large hotel, a huge marble hall, a sweep of polished brass, the walls hung with animal heads, the air soundlessly conditioned, so, in the glorious heat, I was actually damn cold – '... and I ne-ne-never do what I am told. I am speaking to students at the university tomorrow on revolution and counter-revolution in Africa and you are welcome to attend.'

So, it had not even been a row, just a statement of facts and with my little speech done, I pulled the cotton scarf over my head, looped it around my neck, lifted the hem of my dress and walked away. The morning was for me. I visited the Kwame Nkrumah Mausoleum and memorial park in downtown Accra, a place of decaying preservation, curled photos in exhibition rooms, rusted fountains and a North Korean statute of Kwame, also known as Osagyefo, or the Redeemer, striding confidently forward – if only the poor man knew what had come of his legacy, he would drop to his knees and wipe that serene Stalinist calm from his face, and weep.

Afterwards, I wandered between the houses and shacks of the poor, a labyrinth of desperation, until I came to the beach, avoiding the catcalls, and comments, 'You American woman?' 'What you do here lady? This no place for you.'

The human mayhem did not immediately fill me with rage, the emotion I needed to get anything done, no, it was something else. Looking around me a group of children ran into the water, kicking at the waves. I felt despair.

Where was the agency to change this? Who or what was the force that could take these circumstances and turn them around?

I stopped beside the woman sheltering under the parasol and bought a sachet of water, bit it open and tipped my head back, squeezing the water into my mouth.

I shook away the despair, *that* was too easy. I thought of my colleagues, the whole pack of academics, cynics, commentators, the press, who when confronted with human misery would utter, like the BBC correspondent who had questioned me the previous night, 'Bianca, the number of times I have heard the woes of African youth. You know the Hail-Mary-routine, "We are wasted – thrown away in our prime. A generation lost." In one form or another, Bianca, the poor will always be here, misery has always been part of human existence.'

I kicked away a bottle, it spun along the sand, turning wildly. I felt the old rage return again. 'No, they won't,' I said to myself aloud. In a year of organisation, with the right action, this could all be changed – the whole world turned upside down.

How had I allowed myself to despair, even for a moment?

2

Present Day

THE STEEPLY raked horse-shoe lecture theatre was a new extension of the university – paid for and inaugurated by a now-dead Saudi dictator over whom the university had fawned while securing master's and PhD degrees for his children. The small, balding vice-chancellor was officially my boss, a man who, one to one, was awkward and charmless, but, before an audience or when speaking to young women, would flicker into life with sparkling stories and anecdotes. He dined donors, sponsors, executives of FTSE 100 companies and gave to them the flattery and attention they required, feigned interest in their lives, complimented their intelligence and observations – 'What an acute and insightful point you make', 'How astute your opinions. … I wish we had such acumen in our departments …' So, Andrew Ashley, whom I despised, was perfectly suited to the new politics of the modern university – a place of business, funding bids, efficiencies. Andrew possessed the most craven desires, the worst human characteristics, and had therefore been promoted to the heights of the University of London.

For most of his career, Ashley had been an inept colleague, devoid of principles, yet able to access funds from individuals and agencies, build connections, grow MA programmes, fund projects and endlessly, restlessly expand – like the rest of society he thrived on ceaseless agitation. The neoliberal university bloomed a thousand flowers, pushing bloodless entrepreneurs out of the dead earth.

The new lecture theatre was officially named the Euphrates Gallery, but I had informally labelled it Deera Square – the place in Riyadh where the Saudi royal family carried out public executions. I had the unusual honour of being allowed to give all my classes there, an honour that Andrew Ashley had personally conferred on me.

With his smeared, thinning hair, and short, stubby legs, Ashley had barged into my office – knocking and entering in a single action, as part of his daily rounds of visits, like a nineteenth-century factory owner inspecting his machines in a Manchester workshop. Without looking up, my head in my books, my back to the door, facing the window, I shouted, 'Get out of my office, whoever you are, close the door and either go away or knock and wait.'

Ashley tried to interrupt me with a guffaw, a proprietorial clearing of his throat, but I cut him off, 'I recognise those noises,' I said remaining in place, not looking up from the book, 'So in the interest of academic and human impartiality, get out and try again.'

The logic of Ashley's university existence forced him to honour my existence, for I had a power, he knew, far greater than his own. So he left the room and delivered the news in an email – I could have 'Deera Square' whenever I taught, under any circumstances, for any public event I wanted to organise.

Despite this minor humiliation, Ashley had a capacity for regeneration that could only be fully explained by stupidity.

* * *

I arrived late, took large strides down the wide steps – the room was packed, my students a quarter of the number; the others postgraduates auditing the course, colleagues and members of the public who always came along for the ride. The windowless room, lit by a hundred sunken spotlights, heartened me, I could pretend they were buried, the lecture taking place in a bunker under a radioactive horror show on the surface of the planet.

I threw my notes on the table, a bundle of photocopies, blinked, rubbed my eyes with the first finger and thumb of my right hand, my glasses pushed into my hair, swallowed, wet my lips and spoke, 'We're looking at *Germinal* today ...'

Surprising the listeners, never entirely predictable, my topics for my Euphrates lectures, jumped around, depending on my current mood, or what I had recently read. In the university's advertising, in the social media posts sent out by a team of young staff, they now wrote, simply, laconically, *Bianca Ndour Speaks!* The licence to speak whenever I wanted to in the university's new prized underground bunker extended to an agreement that I could speak on *whatever* I wanted – each of my utterances, observations, political declarations and ruminations was recklessly encouraged.

'Zola gets us, messes with us, draws us in and refuses to give us the hit we want. He constantly deviates from his own inclinations, from naturalism, in his attempt to undermine the values of capitalist society. He wants conflict, contradiction, not catharsis or resolution.' I did all of this, the extolling, the lecture, without notes, without even a clear idea of what exactly I was going to do. 'Is the solution some great strike, a collective reckoning – but remember this has just failed, the strike failed, the hoped-for dawn of the new world has not come to be – or is there something else he wants? A new dawn that can only come through destruction, and death, a kind of mayhem, remember the last words.'

When I stopped, I'd been speaking for ten minutes – a typical stream of thoughts without pause, stabbing my finger, asking questions of the text, throwing rhetorical bombshells into the crowd, repeating salient lines, my own and Zola's. This process of exposition – though common across the world of literary studies – was delivered with such force, each point an argument, building to a final inevitable crescendo. Each statement a climax, each climax a beginning.

The gallery was silent. I was leaning on the table – I reached for my backpack, unzipped it, pulled out a flask and slowly, methodically, as if I were doing this alone, not in front of 350 people, poured the black coffee into the lid and then brought the steaming cup to my mouth, let my glasses slip back on my nose and through the steam, streaking my vision, I looked at the audience. I put the cup down and started again.

'Now, I want to talk about something else.' I picked up a sheet from the pile of photocopies and read, 'City banker murdered in his apartment. A respected city banker was found dead in the bathroom of his apartment in what investigators are arguing was a targeted assassination. The police are trying to establish a motivation for the murder of a successful banker. The prime minister offered his condolences to the family of Charles King, "It was a brutal attack on an important and highly respected banker … our hearts go out to his family. We don't yet know the exact circumstances, but it's a tragedy and one that we are determined to get to the bottom of." Charles King was a leading city banker, and had negotiated financing and mergers with some of the world's largest companies, including several in South East Asia and China. He was linked to the large Irish retailer Primebrand and to its outlets and factories in China, Vietnam and Bangladesh. Chris Bollard, former communications director of Primebrand, said, "The company was on its knees when Charles stepped in. There was the whole *major high-street store involved in factory fire* issue, and the ILO investigation scandal, in which Primebrand was alleged to have been directly involved. … I am not sure many people thought the company could have lasted two months and now, due to him, it remains one of the best performing companies on the FTSE 100."'

After the passage, I turned slightly to my right, flicked a switch on a console embedded in the table and the lights in the ceiling dimmed and the screen behind me lit up. My voice echoed through the theatre: 'The faint of heart and mind can leave.' There was a twitter in the room, a nervous collective shuffle. Reiterating, I spoke more adamantly, 'Friends, this is not a joke – a dramatic statement. What I am going to show you is not nice.' The room was silent again. No one left. 'On being convicted in 1918, the American socialist Eugene Debs stated that, "if there are still vast numbers of our people who are the victims of poverty and whose lives are an unceasing struggle all the way from youth to old age, until at last death comes to their rescue …, it is not the fault of the Almighty …" While there is such suffering, we too must be in it, while there is injustice, we must battle against it, and while there is poverty, we must destroy the wealth that creates it. Do we not have a duty to see suffering, and not to hide and then to extrapolate? To make sense of it, to find the pattern? Workers experience the sweatshop, the rhythm of the production line but not capitalist globalisation. You experience private debt and student loans, but not the British state.' There was a titter of acknowledgment: I paused briefly, then I reached deeper in.

'Tenants shiver in the cold, because of broken boilers but not the banking and property system. We experience individual heartbreak, abuse, failed relationships but not the 1 per cent or the media barons who turn our desires into a competition fought out in our love affairs. We experience life as a private grief, not the operations of an economic organization. There are immediate questions and general ones. To see in the immediate every day, the great issues, the meaning – the enormity – we need thinkers and strategists. Those who can wrench from waiting rooms, the broken heating system, the failed relationships, or a collapsed factory outlet in the Global South, the *entire* system of exploitation and oppression.'

I moved around in the semi-darkness as I spoke, I came up to my students sitting behind the first lines of tables at the front of the gallery and placed my hands on my hips.

As I spoke, images flashed up on the screen behind me, jerking, stuttering footage, shot on mobile phones. The members of the audience peered, twisted their heads, struggled to comprehend, to make sense of what they saw – then, almost simultaneously, there was a gasp as it became clear what they were watching. Bloodied people emerging from broken concrete, the camera panning the ground, a severed leg, a torso with no head, a child coated in white dust, being held by a man who was silently screaming, her eyes open, moist, her legs crushed, her life bleeding out.

* * *

When I was done, and the lights came on again, I took questions. Ordering those interlopers, lecturers and members of the public, to wait their turn and let my students speak first. There was always this active 'human contraband' of non-academics trafficked into my lectures – journalists who needed to fill copy, or Bloomsbury residents who wanted gossip. There was also a hardcore of real fans, who hung on my every word, followed each lecture, attended tours and listened ardently to all my proclamations.

A student caught my eye – broad, short blonde hair, muscular, he wore a white T-shirt, black chinos and brogues that he kicked off whenever he sat down and an expensive watch hung loosely on his wrist. Despite myself, I liked Rory, his nonchalance, his confidence; somehow he would always pretend he wasn't listening. Slouched in the middle of the third row, he raised his hand, and I nodded for him to speak.

'Bianca, if I'm right, you started with *Germinal* and French anarchism in the nineteenth century and finished with Bangladesh. What links them?' Rory straightened himself, put his elbows on the table in front of him, 'How do *you* generalise? How do we get from the specific to the general? Are you not just making a case for a *general* revolution?' There was a titter in the audience, 'Using these lectures to make a faintly disguised political point?' Now there was laughter.

I was sitting on the table, my notes around me, smiling, 'There is never anything disguised about my political points ... you must always wear your politics on your sleeve.' Half of the room clapped. 'But you are wrong about my, my proselytising, Rory.' I knew the names of all my students – I'd always had this capacity to recall the full name of each student from its first appearance on the class list. Rory Abbott-Barker. Every childhood friend, acquaintance, colleague, student, I'd ever met, from every period in my life. 'Maybe the point I am making is the opposite' – I surveyed the lecture room, scanned the rows, found the face I was looking for – 'Is that every movement, each revolution, has ended in disappointment, despair and cynicism. If you allow me,' I shifted my position on the desk, 'we overthrew communist dictatorship and won neoliberalism – structural reforms, unemployment and poverty. We ended apartheid and got Jacob Zuma and the murderer Ramaphosa. We overturned Hosni Mubarak in Egypt, Blaise Compaoré in Burkina Faso, and we were repaid by counter-revolution.'

I took the last mouthful of my coffee, put the lid down, licked my lips, continued. 'We' – I opened my arms, embraced the room – 'declared ourselves the 99 per cent, yet,' I levered myself off the table, 'The 1 per cent continue to enrich themselves. Despite our struggles, our endless waves of protest and revolutions … they break on the same sandbank. The 1 per cent are endlessly renewed and the planet destroyed. Our struggles *and* the elite endure – an epoch of glorious combat and shameful failure. And each time the power of the rich grows, lives are destroyed and ruin beckons. Remember how we thought the world would change after the pandemic?'

There was nodding and murmurs from the audience.

About thirty minutes later I felt suddenly overcome with exhaustion. I took a step back and, with a hand behind me, groped for the table muttering, almost to myself, 'A cruel game that continues without end.'

My students didn't know what to do, and sat dumbly, perfectly still. A moment later slightly revived, irritated with myself, I barked, 'Okay, I'm done.' I turned my back to the room and started to clear away my papers.

3

Present Day

IT WAS MACABRE, but I'd long given up fighting against myself – trying endlessly somehow to be less who I was. I realised that this was futile, despite the efforts of an industry promoting a new dawn of personalised inner transformation, with the shimmering, impossible promise of becoming complete or entirely in the moment. I, too, had cashed in on this craze – this contemporary drive of being – and written a book that spoke of regeneration and rebirth.

But today I see all efforts at growth and reconstruction as flawed. Instead, I stand in judgement – I do not let the moment pass, to see injustice and misery all around me, note it, acknowledge it as a mere consequence of the mind's incessant chatter, and then release and let go.

My script is now pure political economy – radical and uncompromising. Capitalism and specifically the capitalist class, the 1 per cent, has to be destroyed. No remnant of it can continue to exist, for wealth survives, grows and is passed on, from generation to generation, family to family – from crisis to crisis. Wealth, and the elite that controls it, has to be destroyed, wiped off the face of the earth – in a word, obliterated.

Individual human beings are immutable, they cannot be changed – it is only in the realm of politics and economics that there can be transformation. Quantity to quality. From acorn to oak tree.

* * *

There is a kind of mourning, even in the height of the summer – the retreat of the day, a hesitant slow death on the trees visible in late August. Then the days shorten in large strides until we have only a few hours of daylight between dawn and dusk. The canopy of light draped over the two poles of the day is so brief that by December we barely glimpse the sun, but in January there is a slow retreat of the night.

Things end, things begin again but it's how they begin that matters – seasons change in a cycle yet a revolution needs to make a decisive break, otherwise it too will be no more than the recycling of a new elite.

I stepped out of the flat into the darkness for my run and looked up. 'How much longer can I do this for?' I felt the darkness of the winter like an injustice.

As I started to run, I found the groove of my thoughts again – even the greatest rebellions, if they don't break decisively with capitalism, will lead to a new enslavement. The rationale of private ownership will expand and a new elite will form.

* * *

Nina was playing loudly in my headphones as I hit the tarmac – the roads were drying slowly after the night rain, the city looked abandoned, only a few dark shadows shuffling, heads bowed, to bus stops, looking up at the sky, wanting not to exist. I needed to say something to them, to eliminate the street and to make a declaration. To tell them the lie, all of them – the women *and* men – that there was a solution to their hardship. Instead I ran. I let my mind wander, let it feast on its distractions uninterrupted. I did not need to think about the route. I knew the city.

As I ran Nina sang to me, *And now we got a revolution, Cause I see the face of things to come*. This was the song that marked her transition, when she turned towards the movement and became political. When she started her career, she had no solution to the black historical problem – though she knew injustice. Between verses in the song, as I ran, I thought about Nina; her singing gave her a certain freedom. In 1958 Nina moved to New York and drove a Thunderbird and would sit over a drink after her set.

I pushed myself hard, ran faster, but still couldn't feel anything – no effort, no wear on my muscles. I moved to the road and hit the puddles, sending a spray of water up my legs.

Those evenings decades ago gave the singer a taste of human freedom – erased the pain she felt. Nina's words were strident again in my head: *All I want is equality, For my sister my brother my people and me*. She could not stop the violence around her, but the joy of singing opened a space of ecstasy. What did she have except these little pleasures, these small freedoms, enough to break open the night, to allow the light to enter?

I passed more figures as I ran, silent, some in pairs, ghosts making their way slowly in the darkness.

Nina's small freedoms created a world where her blackness, her being, ran deep in her veins, and would not be questioned. Human for a moment.

Desperately, even with the sweat of the run being worked up on me, I wanted the night to end, to embrace the people around me.

Black joy is temporary, I thought. As Nina sang her last words, *You don't have to live next to me. Just give me my equality*. After 1964 she could not hide any more from the violence and struggle that overshadowed her small freedoms.

Something gave, something broke.

4

August 2006

I SAW KAARINA for the first time in years outside a lecture theatre in 2004, during one of the talks I gave on my book *The Kill List* (a history of the targeted killings by the United States, since 1960, and my first non-fiction title since *The Elation of Being*) – it was a sunny day in August, only a month after the end of the global lockdown due to the virus.

I had bought two large plastic bags filled with waste paper into the lecture to illustrate the recent scandal that involved binbags filled with $100 million used by the American occupying forces in Iraq to bribe officials, paid contractors, hit squads and thugs to carry out the real dirty work of the twenty-first century. Throughout the lecture, I lifted the bags – 'You see,' I would almost shout, 'it's no more complicated or sophisticated than this,' waving the raised bags, 'graft, corruption, paid-off Iraqi civil servants, local businessmen, killers, jihadis and whole national industries paid in cash from plastic binbags flown into Baghdad on US military aircraft.' I used such stunts, this plastic-bag 'realia', to press home a point, to hammer a lesson into the recalcitrant human brain – to explain the unreformed, unreformable reality of capitalism. 'Do you get it' I remember almost screaming, impatient, frustrated, 'It's as simple as this.' The bags raised before the audience.

The lecture had been organised by Yusuf Habib, a tall 55-year-old friend, who was now a mover in academic circles in South Africa. He was many things this Yusuf, but I had always found him attractive; dark, thick black hair, which he would periodically flick from one side of his face to another. He was irrepressible, his political sense impressive; he had been a full-time militant in the 1970s and 1980s, then ran the Social

Thought Institute to create militant researchers from the raw material of graduate students.

The night before Yusuf had uncorked too many bottles of wine, the back door to his house open, the darkness of his suburban house heavy. In a moment of relaxation, straining briefly with the corkscrew, calling to his partner, Nadine, for another glass: 'I have just recruited this excellent researcher. It was hard. Not a popular decision. She is Indian and from Cape Town, did her MA in New York. She's bright.'

'Did you not have any black candidates?' I asked.

'Yes, Mosa, you know her. You taught her politics a few years ago.'

'But she was no good?' I said.

Yusuf was expansive, delighting in the story, enjoying the end of the evening – recounting this minor triumph. Nadine came in and put down a box of chocolates on the table, a couple of glasses, she had heard the story, 'I'm going to bed. Let our guest sleep Yusuf.'

'I will when I've finished.'

I knew Nadine and liked her. I winked, smiled and blew a kiss.

These two Londoners – whom I had known as activists in Hackney years before, sharing meals and organising campaigns in their modest terrace house, were now living in a large Johannesburg villa, which was light, bright and grand. I enjoyed the strangeness of the evening, and although I had been there many times before, the peculiarity never left me, the sense I had that none of us really belonged.

Yusuf refilled our glasses, too quickly so the wine sloshed and splashed on the tablecloth. He went to the door, locked the grill, leaving the door open.

'So, this woman, Kaarina – very beautiful and gay.' Yusuf paused, stared hard at me – not knowing I already knew her. He winked. 'She was brilliant. Mosa was no match, no competition. Even colleagues who also interviewed her and gave her a hard time had to agree. I tell you, Bianca, she is bright, sharp – she reminds me of you.'

The next day, before I spoke, I was introduced to a group of students and young researchers in the concrete square at the centre of the university, outside the lecture hall where I was due to speak, jackets and conference bags hung on shoulders, holding coffee cups and canned drinks; we stood in a loose semicircle – shielding our eyes from the sun. I identified Kaarina immediately, her smile sweet, broad, natural as I remembered; she seemed younger than she could be, too young even for Yusuf to have made such claims, for him to have winked at me the night before.

As I spoke, I looked at Kaarina and smiled.

Two days later, at the launch of the South African edition of the book, we kissed. The band, from Kinshasa, had been assembled for the launch, and after my talk, and the intervention of a Congolese colleague who argued I had been too sympathetic to Patrice Lumumba, Ben Barka and Amílcar Cabral, and too critical of American democracy – they played late into the night. Eighty people cramped into this downtown book shop.

I took Kaarina by the arm and led her outside and behind the bookshop we kissed – it had been years.

5

1979 – Port Harcourt, Nigeria

AFRICA HAD only been independent a few years and already our father was living the good life with us in tow. He was a Scottish man and a petroleum engineer – ruthless, generous, kind and cruel. My thoughts from that time still come to me in pidgin, the language I learnt with my sister: '*You no fit understand am, him no day straight*.' Our mother was Wolof from Senegal, beautiful and dead, we never knew her except from the painting of her that he placed in his office – wherever this was, it hung above his desk, a large gaudily framed multi-coloured painting of a woman in a boubou of turquoise, that hung to her ankles, her hair in braids, coiled on her head. He placed her in his office in the large house in which we lived for seven years in the Shell compound in Port Harcourt. Our dead mother was the queen, the head of state, the woman we were allowed to stare at in his office, but when we asked him about her, his response was stilted, brief, or worse he would not answer at all. '*Baba no go answer you at all*.'

Maïmouna and I were sitting on the floor of his room – where we were permitted to be, if we promised to be quiet. Maïmouna would be bent over a drawing pad, sketching faces of her friends or of us, and I would be playing myself at chess – hitting the switch at the top of the chess clock after each move. Silent – '*becous we no wan try Baba*.' The phone would ring and Howard – we called him father or Howard, not dad or anything else – would answer and then bark instructions at a subordinate, or pace up and down the large office, explaining in a strained impatient tone, some basic fact about oil extraction, pipeline pressures and the equations that were, 'So bloody obvious man, take your bloody calculator and your tape measure and get out on the fucking rig man?' Shouting with authority – in his deep musical voice – we would look up from our activities on the floor, and stare at him, not in shame at his anger, but pride that he was our father and was clear about everything; knew everything – '*him bi sabi sabi*.'

'These people are such damn fools … "*them bi mumu!*",' he said slamming the phone down, looking down at us, and we knew he didn't mean black people, Africans – he was many things, but not racist. His 'damn fools' referred to everyone, all human beings, everyone with whom he was forced to drink on the weekend at one of the compound's two bars, or the fools higher up the hierarchy – in London, or in New York, or Lagos.

If we were daring one of us would say, 'What has happened father?'

And if he was feeling voluble, open, expansive he might respond – very technically – that some fool had broken a basic, fundamental protocol on drilling and enter into a long description, grabbing a large sheet of paper from his desk, and sit on the floor with us, clearing books and papers, to explain:

'During oil drilling girls, we have to make sure the pipes and wells are closed. If the oil – which you have to understand is not just oil, but contains other fluids and chemicals that we have added at a later stage – is released into the environment, it can cause massive fucking groundwater contamination – *na wahala bi dat ooh!*'

Here I remember him drawing a drill, the sea, the jagged south Nigerian coastline, of which we only had the slightest sense, and then dotted around the coast and a little inland, he drew palms with a web of twisted rivers and creeks to indicate the complexity of the delta.

'Right, you see,' he said, looking down at us eagerly, with such pleading we could do nothing but nod our uncomprehending heads, desperate to keep him talking, and to make sure he would stay with us on the floor – his attention ours, his presence with us. '*We no jus get wetin him dey talk – but we dey enjoy di koko like dat*.'

'So, most companies, including the fools your father works for, have strict controls in place to prevent releases, leaks. If these fluids leak or if we have contact with them, it can cause major issues to anyone exposed.'

If he thought our attention was flagging, or if something needed to be said, he would state categorically – graphically – to fix an idea in our heads. Scar us with a verbal trauma, that we could not erase. 'So, these fools, these idiots, if they do not take care, and there is a leak and people are exposed to drilling fluids it can lead to nausea, sickness …,' looking at each of us in turn, from face to face, 'Inflammation of the respiratory system, and even cancer.' *'Dat tin dey cos plenty gbege.'*

Involuntarily one of us, in those days I was never entirely sure who said what – our thoughts and instincts finely tuned – said, 'You mean die, like mummy died'. *'You wan pkeme like our mama abi?'*

This changed the atmosphere of the entire carpet party, our little communion was over, and the effect was visible on his face – like a master of mime, his countenance changed in an instant. The mask of his smile slipped and his face coloured, the muscles tightened.

'Get your mess out of my office and pick up all those pieces …' as he stood, he knocked over my chess clock, hit the side of the board with his foot sending the pieces tumbling, rolling over the floor onto the hard tiles. I rushed to pick them up, pulling up my blouse, dropping them quickly into the cloth hammock, Maïmouna did the same with her papers, and pens.

As we stumbled to the door, Maïmouna already crying, we heard him rage behind us, his voice coming from the back of the office, the sounds of the large sheets of paper where he had drawn our entire world being torn – before the door slammed he shouted, 'Your mother did not die from a bloody oil leak, or from being soaked with hydrocarbons, you damn fools – she died' he shouted, 'giving birth to you two in bloody Dakar.'

* * *

Nothing really stops children from loving their parents – no matter the cruelty. There is no rule: no three strikes and you are out. Maïmouna and I loved him and needed him. Invariably in the evening, after we had put ourselves to bed, or been put to bed by Fawari, he would come in and read to us, or tell us a story of his recent tour of the off-shore rigs, or in-land to the pipe lines, and there would be a character sketch – a story of a man he had met somewhere near Bonny Island who could carry a single segment of piping and place it better than any 'damn fool' machine, or digger, or the family who were found sleeping inside an abandoned outdoor store of equipment, beds made-up inside the 'bloody pipes'. '*Na for inside pipe dem dey sleep.*'

We preferred when he spoke of his own childhood, growing up in Thurso – a godforsaken place in the north of Scotland, windswept so even trees couldn't grow, and life was lived under a low canopy of cloud, where you never felt the heat of the sun – every day, every month, each 'damn season' a cold, dark, wet misery. The dogs he had kept as a child – most of them semi wild – the boarding school in Edinburgh where he went at the age of seven, and the 'freezing outdoor swims' he took in summer – nothing to us was more exotic. We loved the stories of our grandfather who would hit the elbows of his children with a serving spoon at the dinner table if they dared to rest them on the table.

Everything we got we took, and always wanted more. '*We no dey tire to lisin to Baba tori.*'

6

Present Day

NINA MOVED to Liberia in 1974. She was 41 when she arrived at Robertsfield International Airport, her daughter 12 years old. Leaving America, '*Oh, but this whole country is full of lies, you're all gonna die and die like flies*,' she sang. The black revolution a dream, replaced by arrests, murder – and disco. Then the collapse came, her breakdowns; she lost her daughter and spent years playing $200-a-week gigs in down-and-out clubs in Paris. Unknown.

Life is sand in our hands even while we are still alive – even before death comes. Our lives a long, slow dying. That we resist.

The racists and the lynch mobs killed her. Grasping this giddy, impossible paradox – life and death in everything we do – is the principle challenge we face. So Nina played these dives. Year after year, drinking, squalid, lost. A living death.

I know Paris and France. Twenty years after she lived there, I learnt its misery. The five hours at the piano, tearing into the songs, slurring, missing whole lines, notes, dreaming of the night and sleep, and a final end to all this. Yet there was still something in her eyes – such power in them, something furious and wild. A kind of spell when she sang, half delirious, drunk on her misery.

There is a street where Nina played called Rue Léon, the buildings squeezed together, the façades broken, stores with imported West African goods, black men serving customers, patting themselves warm in the winter, working ten hours a day, earning €20 a shift. An eye on the road for the police raids – since they are without papers, they are hunted. *En France ils chassent les immigrés comme des bêtes.*

What has it done to us to be hunted for so long, for five centuries? Paris is a warren for the hunting of black skins, and it was in this street that Nina played the *Olympia*. Tips thrown into a hat, her pan-African fire driven out of her by the bouts of mania and depression. There was a constant conversational hum over her voice from the venue's customers, whom she could no longer order to sit, listen, be quiet. Pay attention, give way – 'Listen to me sister. I am singing.'

'*My skin is brown, my manner is tough. I'll kill the first mother I see. My life has been rough.*'

Nina understood that the only purpose in life was to rage against suffering – we are nothing in this life if we are slaves to the cause of injustice and suffering. She knew that if there is no struggle to the death there is no change. Power relinquishes nothing without violence. Nina knew that if we are ever to find freedom from suffering, we would have to pay for it. We will pay for our freedom with sacrifice and pain, and with our lives and the lives of others.

Without rage we are nothing – we do not preserve the dead in books, or demonstrations, or win justice in poetry, or epic storytelling, or find peace in *being* and the *power of now*. The past must be seized, learnt from, gathered into our hands and used now to refigure the future.

Justice must be taken, extracted from the flesh and blood of present.

7

24 October 2013

IN 2013 I WAS still recovering from losing Kaarina. Gradually as the months passed, I even allowed myself to remember her with fondness. The memory of her touch and her smell no longer tormented me – most of the time.

Lydia encroached slowly on me – but not because she had a particular charm of her own; she simply filled the space I allowed her. Initially, for the first time in months, it was one night a week, then two, three nights and now we eat together in the day and frequently take lunch together in my office.

There is much still to say about Lydia, her peculiarities and beauty, the inevitable seeping in of each other's concerns, the slow shuffling of our separate feelings and lives into a single pack. She still feels to me as she did in the first weeks – like a headwind, the smell of sea air, salt in the morning, the sounds of seagulls.

I had immediately noticed Lydia Yabara in my Friday seminar on Literature and Revolution. She was unlike the other students – neither a part-teenager, nor a sloughing twenty-year old, Lydia was already 29 and spoke clearly and confidently, sitting up straight in class so I immediately noticed her. She dressed unusually, never in jeans, always ironed trousers, or a skirt. Her father was from Guyana, and her mother the UK. The mother now lived in West London with Lydia's younger brothers and sister. She had smooth brown skin, and her hair was glossy and black, and she wore plain shirts with the top buttons undone, so her deep cleavage was visible.

Lydia caught my attention in the first class, and though I knew I wanted her I held off until the party I threw for the students at the end of the year. Lydia was more earnest than the others, never unkempt or casual, always serious and sober. For years she'd worked as a legal secretary, living with lovers, at home, saving money to study and then attending my free lecture series and reading my books. There was something unsettled about her, though she was older than the other students; she never knew exactly what she was worth.

Still, Lydia was a kind of homecoming, to everything that was important to me – politics, class politics and my short lifetime's ambition to take on injustice. I was reading again and I had managed to push away my emails, the internet, the irritation – the huff and puff of the web, and opened my computer to write each day, then take a break to read the papers, the Financial Times, the New York Times, the Guardian, and after a flurry of correspondence I would spend a couple of hours training.

The old anger – the passion – was making a comeback and it felt good. You see everything in life drives us to compromise, obscures clear and coherent thoughts. Plans, action and hope are smeared along the road of routine – misshapen, unrecognisable. Finally, I was finding my way back.

8

28 November 2013

I WAS PRACTISING my ideas on Lydia, who was sitting up in bed, passive, bemused. 'If we are the children of the great wave of twenty-first-century revolution, in North Africa and the Middle East, and these sites of revolution, like Moscow and Petrograd in 1905, are the anvil on which the century will be made, then the signs are emphatically ambiguous. The concrete actuality of our lives is the failure of this first wave of twenty-first-century revolution.'

I was lying next to Lydia extolling to her on the theory of permanent revolution, the paradox confronting the left. I jump out of bed, and almost shout: 'The best chance we had was 1917, the defeat in the 1920s is still with us – do you see Lydia? Everything else that was done was done in our name.'

She watches the show, her head sunk back into the pillow frowning, 'You're crazy – you are having one of your turns.'

I knew I was showing off, but I couldn't help it. 'The curve of revolution rose after 1905, but today defeat begets defeat. Yet from the ashes of defeat in 1905, in 1906, 1907, there was ascendancy – the road to socialism soared and though practical efforts temporarily failed revolutionary theory was triumphant. Occasionally, theory trumps practice. Let me explain.'

At this point I was preaching, leaping around. Lydia had her hands over her face, laughing.

I continue to dance, flinging my arms and ideas into the room. 'The point, the point …,' I said, aware of my power, 'Is that one hundred years ago defeat existed on a battlefield of rising hope in socialism, revolution and alternatives – of course in the streets and factories it was a question of bodies and the balance of forces, but today …' The more elusive Lydia's attention –

uninterested as she seemed in the subtlety of my thought – the more determined I became to seize her. To wrestle her attention to the ground.

'I want you, B,' she repeats.

I ignored her and dodged her grasping hands and hopped and bounced beside the bed. 'And now defeat, the defeat of our year of fire and ash, our 1905, in 2011, leads not to resurgence – the réjouissance of socialism – but to the complete opposite, namely Islamism, catabolic ideas, new dictatorships, permanent retreat and reaction. Where we stood bold and socialist in 1905, even bloodied and defeated in 1906, and worse in 1914, this was temporary. In 2011 our defeat gives birth to catastrophe. What I am saying Lydia …' I lowered my voice, leant closer to her, fixed her eyes, tried to dig out her arm from the blanket and find her hand, 'Is that our voices, our words, our ideas have gone.' Her focus was on me, her eyes soft, full of desire, her mouth open. I continued, 'So – and this is the point – the theory, the language of social transformation is not present. Where it was, there is only a void, a blank, and 2011, our 1905, has no riposte. No 1917. No revolutionary actuality – no realisation.' I paused, took a breath.

'Actuality,' Lydia repeated, shuffling up a little in the bed, so the duvet slid down, 'Is exactly what we need – now.' She took my arm, pulled me towards her. I fell on her, hooked my leg over her waist, lowered my mouth to hers and slowly cradled her face in my hands, stroked her neck, felt my head empty.

I was normally happy to give her what she wanted, but tonight I needed to take my fill – it was the spirit that seized me, made me speak like this. I felt possessed by desire and wanted it satisfied. Everything that had happened, the waves of memory, the ripple of the past over my body was fading.

9

1996

OVERALL, I HAVE little use for my past, and rarely think about it. However, I need to explain briefly how I came to write my spiritual book and became the famous teacher and speaker that I am now. The book with which I am least pleased – a sort of manual to life, that I wrote almost twenty years ago, in a six-month depressive episode, is *The Elation of Being*, published in 1996. The book was partly my life story: a woman growing up in Zimbabwe and Senegal then moving to the UK, who plunges into a crisis – life, politics, love – and in the midst of a breakdown finds a way out, a spiritual awakening.

I wrote it quickly, effortlessly. My style was sing-song, colloquial, as if – I believed – I was speaking to my disciples, and that I was their spiritual teacher, bringing them enlightenment, after aeons of ignorance, and darkness. Enlightenment, I wrote, was an end to ignorance, hatred and suffering. I thought I had found it in this urban attic, with the birds outside, and inner peace. This is what I wrote – a bliss of love that I was certain would conquer all fear, all extraneous doubt and questioning.

* * *

When I was visited by friends, who sought me out, I would extol my vision, behave like a preacher and probably seemed insane.

'We are not given unconditional love. If we are dependent on someone, our survival is dependent on them. You are exploring different bits of the ego. I can feel it, just sitting here next to you. I know what you are carrying. You need to cut attachments in order to keep moving, yet the most difficult attachment to cut is the attachment to a child. I have no degree of detachment, like iron filings to a magnet. We must clean, clean. …' Nostrils expanded, my arms open, I would motion, sweeping an imaginary table clean. 'This is the mortgage on my soul, these are your authentic emotions, this is perfect, how much energy is required to keep this down? Like a 78-rpm record being played at 33 or 45 rpm, how can you dance to that?'

Nothing I said really made sense, but this was part of the beautiful mystery – tied up in the puzzle of my words.

I was practising the chapters I had been drafting, reading aloud to my captive audience. My visitor would invariably sit with mouth ajar, transfixed – rarely daring to contradict me, to suggest I was exaggerating, to recommend certain changes to my tone or language. How do you tell a woman who is mad that she is wrong? So I continued uninterrupted.

'Memories are the mortgage on your soul. When you cry,' I waved my hands again, 'you are paying off the debts. The danger is that our emotions are buried so deep underground.' My arms dropped, I bent in the seat, touched the floor, '… underground. So closed down. This is why people throw themselves off bridges with bits of elastic. Closed off and alienated, we have to dance with death to feel alive. You see …' I slowed down, moved slightly towards my visitor and stared for the first time, directly into his eyes, 'what we think is love isn't love but fear.' I paused, held my gaze.

Invariably my words, about fear and love, made my listener – and it would seem, my readers, too – want to cry. I lifted a hand like a healer to my friend's face, her mouth twisted into a mask of Greek Tragedy, both ends curled down, the eyes widened and creased. The power I had was terrifying. My unsuspecting visitor, a friend, a colleague, even my sister, who had simply climbed the stairs to enquire if I needed anything, or wanted to eat, would try to cover up her shame, the tears, the fear, the love – which was it? When she did this I would lean forward, pull the hands from the face, 'When you cry like this you are paying your debts …' I repeated, frenzied, convinced. 'The Chinese say that falling in love is bad for you. Unconditional love for yourself is real love. All forms of love, for your parents, for you lover, for you children, are conditional love. The closest to unconditional love is the love of a child.'

Choking, sniffing, she would weep, breathing in, more tears fell, losing her breath, panting, sucking in the air.

Relentless, I continued to speak. 'We all have shadow sides, but we judge these shadow sides as bad. Then we have good and bad. Duality. You have to get back to unity, you see in our spirit there is only love. Why would we be given the choice of good and bad and then be punished for being bad?'

I believed that I could help readjust the planet to the source, to the core of love and enlightenment and find the words to draw out the vulnerability and fear in my readers and audiences, which would save them. Chase away their thoughts, worries, anxiety – and slowly reconstitute them, bring them back together, humankind's face streaked with tears, its throat dry, parched.

Yet even as I was saying these words, or writing them, somewhere in me an incoherent, silenced voice was asking what would the world I envisaged look like? Each of us in our place, loving ourselves unconditionally, re-establishing unity? But what unity? The unity of injustice, the harmony of exploitation – man at the castle, women by the gate, the child under both and the rich? What of the rich?

Is this what I meant? Balancing the exploitative order, the power of kings, potentates, dictators, politicians – re-establishing the organic unities of unequal power?

I kept going, preaching, writing – probably sick, frenzied.

My readers would describe to me feeling the skin on the back of their necks bristle, rise with understanding as they read the book. *We need to reorder society and ourselves, reset to zero. Zero is the point of absolute equality. The messianic zero of radical equality, where everything starts again and where there are no formal structures.* I suppose in my own way, during those months of depression (more on this below), I was trying to tell a story of redemption and revolution: *We are not bound to our past, to our mistakes; the past can be erased if we start from zero.*

'As soon as we split in two, we are lost. If we make those binary judgements, we are breaking the unity. The ego has a huge vested interest in being both in the past *and* the future, so we gallop through the present hoping that the future will be better. Face it, feel the pain, and move on. A bit of the debt paid down.

'Clean. Zero. Remember this. When you get on the bus, on the plane, say thank you to the runway, the tyres, the tarmac. You are just getting rid of some of the mortgage on your soul.'

Audacious, arrogant, I took on everything, adopted star signs, the Buddha, the New Age, Chinese medicine, old scriptures. I couldn't stop. 'Talking therapy just reinforces the neuro-pathways already there. Let them collapse. "How did I feel when she said that to me?" Deepening the pathology, deepening the problem. Find it, fix it. Get to zero, find inspiration and go with it. We don't miss opportunities that come our way – the binary kills us in the end. Once we get fear on the same vibration as love, we can return home. The heart chakra has the biggest electromagnetic charge. The liver is the ego, the liver is king.'

I became rich from the book and this is not a metaphor for inner wealth, but *external* cash – from sales of the book in the United States, in Canada, across Europe, Africa and Asia. I was on almost continuous tour.

My fans would describe staggering down the road after my lectures, a blur of traffic streaking past them, buses and trucks shuddering and beating the air. I had created a radical sort of uncertainty in their lives. My words echoing in their heads, *the liver is king, fear and love on the same vibration, get to zero*. Asking themselves, *if only I can find the meaning, the truth of her words, so I can understand ... then I can start again, find a way out.*

I now had to expunge from the world this gospel I had spent years preaching. Doing this had been my project for a number of years.

* * *

The book, *The Elation of Being*, was one of those books about redemption, a self-help guide to 'Those of you also finding it hard to see the way through ... who need, like me, to escape from a cycle of depression and regret,' as the book's back cover declared. The photo of me, a small rectangle on the inside back cover, radiated the same message: I was smiling, my glasses off, my eyes ablaze, the lighting ambient, revelatory – the preacher, the saint, the prophet. The core of the book spoke of how I had 'transitioned' from theory to practice, from the weight and habits of negative thought, that these patterns, customs, are encumbrances to life and we need to evacuate, clear out our inner lives, find a path to action and practice. Essentially – I was saying – we need to stop thinking, find peace in the blissful stupidity of the rest of the animal world.

It was nonsense, unequivocal nonsensical airport crap. Such 'encumbrances' were exactly what made us human and yet I had written a best-selling book about how to 'rid yourselves of thought'. And, in writing a 300-page life story with a single egotistical message of personal self-discovery, I had hit on something. I never even thought that the bloody thing would be published; I'd thought that my publisher would despair – would beg me to return to my steady, reliable popular non-fiction. Instead, within weeks of its publication I received reviews that spoke of a 'rare passion', 'unusual insights', 'Bianca Ndour, provides us with a road map out of our modern despair' and most ridiculously, printed on the cover of the second edition – out after three months of the first edition, 'a gospel for our times'.

I began to believe the hype.

Quickly, two other changes took place – within a year. The book sold wildly. I had never made much on any of my previous books, at least not more than a pauper's salary, which subsidised my university lecturing, but now, suddenly, I had money, and a lot of it – a ridiculous amount. The second change was that I was asked to speak about the book at events, guest lectures, conferences, seminars, book fairs, self-help groups, around the world. For years I was permanently on tour, often speaking to huge audiences, and what rapidly became clear to me was that I had begun to accumulate followers. I had created a cult and I was happy to play along, lecturing on 'The Origins of the Wheel of Dharma', 'Introduction to Emotional Intelligence', 'Moods and Serenity'. I was promoted like this: 'Best-selling author of *The Elation of Being*, Bianca Ndour, speaks on the mistaken behaviour in everyday life and the five cylinders of the body.' These events would sell out, wildly, ridiculously – and lecture theatres had to be replaced with public auditoriums, in the cities, and even national sports halls.

Crowds of people around the world would attend my lectures – a hungry, exhausted, vulnerable readership who wanted me to speak about the laws of return, reoccurrence and reincarnation and our multiple lives – to comfort them in the face of our brutally short lives; they wanted me to be a saviour to them. To uncover for them the answer to the riddle of life. In the heady first year after the book was published, I was even asked – after I had spoken in Atlanta – 'What, would you say, Bianca, is the meaning of life?' There was silence in the audience, not a single titter of laughter – I was being asked utterly without irony, as if I possessed *the* meaning, I responded with a few platitudes from the book, and the audience sighed, and a few closest to me put their hands up to their mouths in awe.

The freedom the sales of the book gave me was an unmitigated pleasure. I reversed 400 years of world history to be reunited with my own means of production. In a manner of speaking I was free, and I continued to speak at well-paid seminars in North America, Japan, Australia and at public lectures in private universities and institutions.

Around the world there were photographs in the press and posters advertising my talks, stuck to lampposts in every city where I spoke. My middle-distance stare, wise and humble – the smile full of *sagesse*, my brown skin radiant, my fingers steepled.

Today I still speak five or six times a year across Africa, in East Asia, in North America and South America. These activities – promoting a dreadful book that extolled the worst kind of bourgeois individualism at global self-help groups that were initially set up and sustained by foundations that were formed in my name, and royalties that bankrolled my activities – paid me handsomely, over and over again.

* * *

So, the worst thing I had ever written, which I could hardly bear to read from any more, or look at, had done this to me. In my flat and at the university, I removed the book from my bookshelves. These minor truths and clichés, which had simply emerged from a breakdown, from despair and insanity, of the revelation of mortality at the age of 28, were now the only thing for which I would be known – always.

Though now I was determined that this should not be the case.

PART 2

'The only way that we can stand …'

1

Present Day

I HAD STARTED to read the wacky websites, the huge online content of hate, nonsense and occasional brilliance. I was searching for any clues – if there was an answer, some indication of what was beginning to happen, there would be someone, somewhere, on the web, who was talking about it. The difficulty was finding my way through, parting the tall grass to see the path ahead – separating the wannabes, the supporters and the self-aggrandisers from the real. The core. The kernel. One site came up again and again, at first amusing, ridiculous; but gradually my interest was aroused. I recognised the language – adamant and arresting.

www.firethistime.com

Blogpost #1 – The coming storm

The rule of the rich – the 1 per cent – is coming to an end. This year will mark the systematic destruction of their power, their privilege and wealth. They will not be asked to surrender their wealth, nor will they be politely requested to pay more in taxes. The year 2014 will mark the start of a total, complete, full-scale war against the powerful.

The lives of all of us, the 99 per cent, are a constant curse in this immiserating system, which destroys all joy, rest, pleasure, relaxation and time to get on with life and living. Don't we know it! The soaring percentage of our time, energy, strength, life (in a word, our health!) we spend in extra working, on bureaucratic trivia, hassling, fighting, campaigning, 'pleading' and at times grovelling, just to secure a roof over our heads, warmth, crumbs to eat, a job. These are the circumstances for all of us, North and South.

These are the conditions – let us laugh long and loud – in which we, the downtrodden, trivia-burdened, trifle-encrusted 99 per cent must organise, unite, rise up.

The 1 per cent have destroyed the environment, the only real source of all human wealth. Do not believe their games at climate change conferences – they are nothing more than a murderous game of roulette with our lives. Fossil fuel production is not stopping, it's growing. If we do not put an end to their game and they are allowed to pump as much oil as they want in pursuit of profit, we will face climate Armageddon for the 99 per cent. Yet the 1 per cent will protect themselves from the worst effects of the climate emergency. This is called climate apartheid.

Waiting for the rich and powerful – and their politicians and ambassadors – to agree on climate protocols and agreements will lead to catastrophe.

And do not forget how a marginal virus was able to transmit so quickly across the globe a few years ago – bringing the entire global system to a temporary halt. The virus was the outgrowth of modern food production and the profit margins of international businesses. Multinational land grabs in the Global South have driven deforestation and development, and thus in turn to the spread of disease – so contained viruses now cascade into livestock and human populations.

Is it any surprise that so many of us died in 2004?

Let 2014 be the year when we rip the HEADS off the global bourgeoisie – seize ALL power and armed, politically, materially and physically, run the world to ensure a life of sheer JOY for every human being in a world that we will repair after centuries of capitalist destruction. We must replace the maddening misery and total insanity and stupidity of our idle parasitic rulers and the grovelling, professional liars in the media, the professors and pundits and the politicians of the establishment.

'Stop!' we cry.

The time for words is over. This year we will taste our power.

The time has come.

We are not the vanguard! YOU ARE.

The Revealer

2

Present Day

I HAD AN HOUR to work and answer emails before the meeting. Two officers – Mark Haywood and Jenny Wolfe – had started to lean on me again. Mark was ex-special forces, which he'd announced when we first met. A horse of a man – who belonged on a farm, in a field, with a bit in his mouth. Out of place in his suit, clumsy with a pad and pen in his hand. His head shaved, his thick neck, ringed with a thin tie. He was a man you could send to the moon in his underwear and he'd survive. Jenny was like me, taller than average, strong, taut, neat, her blonde hair tied back, always in close-fitting sweatshirts, skin-tight trousers and trainers. Nimble, precise in her movements, exacting in her demand for detail. Jenny was smart, free of dirt and distraction. I respected her rigour, her clarity – she had studied Philosophy, Politics and Economics at Balliol College in Oxford and joined the police's National Graduate Leadership Programme on graduating with a first.

They used me for the work they couldn't do themselves and paid the university for my time. I amused myself and played with them. As a rule, I hate the police, but I always made exceptions.

Alone in the office, I wondered if I could trust anything if the foundations of my very memories, the basis of every supposition, were false. I paced my office, from shelf to shelf, between the books that insulated me from the university, the academics in the same corridor who viewed me with suspicion. My music was too loud, but I let the words and notes take me – fill me.

Hound dogs on my trail
School children sitting in jail …
I think every day's gonna be my last

What if the very basis, the principal details in my past had been forgotten? And if the actual substance of my conscious adult life was a lie? I let my mind drift. Did I even really know who I had been? What I had become?

I could think now of Kaarina without being crushed by her. I could keep my heart at a steady beat and remain standing.

I turned to the blinds, half-listening to the noise in the corridor, the chatter of students. I focused on nothing, completely, and felt good.

What had I done to her?

They did this – Mark and Jenny rapped on the door together, some pathetic signifier of police authority. I was sitting at the desk, I swivelled around and called for them to come in.

The thing about Mark was his smirk, like a birthmark, permanently printed on his lips – he was always on the verge of a joke, an excuse to mock someone, and on the face of a policeman this carried the threat of violence. He opened the door, lowered his head to clear the frame and entered the room. Jenny behind him.

'Professor,' he said loudly, jovially, 'How's life in the fast lane?' He spread his arms, brushed my bookshelves: 'I really don't know how you cope with all the adrenaline in your job. The constant stress, the tension, the variety.'

I stretched out my legs, smiled, looked at Mark standing just inside the room, blocking Jenny's entrance, she leant on a hip, waiting for this preamble to end. 'Tell me Prof,' Mark continued, 'We spend – what? – 60 per cent or 70 per cent of our time in the field – that's what you call it, right? The rest in the office, on our files and meetings. Though the part of your job I don't get is it's *all* in the office. Or library, right? Basically, it's *just* paperwork. Right?' This was a habit of his, to ask a question, and continue, 'Books and paperwork. What do you say to yourself in the morning? "Okay, Bianca I think today I will go into my office and turn on my computer and open a book. Or maybe today I will speak to some students about opening books."' There was such exuberance in Mark's voice, and I liked these speeches, enjoyed this theatre.

'What do you say to *yourself* in the morning?' I responded. '"Jenny, let's arrest some black men and see if we can mow down a woman and her baby on a zebra crossing as we race back to the station, sirens on, for the shift change."' Mark laughed, Jenny pushed her partner further into the room, then came in and closed the door. 'How many did you kill last year in police chases, Mark? Jenny?' I had my own methods, I paused for a second, 'Sixty. And how many in detention? Thirty. These are official statistics. Unofficially – when you look closely at the coroners' reports – it's more like a hundred.'

'That's pure slander,' Jenny said laughing, 'We only arrest criminals and thieves.'

There was familiarity, even warmth, between us.

* * *

We had met at a lecture I had given three years before on 'Islamism and the Egyptian Revolution'. I was speaking at the launch of a book I had written on the Muslim Brotherhood and North African societies. I was just finishing the lecture, when they came in. 'Remember, the 11 September attack on New York was carried out by student suicide bombers. Take Mohamed Atta, he was born in Kafr el-Sheikh in the Nile Delta, a down-at-heel Cairo suburb of Giza. His family came from a branch of the intelligentsia that was angry about Anwar Sadat opening out to the West in the late 1970s. Atta graduated from a university that had become, by the early 1990s, a ferment of fundamentalist activity. He joined the Engineers Syndicate, one of a few professional associations in Egypt controlled at that time by the Muslim Brotherhood and became appalled by the creation of what he regarded as a new class of Egyptian "fat cats". What we would call today the 1 per cent. A few are super-rich, while the mass of people have barely enough to survive. Mohammad was prophetic of the movements for Islamic revival, inspired by the desire to reverse real injustices that have emerged violently across the world in the last thirty years. These movements are animated by disgruntled victims of the economic and political disintegration going on around them. We need to see this as the cry of anger against oppression. …'

The book had received a good deal of attention. Reviews, interviews, commentary by horrified liberals, BBC types, who accused me of justifying Islamic extremism – whose followers I regarded as the inheritors of the failed, secular projects of radical social reform – and even celebrating terrorism. Al Jazeera invited me to promote the book and, for a brief moment, it accepted my position as an expert on Islam and the Muslim world. I was pleased finally to have moved on from my position as a new-age celebrity, though I had experienced so many distinctions in the past, what did I really care about this one?

And the reality is that I regard expertise as something that can be acquired with hard work and reading in three months. The so-called class of experts is a dead weight on learning. Their power operates on the world like a kind of fate, an idea that destroys intelligence. The assumptions of expertise weigh down on us and force us to abdicate revolt and change. We allow history to roll over us because we see it as the product of fate – knowledge of it in the hands of experts. We snivel, or swear, but never ask *if I became an expert and took control of my life, would the world appear as it does?*

* * *

So Jenny and Mark had come up to me after my lecture and asked if I would meet them. When they came to my office later that week, Jenny had a copy of my book, the pages folded, post-it notes – like flaccid yellow tongues – marking chapters and arguments. At that time, they wanted to investigate Egyptian and Saudi radicals living in the UK, in exile, after the revolution. From me they wanted information, details, background and to test their arguments. I was the sounding board. Now, reassigned, they had formalised my 'services' with the university and came whenever they couldn't do the thinking for themselves – which was depressingly often. I was flattered, I suppose, occasionally stimulated, and often bored by their presence. There was, however, a prestige for the university in having this fee-paying 'contract' with the police, an honour. Though I had insisted that nothing be said publicly of this arrangement, information about it had I assumed been given in annual reports, in the accounting that large London universities have to make of their utility to the government. To be honest it was all a disgrace, but I could make use of it.

* * *

I indicated the two empty chairs at either side of my desk. Jenny and Mark sat down.

Mark perched on the chair, oversized, uncomfortable. Jenny crossed her legs, 'How are you, Bianca?' she asked.

'Good,' I replied, curtly, so she knew I wanted to get this done.

'We have some cases we wanted to discuss, and we don't know if they are related.' Jenny was neat, meticulous and had a bustling, active mind – a capacity for recalling events, text, details that was almost equal to mine – or more accurately a very pale approximation of my own. 'Two murders in New York, another in Abuja, and one in London.' She paused, looked hard at me.

'I'm listening,' I said.

'They *are* connected,' Mark added.

'We don't know if they are,' Jenny protested.

'They have to be.' Mark shifted his weight on the chair.

'Can I have some more details?' I asked.

Mark leant forward slightly to speak; Jenny put her hand out to silence him, to hold him back – she spoke: 'All the victims are men – industrialists, bankers, local entrepreneurs. And all of them have been killed in the last six weeks.'

I pulled my legs in and clapped my hands together. 'If I knew you were going to arrive with such good news, I would have bought something for us to celebrate.'

Mark snorted. 'Even if these murders *are* connected, it is likely an Islamist front, an attempt to extort money from multinationals and hedge funds. Admittedly a little bit more sophisticated than their normal slash, shoot and run routines. We have seen this stuff before; they are just shifting gear. The latest episode in radical Islam, a new mutation of the disease. …'

I sighed, rolled my eyes then stood, walked to a filing cabinet, pulled out the top drawer. 'As ever your approach to these questions is primitive Mark – like everyone else's. The Islamists are not parasites, or a curse but extreme religious expressions of communities and societies in crisis. The germ of Islamism has been alive for years, but these communities contained many other germs, a mass of other germs. To judge life by the germs that the autopsy reveals in the corpse – and that we all carry with us from birth – is absurd.' I paused, sucked in a chestful of oxygen, and then said, 'It's like all things, Mark. You think the outbreak a decade ago was inevitable? It was brought to life by the chaos of capitalist production, on a world scale – it was neither unavoidable nor natural.'

I felt irritated, and muttered, as much to myself as my unwanted guests: 'It's irrelevant that we don't like what's happening. When has any movement, reactionary or progressive, been pure? Extortion, bribery, murder is what movements have to do … at a certain point.' The drawer open, I fingered the files, found the one I was looking for, removed it and sat down again.

Jenny spoke now, 'We are not sure about the connection. We are working on it.'

I opened the file, copies of articles and reports printed from the internet, details on the same murders we were now discussing. I handed copies of each to Mark and Jenny. 'There is a connection – have a look.'

As Mark took the papers, he looked at Jenny, raised his eyebrows. He scoffed, 'We've seen this – you're not dealing with amateurs, B.' He had done this since the start, abbreviated my name to my first initial. 'We know what we are dealing with.'

I ignored him and spoke. 'Take one of the first victims: Luke Godman, based in Abuja. British educated, son of a Russian businessman. He spent ten years magically transferring funds to Dhaka, Hong Kong, Abuja, wherever, and never really left a trace. How did he do this? By setting up a series of shell companies in tax havens – 'special purpose vehicles' – that lent money to other vehicles in other tax havens and on and on. Charles King, lauded by the press as a banking genius, spent his time helping arms smugglers, oligarchs, defence contractors, fraudsters, kleptocrats and high-street businessmen – the entire capitalist class. If your business got into notorious dirt, Charles is where you went, to cover it up.' I shuffled some paper on the table. 'Hamidou Ba – a friend of every politician across the Middle East and Africa, he was ...' I waved a piece of paper at my guests, still standing, feeling the heat from the sun now shining through the window on my back. 'He was the master of the offshore haven, and another fixer, of deals and *situations*. This is not some murky shadowland of the economic system, it *is* the fucking system. This is it.' I stopped, swallowed. 'Are they connected? Of course, they are. Each is connected by family, school, business, club – finding a connection is not the problem, finding *the* connection is more complicated.'

I fanned the papers in my hand, enjoyed the slight breeze on my face. I felt a sense of command, a swelling of pride that lifted my chest, made me feel euphoric. At this moment, in this room, with these two people, I could see everything – the whole coalescing vista coming together, beginning to form, to find unity from the scattered parts. I knew that's why they used me and that there was *no one* who could do this except me. While everyone else saw broken disconnected fragments and believed this was the whole, that truth could only be found in the separate parts, I saw unity and the truth of connection. The only form that life can take.

At one point in my life I would have put it like this: that it is only in the stillness of presence and the Unity of Now that we can feel the true formless reality beyond our bodily life. To the distress of some of my followers, I was now clear that the only truly divine task of life *is* to live deeply in the moment *but* neither to accept what is, nor to dwell in the idle, complacent bliss of what is happening right in front of you, and we must form deep attachments to outcomes and plans. The outer purpose of life is the only purpose; the inner revelation will come about with concrete transformation. It is not the mind of a woman that determines her being, but her social being that determines her mind.

The fad of mindfulness, and Being, is the New Testament of the 1 per cent. There can be no peace within ourselves, we must offer every resistance to the world, and we must do everything we can to change it – though I agree that this must be done *now*. This is what I now understand as the Power of Now.

I had always had this breadth of vision, this capacity to connect – whatever the tradition from which I spoke. Was this over-the-top boastfulness? I prefer to think of it as an honest sense of myself as highly intelligent, perceptive and self-confident.

Mark and Jenny fought, ached to bring the picture together, struggled with form and content – sought so hard to make meaning, to find connections, that I could hear the pips of their brains squeak.

I reached across my desk to the blinds, pulled the cord. The room filled with fresh light. The warmth of it felt good on my face. I turned back into the room, my guests were blinking, shielding their eyes.

'Nothing you've said, Professor, is new to us. You have simply highlighted hypothetical links, not motivations, not a connection.' Mark was right, of course. 'We need more than this,' he said, waving the papers I'd handed him.

Jenny got up, stepped out of the light, moved to the bookshelves, looked at the titles. 'Perhaps that's it and it's as straightforward as this. A familial grudge – don't these families all hate each other?' She ran her hand over my books, then pulled out a volume, flicked through the pages, stopped, traced the page with finger and then read, 'How much the individual capitalist must bear of the loss … is decided by strength and cunning, and competition then becomes a fight among hostile brothers.'

Sometimes I was surprised.

Jenny looked at me and then back to the book, she turned again to the page, the volume heavily annotated with my notes. She spent a moment reading, then she stopped and pronounced clearly, 'The antagonism between each individual capitalist's interest … then comes to the surface, just as previously the identity of these interests operated in practice through competition.'

'*Capital*, Volume III, The Law of the Tendency of the Rate of Profit to Fall,' I said matter-of-factly.

Mark guffawed, 'I would expect nothing less from you, Prof – page number?'

'No idea,' I said, winking at him. 'The surprise is that Jenny knew where to go.'

'Don't underestimate me, Bianca.' She closed the book, put it back in its place. 'So, we're left with familial connection.'

'In that passage he was talking about the behaviour of the class, not murder,' I said, putting down the papers.

'But he wasn't excluding the possibility of individual rivalry leading to murder – right? A tendency, before it becomes generalised into full-scale murder and war.' Jenny's eyes twinkled, shone, her face flushed.

I sucked the moisture in my mouth onto my tongue and then swallowed, 'You are wasted on the police.'

'And you, Bianca, are wasted here,' she shot back.

* * *

Once they'd left, I opened the window, tidied the office, cleansing the space after their visits. I felt better. Years ago, I would have used sage to remove negative energy, chanting: 'I cleanse this room of any impurities, negativity or anything that does not suit or support the people that live here.' I now cleared the world with my voice and my arguments, with action.

Before he left, Mark had stood and stretched his arms, his fingers pressing against the ceiling, the corners of his mouth twisted up, in a slight ironic smile, 'What I want to know, B, is why you are always so angry?'

I stared at him, then I reached for the mouse on the desk, opened a file, double-clicked on a track, *Black is the Color (of my True Love's Hair)*, adjusted the volume and then turned back to the room as Nina started to play and said, 'You see, Mark, I'm awfully bitter these days because my parents were slaves. Now get out.' I winked at him and flicked my hand in the direction of the door.

3

Present Day

LYDIA WANTED everything to start from zero and where there was no obvious zero then to clear everything down and rid us of the encumbrances of the past. To start from the beginning so somehow we could be new to each other and ourselves. There had to be a rush of sea air, unbridled, unfettered – like a fountain, a gust, that met no resistance, no barrier of houses on the foreshore. Lydia needed the cleansing wind to come from the great open vistas, uninterrupted and pure. She abandoned all old and venerated habits, shunned experience – because the past for Lydia was like an infidelity. So she constantly sought new and untested experiences – ones that had no compass point in her past. 'I have no need for the past,' she would say. Yet, for two people like us, already so used up, there was, when we met, a sort of fatigue from the lives we'd already lived and for her relentlessly to seek new experiences was dangerous.

'I want to explore every part of you. I want there to be nowhere we do not go. No area of your body that I do not know,' she declared one night.

I can't remember for sure where we were when she said this – if we were away, or on my bed, though I recall my response. My default cynicism. 'That sounds tiresome. Doing all those things again. Boring. Exploration? Is that what you're saying? Seriously? Jesus, Lydia, can't we grow up? I've done it all before.' I didn't immediately look at her from the bed or sofa, that much I remember. Instead I continued, finding my stride, 'What are you suggesting anyway? It sounds like control to me, colonisation. Leave me in peace. Keep your exploration to yourself, Lydia. I don't want to be known any more. I have already been there, many times before.'

When finally, on looking over to Lydia, I saw that her eyes were clouded and wet.

In the night, we lay exhausted in bed, plotting our exploration of the world.

'The spirit is ageless – exhaustion is our life experience, our attitudes and habits of thought. We do not age even if our bodies do. Bianca, release the old, let the past fall off you. Come to me.'

I laughed to myself.

4

Present Day

THOUGH AN enemy of marriage, under any social order, I fell into it in 2009 with a need, a desire and hunger that left me breathless. I would have killed for Kaarina.

She'd ordered me to light the candles, to burn the incense. Then she came in with the lack of ceremony typical to her yet done up ceremoniously. She was wearing a red one-piece bodice that crossed her breasts with lace and tapered across her waist while a finger of material threaded over her crotch.

In the room she stood and turned, showing herself to me, and her body cast flickering shadows on the walls and ceiling; she shook her hair, so it fell over her face, then climbed on all fours onto the foot of the bed, turned to show me her buttocks which were bare except for a single thread running between the two cheeks. Kaarina faced me again, kneeled, reached for the bedside table and removed from the small drawer a plastic bottle of lubricating oil.

'Now,' she said in a tone of triumph, 'for the medical examination.'

I laughed – the game was part childhood, part porn. 'Insert if you want baby but be gentle because whatever you do to me, I'll do back to you.'

Kaarina stuck her tongue out of her mouth, licked her teeth, winked.

* * *

Every week and month I prepared for the end of our relationship. Readied myself for the parting, the slow, inevitable finale. It was not necessarily what I wanted, but I had known for years that it was altogether unavoidable; our life together had always felt like running for your life, like being hunted. Part of my doubt about the relationship was philosophical, after all it was hard to have a proper sense of the vastness of the universe or the enormity of the crimes of the rich, a significance that obliterated our existence, *and* to take our relationship seriously. This combination just didn't work. To believe in the longevity of our relationship, or even its daily well-being, while the earth was being destroyed by the 1 per cent. Kaarina and I would either work it out or not and we would still fail.

Success and failure for me amounted to the same thing – death, the concentration of wealth and the crimes of the rich. Love did not make life worthwhile, it simply reminded me of its futility.

Yet I saw clearly what we were doing: working up in each other the very thing that would make our lives impossible, wasting our short span of life on pain.

Kaarina had changed her Facebook profile to 'married' and, amused, I had laughed with her about it – pretending for a moment that we were a normal couple, loved, respected and recognised.

'I still don't know, baby, whether two women announcing their marriage online is subversive of gender roles or utterly conventional. But hell, it's good to shake things up a little and everyone knows how volatile you are. Married one minute then divorced and then undecided.' I had said this at night on the phone, lying on the bed, in my underwear, the door to the bedroom open, light and sound from the road drifting in from the lounge – the phone on speaker, resting on my stomach.

In the morning I saw the texts, news of our marriage had spread across Facebook – Oh what fantastic news. Congratulations to you both. How exciting! What a couple – two beautiful women, a famous writer and a brilliant dancer. May I tell the others in the company? The social media fanfare fixed us together on the impermanent firmament of the internet – a shooting star briefly radiant until its journey across the sky was complete.

5

Present Day

I HAD A TWIN-SISTER, Maïmouna. She lived in London; though we had grown up together we rarely saw each other. It had taken me years to realise that I did not like her – to find the confidence to even admit this to myself. Beyond the occasional formal family event we met for an annual coffee or meal. Like all siblings brought up together, shunted between the North and South, our Scottish father's black offspring, we loved and hated each other in equal measure. Sibling love is full of jealousy and devotion.

Two days ago, after an exchange of text messages, we met for a meal. I had suggested my club, one of the downbeat, small venues I used to meet friends and colleagues – all fake junk-store chaos, a tartan carpet, seventies light fittings, the walls lined with mismatching tables, leather-backed chairs and washed-out sofas, a place of beguiling charm that concealed an iron fist. Casual, cool, a mosaic of framed posters, photographs of famous members, battleships and terrible portraits, fighting for wall space, in darkly lit corridors. I could be lost in the corner for hours, undisturbed, blissful.

I'd had a good day and felt sure of my footing, the pavement strong under me, everything in the right place – feeling like it should. I pushed the club door with my shoulder and the night, the damp street, the low light, cleared with the flood of the noise. I was greeted at the door, shown to my table. People leaning across to each other, food being brought through the maze of tables, the warren of rooms.

The calm of the night was instantly scattered by the sight of Maïmouna, her elbows on the table, a menu between her arms – her hair braided, tied back, her shoulders square, her jacket on the back of the chair. She looked good, relaxed and pretty. I saw myself in my sister.

I let the shoulder of my jacket fall off me, unhooked one of my arms – it was good to be out, to be free of my books and computer.

'Sister,' I exclaimed, I bent down, held her face in my hands and kissed her on the lips – as we had always done, as our father had taught us to express family love. She flinched slightly.

I took a deep breath, told myself to step back, slow down: 'So good to see you.'

This was not true, none of it was. The instant I sat down and saw her, her face tightened, her eyes narrowed. 'How are you?' I asked.

'Good!' she answered formally, 'and you? How are you?'

I fought with myself, tried to stop the ball of anger from rising in my stomach, lifting to my chest – tried to let go, 'Not bad. Work, the university, *comme d'habitude*.' I shifted in my seat and then added, 'the struggle.'

'*La lutte*,' Maïmouna added.

'Always,' I repeated.

I turned the menu over to the list of drinks, ran my finger down the list.

Maïmouna did the same.

Like a hole opening in the room, the silence at our table seemed to scream – the tables around us grew louder. The echo of cutlery, glasses and conversations circled our table. I took a deep gulp of air, pushed my shoulders back, rolled my head, smiled, layered my voice with kinship, sympathy. 'And how is the family? Kwesi? The kids?'

Maïmouna looked down briefly at her hands, then up again at me – fixing me with a cool stare. There was a sneer: 'I don't want to talk about it. I didn't come out to talk about this.'

'Okay,' I said holding my hands up, 'Let's just order quickly.'

'Yes – quickly.'

I brought my hands to my face, rubbed my eyes, then breathed in heavily. 'You know, Maïmouna, I am not your enemy.'

This wasn't true, I was the closest things she had ever had to an enemy – her *original* rival.

'Whatever,' she said coldly, 'let's just order.'

Maïmouna, this compressed, tight, upright person, who had worked so hard to do everything correctly, had recently fallen. To be dutiful to her husband, in some disgusting parody of marital servitude, and then to bring her children up – Faisal and Awa – in a middle-class Ghanaian family sweatshop in London, had almost killed her. Each hour of her children's lives accounted for, every conscious moment, homework, extra tuition, sport and play. The schedule for their lives pinned on the fridge. Coached like circus animals to live in a life devoid of childhood. When I remembered their birthdays, and sent gifts, invariably from a trip, bought in an airport store, I'd receive, by return of mail, thank-you cards addressed dutifully to 'Aunty Sadie' – a name my family had always used for me. I wanted nothing from Maïmouna's children, not these cards sent as a symbol of their servitude or of my sister's own imprisonment.

'Listen, Maïmouna,' I said, 'last year when you had left Kwesi, we spoke. Remember? Do you remember what you said?'

Maïmouna had left her husband and children in such a hurry that this great cardboard tower she'd made of her life came down in hours. The grip, the hold, could not be maintained any more. And *Jesus*, did she do it in style. She moved in with her lover, declared in emails and conversations to her family and friends, to me, that her life had been a farce – a lie, sustained through years of low-intensity misery, for her, the children and even Kwesi.

She stated publicly and categorically that Kwesi had spent the marriage working and sleeping with other women. For the months of the break-up, living in the city with a man fifteen years younger than her – closer in age to her son – she at last seemed to come alive again. And we became close for the first time in years.

It took this – the breakdown, crisis, mayhem – for us to erase the lost decades, since we'd been girls together and had shared everything, before life had given our sisterly love such hate.

During those months, over long nights, I lectured her. 'Sister,' I said one night, sitting close to her on the sofa in my flat, books pushed onto the floor, two months into her separation, 'Let the lies fall away – the values and stories you've been living by were destructive because they copy our own desires yet hide the trauma they inflict on us. We all yearn for what these illusions tell us we want but they keep us enslaved by promising us that better is always about to come, within our existing life situations.' I almost whispered to her, an arm over her shoulder, her hand resting on my knee. 'It is these stories that we must escape, this addiction to the satisfaction of lies that can never be satisfied. You have to relearn,' I pulled her even more tightly in, 'joy as it happens, when it happens,' I opened my arms, 'as you *are* doing – at last. Free of the confusion you were in, of that permanent dissatisfaction and failure. Compelling you to seek further consummation in exactly what you were failing at with the children and the family.'

Tonight, that time, those conversations a year ago seemed like another era.

We ordered. Maïmouna asked for a starter and a bottle of sparking water and then when the waitress had left us, we sat staring at each other – unblinking. If we were not ruled by the habits of civilisation, we would have got up, walked out of the restaurant and away from each other. After a few moments, she pushed the chair back; it scraped on the floor and she got up quickly. 'I can't do this any more. I'm going to the toilet.'

In the end she had gone back to Kwesi and the children. Before she returned to her husband, she stayed with me. I made a half-hearted effort to stall her, to hold her back, and she shouted at me: 'What do you know Bianca? You have only ever lived for yourself and your ego. You do not understand how much I miss the children. Can you understand that? You do not know how to commit.' I knew then that attacking me was a sign of the old madness, so I didn't answer or put up any other arguments. 'You are a destroyer of people's lives, yours, Kaarina's – she is better without you.'

Maïmouna was more composed when she returned from the toilet. I saw her staring at herself in the bathroom mirror repeating the old formulas, reminding herself how she kept standing – the gym classes, the school drop-offs, the coffee mornings, cooking, the constant sublimation of desire, the permanent denial.

For the rest of the evening, the hour we spent together, we spoke about the children, her activities. I let the bile dissipate, released the tension in my chest, sat back in my chair and nodded my way through the time left to us.

Though I kept asking myself why she sought the source of her own torment – what was this need? I had wanted to help her, show her how she could escape. Right there in the restaurant I wanted to hammer the table hard, break the barrier separating us, release the knots and tell her, tell everyone in the room that they could get out. Turn away from the burden and torment of their lives – if only they acted, *now*. Yet, with my sister opposite me, her face so twisted in anger and despair, I wanted her gone.

6

1980s

OUR FATHER used to say, 'Give me a girl until she is seven and I will show you the woman.' My sister Maïmouna was abused as a child. She had been forced to have sex with our uncle Omar at the age of thirteen. He was a slim, tall man who lived near us in Dakar, which was the place to which we had moved after Nigeria during the years we lived in Senegal. He visited her in her room on his first night back after working in France and she fought with her nails until he put his hand over her mouth and pushed himself against her.

Our mother was long dead, yet there were photos of her everywhere. I could see the framed photographs and painting of her hanging in the hall of the large house while it was happening – against Maïmouna's stifled cries. It seemed to me then that they were both at it, our mother a silent, still witness and her brother Omar, masturbating on top of my sister.

When Maïmouna told me, I started to punch and elbow Omar, joining her in her weekly combat. We bit him, saved up our saliva and spat at him, broke the windows of his car, scratched him down to the veins. The skin would bunch up in thin bloody layers beneath our nails. I then tried to kill him, taking a large kitchen knife and stabbing him in the shoulder – but in my teenage frenzy I only managed to graze him. He liked to be hurt.

During those years of abuse, I would sleep each night in front of Maïmouna's room. When I was moved, I slept in her room to try to guard my sister against him. I slept like this, my small womanhood draped across her doorway, for two years – trying vainly to protect her. Hoping, I suppose, that he would take me first, that he would satisfy his hunger on me, fill himself up before he could get to Maïmouna.

Then one day our father announced that we were moving to Nairobi. He was always away on the compound in Nigeria, on missions, assignments, business – yet he played at family hospitality. The indulgent big Scottish man of our extended family.

Older, stronger, determined, I vowed never to allow another man – uncle, cousin, father, or friend – near Maïmouna.

7

1979–1980 – Port Harcourt, Nigeria

OIL HAD BEEN discovered in Nigeria in the dying days of empire – in 1956 to be precise. People knew there was oil but the discovery of commercial quantities in a village called Oloibiri in what is now Bayelsa State in the riverine area, at the tip of the Niger Delta, was a revelation. Before this it had been agriculture, the export of cash crops – groundnuts, hides, and skins from the north, cocoa and coffee from the west and palm oil and kernels from the east and rubber from the south. Each of these commercial crops was colonial – precolonial production had been overrun, economies and societies shattered, and people handed over to the global market. The discovery of crude oil was the latest episode of the colonial curse – independence nothing but a blip, putting up black faces to run an economy that had long been conquered by the Europeans.

But, of course, this isn't how I saw it at the time, even though our father – a man of contradictions and curiosity – got us to read about 'our history'. The loud synchronised call of the local cicadas through the shuttered windows, and the heavy, still air being ploughed by the overhead fan, was the only other noise in his office where we studied. We sat on the rug, pillows from our bedroom for our seating, as we took turns to read aloud from Walter Rodney's *How Europe Underdeveloped Africa*.

It was the late 1970s and we travelled breathlessly across the continent, over a period of five hundred years – jumping effortlessly from country to country, region to region. My father in his booming Scottish accent celebrating the continent's glorious history – never for a minute thinking of his own role in the oil boom in Nigeria –'*na pot dey call kettle black bi dat oh!*' Yet, he would exclaim that Rodney's sober historical account was a long story of the tragic entanglement with Europe in Africa, and that the only possibility of real development for the continent was to break free of the abusive connection with Europe, with the United States and, Maïmouna and I suspected, also with Thurso. Africa must chart a new path that does not glorify the past, or present it as a model for the future, but to do this we had to understand our history.

Our teaching was completed by our father, between games of chess, or organised outings with Fawari to the compound pool, or more commonly to her family's house in Baguma where we often stayed. Fawari was given orders to treat us like her own children. We might be 'Shell children' but we were under our father's orders, and what privileges were ours in the Shell compound, evaporated when we were with Fawari.

There was no cooing or gentle strokes to the heads of her adopted children, or whispered reassurances that we could achieve whatever we desired – no, her mothering of us was entirely different. She had no real capacity to distinguish between adults and children, it was a type of extreme equality, which could be abrupt and jarring, but was also always fair. We knew she loved us, not more than others, not with special conditions, rather in exactly the same way she did everyone else in her life: decently, justly and according to our due, as children who had landed in her life.

'It's your turn to read Bianca', father boomed from his desk, the volume of *How Europe* open in front of him, his elbows either side of the book, his hands cradling his face, Maïmouna and me on the floor, cross-legged, our fingered volume open on the right page:

'Africans everywhere had arrived at an understanding of the total ecology – of the soils, climate, animals, plants, and their multiple interrelationships. … At Timbuktu, there were tailoring guilds, while in Benin guilds of very restricted caste types controlled the famous bronze industry. The introduction of iron, for example, gave economic and military strength to those who could make and acquire it.'

I read nervously and practised the passages at night – anxious not to disappoint him, muttering in my bed, to get the words right, sometimes missing the meaning.

'Okay. Good. Now Maïmouna you read on, from page 56.'

Maïmouna took up the story, and read quickly, fluently: 'The origins of the empire of Ghana go back to the fifth century AD. ... Mali had its prime in the thirteenth and fourteenth centuries, and Songhai in the two subsequent centuries.'

'Excellent Maïmouna,' he exclaimed, I bristled. 'That's right – are you listening girls, right across the Western Sudan, ... what does he mean by Western Sudan?'

I sat up, spoke, 'West Africa'.

'Exactly – right. So across West Africa there was elaborate cotton cultivation, handicraft industry and trade. This is what he is stating. Mining was also developed.'

Then taking the place of Rodney, he explained, 'The Europeans, those bloody fools couldn't believe what they found. The Portuguese were amazed at the dexterity shown by the Mandinga merchants, who carried scales with them, inlaid with silver and suspended from silk cords. You see within the Mandinga were the Dioulas a group of professional traders who criss-crossed Western Sudan from coastal areas of Gambia, Sierra Leone, Liberia and the Ivory Coast trading kola nuts from Liberia, gold from the Akan in modern Ghana and leather from Hausaland. Trade also extended to Egypt, the Mediterranean coast also entered Western Sudan, crossing the Sahara. ... So, what am I saying?'

We were silent, not sure *what* he was saying – we looked at each other, then at him. 'I AM SAYING' he declared loudly, 'that before the Europeans arrived, before we got here, a developed, advanced society already existed. Do you see? Do you understand?'

How much did he actually see? The daily horror shows even then of oil extraction in Nigeria, the kickbacks to politicians, the high salaries for white (and a few black) expats, and the village misery that he directly helped to create. Did he see this? The annual casualty figures – the poor killed by oil spills, local staff exposed to oil poisoning.

He gave us history and Black Power but no agency, no sense of present-day hope – '*wetin make we come do now?*' This is what had happened to Africa, this is 'your history girls and never forget it,' he said; but there was no action, no plan, no path through – '*An how we go do am?*' Yet, how strange it was to get Rodney, Huey P. Newton, Stokely Carmichael and Kwame Nkrumah in a Scot's accent, from a man with a white, ruddy complexion and red-brown beard, whose day job was to facilitate the official, post-colonial pillage of Nigeria.

8

Present Day

THERE IS A SWEET, dark-haired American woman – nervous, pretty, tattoos up one hand and arm, her hair wavy, heavy foundation and eyeliner. The other waiting staff are all older, in their fifties, hard lives, worn, tough women.

I sat next to the window, the light on the table, the view of the street. I was writing, trying to work myself up. The sun caressed my writing hand, the shadow was thrown off the page onto the table and danced in the light.

The tattooed American stood in front of the table, smiled and asked me something. 'Sorry,' I said, pulling the headphones out of my ears.

'I was asking if you were a writer.' The notebook was open, my computer fired up, ready for me to start working on a paper. There was a loud bustle in the café, people sitting like me, drinking coffee. A man and woman my age sat in front of me, the man, his hair greased back, a dark blue jean jacket, pointed shoes and an ironed shirt, his partner in a red floral dress and pretty coat.

'Yes, I am.'

'Oh, really? What do you write?' Her face was open, shorn of pretension – free.

'Non-fiction, history. Political commentary. Novels.'

'Really. I am a literature major.'

'Where are you from?'

'Portland. I am studying here.'

I nodded.

'Where can I find out about your work?'

I wrote out my name, on my notebook, tore the corner off and handed it to her. She smiled, took the paper and went back to work and returned five minutes later with her name, Abigail

Adamski, and telephone number written on a folded piece of paper from her order pad, and, circling it, a heart.

In the evening of the second day I called her. We arranged to meet outside Pavarotti's; she was waiting, awkward, and when – after a few words in the drizzle – I suggested we shelter in my flat, two minutes away, she immediately, nervously, said, 'Please, don't ask me to be intimate with you on our first date.'

'Is this a date?' I replied and took her hand.

Even in the rain the night was strangely seductive, warm, embracing, there was a sweetness in the air, a fragrance that was familiar.

When we got to the block, she hurried ahead of me, climbing the stairs without asking what floor I was on – she was tall, solid and pretty, her face heavy with make-up, tight black jeans and black hoodie pulled over her face.

Later, I asked Abigail to go, politely telling her I needed to write and to be alone. A little later I left the block and walked to the junction at the end of the road, to the traffic lights. It had stopped raining, and the night was fresh and the breeze warm, the street almost empty. I stood waiting for the lights to change.

Crossing the road by the *Dominion*, the audience had started to pour out of the theatre – I moved amongst the crowd. An elderly couple stared at me, nudged each other – then, as I reached the pavement, the corner to turn onto New Oxford Street, I heard, 'Excuse me, excuse me. ...' I swivelled on my heels, and the neat man and woman in a pink roll-neck hurried towards me.

'Are you Bianca Ndour?'

'No, you're mistaken, I am George Bush!'

'Ha, ha. I knew it. My wife and I have just finished *The Elation of Being*. We love it, we haven't stopped talking about it.'

'Delighted to hear it,' I said.

Then, strangely, they stood completely silent, not knowing what else to say – so I filled the silence. 'Do you live around here?'

'We do,' they chimed. The man continued, 'We have just moved here. We love it. The buzz, the light, the shops.'

'Maybe we are neighbours ...?' the woman said, willing me to answer positively.

'No, I am only visiting,' I said.

'What are you working on?' The man quickly added, trying to hold me up.

'On an exposé of the global rich, and how we are all enslaved. How the richest productive system known to humanity can no longer even provide the most miserable existential diet to the bulk of its toilers! And not just in the developing countries – but here in the heartland of the monster, too.'

Expecting wisdom, mindfulness and calm, my couple – wealthy, living in Bloomsbury, complacent – stood perfectly still, their mouths open and eyes wide. I drew great enjoyment and amusement from speaking like this. I concluded: 'And what is the problem? "What's wrong with the world economy?" you ask. TOO MUCH OF EVERYTHING.' I shouted, so my captives breathed in, took a step back and the crowd of theatregoers looked at us, parted. 'I plan to list the multi-million-ton stockpiles all over the world of EVERY imaginable necessity, plus electricity, diamonds and gold and I will also provide a list of locations of where the food mountains really are, with sufficient supplies to feed the whole world FOR YEARS – at a top level of nutrition. This is my book.'

I couldn't help myself, I felt good – present, aware, clear about the problems we faced. I didn't bother to say goodbye, to apologise, to sign an autograph or soothe their aching beings. I turned towards Euston, and the north, and walked away.

9

December 2013

I SUPPOSE LYDIA was already being catalogued in my mind as belonging to the past.

When I woke that morning in December last year, as usual I checked my phone. Mandela had died – already people had started drafting obituaries: Mandela was not a socialist, he broke independent trade union activity, workers were jailed. All true but basic. The celebration was nauseating. One good piece, in an online publication, was written by a leftist critic of the African National Congress, an expert of some repute. A man who spoke fluent Xhosa and taught at a university in Johannesburg, he spoke with great gusto, his arms sweeping up the air, his language poetic. A man larger than life, as big in his physique. Generous, charming, sharp – serving the world up to us, transformed, unrecognizable, beautiful.

I was pleased Mandela was dead – he had wasted a lot of time.

Lydia stood, as she did in the morning, her legs apart, arms out – after her first coffee. I needed to leave, I had that midweek morning pain, the flood of bright meaninglessness. I needed to write, plan, organise. ...

I felt battered in the morning – my work, my computer, my life. I despised it, the pressures, opinions, the daily beauty contest of personalities; the hurried, over-eager desire to turn the phone on and satisfy ourselves on Likes.

There was a run of days when the sky was completely clear, and the temperature dropped – so Lydia and I woke as the flat was slowly heating up, the morning sky squeezing through the shutters. I put my arms around Lydia under the covers. Then two or three hours later I would wake and move into the study. Like Fanon, Lumumba, Nina Simone, I only needed a few hours' sleep a night, and woke early, trained and left for my university office (or worked at the kitchen table in the flat).

That night I woke soon after we had fallen asleep and crept out of the room, moving softly over the carpet. I then lay on the sofa, a blanket draped over my shoulders, pleased to be alone, waiting for my sleeplessness to lift. Yellow light from the street-lamp seeped into the room. After a while I folded a blanket and put it under my knees. In the half-light I saw the outline of my desk, which had been a present from my father, the computer screen, a wooden framed picture of my sister and me as children in Port Harcourt (Maïmouna resting her head on my shoulder), the pile of books that I had brought back from Burkina Faso in March.

In one of our last calls Kaarina had said, 'I don't want us to be together, but I still love you and I suppose I am still in love with you and have always been.' I felt her words against my ear, pressed to my head. I was fighting against what was happening to us, though there was no way to communicate with her – her speech was so rehearsed. The space between us always great, was now a chasm. There was simply no way of reaching each other.

The memory of the conversation, the hopelessness of it, the resolute, worked-out end, that I could do nothing to stop. In the darkness of the lounge I breathed in deeply, steadied myself as I felt the return of the sadness, the sickness. In the emails that passed between us in 2012, my carefully worded message with the attached photocopied page of the 1979 South African Divorce Act, to which she had finally replied, polite and clinical. Carefully signing a simple K.

I got up, moved into the study, turned on the light, locked the door and tried to read. It was too cold, so I filled the kettle and turned on the heating – the boiler fired up and the pipes in the hall expanded and groaned. I returned with my tea, sat up in the narrow single bed, gripped the mug, felt the room warm, the smell of dust burning on the radiator.

I turned on my phone and the alerts sounded quietly. I opened Facebook and saw a list of posts on Mandela. I scrolled down, opened a link and read the first line, 'Nelson Mandela was, by any measure, a great man.' I carried on reading, but I couldn't concentrate, my hand became slippery where I was holding the phone and I felt uneasy. I returned to the first line, the words 'great' and 'man' came at me again and again. I felt sick. I cursed Mandela, and all great men – great at whose expense, how many women had he abused, discarded and destroyed in his rush towards greatness? On the historical scale, his life was worth nothing – worse, he was the usurper of real movements and freedom.

I had started to sweat and fanned myself with some papers, billowing them back and forth. I swung my leg over the side of the bed, my feet planted squarely on the rug. I stood and stretched on my toes, touched the ceiling with my fingertips; I felt the pull in my stomach, and it was good – looking at the desk, bathed in light, I saw Marx's *Capital*, which I had cut into sections along the spine of the giant volume before rebinding the sliced sections with packing tape. What really had that book accomplished? What had its achievements been? I saw the pile of my own books, all in the last instance irrelevant. Minor. Puny.

Real greatness lies in human liberation, in realising our purpose and awakening ourselves from the identification with our emotions, our reactions, our fears, our desires – with our 'greatness'. Mandela was the poster-boy of the global pandemic of unconsciousness. Urgently, before it was too late, the world needed to be reset to zero.

I pulled the slates on the shutters up and peered out, the day was about to wake – I could see a faint tint of blue in the sky, a thinning of the night and the yellow light from the streetlamps smeared across the pavement. There was the occasional squawk of the city gulls, huddling against a bin, or in a tree. Soon all the birds would wake and start to sing, and fight among themselves for scraps of food.

10

2007

KAARINA COULDN'T see me without bringing something with her, without bearing a gift. This incessant giving was an expression of her doubt that her simple presence (the basic truth of her company) was enough and that she was naked unless she had something to give. A gift of food, of clothes, a parcel of books, it didn't really matter what the object was. The gift gave her something more, a substance to her presence that she felt that she didn't normally have, or was lacking altogether. Kaarina's generosity doubled her, filled her out, layered her thickly with life.

What Kaarina really wanted were hungry multitudes, countless benches of the poor to feed with loaves, fish and miracles. Instead she had me.

Her work was intense, limitless – day after day on the front line dealing with asylum claims, pulling children back from the jaws of the system. She tried to stop the machine from grinding life into nothing, exhaling the dust of destroyed lives. A 15-year-old Somalian girl whom the Home Office declared was twenty, outside their responsibility and ripe for deportation; a boy from Afghanistan with a full beard and deep voice and a trauma so deep he woke in London parks, not knowing how he'd got there. Tormented by visions of his murdered parents, pushed onto their knees and shot. A shimmering on the city's horizons, where under our low English skies the whole world was weeping.

These tortured children that the government and their law courts wanted to destroy, Kaarina tried to save. As the fire consumed houses and fields, threatened neighbouring land, lapped even at her own heels, wet with fatigue, breathless, Kaarina would run in and out of the flames, pulling out burnt and disfigured children. Each human being, every creature disfigured and mistreated, broken and tortured, could be retrieved, redeemed by her outstretched hand (and, infuriatingly, she extended this charity to the torturer – though never the Tories, I discovered).

I would respond: 'God damn it, Kaarina. That's not how it works, not in life, not in history, philosophy or in any liberal fantasy of life. Your children – the ones you try to save – are the blood and flesh that capitalism feeds on, and the cogs and wheels of the system are as insatiable – as incessant – as your naivety and charity. One soul at a time you say is better than talk of systems, global processes and historical trends … but it's not one soul, its thousands crushed under collapsed factories in Bangladesh, expelled and murdered from their land by mining companies in Burkina Faso or it's the years wiped off life expectancy in Western Europe, the thousands driven to despair and suicide across Greece, Italy and Spain in the name of austerity and banking profits. Millions killed every day – a daily, murderous assault on humanity by the 1 per cent … to be precise Kaarina, by the 0.001 per cent. Two hundred and sixty-four individuals to give you the exact figure.'

My problem is that I never know how to stop, how to slow down when I feel strongly about something. I needed to break the wrong thinking, see the error entirely pulverised. So I went on: 'And to these jackals, their heavies, the highly paid managers with share options, who carry out the kills, what do you suggest, Kaarina? Further redemption – maybe a curative course of psychiatry? Prison sentences? This justice you celebrate, ha, these animals will not take to feeding on chamomile tea at a spa retreat. These creatures have a taste for blood, are ravenous for the profits of crime. They must be obliterated. Sadly, very few people have ever realised this … your notions of justice are just the instincts of the unthinking pack – a great mass-media illusion.'

The head is a thick and stubborn organ; Kaarina's was as thick and impenetrable as any.

She kept two mobile phones permanently on her. Email, phone calls, human misery on one and her own personal chaos on the other; she had to hear in stereo – witness statements, medical reports, court decisions, removal orders, judicial reviews, were to Kaarina her daily bread. She fought a daily battle against these things and, as she did so, bought me an entire wardrobe – breaking from her computer for two minutes, pacing her small flat, a coffee in one hand, then hastily preparing a meal between her submissions and slumping again at the computer, opening a page to an online clothing store and navigating the long lists of skirts, underwear and shoes. Order after order – relentless without taking breath, packages arriving the next day, gathering in the hall, waiting for distribution: to me, her family, her clients – to all the people she loved, to those she tried to save, to those whose love she needed.

* * *

Around her Kaarina had built a shell – a presentation of herself, impenetrable – yet beneath it, when the battle with the day was done, she let the carapace fall away; it was only then that I really knew her, and when she truly allowed herself to be seen.

Yet, for all my pretence that I could see the core, the essence, and that only I could break open the shell, I often stumbled over her words and meaning. I could never be entirely sure what she was attempting to say.

There was never an effort to wrap the presents – on the contrary, they were given casually, like bags of shopping. The lack of ceremony *was* the ceremony. Perfunctory, matter-of-fact, Kaarina would place the bags next to me on the sofa, or on the kitchen table – 'I've bought you some things.' Dump it next to me, playful. One night she placed two bags beside me and left the room.

She had travelled across London in the rain, which hammered the pavements and buildings. The tube had not been running so she rushed, panicking that there had been another outbreak, her coat over her head, the bags clutched tightly to her body. Coming into the flat, all apologies, water dripping off her – letting her coat fall to the floor, presenting me with the bags, a pair of trainers, jeans and a checked shirt, as she hurried to the bathroom to dry herself. Amused, entertained, I nodded my silent greeting and while she dried her hair, the hairdryer humming noisily in the bathroom, I changed into the clothes in the kitchen, pulled up the skinny black jeans, slipped the checked shirt over my T-shirt, buttoned it half way up and pushed my feet into the trainers.

When she saw me in my new outfit looking like a mail-order model, I was holding two glasses of wine. Finally free of the winter rain, the day, her child, she dropped her eyes slightly to the table, then lower still to the floor and when after a second she looked up she was blushing and there was something hopeful on her face beyond anything I had seen before.

The core of who she was could not be told from her words – protective, obscure, occasionally inarticulate. For a woman who believed in practice, I could not see the act, the deed, the heartbeat. In the first months I saw nothing of who she really was.

Yet, it was her acts that counted, her smile when she came to me in the kitchen and saw me in the clothes she'd bought, when she took the glass of wine, her hair still damp, ruffled, her face alert and free.

* * *

So, the more I told her to desist, to stand down, the more the gifts came, in greater and greater abundance – however much I chastised her. 'I don't need anything. Not a thing – I have more clothes than my limbs can wear in a dozen lives. I do not need special shorts to sleep in, or another vest to run in. I have all the music, books and gadgets I need. The planet cannot take any more consumption. Please Kaarina, no more!' I was restrained.

* * *

How do you remove a person from your life who gives you so much? Each space in my life had been colonised by her. The bedroom, the bedspread, the wardrobe of clothes (and the wardrobe), the radio, the eye masks, all my toiletries – the moisturisers, shampoos, conditioners (enough bottles to open a chemist) – the new showerhead, large enough she'd said for us to take a shower together (large enough, I'd said, to drain what was left of Lake Chad). Her presence extended from the bedroom to the lounge, and the new DVD player, then to the kitchen, Le Creuset pots, the spices, the packets of Thai green and red curry paste, tins of coconut milk, coffee percolators and espresso machines, teas, green, white, orange and black.

Everything on the planet that could be bought, she had bought for me.

To remove her, to take her away, after she'd left would leave the flat bare. I often slept more often in my office, enjoying the silence and anonymity of the university at night, the security guard sitting behind the counter, his face dimly lit – blissfully uninterested. I ran up the stairs, reached into my pocket for the keys, turning the key ring over in my hand – Kaarina had given even that to me, when she returned from a few days in Paris. A miniature of the Eiffel Tower, the 7,000 metric tons of nineteenth-century puddling iron reproduced in such detail that there was even a tiny, barely visible lift shaft.

11

Present Day

ON THE OCCASIONAL day when the owner of my usual café, Giancarlo, had suspended the profit motive, sacrificed working hours for that minor, inconvenient human activity sleep and anti-capitalist rest, I would use another café to work in. Shunning the chains, the diabolical coffee lounges that have proliferated across London – and every other large and small capitalist city, town and canton in the world – I chose Alacosta Coffee, a tatty, family-run institution on Charlotte Street; the print on the florescent sign above the shop, declaring, 'We are the Original Costa.' Some claim, I thought. I sat down and waited to be served; the only other customer was a woman with a dog.

Disgruntled, irritated, staring into the abyss of my day, I opened my notebook and read through yesterday's pages on Kaarina, on love and regret, for some piece of New Age tittle-tattle I had been asked to write for a newspaper feature on 'Life after Life'. These were the fluff pieces that I normally despised, but just this once I was doing it as a favour to the editor. Rereading it now, I could see that there were so many lies in what I had written, lies in the nostalgia that I had expressed in such soppy, sentimental prose. The decision to leave Kaarina in 2012 was unavoidable – our life was ridiculous: the father, with his wealth and tremendous Zen ignorance of the world; and those years-long contortions to which I was subjected. His grotesque house in Constantia, wealth dripping from the walls, his pride at being the first Indian family to move to the Cape Town neighbourhood. All wrong. All doomed, in one way or another, from the start. Should I write this? Give vent to my thesis that we are *all* trapped in the wrong relationships? That each of our attachments to objects, emotions and other human beings is wrong? Rehash the arguments I had made in *The Elation of Being*?

A man in his thirties with a rainbow knitted hat and a long, greying beard, tall, fashionably dressed, came into the room holding his bag and a coffee. I turned, looked at him and smiled; he smiled back. Distracted I opened the paper, read an article on Barack Obama's call to the Taiwanese president. I recalled the graphic I had used in a class that week, the encirclement of China by American warships, the South China sea a site of intense geopolitical tension, the whole of North and South East Asia and the Pacific Rim ringed by American nuclear subs, aircraft carriers on military manoeuvres and lily pad bases. China's rapid militarisation and increasingly bellicose presence in the region had seen the creation of islands from concrete and rocks, the occupation of the Paracel Islands, the brazen patrol by the Chinese navy of the Vietnamese coast. No one understood what was really happening – no one except me, that is. I slammed my fist on the table, the coffee jumped. Dog-woman and beard-man turned and stared.

Here *I* was, here *we* were, with our pathetic losses, with our café enemies, and the world was facing a fresh Armageddon. American imperialism was readying itself for war and how much longer did we have, a few years, half a decade, a decade? Yet most of us were happy to splash around in the glorious shallows of the present – or as I had once put it, turn away from our ephemeral, unconscious life situations. Ha, it was exactly the ephemeral, fleeting present that was going to kill us, unless we took action.

I recalled the truth, reminded myself of the reality: the world recovers from the horrors of economic depressions not by disingenuous New Deals or the conjuring tricks of Nobel Prize-winning economists in the central banks and universities of the world, but by total destruction and death in a global war. I need to get onto the streets, clear my head and fight.

There is no time for these personal distractions, not at moments like this.

PART 3

'All the evil that will have to end'

1

Present Day

THIS WAS THE first time I had been back to Senegal since *The Elation of Being* was translated into French, then a Senegalese edition was published, and I was invited to lecture. It was fifteen years since I had been home – after all, this place felt like home. Almost twenty years since *The Elation* had been published. The French translation, corrected by me, had predictably been a hit and soon I was receiving invitations to speak in France, Quebec, even the French colonial Pacific and in Francophone Africa.

I didn't recognise the city any more – not a single part of it. And I felt an intense sadness that came from this fact. As though I, too, had been erased, and the streets where I had played, and the houses that I had known, had all been obliterated. The streets and the buildings carried only the faintest impression of the past.

On my first full day, three days before I was due to speak, I sat on a city beach and pondered the life around me. The buildings spread across every spare patch of land, often only partly built, iron joists embedded in exposed concrete pillars. Before there had been a single dual carriageway that led traffic in and out of the city; now there was a motorway, underpasses and toll roads that ran to regional towns and cities. Every building, road and port has been built by a French company, each demanding their share of profits and paying only 15 per cent of the cost.

The neighbourhoods swept by sand, the luxury flats, the apartments where I was staying near the airport were splashed with concrete, the walls badly tiled, the units ill-fitting; the toilet seats slid under you, the stairs were uneven, so you would stumble as you climbed, the roof terrace was impossibly high, threatening always to fall onto the rocky sand below.

Yet the views of the old city made me feel alive with the strange, familiar chill of the spring wind and the smell of the sea, the faintest memories of my last visit and of my childhood.

I craved these strange visitations from my past – so I could maintain some coherence, a connection with who I had been and what I hoped I still was. I had lived in so many places. There was an odd anti-loss to these book tours – a return to the past. As much as I tried to talk about the new stories and books, the volumes I was currently writing, the only book I answered questions on was *The Elation of Being* – though my fame was such that I could usually speak on any topic I chose.

The last time I was here working on a project I taught a course at the university and lived in a small half-built settlement in the north of the city by the sea. The whitewashed buildings gleamed in the sun like pearls and the sand blew through the unmade streets into the great dunes, always changing shape so new tracks would have to be made to the main road for the buses and taxis to pass in the morning.

Ferocious, unkempt Dakar, I knew that the less you fought the city's unconquerable traffic and chaos the easier life was. But I fought and carried my European madness with me, until it, too, had worn me down and I accepted once more a pace of life entirely unlike the stressed world I had come from in London.

Years ago, when I was last here, I knew I wanted none of my old life and dreamed of staying. I had called Joanna, a woman from London I was seeing, to *explain* that I had decided to stay on. We had met at university and through some sort of conjuring, or just simple inertia, we were living together.

'What are you doing there anyway?' she asked, two hours into the conversation, beginning to see what I was doing. 'I mean for God's sake, Bianca, what is this? Some kind of third-world porno kick? And who are you seeing? I bet you are seeing someone.'

Her tone became angry, yet for all the fury in her voice – the genuine hurt – all I could really concentrate on was the activity around me in the phone shop, with its row of cubicles for making calls, the door open, the warm night-time breeze, the naked bulb, the laughter of customers and what I knew I would see when I left, when this call was done: the street awash with moonlight, children zigzagging through the sandy alleyways of the inner-city medina, the noise of families eating together. I would feel a complete and overwhelming calmness. The *rightness*, for the first time in my adult life, of my presence in a place, in this place. I felt the sand between my toes, let Joanna berate me, moistened my lips.

'I mean,' she was saying, 'who do you think you are? We have talked about this before, Bianca, and you are not a fool. You need to get out of there and come back. I mean, what exactly do you mean by saying you are going to stay?'

I knew her protests and anger were about to crumble, and when this happened, there would be a loss of coherence, the pattern was always the same and it made my heart lurch. 'I mean,' Joanna continued, 'if you are staying, Christ's sake, if you are going to be so stupid, I will come out.'

I was woken up by this and jerked back into the conversation. I sat up on the small bench, then stood. There were a few children, a small boy and a girl, the boy with his head shaved, the girl dressed up in a tight boubou, her hair plaited with beads; their faces appeared in the smudged glass of the shopfront smiling and then disappeared. The young man at the desk shooed them away, but they kept coming back, he lifted his hand to me in an apology. I nodded.

All the phone shops have gone now.

Who did I think I was? Joanna had asked. No one can be sure of who she is and nor could I. I liked it this way. I held my tongue. 'For God's sake, Bianca – what are you saying? If you are there I will come,' she repeated.

I pretended I was angry, though now all I wanted was silence and for this conversation to be done. To have Joanna gone. 'Listen, I am not pretending I don't know what it is. What this place does to me, I can't work it out. I don't know. I don't even know what you mean. But you are forgetting something Joanna, something fundamental ... but Bianca,' I did this, spoke in the third person when I wanted to press a point, to hit hard, 'Is black. So maybe it is a Third World kick but it is *black* porno. And I am black. You know Bianca is less an object of observation and curiosity in Dakar, a city she hardly knows any more, than she is in London. She is a pretty black woman with pale skin and if she doesn't open her mouth, no one knows who the hell she is.'

Joanna was silent.

On a dirty, sandy strip of land between the packed low-built houses there were boys in luminous-coloured tops playing football and I could hear their shouts. Half of the pitch was lit by a pool of moonlight and the other half by the flickering yellow light from a street lamp. Buried in the sand were tyres that the children used for goals and behind the field was a shipping container, long abandoned, where – it seemed – two families were living. In the distance the city, which in the day shimmered against the pale blue sky, now only faintly, pathetically flickered with light. Elsewhere, houses and offices were still being built, and everywhere in the city mosques were going up, with scaffolding scaling the minarets. This was the city of the half-built mosque.

Even sitting at the back of the shop – the struggle over, the small boy and girl fully inside and dancing in circles, kicking in the sand from the street – I could see the outline of a minaret in the distance and, though the mosque was not complete, the adhan sung out from speakers hanging on scaffolding, in sing-song Arabic – the words that I had long ago taught myself, *Hurry to the prayer (Rise up for prayer). Hurry to success (Rise up for Salvation). Prayer is better than sleep. There is no god except the One God.*

The call for prayer drifted across the houses and made me certain that I wanted this phone call with Joanna over.

Soon after this she started to cry – 'Darling,' she said. The pattern was always the same, namely accusations, denunciations, followed by anger and tears – and then just tears.

Moving back into the first person, more calmly now I spoke, 'Joanna, I'm black if you remember, from Africa. I feel as though I am at home here, remember this was once my home – like nowhere else.' She still managed to scoff. I paused, breathed in: 'And I've met someone.'

There was silence, her voice was quiet. 'What?'

I continued, 'I have started to see someone.'

Then all I heard was a sob, and a sharp intake of breath. 'How could you?'

Pain, betrayal, death. In that order.

Each acute experience of human emotion generates clichés. To death we say, 'At least it's an end to the suffering.' 'I am very sorry for you.' 'He/she had a full life.' 'She/he was too young.' 'It's such a waste.'

To betrayal we say, 'How could you?' 'I can't believe this is happening!' And, 'You disgust me.'

To pain we say, 'It will pass.'

Joanna said, 'I can't believe this is happening to us,' and between sobbing she also said, more quietly, 'You disgust me.'

Within two minutes the call had ended, and I was walking towards the boys playing football. I had my sandals in my hand, and let the sand splay my feet, spread my toes – massage me. For the short walk my head filled with Joanna's pain at the lie I had told her and by the time I had lit a cigarette and was leaning on the lamp post at the corner of the sandy pitch where the boys were playing football I was thinking about the next day and the work I needed to do. The study.

I didn't think about her again – until now.

* * *

And now I was back in Dakar, and within a few days I knew again that I didn't want to leave. How little Lydia meant to me, even the thought of us together – the perfectly good feelings, the forgetting she'd allowed me – left me utterly blank. Strange, disturbing even, but it was as if she didn't exist, as if I had imagined her, as if she was just a figment, a shadow from a half-forgotten dream.

This is what happened when I travelled, I was lost to the past and to my life in London. When I was away, I forgot Lydia, she had been erased completely from my mind; she ceased to exist. I knew Lydia longed for me and missed me, and this disgusted me – not that I was missed with such force, but that she had pined so visibly in my flat, over my things and in my life. There was a lack of cleanliness about her, her life led so loudly, so hysterically. It was *this* that disgusted me. Her noise.

But what was this capacity I had to forget? To have part of my life cast deep into the shadows, to be expunged, even while it still lived?

I felt the city, the country, the continent embrace me, take me – that is what Africa, all parts of it, had always felt like for me.

After the plane taxied to the terminal and the great, thick, vault-like doors swung open, I smelt the sandy, dry heat, heard the hard rustle of the wind in the palms and I forgot completely and totally my whole life in London – it fell, tumbled into irrelevance, crashed and scattered onto the ground, the plans, the stresses, the absurdities each deserted me.

I have perspective, which comes at the price of loss. How could I ever explain this to Lydia? That I become absorbed in the fragrance of a continent – the temptations, the sensations pull me in, but not as they do in London, with its impotent, crippling rage, but rather with the force of a storm wind. A hurricane that I cannot control.

I pondered, tired, blissful in the sun, sitting on the roof terrace listening to the mosque, the bleating of goats, the cries of the neighbourhood – this entire city cacophony.

I didn't really exist here – at least not that thing, which I used to call the situation of life, which was not me, not really me, just clutter and crisis – and as a consequence neither did Lydia, nor any part of my Northern life. I had travelled to another world, with such divergent organisation and laws that my thoughts, experiences and my life situation had no mooring, no real belonging.

I was delighted by the total anonymity this gave me, the erasure of who I had become, free from any attachment – with only my anger to root me. Yet, I was also acutely in myself, where my blackness both really meant something and meant nothing at all. So, I was nothing here; I was not forced to be a black person, out of some desire for self-identity and self-determination, the quest to make myself known in a white world. There was simply no need to affirm my blackness. And therefore I existed completely. I was not marked out for special treatment, racial sympathy, insult or desire. The gaze that fell on me in this city was ordinary and mundane. I was treated with the same ignorance, lack of interest and irreverence as every other woman. That is to say, not particularly well. After all, I was a woman, but I was not a *black* woman any more.

I dragged hard on the cigarette, enjoying each inhalation – I always smoked when I was here, without a flicker of guilt.

2

Present Day

THE FIRST NIGHTS here were often an ordeal, my dreams vivid when I travelled. Waking between nightmares covered in sweat, I parted the mosquito net, paced the hotel room, then removed my underwear and opened the window and looked at the houses opposite. The weak light of the moon shimmering, the edges of the building, the low buzz of the mosquitoes. My head filled with images from the dream, my heart pounding.

There'd been so much loving in my life, and such pain.

In the heat and dust of Dakar I felt an intense craving, and a distracted, consuming desire. I thought of the look on Kaarina's face in the dream and felt sick *and* excited. This was it! The continued possibility of sex. My body ached. I went to my computer, selected a track and clicked play – Nina sang into the room. I then took a shower and as the water crashed over my shoulders and back and onto the floor.

* * *

The less I did here the better. Apart from my speaking engagements, I maintained my rituals of work, the early starts, the day on the roof terrace, the small birds darting between the railings, the coffee and baguette with two fried eggs. I would calculate the time to spend on my work and the rest on emails, articles and preparation. I held hard to these habits, wherever I was. And if I needed to escape, to travel, to see, I had to earn it. Otherwise I would be lost, and an unforgiving pain would fall on me.

On this morning, I would work until noon and then pack my computer, my notes for the evening, and walk through the sandy alleyways to the main road past the mosque, the fruit stalls, the

Mauritanian silversmith, his eyes always bloodshot, smoking hard, sipping small glasses of sweet black tea, his familiarity with me, in the few weeks I'd been here, '*As-salaam alaikum – viens ici, on peut faire le commerce ensemble*.'

Then past the corner hospital with families clutching their faces, crying, holding on to each other – only here, outside the hospital, in the sun's brutal and honest light, the continent's true barbarity was revealed. I would then walk two hundred metres to the café, sit, order another coffee and proposition the beautiful woman who worked there. Her body young and full, pushing hard against her clothes, her skin dark, her eyes white and clear – her manner insolent. I would ask her if she wanted to see me in the evening, after my talk, and if she agreed I would take a taxi to the airport office in the city and change my flight again.

As I tried to work my eyes fell on a small finch that was being chased by other birds. It flew into the railings on the perimeter wall of the terrace. A swarm of thrushes, sparrows and finches were fanatical, tireless, snapping and nattering around it like flies. When they flew off, the bird sat crumpled and exhausted, unable even to stand on its pin legs. I wondered how long it would survive, with the hazards of the city – the feral cats hunting for food and sport, as numerous as rats at this end of town.

I ordered another coffee, shook my head clear and started to write my talk for the evening.

* * *

There is a particular house in La Pointe des Almadies, an area of the city that had always been a base for the rich, even when I was here fifteen years ago. Like the rest of Dakar, this area is now covered with houses and apartment buildings, yet, unlike elsewhere in the city, they are built with expensive imported tiles, parquet flooring, and by workmen brought in from the Middle East. The neighbourhood is close to the airport and opposite the ocean and between the mansions that have gone up you can see the water. The breeze from the sea bounces off the houses, hits you, kicks up the sand. The main road, Route de la Corniche, runs around this city-island, up from the old town, along the coast to the north and then joins the new motorway and heads east out of Dakar to Thiès and the mainland.

The houses built by the rich have no consistency. This one is a lavish walled palace, with great concrete columns on each side of oversized doors, a tiled roof, a swimming pool built on the second floor – a *piscine suspendue* – the sound of children splashing in the water, their American English echoing through the streets. Around the house is a perimeter wall four metres high and, beyond the wall, the guards languish, bored, in the sun, in front of the unmade roads, the rubbish, the chaos, piles of rubble, cars skidding on the sandy tracks.

I walk past this house every day, marvel at how the underside of the balconies are lined in expensive imported oak. On the drive outside the gate, there are two large Mercedes and two Land Rovers with their windows blackened; the vehicles are parked on the one paved stretch of road in front of the house. In this unpaved neighbourhood, simultaneously squalid and opulent, there are similar small stretches of paved road, built in front of an individual block of flats or houses.

Two days ago, I lifted my head as I passed the house and the sun hit me, forcing me to shield my eyes. Above me, when I could focus again, I saw a flock of sparrows, singing and chirruping without reserve, holding nothing back. I saw them swooping and darting between the branches of the trees, the balconies of the houses, their six-centimetre forms unaware of the rich, whose houses they played in, flying low, skimming the water in the swimming pool. Above them, focusing harder now, I could see other birds hovering like children's kites high in the sky – hawks, eagles, vultures. They, too, it seemed, could see everything, but they hunted alone, planning – they were deciding, I fancied, what of the life below should they kill.

I breathed in deeply, dropped my head again to the road, to the single, short stretch of paved road in front of the house and decided that if I could be one of those birds, I would choose to be the eagle.

What is life without a plan – without a decision to act?

* * *

I pulled up outside the Théâtre National Daniel Sorano in a yellow and black taxi. Groups of well-dressed middle-class students and professionals were queuing on the theatre steps. I got out of the taxi and their faces turned towards me – people smiled, some waved, the crowds around the door parted. I nodded, put my palms up in from of me in apology, tucked the small folder – covered in patchwork cloth, which I had bought in a market a week before – under my arm; it contained my papers, a book, two pens, a small notebook. I looked good in the boubou, the long dress, wrapped tightly around my body, my hair tied with a strip of cloth, the same pattern as the dress, and over my shoulders, a shawl, on my feet sandals, decorated with small coloured beads. I could be Senegalese but I knew in this crowd I was the daughter of a white man who had lived most of her life in the northern darkness.

I saw faces I recognised, a couple I had known for years – the woman, beautiful, from the south, the Casamance, her husband from England, his hair shaved, his beard greying. They had two children. I waved and cupped my hands around my mouth: '*Après*' I shouted. They nodded. Then I was inside, the cavernous interior dark, with concrete pillars and stained maroon carpets – a blast of cold air from the original 1960s air-conditioning system. The place was poorly lit, with flickering spotlights and faint, dying light from the old, recessed lights.

The large auditorium was full, many stood in the aisles. I was flanked on one side by a local publicist who had organised the night – Ndongo Bathily, a man in his forties, his glasses thick, a sly, confident smile – and on the other by a security guard who had taken my elbow, as men do here, steering me towards the stage. The atmosphere was festive, as I descended towards the stage I acknowledged the greetings; Ndongo made short introductions here and there, and then as I climbed onto the stage there was a round of applause – a few people stood, there was cheering from the balcony. I took the microphone from the table, where Ndongo and a woman, Khady, dressed like me in a striped boubou, sat. *'Vraiment, c'est très gentil de vous, mais je ne le mérite pas. Quand même, merci pour la bienvenue.'*

I delivered my talk, quickly and concisely – as clarity and passion, and meaning what you are saying, really meaning it (and preparation, not too much, just enough so it looks natural) is the art of good public speaking. The members of the audience must also get something, they should come away informed, smarter than they were, harder to fool. There should also be a single clear metaphor, to illustrate the central point that will fix itself hard in the minds of the audience, lodge itself there stubbornly – something that is impossible to escape. Or just a concise formulation, which connects with the audiences pre-existing knowledge and is both utterly novel and familiar: 'The period we live in resembles a movie of the 1930s in slow motion … with widening polarisation to the right and left, and the growth of fascist forces,' or 'the great volatility of the world has broken out inextricably since the 2004 outbreak, the 2008 financial crisis and its impact has triggered an era of crisis, war, environmental breakdown and revolutionary upheaval.'

I needed my stories, metaphors, aphorisms to become a habit of thought, a narrative of the epoch as we sought clarity, an explanatory hook – a battering ram against the ruling material force of society and the class that has the means of material production at its disposal. In a word, I wanted to change minds.

The cold air blew hard in the theatre and I saw the audience patting their arms warm, shuffling into jackets. I, too, pulled the shawl over my shoulders as I spoke.

I wanted to stir things up, give the audience members more than they wanted or expected. They wanted enlightenment, answers, salvation; and most of all they wanted me to speak about the book that had filled this room, and every other room I spoke in on my semi-permanent tour, in each damn nook and cranny on Earth. The lessons trite – we must loosen the grip of the past, release the future and find our way back to the present – and the book irrelevant, new-age Buddhist garbage, 'Be an activist, be involved, but also keep your distance and understand that the real struggle is within you.' I cannot believe that I wrote these words.

Clearing my throat, I spoke, unscripted.

'I have come from the dark North of our planet – from that warren of countries called Europe, cursed with hate and racism. The Western ruling classes are busy making headway with chauvinism and hate politics, trying to draw away the raw anger at how lives have been destroyed by crisis. Yet there will be mass struggle, capitalism will see to that. When that happens doesn't concern me tonight, but when it comes we must seize it with both hands – and not let go!

'Yet across the world the anger is the same, in different circumstances. Here in Senegal, too, there is an audience of billions of new potential fighters who see the centrality of politics – and all resulting – quite visibly – from the resolute and quite inspiring determined protest from below by ordinary Nigerians, Ghanaians, Burkinabés *and* Tibetans.' I added this last nationality to the mix for the benefit of the audience, I knew what turned them on, how they had been inspired by the Richard Geres and Spielbergs in their support for Tibet; I knew what titillated them. I had even once made a pilgrimage to visit the Dalai Lama, with all of his petty-bourgeois prejudices and nationalism, though his wealth and luxury sickened me – such enlightenment costs a fortune.

'Resistance is all over the place ...,' I continued. 'I come from a place where the West's crisis is scapegoated onto us and millions face job losses or repossessions. They call this austerity. Years of austerity, the same economic adjustment that they had visited on my continent, on Senegal and every country across this land – that apocalypse of lives and jobs, the massacres of the poor we have witnessed for three decades.

'Though all in all these are exciting times, despite the – as yet – lack of a clear plan of action. It will come. I will see to that!' I paused for the smattering of applause. 'Yet, we need to sift through the ideological hot air from the professors.' The audience laughed; I had been introduced as 'the Professor'. 'To see clearly we have to demolish the rubbish – the lies and half-truths – we have been taught.

'Our art, as I see it, is that as soon as we have unhinged the credibility or gullibility used by the professors of the ruling ideas, the authors, we can begin to argue seriously about the revolutionary agency of the poor – as the only force capable of standing up to, challenging, overthrowing and replacing capitalism.

'But the job of "unhinging", exposing, requires an almighty effort, will and determination.'

So I gave the audience what it needed, and also – here and there – a little of what it wanted. I had turned my appearances into a polemic about global political economy in Europe, in New York, Chicago and Beijing, in Melbourne and Manila, *and* in Lagos, Abuja and Johannesburg. I raged and raged. I was a one-woman, revolutionary band; where I went revolt and riots followed.

But I also analysed.

'Let me speak briefly about the shameless involvement of France in Africa.' I was speaking in Senegal, after all. 'Elf, we know, was used as an arm of the French state. "Sweeteners," sometimes in the region of $15 million, were paid to African leaders to ensure Elf was awarded oil contracts, while French governments shuttled between diplomacy, politics and business – gobbling up the continent's resources. In Senegal – do I really need to tell you this?' I said this with real anger, disbelief that these people, a *West African* audience, might not know the open, daylight robbery that was taking place in front of them. 'Your own government is selling off oil blocks to French companies, in the sea around Rufisque, Mbour and Joal Fadiout in a bonanza that we are told will turn the country into a Kuwait, a Saudi Arabia, the UAE. Or a Gabon. Recall how the ruling family in Libreville was kept wealthy in return for sacrificing independence, with access to enormous amounts of wealth, all in the name of Françafrique. …' I couldn't stop and the more I spoke, the angrier I became – frothing, avid, frenzied.

Suddenly I pummelled the table in front of me so the water in the glass jug spilled. I did not want the audience to feel comforted by simply *ad nauseum* repeating the core arguments of the one book of mine that they *had* already read, *The Elation* – a simple-minded story of individual endeavour, personal growth, private gain and then revelation, in a phoenix-like transformation of consciousness. I had to rub them up the wrong way, to start from zero.

The power of the present *is* in the past. What we are is what we were, and what has been done to us. The dead live in the traditions that weigh on the brains of the living. Just when we think we are occupying the present, creating something that did not exist before, precisely at such moments do we conjure up the phantoms of the past, take their names, their chants and slogans. Yet, the activity and presence of this new scene – this nowness, this isness – in the world is stolen from the costumes and language of the past.

And the only true prophets are those who forge the future – in their declarations *and* plans. Without the past and future, we are nothing, but mindless, dumb machines – *tabula rasa*, void of life.

The hunger for change was insatiable – yet they had it all wrong, and I had helped in the mystification.

The change they thought they needed was what they already had, what they already practised. My contribution eighteen years before had not challenged the world, it cut with the grain of its fake promises and epiphanies. In following the fashion of unique revelations, spiritual truth, I had been utterly and predictably faithful to twenty-first-century ideological trends – without a past or a future, the Power of Now translated into All Power to the 1 per cent.

So, instead, I raged, roared at the faces I could see in the audience and they stared back at me in considerable surprise.

'And here, friends,' I finished, calmer, reaching to the back of my head, tightening the cloth wrap around my hair that had been shaken loose. 'In Dakar, in the new developments, we have to ask what improvement has there really been, what has there been for the poor – who feed from rubbish bins while the rich eat on silver plates – in the new buildings and roads. ...' I knew I was straying on ground that was dangerous. There was a rule that I was breaking, come to the continent, to Senegal, criticise Africa, the thieves and politicians, the whole caste of profiteers if you wanted, but not the country *itself* – not your hosts. I knew this, I had learnt this. 'But we should not fool ourselves, sorry *you should not fool yourselves*,' there was some sympathetic laughter from the audience, '*You* are living in the future. Global capitalism looks like this – the rich in their castles, houses, compounds, built in La Pointe des Almadies, in the luxury apartments on the Corniche, and around them the poor, in their squalor, on unmade roads, mothers and fathers hawking, barefoot children begging outside modern palaces and mansions to the hum of generators. …' I was silent for a moment to allow the description to sink in. 'What does this new anthem to Africa's renaissance sound like? What is the real sound of Senegal that should be sung from the mosques every day?' I stopped here, for a moment, let the crowd wonder for a second if I had finished, and then, at last, I said, 'The sound of our mothers crying.' There was a sharp intake of breath and then a round of applause.

So far, so good.

'We must dedicate ourselves to publicise, promote, support, argue for global resistance – especially the now growing element of the most decisive and by far the most important kind – the resistance of the poor – in North Africa, in China *and* in Tibet, not just Buddhist monks but jeans and leather-jacket-wearing urban youth in Llasa! And we must be clear that our struggle everywhere is against the 1 per cent, the 0.1 per cent to be precise and statistically accurate.'

Before I put the microphone down, I said, my tone soft, conciliatory – entirely calm, 'But what do I know about your lives in Senegal, my friends? I am not from here any more. This is *your* country. These are your challenges.' The applause started, filling the theatre, fuller now, spreading across the entire auditorium. I sat down.

The dangers were all around me here. I could not spend five minutes without a hail of problems. The biggest one was the overwhelming feeling of being, in some way, special – the unearned prize for being from the North, for visiting, speaking and then being able to leave.

I felt the glow of acclamation as the audience clapped. I took my seat as a few people stood up and cheered, I watched myself, my chest swelling, the pride stretching across my body. Yet, beyond this I felt something else, a privilege, an excitement that was entirely unearned – a swagger, a power, a sense, always there, in being different – greater, somehow special. I felt this in the streets, in the heat, waving away the mosquitoes on the roof terrace in the evening, after I had finished my work, stopping in the middle of the sandy tracks between the houses, bending down, prising off my sandals, emptying the sand, then standing again and walking on. For nothing I was raised like a saviour, offering nothing real, except spoken words, words on printed paper, for my useless words I was lifted high on the audience's shoulders ... before I had even properly started my work.

Despite the coldness in the room, I unwrapped my hair, let my plaits fall to my shoulders and wiped my face dry with a handkerchief, gave a self-depreciating smile, bowed my head a little at the audience and slowly tied up my hair again – repeating the action in reverse.

Ndongo took the microphone and spoke – a gush of nothings, praising me incoherently, lavishly. I could not even make out what he said but I nodded and smiled. When he sat down there was applause and Khady stood and spoke. Khady Diop was a friend. I liked her – large, adamant, charming, obvious. She gave nothing to me I did not deserve.

Leaning over the table as though trying to bend down and speak privately to each member of the auditorium, Khady said, 'With a performance like that Bianca, Madame Tening,' something she called me, a type of public pet name that had been taken up in the country, 'you will not be invited back to Dakar.'

The crowd could finally relax as Khady trivialised what I'd said, skinned it of content and action – this was necessary, and probably secured my stay in the country for a few more days.

* * *

I had been with Khady for two months fifteen years ago. I remember her saying, 'I want to boast about what we're doing, tell everyone, explain that I haven't slept for weeks and I have never felt better. The pleasant pain, the ache, that sense, that feeling. . . .' All this came out years ago – when we'd been together in Dakar.

I was leaning on pillows propping me up in bed, I was amused, pleased and satisfied, the sheet gathered between us, her head on my chest: 'But,' she said, raising herself, 'I can't say anything because I would be stoned to death, and because what we are doing is illegal.' Though she loved our illegality, as the only place she could be herself, the lie of our relationship, the 'make-believe' in the coming and going to the apartment I had on the fifth floor of the lopsided building near Fann Hock and the university where I worked. The landlord lived on the ground floor with his children and second wife from Zambia, whom he beat every night. Four months after I moved in, he was murdered in his car in the middle of the night, his head smashed open with a rock. His car had been parked outside a building in a neighbourhood lined with the street shacks of the homeless he had tried to evict, the pavement stalls over which he would drive his imported Mitsubishi Pajero. He was murdered and no witness, not one of the dozens who lived in the shacks on the streets, or of the children who played there night and day – came forward.

After I returned to work in the UK, Khady married a young man with whom she'd never slept to whom she had promised herself as a high-school student. Now she lived a middle-class life, worked in the French embassy, and had three children.

* * *

Khady, Khady how you still make me smile. How I longed for her again, *to hold you once more*. I smiled at her as she spoke.

'Questions,' Khady announced. 'Now it's your chance to interrogate our special guest.' She looked at me and winked.

A young man in his twenties put his hand up, his face fresh, his skin clear and bright. A microphone was handed to him.

I felt elevated even after I finally returned to the UK – to the Northern prison where I lived. My hair was plaited, my gait contemplative, purposeful – I had the knowledge that the development and privileges enjoyed for a few decades in the Old World would soon pass and that dust and loss would then blow across the entire world.

I had seen the future and the coming fall. I had breathed and loved in the South where humanity lived and loved and died; where capitalism had no legitimacy, where it was weak and dependent and constantly on its knees. *Where the chains of the 1 per cent were weakest, there they must be broken.*

I believe that I have a unique clarity in myself, a sense of irreplaceable experience and knowledge. How many people on Earth understand and know, really know, what needs to be done? And if I were killed? If *I* disappeared? I was sure it would all be over for a century or more. An entire dream of the world would disappear into nothingness.

The young man, the boy, spoke confidently, easing his way in, congratulating me. 'It is nice to see our sister back here, back home,' there were a few cheers, 'her book that has given all of us much hope and inspiration. … I want to ask her, given her strident opinions about this country, what her thoughts are about the murder of Monsieur Couper?' I let the question circulate in the silence.

The audience sighed collectively, the question was brief and there was no attempt to elaborate, or to remove the sting. I was relaxed and feigned ignorance, I let it sit, the silence in the auditorium, broken only by the moan of the air-conditioning, the shuffling of people in their seats.

I looked at Ndongo and Khady and sat back in my seat for a moment. I leant forward to the microphone and said, 'Brother, could you repeat the question. I am not sure I am aware of what you have spoken about. What is the story?'

The man smiled, he looked around for the microphone; an usher hurried up the aisle and passed the microphone back to him. Slowly he stood and started to explain: 'Madame Tening, there were murders last night. A Franco-Senegalese family killed. A well-known local businessman from France who had lived in Dakar for twenty years.' He paused, looked around him; there was a stillness in the theatre, which felt strange. 'The man, well-known to the people here – maybe not to you – was a controversial figure, a businessman. He was cruelly murdered in his home near Ngor, in the north of the city, and then it seemed his house was broken into and his three-year-old daughter and wife tied up.'

The effect on the audience in the theatre was predictable, the details sensational and unusual. I saw heads bow; others covered their mouths. Ndongo took the microphone and spoke, 'Terrible though these events are, what relevance do they have for our guest? Can we move on please? Next question.'

There was an uneasiness that I could sense. I stood, put a hand gently on Ndongo's back and reaching for the microphone, said: 'I think I understand the question and its irrelevance. There has been a murder and I think the young man is asking me – given my recent polemic on Françafrique – what my opinion is?'

'Just your thoughts Madame – *if* you have any?' The man was still holding the microphone. There was laughter, tittering, the room relaxed.

'It is true I am known to have a few thoughts – here and there. Maybe I can say in a few words ...,' I replied.

Next to me Khady half stood, moved towards me and whispered, 'Bianca, don't say anything – none of these things has been confirmed and you'll only invite condemnation.'

There was a mild eruption in the room, a few people called out, 'Next question – *la prochaine question, s'il vous plaît.*' Someone shouted to the man to sit down, the same soft insolent half smile on his face.

I waved down the heckler, and stood confidently and – with my shoulders back, my body facing the audience fully, squarely – I raised my arms, silenced everyone. Once more I felt that I could do anything I wanted. I just needed to open my mouth, let the words come out, tell them what I thought – let my eloquence tumble over them, let my presence subdue the auditorium. Slowly I raised the microphone, 'I know nothing,' I repeated slowly. 'Nothing of the murder you speak of. But this man, Couper, if it is him, I know him. We all know him.' Beside me I could sense Khady relax, her muscles relax under her dress. 'I mean I know him by reputation, as we all know him.' I repeated. There was a rumble of agreement. I continued. 'The man was well known to me as a speculator in food products – they call it "softs" in Chicago – and in the price of goods globally, moving funds around to the world where money can be made. He was a market speculator and financial bandit who has helped construct this world of horrors. Hunger has not been down to fate for a long time – it is the product of men like Couper. Remember, my friends, behind every victim of mass hunger is a mass murderer. He also invested in companies, and factories. Let's start briefly with Bangladesh. ...'

When I finished, having given graphic illustrations of the man's crimes, I added a kind of disclaimer, 'None of these things I have said, his crimes – for that's what they are – justify, could possibly justify the man's murder if that's what it is. This goes without saying, but still ...' I looked directly into the face of the young man, 'it needs to be said.'

Relieved, in complete agreement, the audience applauded me for the *one* thing I regretted saying with every cell in my body. The crowd continued to clap so enthusiastically that it silenced the effect of the lie, those words that had left a line of sweat on my brow. I fought to remain standing. I gripped the table as the applause continued, its sound like blows raining down on me, I bit my tongue, then my lip until I could taste the acrid blood – until the wound stung.

3

Present Day

I HAD LIED, and I suspect some in the theatre that evening knew I had. I had listened to the reports in the morning, been to the area in which Couper lived and spoken to his neighbours – the house was a grotesque palace even in this neighbourhood. The sand blowing high between the houses with people hailing taxis, with a hand shielding their faces, a scarf covering their mouths. Around the houses there were police cars and tape cordoning off the property – then around them a line of soldiers fidgeting with their rifles, their heads bent away from the wind. Covering my face, making myself invisible, I spoke to one of the policemen outside the house; he looked at me, wrapped up like everyone that morning, in my scarf, only my eyes visible, he said '*rakk bu jigéen*' (*sister*). Move on, this is a sensitive area.'

I pulled down the scarf, so my face was fully exposed and repeated myself, '*Jaam nga fanane*' (*good morning*), can you tell me what happened here?'

He looked at me, stuttered an apology and then spoke, looking at the ground, then hurriedly staring at me. 'Madame Tening …' It was often a surprise that I was still so well known in Senegal so that even an ordinary policeman would recognise my face like this. Though my fame had long burst the narrow banks of academic circles.

'Madame Tenning,' he repeated, 'there was an attack on this important monsieur. He, he …' the policeman nodded towards the car in the drive with a blanket hastily thrown over it, '… was killed in the vehicle.'

'How?'

'With a knife, madame.'

'How?' I repeated.

'Here …' he said, indicating the space under his chin, 'and here,' he pointed to his two eyes.

'So, he was blinded,' I said without embellishment.

The man didn't reply, he lowered his head and nodded. I was still, the sand blew against us and it stung.

'And the family?'

Looking at me directly, he hesitated; I widened my eyes, loosened the scarf so it fell away from my chest. His eyes dropped, he swallowed and after a pause he continued, 'he, the murderer, took the keys from the man, entered the house, opened those doors …,' he turned a little to indicate the thick metal outside gates, 'Then he tied up the wife and cut her throat in the kitchen. It's terrible, blood everywhere – over the tiles.'

'And the children?' I prompted.

'There is only one girl.'

'The girl?'

'She was found in the swimming pool, drowned.'

'Why the girl?' I asked, more to myself than the policeman.

'Only God knows the cruelty of this man. It is beyond our understanding.'

'So, you know it was a man?'

The policeman laughed nervously. 'Of course, madame,' he said, a little derisively, for the first time looking directly at me. I turned to face the full force of the wind, and walked away. 'Madame Tening,' I heard him call after me, 'one minute.'

I ignored him and carried on walking.

* * *

I should have spent the day working. Instead I went to the beach opposite Ile N'dour, where there is a permanent market of small makeshift stalls, pieced together with wire and tape, scraps of wood, selling necklaces, rolls of cloth, T-shirts, and closer to the shore there are restaurants, open barbecues, halved oil drums filled with charcoal grilling fish, large steel pots of rice, and around them plastic chairs and tables. The sea was worked up, large coloured narrow boats, pirogues, crowds of children and women came and went, carrying buckets of fish. I sat and watched, let my mind spread, allowed it to go without reprimand – I did not try to control the branching, widening thoughts. I gave free rein to the incoherent, wandering thoughts I usually fought against day and night.

And when I closed my eyes, I did not see darkness and words, but images and colours.

I saw the child, naked, her body floating in the pool – what possible purpose could *her* murder serve, I wondered, and the wife, I tried to find in myself sympathy for her but this was harder. A consenting Frenchwoman – was hers the voice I had heard shouting at the children in the pool a few days ago – conscious of the world, immersed in a life of privilege, aware of her husband's crimes, or choosing ignorance, which is no alibi any more? Then my mind turned to the stink of the man in the car, the sun beating on the bonnet, the flies on the gorged eyes – crawling in and out of the bloodied sockets.

Absentmindedly I ordered another drink, a beer. I turned to the most extraordinary fact – it's always the most obvious fact, that is *the* most vital. Like the murder of my landlord years ago, this killing took place in full view of the neighbourhood – there is no real privacy in this city for the rich and poor, this much I knew. This fact led to another – the murders must have been conducted with the complicity of the community and the man's staff, the guards, the nannies and the rest of the slaves he kept.

What of them?

Surely the team investigating the murders would know this basic fundamental, Senegalese fact.

Trying to think authentically, to smell, feel and think *Senegalaisement*, I realised another basic element to the case, that the man, Monsieur Couper, despite his notoriety, the general distaste for his methods, had no security or none other than a gate, a guard, who slept in a shack beside his hideous concrete castle.

And only if you knew Senegal could you understand these peculiarities, the night-time murder of the powerful did not happen – not in Dakar, not in this country. This was not Abidjan, Lagos, Johannesburg or London. Dakar was a place where the rich could sleep peacefully in their beds, with impunity ... until now.

'*Mon frère, dama mar*. I will have a plate of *yassa poulet*,' I said to the man who came to my table. I smiled, then, before he could start a conversation, I took out my notebook and a pen. The wind had died down; I looked out across the ocean, the infinite ripples on the water, and in the distance, on each tiny wave the light burst and refracted on the surface, sending miniature stars fizzing and burning into the sky.

I could relax finally, the vision jarring, magnificent, took me away from myself.

When the food arrived, I had adjusted myself in the seat, drawn my scarf around me, more to hide than shelter. I ate.

* * *

I was with Khady on my last night in Dakar.

Earlier in the day, my eyes were lined, highlighted, my hair flattened and tied back, the colourful blouse I had bought from a city market stall open, matching the skirt with a large split up one side. The young girl to whom I had spoken at the bakery in my best Wolof, smiled at me and came out of the shop after she served me, so we could continue to talk. Her hair was dusted with flour, her T-shirt smeared with fingerprints from her morning labour. Outside, in the morning sun, I felt desire scream inside me. I felt acutely alive next to her. My whole being drawn to a single point, focused into one thought, one feeling, the surge of adrenaline opened something in me, making me feel awake for the first time in weeks – the colours, the sensations and smells of the city street around me were clear, beautiful, vivid. Everything was lifted in the tide of my lust. I was utterly, unavoidably present. As she pointed to the places to eat, indicated the best spot to wait for a *Car Rapide*, she edged closer, so our arms touched, my skin bristled and when she looked at me the insolence had gone and there was a softness – so all that was left was her sweetness. If I took her as I wanted to, as I knew I could, I would be destroying something.

I cursed that part of me that was irredeemably from the North, corrupted and lost, that half of me that was white.

I thought of the birth of the modern world and slavery. The crimes were unrecoverable; there could be no revenge, no revolt or promissory note, no compensation – the tens of millions stolen, murdered, taken, an entire continent broken, against which no European pogrom, holocaust or massacre could measure or compare. The continent – this place that had once been my home – had been shattered into a million pieces and the inheritors, the heirs of slavery, were the same families, politicians, businesses – J. P. Morgan Chase, the thousands of slaves taken by them as collateral on loans; N. M. Rothschild & Sons Limited, and Nathan Mayer Rothschild, the banking family's nineteenth-century patriarch, who used enslaved Africans as interest; or Brown Brothers Harriman, who financed the cotton economy by lending millions to southern slavers. The list goes on and on. And these families still ruled the world, their system of profit still triumphed.

'What's your name?' I stepped away from the girl.

'Fatou,' she'd said.

I tried to control these thoughts. The sun beat hard on my back, I was sweating. 'I am in a rush to take a taxi.'

'Then let me get it for you,' Fatou said, stepping off the steps of the bakery and into the road.

The desire was gone, but still I felt a simple pleasure, the enjoyable confirming thud of my heart – which was now the satisfaction of a clear thought, a pure anger, *of life fully perceived*.

What is *that* feeling that is more than anger and rage? What is the word for that? Because what I felt then was not even fury, standing near Fatou as she indicated to passing cars, shouted roughly to people she recognised, I realised there would be no satisfaction for these crimes – there could never be an answer for the horrors of the past in the simple course of history, the patient, endless game of waiting, for the revelation, the soirée that would never come. Only those with the gift of setting alight the sparks of hope in the present can carry the future away from the crimes of the past. The dead are not safe from the enemy; an enemy that continues in his projects. Only in its disruption, in the working up of the present, was there a chance at redemption – of revenge.

I had marked the line in Walter Benjamin's book that morning, 'The Messiah arrives not merely as the Redeemer; he also arrives as the vanquisher of the Anti-Christ.'

The point was clear, my chest open and head uncluttered, that justice, real justice, had to be taken today – amid the confusion and outcry of life, in the sky's wild noise.

I knew. I knew. I knew.

* * *

There were roadblocks, private taxis, buses, coaches were stopped on the main arteries in and out of the city; and the city spoke of nothing else. The radio sang in righteous condemnation of the murder and politicians declared Couper a child of Senegal. I thought of the daily massacres taking place in Yemen – the reports that followed updates of the murder of Couper, reports that spoke of Muslim solidarity for the killing in Dhamar, Taizz and Marib by Saudi bombs.

The neighbourhood was shut down and now, to access the area, we had to produce IDs, passports. The informal shops and stalls were closed, the shacks of the poor had been kicked away from the walls. So, where they had lived, in this rich man's oasis, there were only piles of rubble and wood.

I swore loudly as I entered the neighbourhood, so the taxi driver turned to me: 'What do you think?' I asked as he accelerated away from the police patrol.

He was silent, then after a long pause he said: 'Only Allah knows.'

'Does this have anything to do with Allah?' I answered.

'Everything does. Everything.'

'*Tout ce que je vois, ce sont les maisons des pauvres détruites et un homme riche mort* – all I see are the houses of the poor destroyed and one rich man dead,' I said.

He was silent again. I turned to him; his hands were gripping the steering wheel hard. 'There is too much suffering in Senegal,' he said, finally.

'Too much,' I repeated.

* * *

Khady was indefatigable. I repeated the conversation to her, and she nodded, 'At least the poor have their faith.'

I scoffed, hit the table between us with my flat hand; our glasses jumped.

Khady had come to my guest house – a French style *pension* – and we sat together on the roof terrace, the sun recently down, the sky huge, open, dark blue, a strip of pale red light on the horizon across the sea. The birds, so restless in the day, now seemed more thoughtful, pensive. On the railings on the side of the terrace that faced the sea, two small finches sat side by side, taking their turn to sing – an ode to the sky with its shades of red and crimson light, exhausted from all their daytime chirping and the battles for food and song. Local tradition says that the finches are the carriers of human sadness, anxiety and sin, and they can set us free.

Khady took her glasses off and smiled at me. 'What do you think happened?' I asked.

'No idea. A robbery – there have been attacks in the area. Foreigners are a target.'

'The place is full of foreigners,' I said, 'whites – the French, Europeans, Russians; the Chinese. …'

'That's not what I mean.'

'I know what you mean. *You mean* the Nigerians, the Cameroonians, the Mauritanians.'

'The Mauritanians have always been here.'

'Okay so it's not the Mauritanians, it's the Nigerians.'

'That is not what I am saying. I don't want to talk about it,' she said, putting down her glass.

I teased her: 'I couldn't care less that he's dead. Long may he remain so.'

Khady sucked her teeth, shook her head. 'Sadie, *Inna Lillahi wa inna ilayhi raji'un* (we come from Allah and to him we will return). God rest his soul.'

'God damn his soul and I mean it.' I leant forward, reached across the small table, rested my hands on her knees. 'Maybe,' I continued to needle her, running my hands further up her legs. Khady's eyes lost their focus, I tightened my grip then pulled my hands back, dragging my nails along the inside of her legs.

'I have been reading about this man for years and so have you. He was despised for his relationship with the regime, and his dealings. He was known by everyone. *Everyone*. You know what the kids in the neighbourhood called him? Papa Macky. The president's father! His corruption – the money he made from the mines in the north, the oil deals, his investments on the continent and elsewhere. The concessions he was granted in the Sabodala mines in the east – you know the place, where the Canadians, South Africans and British are. And the strike? Remember that? In stable, peace-loving Senegal. How many were killed? Hundreds. Unemployed youths trying to get their hands on some of the bonanza, and strikers were massacred and thousands in the local communities driven away to pave the way for an efficient model of capital accumulation. Those who tried to escape, to run away, were killed by indiscriminate volleys of gunshots fired by mounted police accompanied by dogs and helicopters. And it was Couper who called in the police, told the government that they needed to teach the strikers and the communities a lesson. There was the blood of workers and the poor on his hands, Khady. His soul deserves no rest.'

I wasn't excitable, I was calm. I measured my words and searched Khady's face for a reaction.

Her head dropped; she avoided my gaze. I don't know what it was – the fact that we were together again after all these years and that she thought we shouldn't be, or that her face normally animated, alive, was tired and around her eyes there was a great sadness.

She still didn't respond – was it because she knew that what I said was true, and that there was no refutation?

When she spoke, her face softened, untensed. 'We knew, we knew. There were even charges being bought and when the massacre came to light there were protests.' As well as her work in the embassy, Khady worked part-time in a legal firm that received Swedish money, and investigated foreign companies operating in Senegal. 'We even added our name to the petition calling on the government to investigate the killings and ...' – she hesitated – '... Couper's role in it. It is true, that he encouraged a more effective security-force response to the strike.'

I laughed. 'You are too liberal, Khady – Couper described the strikers as criminals and had called for "concomitant action" to be taken. He ordered the killings.'

I had become serious again; I felt the ripple once more of anger. My ankles stung and itched from mosquito bites. I kicked my sandals off and swung my feet onto the small coffee table. 'And what happened?' I added.

'People knew about it, Bianca, and they were outraged. The families of the miners tried to organise a protest last year.'

'I heard,' I said.

'There had been a permanent protest of the families in front of the Town Hall, hunger strikes and even a few reports on the BBC, Al Jazeera, CNN. Their protests, when they attempted to march north from the city to Les Almadies, was broken up violently by the police.'

'I remember,' I said, 'and two women were hospitalised. Mothers of men killed in Sabodala and a child of eight, if I am correct.'

'You don't miss a thing, do you. You heard.'

'Of course, I did. I heard it all – these aren't secrets, Khady, the truth is always in plain view.'

'So, you know it was a scandal, for the government and internationally – for the big companies ... Taranga Gold was kicked out of the country.'

The mosque, an enormous, beautiful, white-domed building that was still being built a few streets away from the guest house, sounded the evening call to worship.

I couldn't help myself. I straightened my posture, slipped my feet off the coffee table. 'A scandal,' I spat. 'The minister of mines arrested, a trial – and Couper's company investigated. A few army officers questioned; some private security guards imprisoned. And the newspapers ran stories for a few months – of course I heard it all, even *Le Soleil* was calling for Couper to be arrested, for there to be regulations against the operation of foreign companies in Senegal. *The enemy within.* I heard it, Khady,' I repeated.

I stood up. I don't know why I was suddenly so angry, or why I was directing it at Khady. I suppose I needed to rid myself of the bile and inertia I felt here – the fatalism that descended on me and pressed down on every living creature in the country. I needed to speak louder, I had to breathe, to push against what this city did to us, '… and all of this noise – and these demonstrations – what did they achieve?' I continued: 'and to get the justice the families demand, what do you propose, Khady? A bit less injustice? To their brothers and sisters who die in Nigerian cement factories, or are killed when factories collapse in Bangladesh, or are shot down by the police for striking in South Africa, we should insist on a little more oversight? Better compensation for the widows and children?' Khady flinched at this – I knew that this was what the NGO for which she worked, with the support of foreign aid money, had been arguing. 'You see, Senegal needs,' here I spoke a little more calmly, 'the whole of Africa needs to destroy, get rid of, wipe out – *so they cannot come back* – every political pimp, all the businessmen and financiers and the entire caste of profiteers. To eradicate them. Instead we insist on compensation for murder and then laud their murderers as natives of the land. Papa Macky! We are not even talking about reforms, or the promises of a slightly better society … because on this forsaken planet, there is no longer the possibility even of reforms.'

My forehead was wet – Khady sat back in her chair. I smiled, dropped my shawl on the chair, came around to her, checked quietly that we were still alone, put my hands on her shoulders, leant down and kissed her. She resisted for a second, and then reached up for my neck, curled her long fingers around my face.

* * *

Lying together in bed, before she had to leave, our clothes thrown off, the door locked – Khady had dragged a chair from the desk and wedged it under the handle – we talked softly, in whispers, as if we were being listened to, watched.

'You know, Bianca?' Khady said, 'I think we have got so used to living in the dirt, as you say, the corruption, the cynicism, that we need it – somehow. What damage can a scandal possibly cause, when we are already living in the gutter? It's in the open, we know where they live, what they do and *still* it goes on. This is what they mean by freedom; a freedom to know our conditions and to be utterly incapable of changing them – or believing they can change.'

'The freedom to know our misery,' I added. 'We live in the blood and dirt and splash around like children on the backs of our brothers and sisters and this, this …' I was lost for words, '*enfer*, is exactly the power of society. We can imagine the end of the world, but not the end of misery.'

'Bianca?' Khady said.

'Yes.' In my need to extol, I had got up again and was pacing between the bed and the door to the balcony.

'Please come back, here,' she patted her chest, tried to reach me, to pull me towards her.

I smiled, laughed and said, 'You are trying to pacify me like that mosque outside.' She reached up to me; I gave way, lay down next to her. 'You see, the revelation, or the media exposé, is always the basis of a new firmer, more enduring power for the state … but maybe this is exactly what they want.'

The memories came to me; how little she'd changed. *How little any of us really change.*

'They do everything to stop the exposé, as you say. Years ago, the government did everything it could to stop us publicising a report into the property deals of the president's son – the kick-backs.'

'*Us*?' I queried.

'The newspapers I mean. He didn't want the scandal, and when it came, he was arrested. So I am not sure you're right. It's not all just a cycle of corruption and cover-up.'

'No, Khady, you can do better than that. I am not talking about this or that politician but the whole edifice, the system of theft, built deep into the marrow of our societies. Into Senegal. The United Kingdom. The United States. The scandal is the meaning of democracy – it's …' I paused, searched for the French word, 'the *engrais*, the compost of society. We don't even need repression – the people are clear about what's going on. Universal misery has already been established.' I was kneeling on the bed and started to look around the room for my clothes. 'They don't even need to keep silent about the massacre – the papers had pictures, right?' I got up, removed my dress from the tangle of clothes on the floor, shook it free of other items, bra, panties, shawl. 'Do you remember the bulldozers they used to dig the graves, the mass pit where they buried the miners in Sabodala (I am not even mentioning the victims of the virus, buried in the same pits in 2004). All of this came out, Khady, all of it, on the TV, the newspapers, every piece of evidence paraded before us.' My throat was dry, I swallowed, '*We* need to get rid of the army, the generals, the government, and especially Couper – the 0.01 per cent – and his system of wealth and control that props up the whole bloody edifice and for eternity – so they can't resurrect. …' I paused, gulped a mouthful of water from the bedside table and continued more slowly. 'No, the system needs these scandals to survive and this is the thing that scares me Khady.' There was in this monastic silence an idealism that appealed to me – only the word could make the act real, if it were not spoken it simply did not exist. In the end there was only the word.

Khady laughed, stood up, her body was still firm, strong though larger, broader, thicker from childbirth. She said, 'We say, "These politicians, who do they serve?" and "Murderers," and then nothing happens. You have a point, Bianca.'

I zipped the dress up on the side, felt my body wet and clammy – it was nice to be without my panties and bra. I felt released, open.

'You know me. I have always known the point, Khady.' I winked at her, blew her a kiss.

4

Present Day

ON THE PLANE I sat as I always did by the window. I could lean against the cold fibreglass body of the plane, bunch up a jumper and rest my head against the window and stare into the dark, still blackness. The thin, panelled layer of aluminium separating me from the freezing jet stream. The shutter open, and the window condensation running down the outside of the plastic pane – the night was black and filled with stars and in the morning, there was a warm pale blue light and cloudless view of the sun.

Beside me were two nervous Senegalese men travelling to Spain on borrowed money and temporary visas.

They spoke to me in Wolof and I answered in French: 'I would like to sit by the window,' I stated to the man, who was wearing a woollen hat.

'Sister' he said, 'you can have the seat, but can you take one of our bags through customs?'

We swapped seats and I bought them a bottle of whiskey and wave away their refusal: 'Sister, we are Muslim and don't drink.'

'Then give it to your friends in Madrid.'

My moods swung wildly, they always had – I fought with it on that journey as I sat next to the two young men taking nervous swigs from the bottle, asking me questions about Europe, as the moaning, aluminium carapace of the plane fought against the stresses of altitude and speed. I felt saturated by nostalgia and regret. Regret that I was leaving Senegal, that I had ever left and that I had not had the courage, years before, to stay – when I knew I should have. The cold, harsh, impossible life I had in London, busy, locked away, miserable like everyone else on the island.

My long exile from Africa needed to come to an end.

I opened the shutter wider and saw the pulsing light at the end of the wing. I looked hard at the light, let its rhythm calm me. The boys had fallen asleep, their bodies pressed against each other, their hands linked. Below me I thought of the journey across the desert of Mauritania, Western Sahara and Morocco, the sea crossing taken daily by my brothers and sisters – taking place now, an endless trek across the sand, each person a segment in a single body; if I stared down at the dunes below the plane, I could see them walking together, in a single line as long as history. How many corpses? Thousands and thousands each year. I stared out of the aeroplane's porthole. I shuddered. All my feelings of grief and loss were already exhausted. There had not been a single moment since the end of slavery when the suffering had ended, from abolition to forced labour to arrest, imprisonment and massacre. I was sick of the suffering.

I leant closer to the window, looked out at the bands of blue light widening as we neared day in Europe. The same families and companies who had profited from slavery continued to live, prosper and kill.

Finally free of regret and nostalgia, cleared of the remnants of these emotions, my thinking brightening with the sky, I felt something that was not even anger, but a hunger, a craving for justice – that was all there could ever be, what there must be. A reckoning. I smiled to myself and fell asleep.

5

Present Day

THE REVEALER had written another blogpost – #2 – it was posted before Couper's murder in Dakar. This time the Revealer was wilder than before – out of control, I thought. I tried to track the IP addresses to give me an idea of where they were, but naturally the blogger was using a Virtual Private Network, which gave the Revealer a virtual address. This was straightforward enough, but then I realised that they were changing their VPN every post. Every effort was being made to bury the IP address, and all traffic was being tunnelled through the private network. But, it would still not take a serious hacker long to get from this traffic to the real address, so the Revealer, I realised, had timed changes of address every day, several times a day. So, anyone hitting the site would only connect to a constantly changing second or third virtual IP address. This was the first serious clue that they were serious. Proper online camouflage would require constant attention, but could this be done by one person? Already the police had started to tighten their surveillance on the quacks who could be found easily, the posers who wanted to show off. The Revealer was different.

www.firethistime.com

Blogpost #2 – 'Go on or die'

The planet is dying. The UN has declared that the world's richest nations will burst through all the targets set two years ago. Unabashed companies are extracting fossil fuels at rates of 50–120 per cent higher than the agreements made in 2012. Oil companies, hungry for profit, continue to pump as much oil as they want out of the sea and land. These companies – their bosses and owners – are playing a game. They continue to increase production and to reassure their shareholders while making promises to save the planet. Yet, these companies plan 39 gigatonnes of carbon emissions, 60 per cent higher than what is needed to keep temperatures below two degrees. They must be stopped.

So far, this analysis was child's play – it wasn't this that I needed, any one of my second-year students could have told me that current emissions were 60 per cent above the limit that would restrict warming to two degrees. It was the Revealer's intent, the commitment, that stood out.

Action is needed. The time for dialogue and conversation is over. We need action on the streets – in strikes and occupations. But, we also need to break the flesh and bone power of the 1 per cent, prise their grip off their wealth and rule. The desire for profit is their alpha and omega – their guiding star – which prevents them from seeing their destruction. They have created a great kingdom of destruction, taking beauty and life and plunging it into a sea of death.

They will be stopped this year.

Let us be clear that we are dealing with class power. The 1 per cent is a class that defends its destruction and power with brutal force. What we are doing to them is simply what they did to come to power.

THEIR class came to power by the marvellous eighteenth-century French invention – applied to the PREVIOUS 1 per cent – the GUILLOTINE! A humane, modern, efficient way of dealing with useless, idle, malevolent bacteria. Their search for profit is killing us. Once more REVOLUTION has been put on the agenda of twenty-first-century humanity by the 1,635 billionaires, led by Warren Buffett and Bill Gates's personal investment arm 'Cascade Investment', which has urged their massive following of wealthy minions to invest in FOOD/Commodity Index Funds.

They have succeeded in getting the market-illiterate aspirant 1 per cent, the greed-obsessed weak, to fling £2–3–4–5 million of their savings into the area of global production and finance over which THEY have qualitatively, ultimately more control and influence, before they risk even a single ONE of their BILLIONS. Do not forget that Buffett has a Himalaya of liquid cash amounting to $35 billion.

The trillions behind this post-subprime stampede into the more profitable 'branch of industry' is, as always, MAINLY from the less affluent. All the risk – and ruinous, catastrophic loss – will be theirs. This is because the idiots believe that the world's richest man – WHO IS their saviour – is the superhero of our time.

In the struggle to save the planet and our humanity, we take the approach that NO ONE is excluded from OUR ranks, except those who will – to the death – defend the global existence of capitalism against the coming revolution of ALL the exploited, oppressed and downtrodden, destitute and desperate.

The coming reckoning, the WHOLE possibility, the WHOLE predication of our future is in the name of 2.3 billion of us, plus dependants. The 99 per cent. Tens of millions of us are condemned to the slow sentence of death by starvation, or from deadly viruses caused by their bets, their production and their profits.

Yet this is the wealthiest, most productive and technologically proficient society in all human history – in 10,000 years since the Neolithic/Agricultural Revolution – and we can feed 100 billion, let alone 6.5 billion!

To the furious, impassioned, impatient, confused, and so forth, who struggle with the discipline of making a rational, calm, clearly argued narrative out of the limitless anger and hope they feel, understand this: we are moving forward. Action and justice are now the order of the day. Believe, witness, step forth.

The new guillotine of our time – with the popular tribunals assembling on the streets – is about to fall for the first time in 220 years. Let this signal the start. We have no other choice but to 'Go on or die.'

'Go on or die,' said the freed slave Harriet Tubman, holding a gun not only at those wanting to capture the slaves she was leading to freedom, but also at any escapee that thought they might run back to their masters.

Let this be our maxim.

The Revealer

I was beginning to work out a style, an undisciplined virtuosity that couldn't be caged. The person – a lone ranger, or some type of peculiar leader by example, perhaps – probably suffering from an attention disorder, from hyperactivity. There was rage and madness. I closed my eyes after I read the post, sitting at my desk, the low ambient hum of the computer. I tried to summon the person up, to build a picture in my mind's eye. Difficulty paying attention, yet an intensity of absorption, hyperactivity and impulsive behaviour – I saw the Revealer kneeling on the floor, the computer on a small coffee table, empty glasses or mugs. The breathing shallow, the pulse racing. I tried to fix my thoughts on the room. I felt the room rattle, the image shake – poor work or school performance, low self-esteem, impulsiveness, restlessness, attention. Then I opened my eyes – broke the spell – and shook myself free of the image.

6

1980 – Port Harcourt, Nigeria

THE 234-ACRE compound – even then, before the monthly security breaches – by a 20-foot-high climb-proof fence, checkpoints and security turrets. The school had 94 children and 14 different nationalities – about a dozen buildings, low rise, white-washed, with state-of-the-art equipment and white teachers employed from France, the US and Canada. We spoke in every language except Igbo, Yoruba, Hausa or pidgin.

Yet, I loved the school, and so did Maïmouna, we were good at book learning, bright and encouraged to be, and we could do all the sport we wanted – in the 50-metre swimming pool, on the running tracks, in the gym, the green acres of playing fields. We would leave the house early, Maïmouna and I skipping hand in hand, the two streets to the school. The palm lined roads, normally free of traffic, the even paving, the tarmac freshly and perfectly laid. This was a Disney paradise in the tropics.

At school I had a friend – we had a friend – Kaarina she was called, and she was beautiful even then. Her parents had lived on Shell compounds for years, her father a personnel director – half South-African, half Indian. Kaarina was the popular girl at school, through sheer natural calm and charisma.

There were two aspects to our friendship – the first was that we – the twins – were invited regularly back to her house, where there was what I realised even at the time, a functional family life. A brother who exuded the same charm as his sister, and a mother and father who spoke civilly to each other. We formed a set, a group, the three of us – and soon became inseparable; we became known as the 'triplets'.

Kaarina's family, like ours – though far less peculiar – was also excluded from the dominant racial group. We were all black, and her parents too were conscious that this absurd universe – like a visiting parasite on the Nigerian state – was unreal.

The second element of our connection was that we shared Fawari.

Fawari was our nanny, our aunt, and for Maïmouna and me, the only mother we had ever had – or wanted. For Kaarina, who though a little younger than us and wise in the manner of a child, Fawari was her lodestar – a model to follow. She was proud, smart, beautiful and just and she dealt with all of us resolutely – correcting what our upbringings had broken. When she cooked, she explained how it was done, and made sure we prepared the meals with her; when she knelt on the floor of our bedrooms, folding clothes she'd washed, we sat with her, a conveyor belt of folding and flattening skirts and blouses. The conversations Fawari had with us were not infantile; she never pretended to be interested when she wasn't, and her explanations of what we did not understand made us feel seen and respected. In the years that we travelled on her shoulders we saw how the world could be navigated by woman.

The whites in the compound – the Shell base was actually called 'the campus' – stuck together and dined together. Every Sunday on a large table on the veranda overlooking the sports grounds, where cricket was played, these 'international dinners' were each week prepared by a different family, but never included any food I recognised, or wanted – no jollof rice, no pounded yam, pepper or egusi soup. 'International' was white European, or American. In the week, when Fawari didn't cook for us, we ate in the campus restaurant, where the cook, the food and the wine came from Italy.

Race was everything to us, and never mentioned. Our father was the heavy drinking, roaring ranter, who when he was sober could beat the collection of hardy white South Africans, or public school educated men from the UK, at football, or tennis *and* break them over his knee in a rare political discussion.

We were children but we saw: a typical evening in the week saw a dozen men, Italians, Scottish, American, French settled at the mess inside one of the campus buildings to watch a live soccer game on satellite television. The campus was not only an abnormality, a pockmark on Nigerian soil, but it was also an expression of the highest technical achievements of capitalism. When the first television signals were sent through satellites, Shell Nigeria installed a thirty-foot receiver on the golf course. We watched Sesame Street on Saturday mornings. '*We too dey enjoy like oyinbo pikin for dere place*.'

7

2010

WE MAY LIVE in a world that has accomplished great and brutal wonders surpassing all previous societies, but our private passions and desires have risen little above those of early humanity.

Jealousies continue to rage, no matter the good and cultivated intentions of our hearts. Kaarina and I fought.

Kaarina sat eating her sushi, bringing the pieces up to her mouth silently. We were sitting side by side on a bench, she didn't turn towards me. There was a constant bustle of shoppers, the tables of the sushi restaurant a few feet away from us. We watched a couple, both blonde and young, drinking sparkling wine, neither paying much attention to each other, talking distractedly, the woman made eye contact with me – her eyes move over me in disinterested inspection.

'Okay,' she answered finally. 'I suppose it's easier to imagine sex with someone I don't know than with you. Another woman.'

Involuntarily I took a breath in. I searched for something to say; I felt slightly sick. 'I think that's fine and its good we can speak honestly at last.'

It wasn't true, of course, not for me. 'It's good to have this conversation. I have been meaning to tell you about the conference in Livingstone. There was a young woman, a volunteer from the University of Zambia, Nyonde.'

Kaarina sat up, finally turned slightly and looked at me, 'You slept with her?'

'Please let me finish. She moved on me and I wanted to tell you I guess, she wanted something.'

'And were you tempted?'

'Yes.'

'Okay,' she turned back to the tray of food on her lap.

'I just wanted you to know. You know, of course, after a while in any relationship something dies – it's just necessary for us to remain honest.' Kaarina remained silent. 'Do you agree, sweetie?'

'I suppose so.'

'Maybe it's good for us, now, unlike everyone else, to upend the hypocrisy of every couple, who lie to each other.' I waved my hand over the tables in front of us to indicate the couples and families – all the hypocrites. 'That we use this time to speak to each other, to clear the tables. To speak without dozens of intermediaries.'

Kaarina was still silent but she wasn't hostile, there was no sharpness.

'I guess,' she said finally.

I breathed in deeply and silently. 'So, do you have anything you want to say?'

'Not really.'

'*Kaarina*' I said, with slight emphasis.

The blonde couple stood. The man was tall, his ease was natural; he looked around, stepped up to his partner and put an arm around her waist and pulled her gently in.

'Well, okay. There is one thing. When you were away, Michelle stayed over.'

'In our bed?'

'Yes.'

I gripped the bench, my hand perspiring. 'Good. I mean I am really pleased you are telling me this. Did you sleep with her?'

'Oh god,' Kaarina said quietly, she shifted on the bench, 'Does any of this really matter? Is sex really so important? These things happen and you are away, *all of the time*.' Her tone was irritated.

I tightened my hold on the bench. She didn't say anything else. The families, the children and couples, seemed to walk past us in silence. I couldn't hear the conversations, the shopping-centre echo of voices. I looked around me for the black families, the kids, their parents who seemed out of place – scared that at any moment they would be stopped, ordered out.

My forehead was damp, looking up at the large atrium, to the glass ceiling, I tried to make out the sky, but it was raining, and the glass was smeared. I tried to find anything that made sense of this place, something that could transport me to South Africa, take me away from here. Give me space, perspective. If I could only shrink us and our concerns, let them find their proper dimension amid the greatness and the suffering of this country.

I flushed and then, quickly before Kaarina looked up, I got up and walked away.

'Bianca,' Kaarina called after me.

* * *

No amount of logic will dislodge love. Neither will time wear it down, nor a rational knowing – when all the facts are assembled – that it must end. Not the advice of friends pleading that it should finish. The love itself must be exhausted, and the course of its life force must be snuffed out by the lovers.

PART 4

'I know they'll say I'm preachin' hate'

1

Present Day

RETURNING FROM Senegal my life found its usual rhythms. The routines on which I depended. The day divided into writing, normally done in the morning, sometimes early when I woke before anyone else was up and I could hear a solitary bird, or the feral cats and foxes that live in the city. I fed a three-legged fox every night, the animal, mangy, ragged, surviving on pity and urban tenacity. In the summer it was different, then the foxes don't look like they need pity or feeding, instead they are always on the scavenge with plenty of food to be stolen from bins. After a couple of hours of writing I would sleep again, then wake, grab my bag and walk the three streets to the gym to stretch and train, practise my katas and spar; or run to Embankment Gardens and from there take a coffee at Pavarotti's – Giancarlo respectfully keeping his distance.

If I had a class to teach, I would make my way to the lecture theatre or I'd sit in my office, my door ajar, and see students and work late before walking ten minutes home through Russell Square, across Tottenham Court Road and along Charlotte Street, stopping for something to eat or shopping at an express supermarket. These were my routines, punctuated by meetings that I tried to resist, or meetings at the local union branch of the university, or a public lecture I could not avoid.

Today I was working late in my office; the day had been bright, it was mid-April, and there were signs of spring – daffodils were being sold in buckets outside supermarkets, coffee shops and petrol stations. Daffodils are of course everywhere in April, but they were now so common as to be almost unsellable. Imported ones are sold in the city in January and February. I avoided them. The last light from the clear sky came through the window, which was the width of the room; there were huge sheets of glass in this modern pebbled-dashed 1970s building. Blocks of concrete, one on top of the other, towering sixteen floors high. I was halfway up and could still hear the street, the voices ricocheting up the building, the sweep of the brushes on the tarmac as the road was cleaned, the occasional conversation that drifted into my office.

The window was wet with condensation. I stood behind my desk and leant forward, pressed both palms against the window-pane, and rivulets of water spilled between my fingers and over my hands. I removed my hands from the window, the imprint of my fingers and palm were quickly overrun by water and swept away. I looked at the darkened sky, in the distance the BT Tower, the low-rise city and, further east, out of sight, were the skyscrapers of Docklands.

'There will be chaos and collapse before anything can be rebuilt, reborn.' I found myself repeating the lines, the arguments of the revolutionary and anarchist Souvarine in *Germinal*. 'Only from the rubble, the death of the old, will we be able to live again. And this death, like all death, will hurt and people will die. In great, needless numbers.' I had said these words to my class of MA students, whom I tutored in the afternoon in a course on *Literature and Liberation*.

The more naïve and absurd their beliefs, the greater the need I felt to pummel them, break their resistance. 'Yet, the actual death of capitalism – for which Souvarine was arguing – and the resulting mayhem, will be less bloody than a single day in the normal operation of society; it's hunger for blood and bones, for total, constant destruction.'

I saw the lights in the small office in the building opposite turn off and heard the shuddering of a bus braking on the road.

2

Present Day

WHEN I LEFT for Senegal, I had forgotten Lydia completely, erased her totally and she had completely disappeared.

The homecoming was strange – the sky had dropped, fallen. Travelling back to Europe we climbed up through the light and heat of Africa that pulled on the plane, tried to slow our advance, to warn us, and then we plunged down into the earth, below the sky, through the layers of light – mauve, red, orange, blue, into the dark English trough. England is Europe's gutter, running up the north-west coast of the continent. To reach the mud and dirt, the plane had to spiral endlessly lower and lower to the grey cavern in which we live.

I plugged my headphones into the phone and travelled in a black cab to my flat in Fitzrovia.

'Travelled far, love?' The thin, foxlike taxi driver asked, his face drawn and pointed, the collars of his quilted green jacket turned up.

'Yes' I replied, 'from a different solar system.' I stuffed in the earpieces and opened my laptop, found the story, the notes, the scattered scenes and started to type.

* * *

I opened the door, dropping my backpack on the floor beside me, the computer bag hanging from my shoulder. I pushed hard, thinking of the mail, the papers, London's detritus, that would have gathered on the mat – instead the door slid open and I heard a noise in the bedroom, the swish of movement, someone getting up.

The front of the flat faces west, the back east and there are windows on both sides. The corridor is long, the rooms come off this central artery, left and right – all of them, the kitchen first, then the lounge, the bathroom and bedroom.

Stunned, trying to understand, I felt my body tighten, dropped the two bags to the floor, kicked the backpack into the hall. Through each open door there were symmetrical squares of light – turning the corridor into a patchwork of light and dark.

Exhaustion normally heightened my senses, it made me more alert, helped me think clearly, clarified and sharpened my thoughts. I worked intensely when I was feverish, and sometimes I fought off sleep in order to write, or to teach free of distractions.

At night a whole new existence began, which I was free to inhabit alone. I was alert, alive, uninhibited in a way I could never be in the day.

I didn't understand what the noise was, what was moving in my bedroom, but I felt ready for it. Unconsciously, my body prepared itself, tensed, drew its senses to a single point.

Then Lydia emerged, her cheeks inflamed, her eyes red. Instantly I remembered my hurried departure, throwing her a set of keys and telling her to pick up the mail and to spend the occasional night if she wanted.

Too upset to speak, Lydia stood in the hallway, her profile lit in a pool of light, her nose running.

'God, sorry Lydia I forgot you might be staying.'

After a moment, sucking in deeply, Lydia spoke: 'You have not replied to any of my messages or emails. Nothing. I had no idea where you were, and you were due back, you said two weeks ago. Two weeks. I was worried. Crazy with worry. I even phoned the embassy and that place you said you were speaking at. Where have you been? What's going on?' She paused, gulped, her mouth wide, desperate; inadvertently she let out a short shrill cry, high-pitched, like a hurt animal.

I didn't respond. Instead, I picked up my bags, dragged them into the lounge, and dropped them on the floor. The room was in complete disarray – everything everywhere, Lydia's things, her clothes, my books open, the sofa a concave of her body. My music, the collection of CDs, vinyl, that were normally neatly shelved, was in chaos – sleeveless discs and records on the floor, mugs on bookshelves, the table ringed with brown crescent stains.

I noticed Nina's 1970 album *Black Gold*, on the floor by the coffee table, the record half sheathed. Issued in 1970, it was her final recording in the United States before her dramatic departure for Africa. The album – my favourite of hers – captures Nina at the very height of both her political brilliance and originality. The quality of the live performance and her choice of material makes *Black Gold* unmatched.

And here it was defiled and discarded.

I was disgusted by the chaos in my flat, but even more so by this display of Lydia's sordid life.

She started to speak again, looking down – the speech practised, 'I know you said you're a simple, selfish, uncompromising, stubborn woman who prefers to be alone. But, I really don't think wanting to hear from you while you're away, after weeks of being worried sick and missing you is too much to ask. Not even talking about the pleasure of sex or dinner or falling asleep together while watching television in bed.' She sat on the sofa.

I now turned around and stood looking at her, standing in the doorway – her snot and tears wiped away on her sleeve – she was wearing my tracksuit, it was too tight on her and her stomach was visible, her breasts pressed flat. 'Not that I don't feel humiliated or embarrassed enough to have wasted so much time caring and being worried.' I clenched my fists, swallowed, felt my pulse thump hard. 'Just to discover how little I and my feelings mean to you. … I knew I would feel silly for being so worried once you were back and I don't think I'm being ridiculous. So, you can be as selfish as you like, I've got too much shit going on at the moment.' Then after a second's pause, 'Bianca, I suppose it's my fault for being so sad.'

I felt now the satisfying complete composure of anger, my thinking entirely clear. I took a step towards Lydia and, sensing without saying another word what had happened, instinctively she moved into the hall, her eyes widening, out of the light I could see her pupils dilating in the darkness.

'Get out,' I said.

3

Present Day

LYDIA WAS GONE and apart from the text messages, and the one visit she made to my office, I was confident she would now leave me alone. I was now working intensely at the university, supervising and writing. Two students were sitting by the door, their essays sprawled on the floor, books open between us. One of the students had been working on representations of violence in the novels of Emile Zola and Sembene Ousmane, and the other on strikes and radical politics in nineteenth-century English fiction.

It was never enough for me to describe, I needed to state, to make categorical, enunciate and polemicise. I was not the master of subtlety, far from it, everything I really believe has to be worn on my sleeve. My teaching, like my politics, was a slap across the face. So, I finished this small tutorial with an exaggeration, and with a truth (truth can only be found through exaggeration). 'But, at the end of the novel, we are left with a clear sense of Sembene's power, his politics, his sheer, effortless poetic virtuosity and clarity, and Zola's floundering, democratic French republicanism – his hopelessness. His writing is a great sentimental, epic mess.'

Then, with my students astonished, the great writer defied, their own judgements contradicted, and Zola's glory brought down to earth, two of the students left the room. The other, Elisa, stayed. I turned my full attention to her, a 29-year-old single parent who had graduated the previous year and now came to me for informal supervision, attending some of my classes, though not sitting the exam.

'You can't mean that about Zola,' Elisa said, shy, nervous.

'I mean every word. The man was a writer of sloppy sentiment – you see a pattern through all his novels, the same details, the same run of predictable, formulaic human emotions and the lavish, lifeless descriptions. The absurdist play on inherited traits. It would have been better if he had stopped writing after 1885.'

Elisa raised her eyebrows, creased her brow and then dropped her head.

I ignored her blushing, the nervousness.

I moved past her to the door, locked it.

Elisa was bright but withdrawn. I had seen this before in black students, a willingness to let her slower, white classmates dominate. Yet, I also knew that there was a limit to what I could do. I couldn't be an entire social movement, an uprising that would lift her, too (most life passes without transformation, after all). Before these revolutions take place and if they do not come, most of us are obliged to take small steps.

The light was fading, the office warm, and I could hear other rooms in the corridor being locked – the days had lengthened, the skies were low.

There was a confusion in the city, an unusual humidity that clung to people and confounded them. Our clothes stuck to us, the days foreign – there was a certain chaos and disruption brought by the weather. A strangeness reigned in the heart of London, driving out England, confronting us with unusual possibilities.

What else could we do but love each other?

I went to my computer, found the track and turned up the volume. Simone shouted into the room, 'To be Young, Gifted and Black.' I let the music build, my head nodding to the music. I then swivelled around on my heels, faced Elisa and we stood listening to the music, looking at each other. I kicked off my shoes. Elisa swallowed hard. With Nina I muttered the words, 'There are times when I look back and I am haunted by my youth.' I smiled at her and, as she lowered the hand that had been gripping her shirt, a few tears rolled down her face.

I went up to her, took her chin, lifted her face, wiped the tears and held her – pulled her to me.

Our bodies linked, my brown, pale body against her darker one. She continued to cry, softly weeping, and each time the song ended it started up again and soon, on the third or fourth turn we were swaying together, holding each other, but then we started to laugh. I pushed us apart, took both her hands in mine, 'Look up, Elisa.'

We were rocking together slowly, smiling into each other's eyes.

On the next turn of the song I dropped to my knees, pushed her legs apart.

I whispered, my voice husky, loud enough for Elisa to hear me, to break into Nina's singing, '"I don't care where we've been, I don't care where we're going." I am here now, with you Elisa, and right now you are mine.'

* * *

Elisa was beautiful – a beauty that was dangerous, it came out always in front, it pre-empted her, eclipsed her, told a story before she was able to say a word. Her slightly sunken eyes, her high cheekbones, her broad forehead that creased when she spoke and her nose that stretched and widened when she was excited or agitated. Her face was paler than the rest of her body.

It is seared into me how the world shuts down when we are together in my flat or in my office, lying on the bed over the covers, the light low, quivering over us. Resting on our sides, staring at each other, the dusk moving across the bed, blotched and uncertain. Then, as she slowly prepares to leave, to get back to her daughter, she would stand by the chest of drawers near the window, pulling her hair back, fixing it down with clips.

That is how I will always remember her, tall, almost stiff, turning to me, smiling, joking, enjoying how I looked at her – satiated yet still full of desire. Her straight legs, her small breasts, her square shoulders – her beauty.

Elisa fought to be seen and it was a fight I understood – as if she had already been written and there was nothing more she could say. To be black and beautiful was her gift *and* curse. Elisa fought against obliteration. I couldn't make her visible, change the way she looked, or the colour of her skin, but I could provide a refuge where, sealed away together, liberation might take place for a few moments – achieved and lost in a single night.

* * *

In that first dusk together in my office, the night flickering across our bodies as I listened to her as she spoke freely, Elisa brought her head to my chest and I cradled her face with its tension, its defeats and hurt. Her cheeks flushed, eyes wide and moist and mouth open. She spoke about everything – it came out in great gusts, an immensity of history from her childhood.

Nina was playing, I Loves You, Porgy, 'Don't let him take me, don't let him handle me and drive me mad.' Her words skipped and danced around us, encircling the floor where we were lying, giving Elisa the strength to speak. There was very little to it, just Nina, the piano, a few words. Nina wanted all the singing done and finally to rest, yet I knew it was a rest that women like Nina and I could never have. There could be no calm in her lifetime, no peace, no let-up from the disappointment – no final reckoning. Her great life would always feel like a defeat.

As the final lines of the song played – 'If you can keep me, I wanna stay here with you forever' – and as Elisa spoke about her mother, I wanted to tell Nina to stop playing, to lie down and listen to *me*. I have found an answer to failure: *Watch me Nina – it's your time to rest.*

The light now almost completely gone, leaving an outline of Elisa's face. I closed my eyes and felt her words on my face. 'For a second, more than a second, my mum was completely silent. Stunned. I had not seen her like that. She said that she had only loved one man. He was Angolan, and she'd met him in London in the 1960s and he'd died in the early 1970s fighting for the Portuguese – I think. When he died, she took his signature as hers and has signed her name as his ever since.'

Elisa stopped – her breathing had quickened. I could feel a tightening over her, I put my hand on her side. I liked how she responded to me, she caught her breath, sucked in, found her control again.

'This was how she remembered him, every week, every month, dozens of times a year. She'd sign him on letters, forms, applications to bring him back to her, with his signature.'

Nina sang 'I Loves You, Porgy' at the Playboy Mansion in 1958 to an audience of American pornographers, racists, white boys and girls. A black mascot – a slave singing to her masters.

Doesn't every life have two deaths? Nina first died in 1958. She died the day that she performed to those people in Los Angeles, but she also had her resurrection. A few years later she called for violent revolution – violence that she never renounced.

Most of us never fully return to life from our first death. Nina did.

Elisa reached up and kissed me – her hot breath enveloped me. She put her tongue into my mouth. There was something about the sex we had that stripped us of the past, stood us free of our lives.

Back to zero, raw, we were nothing when we were together. As Nina continued to play the piano, we made love again.

* * *

Life moved quickly with Elisa. The first time in the flat on the sofa I pushed her onto her back in a single movement – for a few seconds we didn't even know what we were doing, those moments that are entirely free of thought.

Through the shutters of the bedroom the moon shone on us, a quivering light that broke up our hard form. In the light Elisa's face swam, was muddled and unfocused.

The covers bunched around her on the bed.

Elisa's head to one side, her mouth open, she sighed, she squeezed her eyes closed, her face clenched – she let out a soft, slightly plaintive cry, a whimper.

It was this sound of surrender that I wanted.

'Isn't it all connected, children, birth, sex, sensuality – our bodies?'

There was a pause, the pale light had moved off us again, so we shimmered in and out of focus as clouds crossed the moon.

'But you wouldn't know, you haven't had a child.'

'I had a child who died,' I said calmly.

'Really? No!'

'Really, yes,' I answered, 'with a South African woman.'

I lifted myself a little in the bed, adjusted the pillows. I fingered blindly for the remote on the small filing cabinet beside the bed that I used as a bedside table. I pointed it into the room and pressed play. *Belle* started up and the room filled.

'Al Green,' Elisa declared. I bent down and kissed her hand.

'I need him sometimes to feel,' I said, 'a straight black man singing about his love for God. And if his lover can't understand this then they should not waste each other's time and she can find another man.'

'His one true love, I suppose. He doesn't have the rage of Simone though.' Elisa nudged me, there was a slight teasing in her voice.

'There is no comparison,' I continued. 'But a black man singing about love, sex and the freedom to love and have sex, was … and still is subversive. Though he was a notorious wife beater and preacher and for that he is normally confined to private listening only.'

Elisa didn't answer, she inched up the bed, so we now lay next to each other on the pillows, 'I want to say something,' Elisa said. I heard her swallow.

'You don't need to,' I replied softly.

'Don't silence me,' she chided, elbowing me. The light from the hall came into the room, it was warm, and caressed us. Elisa tilted slightly towards me, our arms crossed, her dishevelled hair streaked across her face, my braids and beads hanging over my shoulders and breasts.

I had been away from myself for too long, I thought. Lost in my work and in a world that I didn't belong to – those years with Kaarina, all of that loss and denial. I turned onto my side to face Elisa, and for a second buried my face in her hair and breathed in deeply.

Elisa was part of the journey back to myself.

'Go on, Elisa,' I whispered.

'I wanted to say, just so you can hear me now, that I wasn't prepared for tonight. I mean that it would be unfair for you to pass judgement on what sort of person I am. You must reserve your verdict until at least our next night together.' She stopped suddenly.

I laughed.

'Why are you laughing?'

'Because tonight was perfect – look at us, we're sisters Elisa. Made to be together.'

Elisa dropped her head. 'Can't you please just confirm that you will?' she said.

'"Will" what?'

'Reserve judgement.'

'No. I refuse. That's not how I do it. Judgement, measurements. It doesn't make sense to me. I can say now that I don't want anything to be different – nothing. Tonight was perfect.'

* * *

I made us something to eat – salmon, salad, sautéed potatoes. I roasted a full Camembert with garlic and rosemary, cut slices of the olive bread I'd bought that evening from Pavarotti's. I had given Elisa my gown and I wore my tracksuit – there was a deep stillness between us, we were interlopers in the night. I felt as though we almost didn't exist in this pocket of time, cheating life, the flood of loss had somehow been stilled.

With the food on the table I rested my foot on hers. From her lowered gaze, Elisa looked up at me furtively.

'I am leaving soon for South Africa. It is a dreadful place – the old white, racist world undisturbed. Yet it is beautiful … though it's a beauty that needs to be burnt to the ground. I am speaking at the university in the city and a few other places on this new thing I am writing. There are some readings, some lectures – easy.'

I tore the last slice of bread in two, dipped a corner in the melted cheese and brought it to my mouth.

'How long will you be away for?' Elisa asked.

'About three weeks, a month' I said.

Elisa was still, her head down.

'I want you to come, not for the first two weeks but after my engagements. I want to show you around. I know some places north of the city, where, this time of the year, you can hear the whales sing. I will also take you to caves at Mossel Bay where the human story started 160,000 years ago. Where *we* – black women – launched the world. It is an amazing place – the whole culture, woman-led, of symbolic behaviour in drawings of scraped and ground ochre. The very basis of modern human behaviour, abstract thinking, planning, music and dance, the hunting of large animals, all of this can be found in South Africa. The real first complex civilisations of human beings, run, directed and reproduced by the activities of women. This is where I want to take you, Elisa. To show you. These were not basic communities, but ones of immense sophistication, technological innovations, cultural diversity – as even the most imbecilic scholars, with their inherent prejudice and misogyny, are now all forced to admit. I mean, Elisa, *these* African civilisations were run and organised by women and survived for tens of thousands of years based on extensive cooperation beyond kinship groups – competition is a historical human blunder, a momentary anomaly. This is what I want to show you, Elisa, not the travesty of the country's modern conditions and misery. Not the development of the cities and mines and factories, but the historical victory of woman, black woman, that lasted for aeons.'

Elisa pulled the gown more tightly over her shoulders and across her chest. I couldn't stop – I have never been able to, what was the point of all this knowledge, all my learning, knowing the truth and not changing the world with it? I stood, pushed the chair back and went into the lounge and grabbed the folded green cover draped over the back of the sofa. I came back into the kitchen and wrapped it over Elisa's shoulders.

'I don't have the money, Bianca.'

'I have money.'

'I don't know. My daughter.'

'Leave her with your mother.'

Elisa leant back, tilting the chair on its legs, she looked at me unabashed, bold. Finally, after a moment, she smiled – open and broad. 'Okay, sister,' she said, 'I accept. Take me to South Africa, take me home.'

4

1980 – Port Harcourt, Nigeria

BESIDES OUR FATHER'S wild reading habits, and peculiar tutorials, he combined forces with Kaarina's parents to 'share' Fawari. The idea was simple: she was to teach us about Nigeria, not through book learning, which he understood had limited value, but through visiting her family, and spending time outside the compound. This time I remember as a freedom that I never knew I needed, a freedom to experiences places where life was abundant and rich – uncontrolled, noisy, joyous and loud.

Fawari – we called her aunty – treated us like her own when we left the compound, the three children, the triplets, became hers. As soon as we left the campus, even our language would change, with aunty reverting to pidgin.

'When we are in *Naija*,' she would say, as we approached the gates signalling our departure from Shell, 'We speak in pidgin, when we are in this Europe, we can speak English'.

The three of us would chirp obediently and invariably she would say, as we crossed the threshold and entered the city, '*I wan chop*'.

And, in order, we would say, each trying to outdo the other, '*Hunger dey tear my belle.*'

Kaarina adding, '*Hunger wan kill me.*'

Fawari teased us, urged us to be more expressive – insisting as we approached the road that we hold hands; the road where we would wait for a bus was potholed, and noisy, traffic progressing along it by horn not sight. She shouted, gently mocking us, '*You sure of dis tin wey you dey talk so? Dis matter e get k-leg. You no need food, you don chop up, you oyinbo.*' 'Are you sure of what you are saying – this can't be true. You are prosperous Europeans.'

Aunty was everything to us. To all three of us she a real mother, who spoke to us like she spoke to her children; she was kind and rough and loving. We took turns to sit next to her as we travelled to her father's house in Port Harcourt, or to carry her shopping and her bags.

The campus was an oasis compared with the chaotic cluster of five million people in the city. Despite 20 years of service as a cleaner, nanny and servant at Shell, Fawari Clark, lived with her father and daughter in the town and sent two of her children – two boys – to a small school in her village, Buguma, three hours by road and track. In what Fawari named Pitakwa – as Port Harcourt was known – she lived with 'grandfather' in a tiny two-room, one-storey dwelling near the Old Port on the Bonny River. At the back of the shack where the three of them lived, was a small courtyard shared with other families; here there was a basic toilet and sink. Cooking was done outside on a kerosene stove.

The first time we went to her city house the three of us fell silent, we might have been black but that made no real difference – with our pressed and ironed clothes, our clean shoes and polished faces, everyone knew where we had just come from. There was a shame we felt, for who we were, and the crime of where we lived, yet we found solace, on that first excursion by squeezing each other's hand tightly in wordless communion.

Awkwardly, Fawari indicated to us to sit on a step in the courtyard, and she shouted to her father – '*Go slow dey wel wel for road as we dey com.*' 'On my way here, we were held up in a traffic jam.'

The bustle of activity in the yard was amazing – the smells of the food we would be eating, the jumble of life, chickens, small children, and the rooms that opened to the outdoor space, with the doors wide, people spilling in and out. Loud and demonstrative conversation – pidgin spoken so quickly, like rounds of bullets from a gun.

When uncle – Fawari's father emerged – smart, a shirt and tie, he smiled at us, and knelt where we sat, lined up like dolls. The noise, the chatter, the conversations ungrasped by us filled the air. He faced us, listened to the tumult, and then his broad lined face broke into a smile, and he spoke in slow well-enunciated English:

'Girls, you must understand that for us Nigerians, we use pidgin to show that we are everyone, to, to …' he moved his right hand in circles, coaxing out his words, 'to show that we connect with everyone, heedless of your status. As visitors, learning pidgin will show us that you want to be with us. Do you understand?'

We all nodded our heads; he then shook our hands in turn and asked for our full names. By Christmas – three months later – each of us spoke pidgin, properly, in full sentences, taught under uncle's patient instructions. At school, in the white compound, we had our own language, that no one except the cleaners, the lawn cutters and security guards understood. The bloody fools probably thought we had made up the language, some unknown childish patois. Not the furious beautiful language half-sung, half-shouted metres from our perimeter fence.

When we had returned, after the first visit to Fawari's city home, I clung on to Kaarina's hand, and then whispered my normal departing childhood love to her, and ran with Maïmouna on the neat, trafficless road the two blocks to our sprawling bungalow. Everything to us suddenly seemed sullen, our lives in the residential compound restricted and confined – the taken for granted luxury an abomination. Maïmouna and I seethed, in our different ways.

In bed that night I sobbed into my pillow for everything that I had seen – the realisation of our wealth surrounded by poverty. Maïmouna came to me, and we lay together silently, holding hands, knowing that we could not talk about this to our father – for all his radical conversation and chatter, this was his world.

For me, that night, I was also tormented by another horror – something that had never really occurred to me before. I was intensely conflicted about how I could share my love for Maïmouna, Kaarina and Fawari. How could I protect them all, and make good on their pain and suffering? How could I love them all?

5

Present Day

WHO AND WHERE are they? I asked myself when I had finished reading the third blogpost. Who were they addressing? This governs, for me, how something is written. Was the aim at the West? It seems to me – prima facie – yes. This was the audience for the posts I was reading, I decided that they were part of it. She/he was a Westerner. BUT the posts were being rewritten, the whole thing, to orient directly to the protestors in Egypt, South Africa, Nigeria, Haiti and Bangladesh (where they had so wonderfully battered 50 police to death for dispersing a food protest!) and Mexico – where demonstrations were taking place against rising (quadrupled) food (cornflour) prices. How did I know this? The blogposts had recently appeared in Spanish, Arabic, Yoruba and pidgin and had been syndicated simultaneously on local newspaper sites, and independent blogs in Mexico, Egypt and Bangladesh. The pieces were being shared, widely, wildly. I translated one post from Zulu.

www.firethistime.com

Blogpost #3 – 'Let the fires burn'

There can be no retreat – for those in battle, or for the rich. There is no path behind us, no Eden in the centuries past. The environmental emergency – the final, definitive destruction of the planet by the 1 per cent – and the struggle against the rich, are connected. Their world, their priorities, are destroying us and the planet.

Who are these people? They are fossil fuel capitalists and the global food capitalists, ADM, Cargill, not only hoarding millions of tons of rice, wheat, corn but running down stocks since the last crisis – paying US and EU farmers billions to grow nothing in 'set-aside' policies and then exporting surplus grain to the poor, in emergency food shipments to those already starving because of their speculation.

Not only will prices continue to soar, and millions die – there is a global policy of 'let them starve' – but there will continue to be uprisings, a global wave of struggles.

Billionaires like Buffet, Gates, Branson have leapt into agricultural speculation as a new avenue with high profit potential, intending of course to carve out this profit to the exclusion of rivals. That ensures the continuing jeopardisation of food supplies, but new price rises mean new struggles.

We have now entered an uninterrupted, *open* fight with the 1 per cent, who have exposed themselves as endangering billions of lives by climate change, environment wrecking barbarism, poverty, inequality and war. They are risking the resources of the two greatest needs of humans – an assured food supply AND an environment that can provide it.

Who is doing the fighting in the cities and countryside's of the world?

It is the poor, workers, the landless, the unemployed and graduates. Graduates who end up in informal jobs, with low pay, unable to afford a home of their own. In the North, many 30-year-olds are still obliged, in the end, to live with parents with whom most of them do NOT want to live, and thus have no sex life. It has long been the same in the South.

We rarely talk about the personal, intimate needs, wants and yearnings of teenagers and youths! But they are PART of the revolutionary impetus we are seeing.

Once we were tired, weak, pathetic, but no longer. The rich will have their turn – all of them know, in their hearts, that we are coming for them. Their game is being played out.

Real power has never been up for election, it has resided unchanged, in the same hands, for centuries. Not in the parliaments and assemblies of their democracy, but in the boardrooms, skyscrapers and banks of the 1 per cent, in the editorial offices and the executive suites of the major media outlets. To secure real power the class that controls and devastates the planet needs to be broken and *destroyed*.

We must be honest.

The world we inherit will be a desert. We have no illusions about what we will need to do, and what we will have to rebuild. The greening of our cities and towns; the immediate banning of all carbon-based industry; the junking of all private motor cars; the grounding of every plane, but on the foundations of the total socialisation of production. The complete expropriation of the rich, their homes, their wealth, their factories and offices – all, ultimately, created by us.

We inherit a world that for four hundred years has been systematically plundered, looted and pillaged by the vilest, cruellest class of pirates and slaveowners know to civilisation. The 1 per cent has never been up for election and no notice is being served. They will, each of them – the grey-haired grandfathers, the jovial uncles, the talented aunts and the dynamic, brilliant wide-eyed young executives – be destroyed, killed.

Do not cry.

We do not cry for the houses of the rich that burn, for the golf courses, the vineyards and the racists, who WILL be destroyed. This is just the beginning.

Go on or die.

The Revealer

I did not know whether to laugh or cry; this was a series of statements, not even an argument. Wild and unstructured, frothing, incoherent – how could they carry through a plan if they battled to write a coherent blogpost? No sooner did I think I'd found the group – the propagandists, the blog-posting rear-guard – than I found myself sniggering at the references to sex, and the naive promises of 'destruction' and golf courses. This wasn't a sophisticated group capable of taking on the 1 per cent – 'the pirates and slaveowners', a characterisation I quite liked – of the twenty-first century; they were amateurs, I thought. I thought I had the profile – a thirty-something graduate living at home with her parents, in an English suburb, dreaming of sex and revenge.

But then, once more, there was the small fact of timing. The original blog, not the syndicated copies, neither the Zulu, nor the Arabic translation, had been published before the fires had started in Cape Town.

PART 5

'I'm the keeper of the flame'

1

Present Day

THE PUBLISHER with whom I had worked in South Africa, who had published *The Elation of Being*, had been urging me to visit for another tour, a series of lectures and talks. He spoke with exasperation – everything he said was hyperbole. A nervous, small, neurotic man, insecure, flighty, dangerous, Jeremy Wale expressed the impotent white rage of a man who spoke about his role in the 'struggle' at working lunches with his authors and at cocktail parties and sundowners in his Hout Bay mountainside mansion. His rage was full of liberal confusion. He had made the journey from white, apartheid privilege to join the African National Congress in the 1980s and now floundered and flapped around like a fish on dry land. Revolted by the government, Jeremy frothed with betrayal – the smell of alcohol permanently on his breath.

'Come,' he'd urged me on the phone a few months ago, fluent, flattering, 'I will set up lectures, prepare the way, something of an entrée to the Global South for your new book. You understand, Bianca, that today when a book is published it's already too late. The thing today is publicity months *before* publication, a year even before the book is even out, or finished. Come and speak, read from your draft, comrade.' (Imagine, this man called me 'comrade').

'Draft scenes,' I said, only partly listening, unconvinced – pondering the possibilities of a trip, what I could do, how long I'd stay. It was the end of the day and I was reading a slim volume of poetry, in Pavarotti's, the book open as I waited for the pasta to arrive. I read and ate alone in this restaurant twice a week – Tuesdays and Thursdays. I read a few of Stella Nyanzi's poems, such power of description, such terse, perfect control – not a surplus letter, nothing unnecessary. I found the energy, the precision exciting – irresistible.

The Bucatini all'Amatriciana arrived, I turned the book over, lay it opposite me.

'Your drafts will suffice – passages linked by a narrative, the story. Christ, you can talk about whatever you want, you know that. We only need to put your name up, your photograph and people come. Say yes, Bianca!'

'Yes,' I said.

'Excellent,' Jeremy exclaimed.

'Yes,' I repeated, 'Set it up. I can come for a few weeks. My food has arrived Jeremy, let's speak later.'

Jeremy spoke quickly, tried to stall me. 'Listen, Bianca, I am also coming to London and then Paris next week for a book fair – the City of Light. I am then going to see my daughter in Venice. I will be there in a fortnight.'

'So, give me a call Jeremy. I have to go.' I hung up; I had no intention of seeing him – this diabolical little man.

* * *

Jeremy had a daughter who was learning Italian in Venice, at a language school. Yet, the story this preposterous South African man told the world was that she was living there – as though Italy counted for something, *as if I would be impressed*. Venice, Rome, Paris, Berlin, London – for this class of South African whites, European cities were the apex of real history, the civilised climax of our species, where, they believed, the old buildings housed an ancient people and culture.

I chuckled to myself.

I'd lived in these cities. Their past, this 'ancient past', didn't even count for a second on the human clock. Measured against Africa's history, Europe was puny, pathetic, terrible – a pile of blood-soaked rubble. Yet, the white ghetto where Jeremy lived in Cape Town, on the balcony, on the decking of his mountain-side house – where he opened his arms to exclaim at the wonders of the Byzantine Empire – stood on top of a civilisation tens of thousands of years old, one without mass wars, slavery, colonialism, holocausts, environmental annihilation. But he said nothing of this because he knew nothing of it. I saw the mountains, the mansions, the English countryside grafted on to the lush, verdant Cape and I wanted to bring it down; these white men in the southern sun, who couldn't even see the world under their feet. The oldest civilisations on the planet, the most ancient intelligence in our solar system, in whole bloody Milky Way – where all the great blackness began, and they knew nothing of it.

* * *

Four days later I arrived on an early flight in the bright thick heat of the city, and felt the sun grip me under the arms, lift me skywards.

2

Present Day

THE ROUTE from the airport, the roads that lead out of Belleville run past the endless shacks of Khayelitsha, built on sand dunes, hidden behind a concrete wall that borders the motorway. The paths between the shacks are like a maze – the colours of the township a permanent autumn, the rust on the corrugated iron, making this informal city look stricken and beautiful. An endless smear of amber decay flung across the great foreshore of the Cape like the carcases of shipwrecks.

Bittersweet, the anger in the city was diverted and confused.

The motorway sweeps into the city, past the university on the slopes of Devil's Peak then along a wide curving, treelined avenue through Newlands and Constantia. Hawkers standing at traffic lights selling inflated rings for swimming pools, sunglasses and bead animals.

I pulled up to the cottage, a small inconspicuous brick house in Woodstock, built on the steep hills above the harbour and the high-rise blocks below. I turned the car into the residential street, pulled up, parking the car, two wheels on the pavement. I swung the door open, stepped onto the road, the tarmac softened by the sun. The heat caressed me; I let it hold me for a second. Then, as I took my backpack from the boot of the car, I heard a voice.

'Bianca, Bianca!' Jeremy shouted, moving quickly down the path towards me. 'Let me take that – and welcome.'

I held out a hand to stop his approach and to turn his kiss into a handshake. 'Why are you here?' I asked.

'To welcome you, sister – that's how we do it in Cape Town.' I saw behind him a box left by the door of the cottage, shopping, supplies – as I had requested. He bounced alongside me, like a child. Despite myself, I warmed to him, I enjoyed the politics, his silliness. He pointed to the food I had just picked up, 'This damn government, leaving everything in full view of the world The president naked, as Dylan sang. His dick out. Disgusting. His henchmen, loyalists dividing up the spoils, its full capitalist thief in the Global South, Bianca.'

We reached the door, I gave Jeremy the box of groceries and counted the large stones by the path, kicked the fifth one over, bent and picked up the key. As arranged the key was left in the front garden.

As in many of these houses in South Africa, built in the 1920s, the corridors were long, leading from the front door along the side of the house. The first door on the right opened to a small lounge, comfortable, nondescript, the second door, a bedroom, and at the back the dining room and kitchen and a small glass conservatory and garden. From the conservatory you could see rising above the house, the mountains, spotted with trees, pines and gums; the side of the mountain was dry and the whole city parched and scratchy. I felt it when I arrived, the hot air too harsh to take on. I shielded my eyes and told Jeremy, who followed me into the cottage, to put the box on the kitchen table. As I entered the kitchen, I felt the blast of the sun through the window, sudden, still, impossible. Glorious.

'The whole city, the Western Cape, is dry. A tinderbox. No rain for three months. The mountains look as though they are ready to blow. And there are water shortages in the major dams. We're the canary in the mine. Climate change is upon us and we are dying. The city's infrastructure is broken, millions of litres of water lost to leaks and waste ...' I let Jeremy continue like this, a tickertape of news, updating me in the background as I put away the food.

I went to the fridge and pulled out a chilled bottle of water, took two glasses from the counter, sliced a lemon, dropped a slice into each glass and filled them. I handed one to Jeremy.

Jeremy was always busy, uneasy, self-important – he radiated unease. His energy was scattered and spread out like the hills and mountains of the city. Bustling with opinions he wanted to preach, to demonstrate his power to his famous guest.

I chided, 'Are you dying Jeremy? The infrastructure is fine in Hout Bay – when was the last time you had a water shortage, comrade? No problems filling your pool this year, Jeremy?' I leant on the table, my glass down, looked at him directly and winked.

'You are right, right ...' he exclaimed, too eager. 'Colleagues are stockpiling bloody water from the supermarket in five-litre plastic containers. One friend even explained to me how she had started pissing into yoghurt containers and emptying them into the garden, another announced proudly that gone were the days of luxurious bath towels. I mean, what the fuck? Someone else declared that he had mothballed the washing machine and now carried bottled water to public places to save on municipal water for washing his hands. And Bianca, one of our writers at the university told me that she had stopped taking her vitamin supplements to avoid her urine taking on a yellow tint, which she thought might be offensive in the unflushed university toilets. Jesus bloody Christ! I have *also* heard of colleagues cutting their hair short in order to save water by not have to wash.' Jeremy ran his hand through his short hair. 'Others boast how long it has been since they last washed or how they had changed their diets and have taken pasta completely off the menu and replaced it with water-neutral food. I mean, it's insane – do you hear me? Water-neutral! For fuck's sake.'

Breathless, impatient to get everything out, Jeremy added, seeing my questioning, furrowed brow, 'Yet. the majority of people in the city have never had the luxury of water flowing from a private tap in their home and have never had access to more than twenty litres of water a day. *Crisis, what damn crisis?* The water taps are still open! To them, these water-saving tactics are just another white quirk, like veganism, or driving small cars. I mean, this, this ... this pee-in-the-yoghurt-pot mentality and this dirty linen and oily hair, is just a nasty insult. But the drought signals environmental catastrophe and human extinction, nothing more, nothing less.'

Jeremy was proud of himself, he stared at me like a child seeking approval. Perched on the corner of the kitchen table, letting the sun envelop me I answered, '"The man jus' upped my rent las' night. ('cause Whitey's on the moon.) No hot water, no toilets, no lights. (but Whitey's on the moon)."' Before he could interject, I continued, 'Unevenness. The middle class have their chilled water and the rich their swimming pools and the poor have the drought. And die. We need to create some *evenness* in the dying Jeremy. ...' Then, mocking him, 'Not just this, this,' I tilted my glass towards him, 'this liberal indignation.' I paused, took the last sip of water from my glass, put it down on the table between us. 'And on the subject of extinction, black and brown bodies have already been subject to innumerable acts of extinction for hundreds of years. So, this raises the question, when you speak of extinction, Jeremy, which human beings are you referring to?'

'Are you following the news?' Jeremy continued without stopping, 'people are talking about the murders. The killings. The speculation, the good money here is on a political motive. That it's not some feud – it's something else. As far as I can see, it's an attempt to take on a global criminal elite, but no one can figure out the links yet. Whoever is doing this, whatever group is involved, it's an anti-corporate act ...beyond our reasoning.'

I scoffed, '*Beyond our reasoning*,' I repeated, 'there is nothing *beyond* reasoning Jeremy. Not when it involves human behaviour.'

Jeremy stretched on the chair. 'I have a theory, Bianca, listen to me.' Despite his edgy, nervous energy, he still had an expectation, a firm belief that he had something to say and that people should listen. This was his South African whiteness – his privilege. I gritted my teeth, swallowed, yawned loudly. 'Four years ago, the provincial government started to reintroduce baboons near Cape Town, in the city, and further out, setting up baboon camps in Grotto Bay and Jakkalsfontein Nature Reserve, you know, off the R27. Since then there's been a battle with locals, small farmers and the owners of big estates who have complained that their property, cattle, land, is being destroyed by the baboons. They were all terrified that their livestock would be killed, wiped out. Though there's no evidence for this. Yah, well, screw it.' I was barely listening, I wanted him gone. The desire to be alone was beginning to overwhelm me, his presence had begun to hurt.

'Jeremy,' I said, my voice taut, controlled, 'I need to shower and sleep. You will have to leave. Sorry Jeremy,' I took the schedule from the table, folded it.

'I'm going, Bianca, but just hear me out.' I sighed, he continued more quickly now, slipping, stuttering, then catching his tongue on his words. 'The conservationists were excited that the number of baboons – perhaps 200 in West Coast National Park alone, were clearly thriving. There had been talk of annihilation – in the Cape a few years before. The attacks on the cattle, and livestock are probably caused by wild dogs not the damn baboons anyway.' Jeremy sat up in his chair, he noticed I was listening, so he spoke quickly and clearly. 'So the Western Cape legislature orders an investigation that simply states what we already knew – the numbers. The baboons are thriving and that the cattle and crops are being attacked.'

My reputation either provoked silence – a sort of reverence, so that what I actually did or said was washed away by the force, the simple, incontestable preamble of my fame, or it provoked, in certain people, an abundance, a loquaciousness. Unwanted and tedious, Jeremy fitted the second category and temporarily in my presence he became more than himself. A great mass of dormant sense was momentarily excited into action, as he tried to reach me, as he stretched his hands up to the sky.

I was now listening.

'Yet, the cattle continued to die, and the baboons continued to roam and consequentially tension continued to boil. There were hit-and-run attacks on the baboons by farmers taking the law into their own hands. Yah, shit – are you following?'

I nodded, 'But hurry up and get to the point.'

'So, the conflict with the authorities reached boiling point; three months ago the provisional government released the numbers, they'd found that two and a half thousand head of cattle had been killed by dog or baboon. A week after this statement in Yzerfontein, you know it, an hour from here on the coast, three baboons attacked a herd of cattle, which resulted in 380 dead animals. Yet, only six animals were actually bitten by the baboons.' Jeremy looked triumphant, he knocked back the last mouthful of water, paused, knew he finally had my complete attention, then replaced the glass slowly on the table, moving it in small concentric circles, smearing the drops of water on the surface. 'Unlike dogs or large cats, baboons only kill to eat, right. So, the other cattle, three hundred and seventy-four, in horror had flung themselves off the cliff and were killed on the rocks below, some were washed out to sea in the surf. The cliffs around Yzerfontein are eighty bloody metres high. It's a sheer drop. I saw the photographs – piles of cattle bloodied on the beach. Completely surreal.'

Finally, Jeremy stood for dramatic effect to deliver his finale. 'Then it was open season. The state turned a blind eye as locals, mostly big farmers and their Afrikaner friends were allowed to kill as many baboons as they wanted for a week. Three municipalities even hired teams for a temporary cull. Yet the baboons hit back a few weeks afterwards, and there was another meeting of baboons and cattle and this time an entire herd threw themselves into a ravine. Within two days most of the carcases had been cut up by the poor, men and woman, children from local squatter camps, hacking away at the free bounty, some even having braais in the ravine itself – poor fucking entrepreneurs, set up garden restaurants serving pap and steak.'

I knew what Jeremy was trying to do but I played dumb. 'Interesting story and your point? That baboons and cows follow their immutable nature.'

Jeremy was in charge now, his whole life lifted – how long I wondered had he practised this party trick, repeated this story, his theory?

'No, no, Bianca, it's not about the baboons at all. There are reports that most of the real killings have been carried out by dogs and poachers. No, Bianca, the central point of the story is that it took – let's say three or four baboons and a few dogs – targeting choice cuts of beef for the rest of the herd, in panic, to throw themselves over the cliff. Yah, fuck! Do you see?'

I had pushed out the chair and sat with my feet crossed. I summarized: 'A few murders and the whole class, the 1 per cent will commit suicide. Your theory is hilarious, Jeremy. Terror and mass suicide succeed where radical social movements have failed throughout history.' I leant back in the chair, pushed hard so I slid a few centimetres across the floor, away from the table – out of the shadows, into the light. The sun shone through the conservatory glass. I basked in it, felt it envelop my head, curl around my neck and shoulders, 'Sadly, the 1 per cent can tolerate a few murders without resorting to hysterical mass suicide. Though your hypothesis is cute.'

This was just the response that Jeremy had counted on, he exclaimed, 'Don't read the story so directly, so crudely. I see, in the herd suicide, yah fuck, of the cattle, simply *a possibility*. The longer these murders go on, randomly picking off the rich, the panic is spread. Generalising fear, yah shit and the rich become nervous, their behaviour defensive, erratic. They are – Bianca, are you listening? – already confused and then they start to build higher fences, colonies on islands, in space … I don't know. They become easier to target. And the whole class begins to feel hunted, you see? There are not so many of them. It could happen.'

I didn't want him to stay, so I stood, calculating the time he'd been here, I said at the end of his last sentences, 'It's good to see you – do we have anything to discuss, specifically?'

He sat up stiffly, pulled his chair into the table and sat down. 'You received the schedule?' He unfolded an A4 page, the list of speaking engagements, the gigs he'd arranged and slid it across the table towards me.

'Five events over fifteen days' I said, still standing. 'Tomorrow the public lecture, a reading and public interview at the university. "Political Fiction with Bianca Ndour"? A signing and reading at Clark's Books on Thursday. What am I signing, by the way? The events next week, one in Johannesburg, another in Durban.' I went back to the fridge, refilled my glass.

A few minutes later Jeremy left.

3

Present Day

IT WAS ONE of those mornings, tight, hot, the night had been still and the temperature had hardly dropped. I slept solidly for four hours and woke rested. I pulled away a banana from the bunch on the kitchen table, poured a glass of water from the fridge and stood on the wooden decking in the garden. The sun was already beating down hard and unyielding, the stiff leaves of the small palm rubbed together in the breeze and the earth sounded to cicadas. The mountainside shimmered, struggling to focus in the heat. The morning sun burnt away the night, took over the city. For a few moments I let it take me – permitting nothing to enter me except the blinding light and heat.

I pulled off my shorts and top, leaving them on the ground, and stood under the outdoor shower at the side of the house. The tiles were hot, the water – rainwater collected in a tank on the roof – hit the ground, and steam billowed up. I had turned up the volume of the stereo in the kitchen, so I could hear the high declaratory words:

The way they do my life.
This ain't living, This ain't living,
No, no baby, this ain't living,
No, no, no

I felt good.

The journey to the university, where I was speaking that evening, was easy, a ten-minute jog or a short walk. I had a day to work. I packed my rucksack, a bottle, books, pens and, before the heat forbade any movement and chased me into the shadows, I ran, slow, steady at first, finding a gentle pace, that would wake me up, open me out. I plugged myself into my music.

The city struck me hard, as it always did. I ran down the hill, through the residential streets and saw families, mothers and children sitting on street corners, walking lethargic, knocking nervously on the doors of the white neighbourhood with the same question – 'Work mister, madam, any money for my children?' 'Please, sir, miss, help me.'

The streets were teaming with the poor.

Rockets, moon shots
Spend it on the have-nots

I moved into the road and ran, hugging the pavement. On the main road there were men, standing between the traffic selling flowers, beads, chargers, beachwear; some stood lame, too exhausted already even to tap on the windows of the cars that had pulled up at the lights. Above us were the mountains, forested, and mighty, the sheer Jurassic cliffs that marked the Western limit of the Cape. I moved onto the pavement again, ran faster, tasted the salt of my sweat, the moisture. I felt as if this whole barbaric, beautiful city was below me.

I saw men and women park their cars, and either ignore the hawkers and their appeals for money or dig out a five-rand piece from their pockets, holding it out and dropping it into a palm.

Marvin sang on loudly, playing over and over again.

Oh, make you want to holler
The way they do my life

I had a few more streets to cross, another mile to run. As I hit the ground hard, I felt good. The road was broad, wide, open, and on the pavement, families slept – a man and woman and two children in a doorway, the children having their trousers brushed down by the man, their shirts buttoned. Tired, worn-out, the street had already started its work on the children, hardening them. I ran on and on. I could see in the distance, the petrol station, the turning I would take. A couple had made a bed on a blanket in the recess of a large doorway. I was pleased to see the city's poor waking early, forced to come out, unable to hide. I ran harder.

And it was never pity I felt, it was always anger. I had always believed in anger. Is this not the time for anger? It was the opposite of inertia, of academic pontificating – anger worked up action, and only through anger *and* action could justice ever come.

I turned at the station, the tight cluster of houses and cafés. I knew I would be working soon – I felt the glow of rage inside me and a joy that was hard to hide.

4

Present Day

I REMEMBER how strange the autumns were in Cape Town. The days would sparkle, the skies spotlessly blue and, standing in the line of the sun, you could feel the heat, broken by a passing shadow, a cloud, a bus, a building. Deciduous trees lining the city streets, shedding leaves in the storms.

In the open, bare vistas of Khayelitsha, there can be no poetry, no lyrical passages about the changing seasons, the beautiful sunshine, the dramatic South Atlantic storms that hit the coast. Instead, there are months in the winter when nothing dries, when clothes are sodden and the mud-clogged, unmade roads and paths between the shacks are turned into trenches. Then, the winter sunshine does not raise up a hidden beauty, just the smell of the open gutter. Only then, as the sun shines downs hard on the township between the storms, do you really know it's winter.

As I have learnt, there is no natural beauty untouched by what we have done, *by what we do*. We have reached into everything – broken down all resistance and taken life and turned it into death. Knitting our destruction into coastal shelves; ploughing our ruin deep into the planet's crust.

Before I left Kaarina she gave me a book of Buddhist teaching and inside the cover she had written: 'You once taught me B, that on the auspicious day of Saga Dawa, the night's full moon brings clarity and the wisdom of moonlight into our hearts. May we both achieve happiness and liberation in this lifetime, love K.'

There can be no liberation *in ourselves*, without taking the whole world with us, without being *taken* by the world. Incremental, partial change is a dreadful lie. There is no individual release, no letting go or freedom, in a world that is enslaved. Our own freedom must entail the liberation of the entire species; and if they remain in imprisonment, so do we. Eclipsed by their suffering, our humanity, our enlightenment is a shimmering, distant lie.

The liberation I once espoused was a trap; like most people, I had been blind. There is no place in the sun for only part of humanity.

I left the house, my hoodie under my jean jacket, my hair bunched up under my baseball cap, Nina playing into my headphones. I stepped out from under the porch and stood in the sunshine, felt the light embrace me. I pushed the gate open and started to run to the university. I moved into the shadows cast by the houses on the street. I pounded the pavement, turned onto the road and tried to find my rhythm, my pace.

There was no comfort, no assurance – nothing. I moved in and out of the light. I knew that there could be no promises, no private joy. In this truth, I felt alive.

5

Present Day

I SPOKE that evening, the event was full, in the largest auditorium at the university, the aisles packed with students and staff. I arrived late, walked down the stairs to the stage, the microphone set up, a table, two chairs, water. For all its recent struggles, the university was still overwhelming – a late Victorian monstrosity.

A moment after entering the room, there was a cheer, a round of applause and half the audience stood. I blew kisses, stopped halfway to the stage and took the outstretched hands, seeing a friend I stepped into a row and embraced her. A white student saw me, she was ecstatic and reached her hand out to me, saying, 'Tell me Bianca, what can I do?'

I had asked for the organisers to play a video, Nina Simone singing, *Love Me Or Leave Me*. The music started, there were a few cries, still standing some of the audience started to dance – I felt a rush of excitement, at last I was back. I felt like I always did in these moments, as if I had just stepped out of prison. Fully, truly, momentarily free.

When I reached the front, looking up, there were more cheers – I took the microphone, removed my folded notes, put them on the table, then – still standing – I spoke, ignoring the academic who had been given the responsibility to introduce me.

Briefly I looked directly into the cameras, assembled in a cluster in the middle of the stage. The lecture was being live-streamed and broadcast on two channels; there was a pack of journalists and photographers.

'Thank you, friends ... sisters, brothers.' There was another cheer. I turned to the screen behind me, the frozen image of Nina at her piano: 'Thank you Nina,' I said. There were shouts. 'I also want to genuflect to you, students, young, gifted and black –

each of you – and to say that what you have done in the last few years, the fight against Rhodes, the unrattled apartheid establishment and its black supporters, the defenders at this university, the racist curriculum that you've overturned, to this, to these challenges. ...' I raised my voice, lifted my arms, 'YOU have raised your voices and your rage. You have fought and ...' once again, I paused, 'started the process of burning down the old, the statues, the Grand Masters, the oil paintings, the white thinkers.'

There were cheers. A young man in the middle of the auditorium jumped up and punched the air: 'Yes sister!' he shouted. Others stood, the photographers moved forward, aimed their cameras, clicked, the room was momentarily a blur of white light. I let it disperse and continued.

'And to the authorities ...' – the vice chancellor and senior academics were sitting at the front of the hall; proving they could take this, they all smiled. The VC, a man of minor poolside opposition to apartheid in the 1970s and 1980s, who had given gentle support to the struggle, stretched out his legs and winked at me – 'who were offended, disturbed by the black rabble, the mass, by the destruction and the refusal of the movement to be cowed, I say the real cleansing hasn't even started yet. I also say that there is no pure movement, no virginal moment, without blood, except in the fantasies of university teaching, in the absurd manifestos of the academic world.'

I threw my arms open: 'This is the age of justice – the time to move against the rich, to set fire to the old. The 1 per cent.' I spoke directly at the camera: 'I know something of history.' I smiled and laughed, the audience laughed with me. 'Take your slow evolution, your gradual development and your peaceful means, and I will show you the bodies of our parents and ancestors. What is this approach exactly?' I stretched my arms out and weighed the air in my two hands, 'Simply a war against us that goes by another name, and that has been raging for centuries.'

I took a gulp of water, looked down briefly at my notes, folded them and pushed them aside – I rarely really needed my notes to speak, I looked directly at the cameras again. 'Light the fire in every corner of the city – in every city in the world. Then take the destruction to the rich, to their mansions, their second and third homes and take what is yours. When and only when there is nothing left of their world, nothing, can we build another one.' I breathed in, swallowed. 'I arrived a few days ago from London and you know what I feel in my heart, and my mouth, and in my fists?' There were shouts, stamping feet, clenched hands thrown into the air. 'I feel anger. I feel rage. When I see our mothers and fathers, their lives destroyed, my sisters and brothers, on the streets, in doorways, in shacks – where some of you live, I say, shame on you' – I now looked directly into the camera – 'for not feeling this rage. I mourn for your lost humanity. And the only answer to that rage is action. We cannot wait, not another minute, for life that will only come when it is taken. To take it we have to reach into the fires, feel the heat, let the flames burn our flesh and still not flinch. There is no salvation in our governments, no answer in our patience or in our gentle entreaties. To those living on the streets, there is no tomorrow.'

I sucked in through my nose, slowed my pulse – wetted my mouth. I needed to throw the liberals something. 'MLK spoke of this when he talked about the fierce urgency of now.' Predictably there were nods, a flutter of applause. I continued: 'The earth must be cleansed. The radical destruction of the existing social order must take place, so that from these ruins, *and it's only from these ruins* that a new world can come. No more nations, states, political institutions or private property – the rich not taxed, controlled, or herded by social democracy but eliminated.'

Then, suddenly, momentarily, I felt overwhelmed, exhausted at the thought that I had to stand here, and explain the cause of the poor. I leant on the desk. Even this act of speech about the millions living minutes from the hall where I now stood – comfortable and secure – whose struggle for survival and life ought to have commanded automatic support temporarily defeated me. I felt a second's frustration at the weakness of words, the powerlessness of descriptions and argument to change anything. 'And what I am saying,' I said finally, 'is simply the realisation, the practice, of the theory we are taught in universities, and that there is an answer to the suffering of our species and planet.'

'None of this, this preamble is what I was planning to say. I have told the publisher, Jeremy …,' I extended my hand to indicate to the room the man sitting in the middle of the auditorium, 'that I would keep to my script, read from the new book I am writing. But you know, there is so much more to say.'

Jeremy sat up straight, raised his shoulders, turned his hands up and lifted them. He mouthed 'I give up.'

'I will get to that, but there are two things I need to say first. One, in all of my work and writing, there has been a single objective. The one aim has been to bring about the destruction of capitalism – which is the back story to all the oppression, hardship, mayhem that we see around us, and that has engulfed the planet and its people in a catastrophe lasting for five hundred years. It is a collapsing sun, a vortex that sucks in our continent. Capitalism has destroyed Africa – again and again. Yet, it's a destruction that keeps coming, generation after generation. Barbarism, disease, viruses, is not a moment, an incident, even an end point that may occur in the future – it is a recurrent, lived nightmare. The daily life of capitalism. Barbarity is the modus operandi of our world system. The dawn of capitalism on this continent has involved continual mass genocide over five centuries.'

The room was silent, the audience was still, every one of them under my spell. I never feared the university, its professors, its disciplines – in fact, it was in this environment, and only this environment, that I really thrived. Only when I was alone on the stage, with an audience of attentive students, ready to listen and learn, and in front of scholars in politics, literature, philosophy, history, theology, physics, chemistry and mathematics, each of them staring at me, coming at me, from the ghettos of their own specialty, did I feel truly alive.

I also had a power – rare among speakers. I had always been able to sense an audience's attitude, its temperament. This is the skill of mass intuition, an ability to penetrate a crowd's thinking. To tap into its psychology. I could feel the pulse, the tempo in the hall and gauge what was being thought. I always knew how my words were being received – the level of agreement, a psychic connection.

But I knew I was just the discharge to the dynamite that lay under the topsoil of their lives that forms from the conditions of our world – the poverty, suffering and violence. Shamelessly, boldly, I exploited this 'explosive', slowly, methodically priming it.

'For centuries owners of multinationals, corporations, the same families, builders of slave ships, owners of plantations, based in Europe, then North America and today also China have plundered the continent on a colossal scale – and you think the barbarity has given way to democratic niceties? That puny elections have absolved these horrors into the simple crimes of the past? The Barclay Brothers, Barings and HSBC, the Bank of England, the Bank of America, the Church of England, and every major mining house, all have been built on the profits of slavery. Slavery, you remember, was the commercial hunting of black skins. We became animals captured for our value. Our colour an identifier of our persecution, a tag of our enslavement and the impossibility to hide. Yet, in recent decades, since the late 1950s, a Westernised, capitalist elite on the continent has shared power with a global class from Johannesburg to Cairo, Rabat and Dhaka. This class, now in power here, has joined the global elite, the 1 per cent' – I spread my arms, then prodded my index finger onto the desk in front of me – 'Representatives of this class here have betrayed their people and they must be overthrown in the north *and* south of our continent. But, since we are in South Africa, for now, this is where we must start – right now.' I could see the questioning, the doubt in the eyes of the audience, of the students. *Did they think I was I telling them to start the movement tonight?*

'The second thing I need to say is this: you have already read about the murders in New York, Dakar, in Shanghai, Hong Kong and London – fourteen in total, so far. Let me explain. …'

* * *

The fires started before I left.

6

Present Day

THE CHAIRMAN of the University Council was called Jack Prichard, and, in my honour, he had invited a large group of friends, comrades and colleagues to his Constantia house for drinks after the talk. This little man, short hair, round glasses, overconfident, had survived the insurrection of students at the university by hiding, and, when forced out of his wood-panelled office, by conceding just enough to keep alive. When pressed, he compromised, when possible, he condemned excesses, and when he saw his chance, he pulled back and found cover. He was a guerrilla fighter and had learnt how to fight in Cape Town's middle-class anti-apartheid struggle of the 1970s.

Jack was a representative of the South African bourgeoisie, a communist who knew how to have a good time, his radical rhetoric a party trick that made him seem more interesting than he really was. The struggle was a cocktail debate with comrades.

Shameless about his life, dismissing his estate on Beaumont Avenue, Constantia, with a flick of his wrist, the hills and mountains soaring above him, the sea and city in the distance below him. The garden, acres of it, a huge cosmopolitan ecosystem, indigenous and imported – palms, proteas, fynbos, gums, willows and rose bushes, separated by a small landscaped hill, a pergola, a swing hung from a tall tree. The terrace, where we sat, was at the back of the house, which spread out like a splayed hand, the corridors stretching from the building's palm, tributaries connecting living spaces, bedrooms and bathrooms. There were suites, guest rooms, six bathrooms, a sauna, a Zen meditation room and two outdoor pools. One, a narrow single 25-metre length of water, lined with marble and heated. The other, a small plunge pool and jacuzzi outside the French doors at the end of the meditation room. The walls of the house were hung with African art, stone Shona carvings from Zimbabwe, Yoruba masks from Nigeria, framed Akan cloth from Ghana, a djembe drum from Senegal.

Jack and his wife, Gabrielle, from Mozambique, proclaimed their Africanness, asserted their belonging to the continent as an act of possession and ownership. Beautiful and obscene, the house made me want to gasp and vomit. It was an exhibition and a declaration – a statement of control and domination; everything you can see we own.

With a crowd of black and white faces around me, I stood on the wooden decking to speak to them – the sound of water from a fountain in the garden behind me, water cascading down a granite wall into a small pool, and over a stone Buddha.

* * *

There is a side to me that is showy.

I spend so much time alone that when I am in company I can lose control. There are several ways in which I do this. First, in argument – I would take on all established wisdom, challenge a prejudice and show how conventional opinion was entirely false: the real reason behind Russia's invasion of the Ukraine; Uganda's support of the UN peacekeeping mission in occupied Somalia; the jostling for position of the Egyptian ruling class and its relationship with the American elite; and capitalism's need for war.

Furious, in a rage against Prichard, his wife, their hospitality and the whole of Cape Town, I tore into everyone present. There was a small semicircle of guests around me, acquaintances, some friends, each taking their turn to speak in the pretence of a conversation.

Since the publication of *The Elation of Being*, and then in my novels, and non-fiction, every time I spoke, the audience would fall silent. I constantly pre-empted every gathering. I came forward before I had even taken a step, breaking forth, pushing through before I had even arrived.

The night was warm, heat rose from the earth.

On the hills of Constantia were large houses, farms and wine estates, and in the dead of summer – during the droughts – when the rest of the Cape was parched and desiccated, on these hills a breeze from the ocean would take the sting out of the sun.

Behind me, as I spoke, the wind gently filled out my skirt, flapped the sleeves of my blouse, threw up wisps of my platted hair.

In the crowd were three students I had taught years ago – Odwa, who worked for an advertising firm in the city was short, round and boastful; Kristy, a bright, slim white woman worked for her father's law firm; and Julius, born in Khayelitsha, Site C, was still so angry that he couldn't find his words in English quickly enough to damn the world. He worked for an NGO. With them, my prodigies, my disciples, I spoke – around them were others, academics, colleagues, neighbours, who had come down from the house; in the background was a Congolese band playing Papa Wemba songs.

The group fanning out in front of me, listened, laughed, sighed like a Greek chorus as I spoke. Then, when I stopped speaking, they would question me – I felt like Mandela, Lenin, Malcolm X.

'So, Obama,' I posited, exclaiming to the crowd, 'is nothing more than an instrument … and almost certainly unaware of the tendency of capitalism ceaselessly to destroy the means of production. His drive to war, the nuclear fire and fury he threatens, the encircling of China with American gunships, is a dynamic at the heart of the system. The real need of American capitalism is war, that is the instinctive drive to destruction inherent in capitalism. To clear the ground for the creation of new wealth and profit, the system must be periodically destroyed, burnt to the ground. The falling rate of profit across the West in the last fifty years necessitates the destruction of the obstacles to accumulation. The weight of dead capital. …' I felt more like a magician, a conjurer, in front of this crowd, whipping up the wind, turning it over, hurling out the truth into the soft bodies gathered around me.

'We know there will be millions killed – though this is irrelevant, not worthy even of comment.' There were a few intakes of breath, gasps (how well I understood liberal shock, the sound effects of the middle class – like the bleating of lambs). 'In fact,' I continued, 'the war is a time of great creativity, even if the destruction unleashed by capitalism contains the seeds of further destruction. The eventual assured destruction of the earth is guaranteed by the climate apocalypse.'

Below us, I could feel the full weight of the city, the real city, its millions below me. In the heat people dragged their beds out of their homes, lined them up outside their shacks. Through the night there was the sound of children crying, couples fighting, the speckled light of television screens and a tangle of electricity wires like a cobweb over the entire low-built slum.

These voices, *this* life, rose up, tumbled and crashed over the Constantia hills, until the suburb was occupied by them. Lapsing into poetry, into Marx, I continued, 'like a sorcerer who is no longer able to control the powers of the nether world whom she has called up by her spells ... in these wars a great part, not only of existing production, but of all life is destroyed.' Then, pausing, assuming the pose and tone of a schoolmaster, I said, 'And the key to these crises, the drive to war of which even the sorcerer is unaware, is the endemic of overproduction. There is too much and the more there is, the further and quicker prices fall and profits tumble.' Swinging around to the brow of the hill and over it to the glitter of the city below, 'The problem is that capitalism produces double, triple the needs of our entire species.'

Even as I spoke, I grew angry, tired of the tricks I performed for the pampered global elite.

I took in a deep breath of warm air, focused on Odwa's face and said, 'Suddenly society finds itself thrown back into a state of momentary barbarism, and famines, universal wars of devastation break out as we are cut off from the supply of every means of subsistence.' Here I was entertaining the very people I despised with an 1848 text, in a city that didn't need more rhetoric and where history had already emptied Karl Marx into the South Atlantic. Still, I continued: 'Marx says, because there is too much civilisation, too much industry, too much finance, war must come. War – and even the super-rich know this – is the sole means of restoring profit. The momentous annihilation of capital is the only path back to the point where it can engage its productive power once more – and profits resume. The war is coming, and the destruction will be felt here' – I flung my arms out – 'in this suburb of the minor wing of the global elite.'

* * *

The second way in which I burnt off steam, let myself go, was by fighting. I like to fight.

* * *

As much as I put it in its place, arranged its psychological causes, filed my behaviour into categories, it slipped away from me, defied my grip – challenged me to come up with a new method of categorisation.

Kaarina had wrenched apart my calm, severed the order I had imposed over my life, so now I knowingly sowed destruction. I pulled women towards me, sought solace and company and then, once secured, tethered tightly to me, I cut them down. I could feel the heart pounding in the palm of my hands. The moist fragile organ, beautiful, pathetic, vulnerable – pleading to my touch. I severed hearts and hung them from my waist like a warrior, a conjurer – my hands dripping with blood.

Elisa was arriving in a few days. I felt a certain dread.

* * *

Suddenly, tiring of the games, the role I seemed to play of town crier, predicting destruction and war, I came off my soapbox, put an arm around the shoulders of both Julius and Kristy, called to Odwa, 'Come friends, let's get away from the parasites before we're infected.' Ushering the three of them to the fountain, across the lawn, we left the crowd. The garden had been laced with fairy lights, small pools of white light dotted the flower beds, paths and hugged tree trunks, hung from branches, like frozen, luminous droplets of rain.

Julius, his voice gruff, deep, looked around and said, 'Fucking wondrous isn't it.'

Odwa answered, 'I think it's pretty.'

Kristy scoffed, 'This has all been done for you, B.'

We were a few steps from a fountain tucked behind two small Japanese maple trees and some large terracotta pots. I was tracing the filaments of light that tracked the path and then ran along the border of the flower beds, the wires converging beside the fountain, where they fell into a sunken manhole. I guided the group so that we stopped just above the plastic cover where the tangle of wires crossed and plaited before falling into the hole.

'The HQ,' I said finally, pointing to the wires. I knelt, 'If they did this for me …' I fumbled, ran my hand over the square plastic lid, fingered the catch, and pulled it open; in the faint light I could see a large power pack, then a series of plugs in a sealed, waterproof box, 'then …' I continued, looking up at them, 'surely they won't mind if we end their wondrous display.'

Only Julius responded, 'Yes, let's mess it up.'

'I was once in Tunisia' – still kneeling, I removed from my bra a small penknife, opened it and placed it beside the plugs – 'and for two nights I couldn't sleep because the hotel in which the conference was being held played 1980s pop late into the night … the normal crap, Duran Duran, Wham! … on giant party speakers.' I unfolded the blade, looked at the faces around me, their eyes intense and wide. 'Then, on the third night, after asking the hotel manager each night to turn the music down, at 2 a.m. I left my room and walked to the pool.' I was fingering the casing over the plugs, I snapped open the box to expose a line of plugs. I could hear the slight buzz of current humming in the wires. Looking up again at the faces, I continued, 'I realised I needed to do more than turn the music down, I needed to disable the entire system. So …,' I turned back to the sunken cables and plugs, put my fingers on a switch above the plug on the strip of sockets, 'First I turned off the power.' I clicked the switch, then did the same to each of the plugs – first the water to the fountain stopped flowing, then around us, patches of the garden were plunged into darkness, until the garden disappeared. There were sighs from the guests in the house, who suspected that this was the prelude to another show – the darker the night, the brighter the stars.

'Then, when the music had been shut off, I took a knife,' I picked up the one I had placed beside the trapdoor, 'and cut the cables.' Concentrating, bending closer to the plugs, I looped each cord in turn and brought the knife between the loop and quickly and firmly sliced through the wire. Returning to the story, I said, 'When this was done, I went back to my room and slept.' The noise of guests had started up again, battery-powered lanterns began to glow in the distance. I folded the blade, slipped it back into my bra, stood, hooked my foot under the cover and kicked it closed.

'Let's sit over here,' I said indicating a bench a few metres away.

'There is a rumour about you, B,' Kristy said.

'Many rumours, I hope,' I said.

'A rumour that you know Kung Fu,' Kristy persisted.

I laughed. The three of them were drunk and lined up neatly on a bench by the silenced fountain with me sitting on the ground in front of them, embracing my bent legs. There was a freedom that felt like a fresh breeze with them – they were themselves, open with me. Odwa stretched out and crossed his feet. Julius rested his chin on a bent leg.

'So, tell us, sister,' Julius asked, 'Is it true?'

'The one debt I owe my father,' I said, 'is that when we moved to London from Zimbabwe, he insisted his daughters learn how to fight. We needed to defend ourselves in the big, racist city – like he'd learnt to fight the racists in Rhodesia, I suppose. We could be sick, injured or exhausted and he'd insist I had to train. I hated it. And then I loved it. Now, it's a part of my life, like sleeping or breathing.'

We'd been left to ourselves, sitting on the bench behind the fountain. The party continued – light from the house now lit the terrace and balcony, flowed onto the lawn.

Kristy asked, 'And the fighting was Kung Fu?' She was the least confident, I remember her coming to me years ago to speak about the course and her absences, the end-of-term papers that had not been turned in. She came with her mother, a poor woman, bent over, lined, though probably not much other than me. I was polite and closed my office door, heard them, the mother stuttering with a heavy Afrikaans accent, a complaint about fees that couldn't be paid.

'Kung Fu,' I said gently to Kristy, her face lit by the pale light of the moon, 'is a Cantonese term for practice or learning. Discipline. Only in the North, in Europe, has it morphed into a distinct form of martial art. Kung Fu is just a skill, a practice. It is meaningless really … in a real sense.'

'Then, what is it you do?' Kristy was wearing a striped white and blue top and I could see the lines even in the moonlight. Her profile, her thin arms, the sweatshirt tracing her breasts. When she sat opposite me in my office all those years ago, trying to focus on her mother's halting, nervous sentences, excuses and apologies, I stared at her – desiring her, wanting her.

'Show us something,' Julius said – eager, excited, he reached for his beer, drained the can, 'Do something for us.'

'Like a performing monkey?' I answered.

'No, like Bruce Lee,' Odwa added.

'It's rather boring to watch – there are the drills, the katas' I said, 'but otherwise it involves a lot of breathing exercises, repetition and meditation. Philosophy really.'

I never needed much encouragement to perform. I stood.

This, then, was another weakness – I needed to perform.

I stepped back on the grass, assumed a basic practice stance, the left leg forward, bent, the right leg straight, my arms open, my right hand unclenched.

I breathed in. 'Martial arts are highly localised. They only came out of China after 1949 – Mao's chief export crop for a time. Different locations have different styles, classified to cities, provinces, even towns.' Quickly, I brought my right leg up, hip height, then keeping it there I flicked it up, brought it down, swept my left leg around to the right, so the twist lifted me and I used the momentum to turn. I landed on both feet, in a crouching positioning, rose, jabbed with my fists – the sweep, the rush of movement created a small gust of wind. I punched the air just in front of the bench – centimetres from my friends' faces Startled, the three students pushed back against the bench.

'No one takes the regional differences seriously any more,' I continued, standing, bringing my hands together. 'The northern styles had focused on fast and strong kicks, high jumps,' I bowed slightly over my steepled hands 'the south on strong arms and hard techniques, fast footwork.'

The group remained silent, impressed – then Kristy straightened herself on the bench and spoke, 'Have you ever hurt anyone?'

* * *

The bench was tucked away from the manhole, behind the fountain and couldn't be seen from the main house. I sat down again on the grass and we continued to chat. From the house two men walked towards us, stopped in front of the fountain and bent over the plastic cover of the manhole.

We laughed into our hands; I patted the air to the group to indicate to them to be quiet. The men had prized open the cover and were now shining a small torch into the hole – unaware of our presence.

'It's completely fucked up.' One of them said: 'look, it's all been cut, every damn wire.'

They were big men, hungry, muscular, in their forties – I had seen them in the crowd while I had been speaking. I knew the type – no country has such clear and defined types as South Africa. It is a nation without clichés, only facts. The guns, the hunting, the opinions, the vision; I could calculate their trajectory in the universe instantly, knew who they were and exactly where they were heading. Men like this, robust, strong, large, had been eating black people for centuries.

In public, they had learnt to speak the new constitution; in private, they could let the old racism rip.

The man who had peered into the abyss, with a mop of blonde hair, thick and weighty, was now kneeling on the grass, looking up at his friend. 'It was that group of god-damn kaffirs and that white girl, you saw them. They came down here with that black bitch.'

I sat up, felt my pulse race.

The dark-haired man who was standing, put his hand out, his friend reached for it and was hauled up. 'We don't know it was them … it could as easily have been someone from outside. We should tell the others, call security.'

'Security,' Blondie mocked, 'useless fucking security, some black man who doesn't know how to shoot and turns up too late. Jack is such a queer he won't have any guns, but I have my Glock in the car.'

'Steady on, Anton – we don't want to frighten the guests. Maybe we should just mention it to Jack and Gabby.'

There was an intensity in Julius's expression, a heightening of his senses. There was nothing now on his face except anger; on Odwa's and Kristy's faces, I saw confusion and fear.

Julius acted quickly, got up from the bench before any of us could stop him and walked the ten paces to the fountain and the men.

'Am I the "kaffir" you are looking for?' he said, stopping two paces from the pair.

The men were startled – though much bigger than him, both of them instinctively stepped back. More calmly I followed Julius – one or two steps behind, indicating to the others to stay seated.

'And I suppose I am the "black bitch",' I said.

The men continued to stumble, Blondie almost losing his footing grabbed his friend's shoulder to steady himself. The dark-haired man spoke, 'We were just wondering what happened here.'

'What do you think happened whitey?' I asked.

Julius's breathing was heavy, quick. 'We should mess you up for using those words. Teach you how to speak.' I felt him strain, his muscles twitch, ready to step towards the men. I put out my arm, rested my hand on his chest, gently restraining him.

The two men now recovered, found their footing.

'I cut the wires,' I said.

'I knew it.' Blondie said. 'Bitch.'

He stepped forward and tried to grab me. I moved slightly, causing him to stumble again. Then, more aggressively, he lunged at me with both hands. I swiped his hands away, moved quickly to his side and, side on, raised my right leg and bought it down hard and quickly on his knee. There was a clear, crisp snap and then – what always happens – a pure, momentary silence that always come before acute pain. He continued to stand for a second, then tottered and felt the sheer deafening agony of the broken ligaments and shattered, dislocated knee ripple across his body and he fell.

His friend caught him and under the weight he also fell to the ground. There was a pile of white limbs, a mess of bodies and muscle – pathetic, impotent.

My only surprise that night was Julius's reaction.

As the howls of pain began to echo through the garden, like the cries of a dying dog, Julius calmly walked up to the crumpled man, who was clutching the top of his leg and jumped on his outstretched limb.

I took his arm, and pulled him away, 'Let's get the others and get out of here.'

7

Present Day

ABOUT TEN DAYS after I arrived, the fires started. I had spoken three times, each time to groups of students, and youth, hungry to hear their anger worked out as a programme, the logic infallible, the defences impenetrable. When I spoke, I felt their force and life in me, the sea of hungry eyes, the open mouths. Each of the black women and men were inside me, with their voices and dreams. I didn't care if they remembered who I was, who exactly had planted *the plan* in their minds. I was only concerned that they would begin to see themselves and understand the unconditional love that they must have for themselves. When I spoke, I felt larger, swollen by the pride and love I had for them.

There was nowhere else in the world that made me feel like this – nowhere except South Africa, where I was completely understood. A country that knew violence, understood its necessity, its role.

On the third occasion I spoke in a bookstore in the city, the sort of pretentious dusty old-world bookshop, where the books were piled high like pillars, each room more impenetrable, a labyrinth of first editions, lost manuscripts and dust.

The store was ambushed; there were hundreds of people trying to enter, queuing outside. I said I would refuse to speak unless the meeting was held in the street, so everyone who had come could hear me. In the end the windows on the first floor were flung open and I was given a microphone, and a speaker was commandeered and finally I was told to speak.

Three, four hundred people gathered on the pavement and street, temporarily shutting off the road. I felt like a prisoner freed after twenty-seven years in prison; the sun beat down, cutting the street in two. I had to shield my eyes to see the crowd below, sweating in the heat. The tall city buildings, 1970s office blocks, and older three-storey redbrick shops and flats, cast uneven shadows over the crowd.

'Sisters and brothers, this is unusual, I feel like the pope or Mandela but, unlike the pope or Mandela, I will tell you the truth and then we can turn our minds to what we need to do. Once we have diagnosed the problem – brought the disease to the surface, seen the layer of perspiration on the skin, can we decide on the remedy. You see, once we have identified the 1 per cent, the rich, the thieves, the elite and their agents, we will have solved 90 per cent of our problem. The right question contains within it the seeds, the germs, of the answer. Why are they rich? And why are we poor? You see, posing the question, the simplest question, takes us directly to the answer. Do you see?' There was a murmur, agreement. I dropped my hand from my eyes and gripped the microphone, with both hands. 'When the English scientist Isaac Newton asked the question, why does the apple fall from the tree, he was immediately a single step from the law of universal gravitation ... always the question, the riddle, and then, only then, the answer. You see?'

Again, there was a murmur, louder this time, a few students shouted, 'Yes!' One young woman, right under the window standing on the pavement two metres below, shouted, 'Tell us sister.'

As I spoke, I saw the fires for the first time. The city is shielded by mountains and below the forested cliffs are the flat plains where the poor live and the central business district built on the shoreline. On the side of the mountain that I could see from where I stood on the balcony a field of pine trees, growing from the steep bank. It was here that the flames burst into life, consuming the trees like kindling, the mountain above us, a mile away. The flames spread across the side of the mountain in minutes – sending orange and red light into the sky and a wall of smoke that obscured the skyline, darkening the street, changing the day to dusk. The beauty was undeniable – the destruction total.

Transfixed, astonished, the crowd stared at the wall of fire, motionless, in revelry and awe. I stopped speaking and looked directly into the flames, then after a pause I said, 'Nothing can be built from the old. It must be destroyed, bought to the ground. Decimated.' There was silence for a second, then a cheer – more a roar than a cheer, which continued as the crowds spread further over the road, and the adjoining streets, spreading out for a better view.

As the fire burnt – the sound of the flames on the wood a mile away, of an open furnace cracking and popping – the crowd started to move, shake, dance.

There was something primordial in the power of the fire. Its wild, uncontrolled energy stirred us. We could hear the dry, hard crackle as the trees were engulfed – the sheer force and energy of this rudimentary element to obliterate the mighty sun, to create darkness out of light, to turn our own star temporarily into a mere luminous disk.

The fire made all of us who witnessed it that afternoon joyous.

If we chose, we could eclipse even the sun with our rage. We could do anything, the power against us was nothing. What was the state, the rich, their institutions, companies, wealth, even their media, their armies and police, their mansions and palaces, compared with this? The 1 per cent could be destroyed – with fire, with the rage of our beautiful destruction.

For a few moments, as we danced in the darkness, it seemed that the whole world was being questioned.

Back to zero.

* * *

The fire that raged for weeks in Cape Town, long after I had left, was like a storm. Imagine a hurricane, upturning the land, crossing all human-made frontiers, leaping like confetti from one hillside to another, one leafy mountain suburb to another, throwing everything up, felling trees with the deepest roots, houses with the heaviest foundations – turning all that is solid into air. The fire did this, its destruction was great, methodical – the sweep of its power more systematic.

The rich live on the mountains and in the rolling, hilly glades over the mountain range – the trees all imported more than a hundred years ago from Europe are flammable pines, oaks, sycamores, dotted around the properties of the wealthy, the parks, nature reserves and city forests. The poor live in the great Serengeti-like plains between the mountain escarpments and the sea, in shacks. Kaarina's family lives in Constantia.

For weeks, the poor watched the mountains burn – the flames insatiable, demented, the fire constantly erasing the conditions of its own existence, impatiently leaping over trees, leaving them untouched, burning only their outer branches, shearing a few leaves, but then consuming a neighbouring grove. Then the fires fell on new trees that had seemed out of their reach with a voracious, frenzied appetite, but only then when it seemed that the fire was satisfied would it flare up again, fall back on the mansions, estates and houses that it had spared only days before.

For the poor who watched from below, from their townships, a new activity quickly developed in those weeks: in the evening, families and friends would stand in the street, bringing their evening meals, and watch the progress of the fires, point at the rich neighbourhoods they knew, Constantia, Tokai, Bishopscourt, Clifton, Table View, and Camps Bay, where they had only ever cleaned or guarded. Revenge, true sweet revenge, is rare in life. For these weeks, the poor had their revenge.

The uninterrupted fire storm tore away what had seemed permanent. The fire was pitiless. Everything that had been immovable was swept to the ground, all new virgin terrain destroyed. Everything in the path of the fire was compelled to obey – subjected to its rule of extinction, forced to yield, to kneel and to accept defeat. Stripped of its façade, forced to stand alone, Cape Town found itself in a state of temporary barbarism; a civilisation once impermeable was, in a moment, burnt to the ground. In the first weeks nothing could satiate the flames – the efforts to douse them, control their movement, seemed only to provoke their anger, causing the fire to spread more rapidly, to elude capture.

All rich, developed neighbourhoods, long built up, invested with the wealth of white families for generations, and the exclusive shopping centres, restaurants, cafés, gyms, pools and parks servicing the rich were reduced to dust.

The crowds who gathered below in the treeless plains, where the fire could not spread, mapped the progress, destruction, at the end of each day. They saw – in the destruction of the wealthy mountainside neighbourhoods, in what passes for the Cape's civilisation – a necessary sacrifice, even a holy one, ordained by God.

In the fifth week, as I followed events in London, I read that among the poor the fire had acquired the name 'comrade'.

8

Present Day

BEFORE I LEFT South Africa, on the days I had with Elisa, we drove to the coast and walked along the pebble beaches, past day trippers, ice cream vans, elderly couples, coloured beach huts, until they gave out and we were almost alone. The beach now swept forward undivided by breakwaters; pebbled mountains fell steeply into the beach and calm flat sea. The clouds were low, twisted and sinewy. The size of cities. Above the clouds, the sky was deep blue, and the sun shone unobstructed.

I was distracted, my shoulders ached, the day was a concession to Elisa. I was not present and only spoke when it was unavoidable – as the sky tinted through my sunglasses we passed a couple with a dog, a man wheeling ice creams.

Elisa pointed to an object in the distance as I spoke, 'We only see anything when we are about to die …,' I said, as we crossed a small wooden bridge over a still stream, two ducks moving on the banks, 'or at rare moments during pauses in our days, when we can step away – breathe, stop, see. I wrote about this in *The Elation of Being*.' I took Elisa's hand and stopped in the middle of the bridge. There was no one else around, no breeze and the sun was momentarily hidden. When the clouds cleared, I closed my eyes, lifted my face to the sky, felt the sun's heat. I had no need to speak, to see, to do. I squeezed Elisa's hand.

I could feel the sun reach my chest and heart and hold them, still them – allow them for a minute to stop striving, to stop blindly moving through life. In that moment I wanted to tell Elisa that I loved her. The beam of sunlight was broken again as these giant city clouds crossed the sky. Elisa flickered back into focus. I dropped her hand and turned to the water, held the side of the bridge. I shook my head slightly, cleared my vision, 'We are so battered by life, by the struggle to live – so often our lives are not really ours. What happens when life, when our own lives, are completely driven out of us?' I turned back to Elisa, who had not moved, she was looking at me motionless. I stretched my arms out, turned slightly to my left and nodded towards the far bank, the heather, the sandy dry patches of lavender, the clumps of evergreen plants clinging stubborn and beautiful to the earth. Beyond this, in the far distance, a town in red brick and then in front of it, in the sea, two or three hundred metres from the shore, the end of a pier, the wooden walkway washed away years before – only the black towering husk remained stranded in the water, like an oil rig. Around us, in the grass, bobbing in the water, there was rubbish. This coastline on the western seaboard of Africa was dying, though still beautiful.

I breathed in and let the sun enter me again – 'How do we get back to zero, Elisa?' I asked.

'Zero? What do you mean, darling?' she said reaching for my hand. 'You have such strange ideas.'

'I haven't even started yet. The danger is that our emotions are so underground. …' I dropped my arm, bent down and touched the ground, '… underground. So, closed down. Closed off and alienated, we have to dance with death to feel alive. You see, Elisa …' I slowed down, moved my body closer to hers. 'What we think is love isn't love, but fear.'

Elisa started to cry, she lifted a hand to her face, her mouth twisted, both ends of her mouth curled down, her eyes widened and creased. She tried to cover up her shame, the tears, the fear, the love – which was it? Then, between the tears, she said, 'I'm crying because I love you.'

I replied quickly, 'When you cry like this you are paying your debts.' I said, 'The Chinese say that falling in love is bad for you. Unconditional love for yourself is real love. All forms of love, for your parents, for your lover, for your daughter, are conditional love.'

I don't know what made me speak from such an old script like this, from work from which I had long distanced myself, or why I had wanted to tell Elisa that her love for me wasn't love but fear.

I took her hand and we crossed the bridge, walked along the gravel path. A man in a white cap was pushing a cart – an icebox on a bicycle, wheels weaving between the heather, his brow wet, he stopped twenty metres from us, set the trolley on its legs, opened the umbrella and waited for us to pass. I bought two ice creams, handed one to Elisa.

'Sometimes' Elisa said breaking our silence, 'I feel intimidated by you. I don't know what to say. I don't know if I have anything to say.'

PART 6

'There's a great truth you should know'

1

Present Day

I DIDN'T WANT to take the call. I had left my phone on flight mode – the journey still rang in my ears, the exhaustion stung me. I was dropped at the flat and changed quickly into my shorts and trainers. The sky was low, the thick cloud cover was punctured, here and there, so a small patch of pale blue light was visible, but there was no real resistance, no fightback, so the city, as usual, had the look of defeat. As I ran, avoiding Tottenham Court Road, running as usual in the street, I sent the rainwater on the street into the air.

I felt awake, the journey working its way out of me, the throb and pain of the run in my legs.

I knew I was back – around me new apartment buildings, small supermarkets, bundles of newspapers sealed in plastic dumped outside newsagents, crates of food being hauled into restaurants and shops. Already I could see small queues of commuters in coffee shops – dog-tired, miserable, all of them.

At least I had Nina – Nina, Nina – she understood. I turned up the volume.

I felt a fury, a surge of adrenaline. I turned the corner from Goodge Street to Charlotte Street – a car sounded its horn behind me. I stopped, turned, the driver hit the brakes, the man, his face fat, loose, cruel. I shrugged my shoulders, palms up. *Once more please, just one more time, sound the horn again, dare me and you will not drive again*. I was in one of those London moods when I wanted to punch someone hard in the face.

As I continued to run, I thought that this city needed to be destroyed so there was nothing left except rubble. I laughed at myself, passed Pavarotti's: Giancarlo was outside arranging chairs and tables on the pavement in a stained apron, a tight, short-sleeved Hawaiian shirt with palm trees waving in a tropical breeze; he bellowed at me and beckoned. I slowed down pulled the headphones from my ears and opened my arms – we hugged.

'Giancarlo, you are huge. You need to exercise, or you'll die.'

'We're all going to die Bianca … very soon.'

'Now that's true – at last a man who knows.'

Giancarlo was a Londoner though he spoke in a heavy Italian accent, and occasionally with me he would let his guard down and switch between Naples and Stratford. 'Where have you been? You look tired.'

'Away,' I answered.

I could feel the cold air hit my back – a gentle sweat bristle on my neck.

'Well, you need to eat.' When he was speaking of food, cajoling regular customers to eat, Giancarlo reverted back to his Neapolitan English. 'Come for lunch today Bianca, I'm making pasta alla Genovese. It will fatten you up.'

'Like a lamb to the slaughter.'

'No like a famous woman who needs her sustenance.'

I needed this familiar neighbourhood love. The sort of affection that I didn't have to think about, reciprocate or tend to and that came because I bought it, because I was a regular customer.

I showered in the university and changed into a clean set of clothes that I kept in the office. When the run had worn off, I felt just the plane exhaustion, the sound of the engines still ringing in my ears – I needed to sleep but wouldn't until the night. I stood at my desk, a student's PhD open, resting on a pile of papers – my office altar.

There were three knocks at the door, I knew who it was – much can be said from the sounds of a person knocking. Jenny knew what she wanted – and there is something unmissable about the knock of a police officer. Seconds after the first trilogy, there was another – a quick, urgent hammered trio. I answered the door.

* * *

Jenny came into the room with bluff, bombast – stood two steps in, her hands on her hips, adamant, accusing. 'You've been away,' she said.

'Hello, Jenny,' I replied.

Jenny was wearing a dress, a black gown and heels, on her arm a grey, woollen coat. She saw me looking at her and held out her hands, palms up to the ceiling and laughed, 'I'm sorry. I am dressed like this, ridiculous I know, I have a press conference in an hour.'

'You look nice,' I felt my pulse quicken slightly.

Jenny reddened, looked at the floor, then up again at me. 'I should have phoned; I tried a few times and you were away.'

'South Africa,' I said.

'Where were you?'

'In Cape Town.'

'For the fires?'

'Not specifically for the fires.' Jenny smiled. I could tell she felt self-conscious, exposed – suddenly, unexpectedly weak.

'Social cleansing … they're calling it, of the rich neighbourhoods,' she said.

I interrupted, 'Forty per cent of Constantia destroyed; not a single person or shack in the slums affected. Four hundred million dollars in damage to property, rich families, generations of wealth, vineyards – all gone. Now …,' I shuffled the papers on the desk, found my folded newspaper, held it up, 'they are saying that there will be an exodus of the rich. Capital flight.' I slammed the paper down.

Jenny was smiling broadly, her hands still on her hips. 'Arson,' she said. I winked at her, yawned loudly, stretched, felt my back click. She continued, 'It was planned, all of it – three fires set within hours, at different points in the Cape, to make it impossible for the authorities to respond systematically to any of them, and then subsequent fires set in multiple points across the city, houses, gardens, parks. This was a complex plan.'

I needed to finish the PhD, write the report. 'And you know what …,' I continued ignoring what Jenny had just said, 'as the flames consumed Constantia, as the rich hills of the city burned, there were celebrations in the slums, dancing, parties, braais – a South African barbecue.'

Jenny put a hand on the back of the leather recliner, placed her coat on the seat. 'And when the poor riot,' she said, 'they burn down their own supermarkets, schools and streets. What do these celebrations really mean, Bianca?'

I breathed in deeply, slowed my heart. 'Two things, Jenny. First, I am tired and have work to do and second, I do not have time to correct undergraduate clichés, and newspaper tropes about South Africa. You will understand it doesn't do my reputation good receiving visits from the police.'

I did not lessen the words, my harshness, with a smile – I wanted her gone. She was mute.

'Oh, and for your information,' I added, 'it was only the large stores, the ones that have ripped off their black customers for years – Pick n Pay, Spar, Checkers and ShopRite – that were targeted, and the small shops, the townships spaza shops were left untouched.'

Jenny took her coat from the back of the chair and pulled it on and held it tight to her body.

* * *

Jenny explained that once more there'd been a murder. She listed the circumstances – as if the crime could be solved with data. She stood stiffly, her coat buttoned up. 'The man was middle-aged, an Italian banker, Matteo Romano: he'd worked on acquisitions for Merrill Lynch, and two years ago he set up his own fund – small, only $400 million. He was investigated by the Financial Conduct Authority in 2012. Nothing happened. He was found dead in his Kensington house two nights ago. The media haven't even been told yet – that's the press conference I'm going to.' Jenny opened her arms, to indicate her attire. 'He was found by the maid. His legs seem to have been broken first and then his throat cut. Nasty. Papers are missing. Our staff are going through his office and apartment now,' she paused.

I quickly interjected. 'And your theory?'

'He was a successful banker and seems to have been liked – excessively.' Jenny pushed a hand into her pocket and removed a folded piece of paper from which she read, '... "Matteo Romano received the London Business Standards award for community outreach and ethical trading," blah, blah, blah. Collecting the award, he commented, "We must endeavour to uphold the highest standards of business ethics in all of our activities." I thought you'd like that.' Jenny looked up at me and folded the paper.

I sniggered – rubbed my face and yawned again. I dropped my hand and my vision cleared, Jenny was staring at me.

'Come on, Jenny,' I mocked. 'You didn't come here for my sympathy. A dead banker – no doubt the man had a family who loved him. Maybe he could even cook decent pasta. I do not care about his humanity. Objectively – and all that matters in life is objectivity – he was a banker. Western bankers, financiers – ALL from the capitalist class are guilty. The whole class has chucked its spare mountains of cash and liquidity after withdrawing all it could from the catastrophe that wrecked the housing needs of millions – into speculating, betting and bidding up the global food industry. And, to even a hint at any regulation, it has reacted by simply buying huge swathes of the global food industry – even from Cargill and the Archer Daniels Midland Company, and worse – vast swathes of land – whole regions of Africa, in particular.'

I cupped my hands around my mouth and called out, 'Cheap land, cheap labour, easily amenable governments, no planning or infrastructural controls, buy Africa anew! All the crooks are at it. Richard Branson has bought swathes of Kenya and South Africa, Warren Buffett likewise and the whole point of the Bill and Melinda Gates Charitable Foundation is to buy land, I mean whole regions of whole fucking countries. They try to be secretive so that we can't find out which countries and where and how they are doing it, but it is happening.'

Once I had started, I found it difficult to stop. 'However, they are playing with fire. These bankers and financiers go to the poor, who are already practically up in arms, posing as entrepreneurial rescuers from starvation and, with multinationals from communist China, they quickly reveal themselves to be the guttersnipe thieves and brutal overseers of slavery and grubbing of profiteers that they are. Your man Matteo is dead and let's hope he stays dead.'

I realised that I was in a bad mood.

Jenny smiled patiently through my little tirade – this venting. Then, softly chiding me, she said, 'Thank you, Bianca, but I came for your help not your opinion about capitalism. You want to know my theory? I don't really have one – but these murders in New York, another in Senegal, everywhere, all since the start of the year … are of wealthy businessmen, bankers, financiers.' She shifted her weight from one foot to another, wetted her mouth. Jenny was tired, she hadn't slept, lines deep and dark under her eyes. 'So,' she said after pausing briefly, 'they are connected. I don't know how but somehow.'

'Not necessarily,' I said, 'Take the last three murders, three rich men – presumably plenty of distinct reasons to murder them.'

'Now,' Jenny laughed, and her eyes glistened. 'Bianca, this doesn't happen, and you know that. The wealthy are *not* assassinated in the normal course of life. The rich, as you know, as you teach,' she threw her arms open, looked left and right to my files, my books, 'live easy, comfortable lives and they are *not* murdered, do not die of the viruses that kill the poor. …' She stopped suddenly, and made a decision to tell me something she had not planned to say: 'okay, if I were to say that they knew each other in business and that they had contributed money to a fund they jointly managed and were involved in investments in the garment industry, what would you say?'

As Jenny continued to speak, I walked to the small coffee machine, next to my bookshelf by the window, removed two cups from the windowsill, placed a coffee cartridge into the top of the machine and pressed the green light. Jenny continued to speak; I gave her the coffee.

Eventually, she got to the point 'I need your help Bianca. …'

I took a marker pen, picked up a small pile of notes, walked to the whiteboard, wiped it clear with my sleeve and quickly started to write down everything I'd just been told, what I already knew, of their names, ages, work. Around the edges of the board, next to their names, I wrote the location, the manner of death and their work and, in the middle, the shell companies, banks, investments and tax havens.

Jenny was silent as I wrote, the pen squeaking on the board, at last I heard her behind me, the clink of the cup against the saucer. When I was done, I turned back to the room.

'How did you know Romano's age? I didn't mention it.'

'That's why I'm the professor,' I said. Jenny raised her eyebrows. 'I guessed,' I added quickly.

Jenny knocked back the last small mouthful of coffee and put the cup and saucer down on my desk.

'I will entertain you,' I said with a flourish, spreading my arms to indicate the whiteboard, words and arrows. 'Bear with me, let's see if I can make anything of your theory. Though one word of essential political economy.' I took a couple of steps towards her so we stood a foot apart. 'The one indispensable fact of capitalism is the link between everything – universal interdependence, the means of production concentrates property in fewer and fewer hands. Right?' I took one more step and put a hand on Jenny's shoulder. 'One code of laws, one set of class interests. Your Romano and these others,' I nodded towards the board, '*are* connected, of course they are, that's the point. Interlocking directorships, financial institutions, global clubs, the rich, their bankers and political backers, are a tiny tottering, connected class.' I stopped, smiled, felt for the first time that day the exhaustion completely evaporate and my heart race. 'Establishing a link is easy, finding *the* link is always harder.'

Like a real policewoman Jenny removed her notebook, flicked the black cover over and removed a pen from her coat pocket. Dutifully, quietly, she took notes as I spoke.

After half an hour Jenny said moving to the door, 'We're depending on you.' Her mood had changed – she'd relaxed, there was more warmth now – the return of that shy desire.

'By "we" you mean the Confederacy of Idiots, the Met and the rest of the global policing mafia for which you work? I do this work,' I turned back slightly to the board, 'for you, Jenny.'

When Jenny left, my heart was still racing, it felt good; I was alive, my thinking clear. As I looked at the names I'd written down, the clouds broke, and a strip of sunlight burst into the room, a line of bright light crossed my desk and cut the whiteboard into two.

2

1981 – Port Harcourt, Nigeria

WE SPENT A WEEK with Fawari at the end of March. Expansive, wide, generous, it was to her that we ran after school – her embraces enthusiastic, her interest in us unending. Our chatter in English and pidgin competing with the crickets, even louder, more adamant.

She suggested we attend her real home in Buguma for Easter in 1981, addressing our father, her head slightly bowed:

'Ọga, sir, I said to Bianca and Maïmouna that they come home with me for Easter.' She was standing on the threshold of his office, maps and wall charts – the entire kingdom of the Niger Delta pinned on the wall, every inch mapped, small Shell emblems indicating conquered territory, and other areas ready for exploration marked with black crosses.

Fawari leant on one hip, stared at the carpet – we stood behind her, in agony that our aunty, this brilliant and proud woman was laid low when she addressed her master, our father. He barked, not looking up from his paperwork. 'How many times have I said: don't call me "*ọga*", call me Howard. …'

'Sorry, *ọga* Howard,' Fawari said, not lifting her gaze.

'God damn it woman,' he shouted, then the content of her first sentence reached him, and he finally looked up, saw us – my face stern, unmoving behind Fawari. 'Yes. Yes, of course,' he said, waving his hand, 'Take the bloody bairns but return them before school.'

'Thank you, Sir,' Fawari nodded and retreated, closing the door, and turning to us she smiled – we ran into her open arms. '*Aunty, you don win*!' '*Na awa Aunty be dat*!' (That's our Aunty!)

* * *

To anyone watching us skipping out of the compound, the scene couldn't have been more normal: three happy girls, their bags slung over their shoulders, without a thought or a regret, life with its muck and experience barely unable to find a grip. Fawari led the escape from our gilded prison.

Outside, on the bustling main road ringing the campus perimeter, a small bus had pulled up, and standing beside it was Fawari's father, ready to bundle us in for the three-hour journey to Buguma. Around him pedestrians pushed past, passengers on the vehicle shouting for us to hurry, and for the journey to start – along the road were peanut sellers, stalls of mangos, oranges, and then everything else anyone could possibly want – spirits, sachet water, Coke, Fanta, seafood, peppered snails, other meats, vegetables, pastry, confectionery.

As we crossed the road passengers leant out of the window haggling for supplies – the vehicle was consumed in a human embrace of traders and beggars. We found some seats, squeezed together, and the journey started – uncle keeping up a constant account, of the countryside, of the misery of the Niger Delta, and its tremendous mysteries, everything he was going to show us. '*Beta beta tins I go sho you*!'

He had worked for the British in the colonial administration, and was no fan of the whites, or the new faces, or the military – 'where we are going there is beauty, you think you have seen Nigeria, but you have not. I say beauty – pure green beauty. But they – your people – are trying to ruin everything. In the villages we can't enjoy our sleep at night due to the gas flaring. The rain kills our crops and water, and we are getting ill.'

There was loud laughter in the bus, jeering, agreement, and Fawari kept interrupting – 'Leave the girls, they are here with us – they will see. Don't scare them with these stories.' '*I beg leave dis talk now o!*'

Uncle waved his hand, spoke louder, 'If you park a white vehicle overnight the yellow oil and soot will cover it by morning. You wake up and your nose is blocked with soot. It affects your eyes too. The British never left and they still suck us dry.' He was an entertainer, and at this last image, he lifted himself in his seat and puckering his lips and sucked in the air – 'suck, suck, suck' he shouted. We laughed, feeling the warmth of the bodies beside us, the connection at last with the world around us – Kaarina took my hand, threaded our fingers together.

3

Present Day

IN THE FLAT I pulled down a print I had in the lounge, a framed poster advertising an anti-apartheid demonstration in 1987 – the first protest I had attended as a teenager when we had just arrived in London from Zimbabwe. On the now bare, white wall behind the sofa, I stuck articles about the fire – charting its origins, its progress, where it spread and what it did. Article after article, photo after photo, fanning out across the wall – telling the story from genesis through to destruction and resurrection. A Cape Town bible story.

At the end of the day, tired and ecstatic from my evening run and workout, I would sit on my Chicago recliner, swivel 45 degrees so I faced the wall, my legs out, the foot rest out and scan the photographs and articles – consider its geography, each hypothesis, reaching across the wall, like the splayed fingers of a hand, indicating a new direction the fire had taken, a fresh motivation, a new lead.

So far, the Cape Town wildfires had burned from early May across the peninsula, starting in the white seaside suburb of Hout Bay. In the first days the fire burnt 7,000 hectares, destroyed thirty mountainside houses and killed fourteen people – eight of these were the elderly residents of a rich suburb who had refused to be evacuated. Within days the fire had spread north up the peninsula to the hillside roads and houses of Muizenberg, then to Lakeside, Tokai and Constantia. On the first day that the fires reached Muizenberg, the flames took down the old wood-framed buildings built high on the mountainside.

Almost with a human consciousness and a sense of justice, the fire – despite the frenzied efforts of Cape Town's fire service and local volunteers – consumed Cecil Rhodes's Muizenberg cottage. Videos of the incineration went viral on social media, with comments labelling the destruction 'decolonisation'. By the end of the day sixty properties had been destroyed in the suburb.

The regional government was powerless to bring the fire under control; as the flames encroached on Constantia, efforts to pacify the blaze were intensified, only for the flames to flare up again. Night after night after I had returned from South Africa with Elisa, having taken one of the last flights to have left the city, I followed the course of the fire, charting its fits and starts where it died down, then where it burst out again – as though the whole thing had been orchestrated, as if there were someone conducting it, indicating and pointing out a new direction for it to travel.

On those evenings in May, I would sit back in the chair, my hands on its armrests, repeating to myself the course of the fire. By noon on 4 May, seventy people from lower Constantia had been hospitalised from smoke inhalations and seventeen large family estates had been destroyed. A retirement village in Noordhoek had been burnt to the ground. Nothing was spared – the city's infrastructure for elderly white Capetonians had been completely obliterated. Chapman's Peak Drive was closed, the road declared impassable – the tarmac turned into a melted, molten track. The Cape Town Cycle Tour was cancelled, and the mighty South African Naval Base at Simonstown evacuated.

Unquenched and inexhaustible, by the end of the fourth week the fire was still burning – ferocious and feared.

I reached down for the bottle of sparkling water on the floor next to the recliner, topped up my glass. Nina sang *I Put a Spell on You*. My phone was off, and I had a pile of clippings on my lap – 'Investigators Close in on Cause of Cape Town Blaze', 'Cops Pursue Arson Claim'. These had to be processed, pinned in their place on the wall.

So far, my theory, my conclusions, indicated that there was no single origin, no one genesis – it seemed the new lines of enquiry posited multiple origins, simultaneous 'creations' across the Cape. Organised arsonists were lighting fires, hours or days apart, from Scarborough at the extreme southern point of the peninsula, through Muizenberg and Lakeside and the city. What was clear was that these arsonists knew about fire: they had made a study of it and knew how it would catch, how it would burn and that fires lit in different places in the city, across its richest neighbourhoods would quickly render the fire service, the scrambled air-force aircraft and the civilian army of almost entirely white volunteers impotent. This group, these individuals, I decided, were lighting fires in a way that kept them almost entirely away from the poor living in the city's shanty towns and townships.

Like all things in South Africa, the arsonists had become insurgents, the fire a political emergency – potentially triggering a wider social explosion. The movement of movements, as the academy was now calling it – reclaiming, purging the environment from the rich, with a movement of the poor.

My restlessness exhausted by exercise, stretched out on the armchair, I felt a profound pleasure, a sense of peace at the chain of events as they spread over my living room wall.

4

2011

WE FOUGHT like children, like siblings – hating each other for a moment, and then making up. Living together in Cape Town, the city of a thousand invisible slums, 2011 was a typical year, our love and quarrels had no purpose.

It was late and the day had been long. There was an evening meal with her sister in a restaurant where she knew the owner in downtown Cape Town – a place panelled like a sauna with black-and-white photos of Vietnam from the 1920s, the colonial heyday. The owner was a small man with charm and recipes he gathered on annual field trips to rural Vietnam and China.

We had exhausted ourselves on the routine of lover's questions – throwing feelings back and forth through a haze of exhaustion.

'You seem different. Tell me what's wrong?' Kaarina asked.

'Nothing's wrong.'

'I can tell that something is. Your energy has changed.'

'No, it hasn't.'

'I think it has, baby.'

The pantomime continued until I said, 'You are fishing for a fight – is that how the weekend ends, a nice morning, nice afternoon and to round it off a row. You want a row.'

We were picking up her brother from a friend. We'd pulled up and Kaarina got out, rang the doorbell, called for her brother to come out. I sat in the car breathing hard – 'Let it pass, let it pass.' I muttered over and over.

Kaarina's brother who, I had been told, was a monster of gargantuan scale with a reputation for careful destruction, was harmless – his brutality pathetic. He mumbled incoherently about Zen Buddhism and the one hundred thousand mantras he needed to say every year – his ferocity a rumour. Doubting loudly across the restaurant table the longevity of his current marriage, we even managed a few sentences of reminiscences.

Then, when it was all done and the night was finally and thankfully present – deep down we all long for the darkness, the final close of the day – Kaarina came into the bedroom in a towel. I was reading, my glasses on the bedside table, the blue pages of the news-sheet centimetres from my face, the covers around me, cocooned like an infant.

The towel was placed on a pillow and Kaarina gave me firm instructions to lie in place. I put the pages down and placed myself in the instructed spot; she then brought a small rolling pin dotted with tiny needles and, after rubbing oils on my skin, she rolled the device across my forehead, temples and cheeks. I shuddered with the sensation.

When she was done, I moved back to my side of the bed, 'Baby, can we talk about what happened today? What was going on with you?' Kaarina asked.

I could hear the washing machine muted behind the kitchen door.

'Can we sleep?' I answered. After a few seconds of silence, I hauled myself up, readying myself for the discussion, 'You know Kaarina,' I said, 'if I tell you, you must listen.'

'I will.'

'Nothing was wrong. Yet, in a day there are moods and most of these are nothing. When you kept asking me if I were okay, I thought you wanted a fight. I was tired. Then suddenly when I kissed your arm to reassure you and said, "I am so happy to be with you," you replied, "Why do you keep saying that?" You are, you must see this Kaarina,' here I stroked her arm, then resting my hand on hers, 'a little perverse. When you …'

'That's not fair …,' she interrupted.

I patted the air in front of her, 'No, let me finish. When you tell me that you love me – I do not ask: "Why do you keep saying that?"'

Kaarina sat propped up on pillows listening to me – I was calm. Her eyes filled with tears, she was silent and didn't reply. I lay down again. She got up and left the room, opened the kitchen door and transferred the washing to the dryer. I heard the drum start to turn, the thud of the damp washing rising and falling.

Kaarina came back into the room and her mood had changed. She was playful and got into bed, peeled away the cover I had laced around my body and wriggled up to me.

'You'll wake up with your face swollen,' she laughed.

'Then you should use the device on my breasts.'

'Yes,' she giggled, 'all around them.'

'A full treatment.'

'I could increase the size – at last you'll have a proper cleavage.'

I pushed myself away from her. 'A proper cleavage?' I repeated.

'Wouldn't you like ...?' she asked smiling.

I spoke firmly. 'I want to sleep. This is not a good conversation to have. Do you see that Kaarina? There are things that should *not* be said. I would never mention your weight, for example – so why do you think it's all right to joke about this?'

I pulled my body away from hers and pulled back the covers. 'I need to sleep,' I turned over.

Kaarina left the room again.

When she returned to the room I was wrapped up, layered in the blankets, sealed away. She got in, her back to me and lay still. *How we destroy the sweetest, most necessary things in our lives.* I breathed in. I tried to distract myself, to bring oxygen and perspective to my thoughts.

That day I had heard about Saturn and the probe launched twenty years ago, hurtling through our solar system at 125,000 kph. After seven years' flight the probe had arrived at the ringed planet, where it had spent thirteen years in orbit. I tried to picture the spinning countless ringlets, the dozens and dozens of moons – including Titan, Pandora, Prometheus, Mimas – and the enormous radius of the planet, nine times larger than Earth. The probe had just burnt up as it plunged into the planet's atmosphere.

I repeated the facts of the mission and tried to see the blackness of space, dotted by the Milky Way – the distance, the vastness and our insignificance; our planet, tiny, vulnerable and perhaps the only place in the universe we could love. I moved in bed, tried to find a more comfortable position. The radius of Saturn was 60,000 km. Maybe I thought only Saturn could satisfy Kaarina's needs. Maybe Saturn had the deep, plunging cleavage she wanted. She was a woman from Saturn, unearthly, and needed a woman in the proportions of a Saturn, or Jupiter, Uranus or Neptune.

I couldn't sleep, I got up. I took my clothes, traced my way around the bed to the door. Kaarina sat up suddenly, 'What are you doing?' she asked.

'I think I need to sleep in the lounge.'

'What?' her voice was brittle, she snuffled up in bed, 'You can't. You mustn't,' she cried. Quickly her face twisted. I sat on the end of the bed, 'I'm not leaving you baby. I just need to think, and sleep and I can't here.'

'Don't go.' She tried to sniff her tears up – her words came out jumbled and confused.

Such terrible misunderstanding – as we get older we become more of who we are, more of what has been done to us and what we have done. What we do continually works up the past, and destroys what we try to make in the present.

I dreamt of the moons of Saturn; the cloud-shrouded atmosphere of Titan, the riddled pock-marked Phoebe, and the tumbling strange surface of Hyperion.

Kaarina and I stood on separate moons, alone, speaking to each other into the blankness of space.

5

Present Day

IT WAS the first time in the office since we'd returned from South Africa. Lydia hammered on my office door late; I thought the college had been closed. Elisa and I were lying on the floor. She pounded repeatedly on the door, 'For God's sake,' I said, stood, pulled on my tracksuit bottoms and faded red hoodie, held out a hand to Elisa, who pulled herself up. I waited. The room was dark. My computer shone a hazy blue light into the office. The window open, the night mild, and a distant siren echoed through the streets.

I opened the door, Lydia looked hounded, drawn. I put my foot on the door.

'Lydia,' I said, 'What do you want?'

She smiled – her mouth thin, her eyes clouded. 'I came to see you.'

'I can see that.' Elisa moved in the room, sat at my desk and picked up a book.

'You have someone with you?' Lydia asked.

'What do you want?' I repeated. Lydia put a hand on the door and tried to pull it open. I held it firm, turned my head into the room and said, 'I will be back in two minutes.' Elisa looked up, nodded and smiled.

Then, in a single movement, I stepped out of the room, pushing past Lydia so she was forced to step back quickly, stumbling as she found her footing. I closed the door.

Forced against the wall of the corridor, Lydia put a hand out. 'Who's that?' she asked.

'Come on, let's go.'

'Go? I am not going anywhere. I've just come. You can't do this, Bianca – you don't just push me aside. I am a person.'

I laughed, took her arm and tried to walk her along the hall.

'Get off,' she shouted, jerking her arm free. I felt the anger in me swell, my chest lift and open.

I dropped my hand from her arm and stepped quickly behind her and, taking her left arm by the wrist, I twisted it, pulling it around her back and up. The pain would have been sharp and sudden and, as Lydia processed it and tried to take a breath, I pushed her forward, driving her along the corridor. As the pain hit, took her breath away, she began to whimper. I kicked open the door to the stairwell, shoved Lydia through and let the heavy door slam behind me. Then I released her, pushing her hard against the wall.

Breathless, she let out a shrill, short cry, 'What are you doing? You're crazy!' Lydia slumped against the wall, winded, she looked like a blooded animal, her face alert and puckered red. 'I'm going to bloody report you.'

As I took a step towards her, Lydia stupidly, clumsily lurched forward with her hand out. I moved aside but a nail, her fingers curled into a claw, caught my neck and scratched me on the left cheek.

I then worked quickly. I stepped forward, grabbed her by both shoulders and turned her so she faced the wall and then slammed her against it, her head hit the concrete, the thud resounded down the stairwell. I held the back of her neck, tightened my hand and squeezed hard. I checked her pockets, found her purse, keys and phone. She was now completely silent, her breathing deep, I bent forward so I could whisper into her right ear, so she could feel my breath on her face, and the heat of my words.

'Lydia, you will not come here again, phone me, or visit the flat. If you do, once more, I will really hurt you. Properly and fully. If then, after that, you come again, for a third time …,' I swallowed. I could hear a door open several floors below, voices, steps and then the sound of another door slamming. 'I will make sure you are permanently hurt, so you can't paint your ridiculous, pathetic art. I will hurt you so you can't hold a brush or a pen or a fucking straw.'

When I stepped back, Lydia was silent at last and stared at me mute. I noticed the imprint of my hand was outlined on her white neck.

6

Present Day

WITH ALMOST no warning, less than two months after we first got together, Elisa told me once more that she loved me. Seven weeks in and she announced that she wouldn't let me go. We were lying on my sofa, pillows piled up, our shoes kicked off, the blinds down – it had rained all day. She had come to see me, and we had taken a coffee in one of the bland, airport-style lounge coffee shops on Tottenham Court Road, full of fake character, pine tables, cocktail chairs and chilled croissants. When we left the building, the road was wet, yet it was warm – strange to have rain in the city and not to curse. The interlude between downfalls lifted me.

Outside the main entrance of the university was a group of strikers, pickets, cleaners and security guards, with a portable speaker playing chart songs. There were about thirty pickets, waving to passing cars, dancing, splashing the rainwater – subversive, belying themselves, the weather, British protest protocol. All traditions erased in this lather of life. I walked Elisa to the picket to introduce her to a few of the strikers I knew.

Elisa gripped my hand tightly. One large woman was holding one side of a banner, *We Are Treated Like the Dirt We Clean*. Her name was Janice; she had taken a microphone and was speaking, the music off – she spoke in a strong Jamaican accent, people stopped and watched. 'All you guys who are here, look at us. We are the ones who clean – when you go to the toilet, we're the ones who have to clean it in the morning. They are the ones who are making the dirt and we are the ones who are picking it up in the morning and we will continue this fight until they hear, until they listen because we must get justice.' When she finished,

Janice held the microphone in front of her, offering it up: 'Who speaks now?'

Elisa nudged me, 'Go on Bianca, speak.' There were others who recognised me, cleaners, a security worker, who started to call out loudly: 'Let Bianca speak.'

'Your turn sister,' Janice said offering the microphone to me.

I felt immense pride to be known as a sister by these people, that despite my office, my books, my status – these items of my professional failure – I had succeeded at one thing: I had, and I knew this, always been on the right side. *On their side*.

I dropped Elisa's hand, stepped forward, took the microphone Janice offered, turned back to the pickets and spoke, 'sisters, brothers, we have a question: "can we ever win?" Now, I don't mean this or that strike (because we will win *this* strike); I mean can we win another world, a just world? For this is a pressing question for the young, for those I teach who haven't yet lived through struggles in which our power is obvious – as you are feeling now on this strike. I have known excellent young militants who, despite being excellent activists, doubt we can ever really win!

'My attitude is the opposite: the only way to enter a fight is to know you will win. Anything less is to limit oneself at the outset. Of course, we should have exit strategies, that is sensible, but the whole approach to the enemy must be to smash him to pieces, to annihilate the university bosses – totally.'

I paused, looked around – there was silence, the whole crowd of faces was still. These people, many from the Caribbean, India and South America, had for years been so abused and ill-treated that had I then and there called for the mass extermination of London's rich elite, they would have followed me with knives and clubs into the houses, offices and palaces of the city.

'So great has been my anger towards the rich bosses that once I would have advocated locking them all up indefinitely, or dreamt of making them clean toilets for life.' The small crowd cheered. 'But now, I'd personally volunteer to machine-gun the whole lot of them dead – just to make sure. No hesitation at all, despite being brought up a pacifist! But, you know, what I have realised from history, from colonisation, from the rape of my continent and people at the hands of the rich is that we must have better guns than theirs.'

There was laughter and cheering. I knew that there were, or are, many ways of speaking in public. One can be cautious, use nervous small gestures, prod a crowd, gently encourage an audience to think in a new way, to consider different facts, or one can do it my way, head directly for the main artery and then rip it out of the body. That is what I wanted. I wanted to wear down any resistance, to deny it, to channel the anger and create new ways of thinking, take the impossible, rub it up the wrong way and hurl these people into the assault.

I knew that some people I encountered resisted the superior way in which I told everyone what I thought. I was, in certain respects, a very arrogant woman and this put some people's backs up, yet, among those with whom I felt a deep and kindred connection, my approach was different – I would always acknowledge their authority and listen carefully to what they had to say.

'Yes, I know those of us who are poor are getting hammered and, as the crisis worsens, so will our punishment. But, for me, I say bring it on. I can't wait to see what the German philosopher Friedrich Hegel called "the blank pages of history" turned over, so that we can get on with the battles we must fight and win now! And sisters. you know what? The wheel of history turns so damn slowly at times that we must be prepared to give the cogs and wheels a kick! The racists and right wing, the fascists waiting in the wings are what threaten us. But we haven't spoken yet. There is as yet no channel through which really to express ourselves. We have yet to cut it. Remember, though, that we don't choose to struggle – we are forced to – by capitalism! The answer to everything I have said, to our poverty, our struggles, to planetary collapse, our daily – and nightly – exhaustion, can only be the total expropriation of the capitalist class which is unfit to rule. But those wheels of history need to be kicked.' I repeated, then shouted, 'We can, and we shall win.'

The cheering that followed was now as joyous and exaggerated as my speech. The leaden skies were free of rain, and there was even a glimmer of blue between the broken clouds. I took Elisa's hand, and introduced her to the strikers; she was natural and unaffected – her charm simple and easy.

Elisa had never seen me like this, in the flesh, in my element – spontaneous and angry. As we walked away from the strikers, she was silent, and then spoke. 'I don't know much about them, Bianca,' she said, her voice quiet, soft, 'but sometimes I wonder whether your views are occasionally uncomfortably close to those of the Khmer Rouge, in Cambodia.'

I laughed loudly and squeezed her hand. She continued, emboldened by my laughter. 'I mean all that, "volunteer to machine-gun the whole lot of them dead" – you must admit there is something in what I say.'

I liked the challenge, this goading.

'I am too good a radical to believe in the genocidal nonsense about the Khmer Rouge.'

Elisa elbowed me and chuckled. 'I am not convinced,' she said, 'so from now on I am going to call you Bianca Rouge.'

'An appellation I will gladly accept,' I said.

The problem with Elisa, I thought, was that her loving was too quick, too present. There was too much frailty and she could be snapped.

7

Present Day

ABOUT TWO weeks later, late at night, after midnight I went for a run. I needed to clear my head before I could sleep. I took the normal route, the roads through Fitzrovia and Bloomsbury were empty. There was a summer chill in the air, the road wet. I ran gently up Goodge Street, past restaurants, furniture stores to Tottenham Court Road. I looked down the long thoroughfare to the traffic lights and the junction on Oxford Street. The lights, timed to change, signalling red to the empty road. I stopped, took off my glasses, wiped the few drops of water from them on my T–shirt. In my blurred vision the red, yellow, green light streaked and stretched across the road. As I started to run again, I filled my lungs, then released the air slowly; I put my glasses back on and the empty road jerked back into focus. On nights like this, I loved the city. A taxi indicated, I moved onto the pavement and passed the music shop on Store Street. I opened my arms; the city felt as if it belonged to me.

I had done two things that day – (1) planned my last Euphrates lectures of the term, and (2) reread the report that Jenny had left for me; she had got it right and wrong. Behind the random attacks, the killings, she still couldn't see the pattern. I had told her that in a phone call a week before.

'I keep saying this to you, you need to connect them, not just as a family – that is easy – the rich are, like the Bourbons, like the Windsors, connected to schools, clubs, businesses and often by blood. And those who are not part of those families, the children from minor families are connected by banks, companies and investments. We have to be sophisticated – it's not only class origins, its class position. So, step back from the details, which are interesting but ultimately useless. Look for the picture, the pattern.'

I had to say this again and again – the police brain, even of the smartest policewoman, is slow.

'Bianca,' Jenny had replied, 'listen to me, these connections might be clear to you, but they are not to everyone. Not seeing the blindingly obvious, what is in front of your nose, is perhaps your one weakness. You are too sophisticated for most of these murders, for most of us. Murder is crude and murderers leave obvious crude clues.'

I enjoyed her familiarity with me – these calls, her prodding and the ridiculous visit to my office. I was having breakfast, standing in the kitchen, the phone on loudspeaker.

'Surface reality is pure illusion. Look deeper – what is the connection? The *actual* connection. Remember your theory, Jenny, your training, not a simple dialectical approach, but the method of successive approximations. There are three stages to all investigations – observation, model formation, then testing and revision. This was Karl Marx's approach in *Das Kapital*. He moved from the complex, abstract, hidden genesis to the most open, naked forms of capital. One opening up to the other. This should be the approach to all murder inquiries.'

'Why do you make me feel like one of your students?' Jenny asked. I imagined her perched on her office chair, in her shared office, her colleagues around her.

'I would never allow such shoddy thinking from one of my students.' I answered. I stretched up, then twisted to my left, and right.

Jenny laughed but I could tell she had been offended. 'So, you are telling me to apply the Marxist method to the investigation of these killings?'

'Yes – to all things.'

I had now reached Malet Street and I ran in the road and felt my body loosen, my steps on the road were light. I knew if I wanted I could continue running until the morning, nothing was stopping me – the air was warm, the drizzle slight and on the surface of the bright moon I thought I could see the whole topography, the visible depressions and hollows and the giant craters.

Nina was singing to me, *Ne me quitte pas / Il faut oublier / Tout peut s'oublier*. I ran. I approached Russell Square, then turned towards Holborn and continued to the Aldwych, this was my normal route, a great loop, along The Strand and Trafalgar Square and then right and up Charing Cross Road and back to Fitzrovia.

I felt my calves burn and the rainwater on the street splash my legs. Sometimes I felt I could do anything I wanted – run as fast or as far as I needed, solve any problem, penetrate any question through its hard bony skull to its soft flesh. I felt an exhilaration, a sense of being indispensable and I did not cower from myself. I stood in life *and* acted.

Slicing through the doubt, the hesitation, the principled, useless waiting – the *lente impatience*, as the French philosophers would have it – for the probable, inevitable historical failure and defeat. In place of their doubts, I acted.

I ran down Villiers Street and climbed the fence into Victoria Embankment Gardens. I tightened the straps on my backpack, jumping from the fence into a flower bed. I unpacked the gloves and weights and spent an hour training. The Thames, only a few metres from me, was crossed by the white light of the full moon, marking out the water rippled by the wind.

* * *

'I want to be clear about something.' We had the conversation in the hall: I spoke, standing close to Elisa minutes before we left the flat together. 'You can say anything to me and between us there doesn't need to be anything, any exclusivity, no ownership.' I let it all out and didn't stop. 'I ask only that you tell me who you are seeing. …' I held her close to me, pulled her into me. Elisa was stiff, we held each other, her head over my shoulder.

'That's not exactly what I want. I mean what I wanted to say is that since my daughter was born, I haven't really been with anyone, and the dad ...,' she stopped here, tried to find the courage to go on and to make this – me, the moment, the night we'd just had – unlike anything else she'd done. She wanted to break her habits of the past, her old relationships, that clung to everything she did.

'You know,' I said softly, 'that you can tell me anything and I will not judge you.'

Summoning the courage, letting it build in her – gathering it all up in a single breath, knowing that this would be the only way she could get it out, she finally released the words, and let them tumble over my shoulder and down my back: 'Well, the dad, when he comes over we sometimes sleep together ... we sleep together when he comes over and this has been going on since he left.'

'For eight years?' I added, calculating quickly from the stories she'd told me.

'Yes, eight years.' Her grip tightened on me.

'Is that it?'

'Yes, that's it.'

I released my grip, took Elisa's shoulders, pushed her gently back and looked hard into her eyes. 'Elisa is that it? The limit of your revelations?' I shook my head slowly. 'We need to survive loneliness anyway we can and live. *And live, fully*. This, this ... honesty, is not something you need to run from or feel ashamed of. Even if he satisfies you only for a moment.'

With her head still down, she let the last exhalation of words out, the final revelation, 'And I love him ... still. He has always been there for me, strange I know as that sounds.'

'Of course,' I said, encouraging her to go on. Through the doorway, I could see the new sun lifting the dawn, surprising the city. I knew how the day would be when we finally left, hot in the path of the sun, cold in the shade. In England the heat never lasted, never really penetrated – it was a stranger who left only the faintest outline. I continued, 'If you didn't love him what good would that be? What else are we without love? I am happy you told me.'

'You don't mind?' Elisa's face creased, questioning.

'Why would I mind? No. On the contrary, I am pleased you haven't been alone.'

'You don't want me to leave him?'

'Elisa, will you hear me?' I continued to hold her, her head raised a little to look at me from under her lower eyelids, her bottom lip trembling. 'This makes no difference to me. If you want to leave him than you should, but love takes a long time to find its end. Let him go when you are ready, and only if you want to.'

To hide her tears, she moved into me again. I dropped my hands to her waist, then I wrapped my arms around her, felt her lower back, the rise of her buttocks. The firmness of her. She wept. 'I have never met anyone like you,' she said.

* * *

I found the narrow willow in the park, the one I always used. The breeze crossed the river, rustled the top branches of the trees and scattered dead leaves across the paths. I let the wind cool me, take off the sweat. I put on my Muay Thai gloves, and started to pound the trunk, ducking, turning, kicking high and low against the side of the thin tree. There was nothing except me, the sound of my breath, and the thud of my fists and feet on the wood. As I picked up speed the stem groaned under my blows – I was never satisfied, I gave, I hit, I tired but still I wanted more.

I stopped briefly, rested on my knees, steadied my breath and felt my feet and fists throb. I took the shin guards out of the bag, strapped them on. I couldn't afford an injury, not now.

I thought about Elisa and her ex. The advice I had given her.

Behind me something rustled, broke – I turned, my heart beating fast. I crouched quickly, tried to look through the undergrowth, inched forward. Beyond the bushes ringing the perimeter fence, taxis and night buses, shuddered along the river, a cat darted out and ran across the grass.

'Fuck,' I muttered, a tingle of excitement in my mouth.

I swallowed, turned back to the tree, and continued to practise until the entire tree swayed to my blows – the wind stilled, the moon lying flat on the river, reaching towards me.

8

2011

WE TRIED hard to unscrew our marriage. In 2011 we dabbled in therapy – like another couple might have toyed with the sex toys, nervous, uncertain and never entirely serious. I suppose we already knew it was over.

We had a system for communicating developed over the trips I'd made, the regular, unvarying journeys to Europe, America, South America, that punctuated the years we were together. For a time, the phone was just a source of conflict and misunderstanding, so we had started to send each other voice messages. Throughout my month-long lecture tour of Australia in January 2009, this had become our routine.

Before the trip, we visited our counsellor Judith – Kaarina had insisted we acquire a counsellor. Judith Jacobs lived in a purpose-built gated community on the dry mountainside close to our house in Cape Town. Guarded by a small army of poor black men in ill-fitting uniforms, ringed with a four-metre perimeter fence, alarmed and monitored twenty-four hours a day, each of the houses on the estate magnificent and grotesque, like everything in the city. Each house was built around a road that spiralled through the steep estate, according to the specific guidelines but with certain flexibility allowed for the owner's own tastes. Apart from a few Indian families and couples, this voluntary prison was almost entirely white.

Judith was tall, overdressed, her face thick with make-up, always formal even when she was talking about sex. We sat in an annexe attached to her house, her therapy suite, on opposite sides of a sofa, facing her. 'Bianca, I am not convinced by your objections to adopting children with Kaarina. Do you not think for Kaarina *and* you a child would actually enrich your life?' She studied her notes, 'You have said that you think there is a stage, a phase, when children feel like a drive and ...' she looked up again at me, 'this has now passed for you. Perhaps you are placing your needs in the way of Kaarina's? Why do you think you don't want to move on?'

'That is not what I mean.' I moved on the sofa, tried to bring my feelings under control, to disguise the irritation. The room was cold, the air conditioner blew into the room silently, the blinds were draw but the sun was insistent, dogged, burning hard against my back. I breathed in deeply, spoke: 'When we first came here, we both complained about our relationship being volatile. So, my worry – and this is from experience – is that a child will add to the volatile tendencies we already have.'

'Well, what I see,' Judith said, ready for this, 'is two people who speak their truth and listen to each other.' Kaarina had taken to wearing her contact lens every day; her heavy features, the jaw, nose, chin, were more prominent, and she looked good. She was wearing her pink skin-coloured blouse, the one that I had bought for her days before we left London three years ago.

Kaarina interrupted: 'I think we are many things – like all couples. We are sometimes extremely respectful of each other and when we work, we are better than most couples. We are generous and give each other space. I think Bianca – darling, you don't mind me saying this do you? – has been traumatised by her experiences as a child and as a young adult in Zimbabwe, Senegal and the UK. But she needs to know that I am not her past.'

We had been married in South Africa two years before – one of the only countries in the world, at that time, where two women could marry. Two years later, we were living in South Africa.

I believe that each thing, every reaction and feeling has its origin in a logical sequence of events – from love or trauma to consequence. I was fucked therefore I am. Kaarina took the shock of my withdrawal, the full force of it, even though I had initially agreed to have children. To try and adopt. But I kept putting it off ... refused the appointments, flicked through the catalogue of black children in the 'adoption directory' and scoffed.

Judith's consulting room was surrounded by framed photos she had taken – all glorious, high-colour clichés of African wildlife. A herd of water buffalo stampeding down an embankment to a waterhole, pushing each other in an immense frenzy of movement. The others were all equally impressive and predictable – dusty savannas, lazing lions, Victoria Falls, black children in the Congo spinning bicycle wheels on unmade roads. This was her Africa – the Africa of the white woman, human beings indistinguishable from the continent's wildlife. Each was one part of an entire vision – unchanged, picturesque and exotic. Buffalo, waterfalls, rhinoceroses and black children, each one fixed in its place on the wall in Judith's therapy suite.

After our first session, I jokingly named this the 'Rhinoceros, Waterfalls and Kaffir syndrome' – no coherent picture of the continent or its people possible outside this racist narrative. I felt disgusted, and dirty sitting there.

Even then, I knew somehow that Judith – and all the South African Judiths, Janets, Antons, and Letitias – had to be stopped.

* * *

The sessions with Judith continued for weeks, for more than two months. They were regarded as a final answer to the long open sore of our relationship and she delivered.

In the final fortnight we were told to draw a flow diagram with the problem at the centre of the page. So, we wrote children in the middle of a large sheet of paper and I spent fifteen minutes drawing arrows north and south. North was positive and south negative – the exact reversal of my normal moral and political economy. I snatched the minutes before our session to complete my diagram while Kaarina had dutifully and fully completed her one days before – with coloured markers and illustrations.

The grains of sand on the wooden floor stuck to my feet as I wrote on the large page. The dog – Honey – was on the sofa, another fight I had lost. The animal had worked herself into the most comfortable, forbidden places in the flat, the sofa, the armchair, the bed, stretching in the morning sun that came through the partly drawn curtains in a long angled reach of light. The day was hot and a sea of dust danced in a beam of sunshine that streaked the room.

I had moved Kaarina's clutter from the table, the poster paper unfurled. I wrote quickly – arrows pointed north and the words pain, exhaustion, age, death, racism, capitalism, exploitation and resistance written in capitals. On the table there was a large glass milk bottle filled with water, the light from the window shone through the glass so the water quivered when I wrote and cast a flickering shadow across the table. The light refracted and split through the bottle so in the shadow it cast there was an explosion of ribbed colour like the wings of a butterfly. The table was stained with the rings of countless glasses and mugs, marking all the meals we'd had – preserving the time we'd spent together.

I breathed in and gripped the marker and wrote at the bottom of the paper – life, hope, distraction, love. Clichés to the north, clichés to the south.

The horn sounded outside, I rolled up the scroll of paper, walked into the kitchen, checked that Honey had water – forever expectant, the dog jumped down from the sofa, her whole body wagging. I slipped my feet into my sandals, opened the metal door and left.

9

Present Day

IT WASN'T enough that we had names and that these names had served us well; apparently, we needed, Elisa had ordered, nicknames, pet names, lover appellations. These new names would, in all communications, replace the ones we had not chosen and they would, somehow, properly represent and mark out who we were to each other. The first day this had been decided, only weeks after our first night together, it was Sunday and I had woken late, surprised to find that we were still together and for my bed to be occupied, the unfamiliarity like a dream; the shutters were down, the cracks of light indicating the time. Nervously, Elisa had got up, hurried to the bathroom and gargled with the mouthwash. Then, without a word, she returned and fell on me as if sleep had not happened and the evening had continued without the interruption of the night.

The light was faint, I tilted the slates on the shutters, so the room filled with a dull glow. Elisa sat up in bed. Three days of sunshine had turned the city into a holiday camp – lifted our faces from the pavement, raised all of our moods and turned us into more than we normally were. There was a secret or conspiracy in the heat, a sense that something was about to happen. When the sun shone in London, the natural order of things changed.

But now the sky was sunken, dirty white and the rain unrelenting. I felt the defeat of the entire city and sensed a vulnerability in all of us. The strange hope that a few days of summer had given us, a vision of another life, now deepened the sense of despair as the sun dissolved back into the firmament. Darkness is a not a twin of the light, it is a beast – an infinite abyss all around us.

What else could we be, I thought, slamming down the shutters, turning back into the room, except an island of manic-depressives?

'Even if we get rid of the rich, we'll still have to relocate,' I said, my tone annoyed, as I stood in front of the bed, Elisa wrapped up in the covers, 'Coffee. We need coffee,' I announced.

We sat in the bed, opposite each other, crossed our legs, our hands around the mugs I'd brought into the room.

'We need names, baby.'

'I thought we had names Elisa – baby.'

Already she'd started to call me 'baby'. Normally, when this happened with other lovers I'd make it clear that I wouldn't stand for it and I would make some sort of speech: 'My sisters and brothers fought to have their own names, not the names of a master, or a slave owner. When Malcolm Little or Cassius Marcellus Clay erased their names, replacing them with an X or Muhammad Ali, they did this because their birth names were *not* their own. My name, my full name is Bianca Natsai Ndour, mine, my family of traders and merchants from Zambia and Senegal is generations old. They resisted and fought the British. Do you hear me – Zoe, Josie, Joanna, Yolanda, Lydia, Kaarina (or whoever) – my name is my families, my roots, my blackness, an anthem to me, to us and our glorious past and it cannot be replaced, with baby, or darling, or sweetie.'

Yet, facing each other now, taking small sips of coffee, like a ceremonial rite in a naming ceremony, I acquiesced.

Elisa said, 'We have names, but these are for everyone, clients, students, colleagues, family, so we need a way of distinguishing ourselves. Do you see?' I smiled, brought the cup to my lips, and took a sip. 'Our options,' Elisa continued, 'are "baby" or "sweetie". My preference is "baby".'

'And for you?' I said.

'Baby as well.'

'So, baby, baby?'

'Well if you want to distinguish us, it could be E-baby and B-baby.'

'As in EB and BB – or maybe you could just call me BB Queen,'

I joked. 'Don't you think that it infantilises us a bit?'

'Well, if not baby, how about peanut or honey?'

I put my coffee on the floor, stretched out on the bed, my feet reached the pillows where Elisa was leaning against the bedhead.

'Seriously,' I said chuckling, 'peanut? Why not cashew, or macadamia? Maybe, baby –peanut – honey – depending on the time of day.'

'Baby, I am being serious.'

'Then what's wrong with darling, or sweetheart?'

'No,' she said, adamantly. 'That sounds like you're selling fruit and veg from a market store in Woolwich.'

So, we settled on baby and used EB and BB for shorthand in messages and notes we left for each other.

That morning in July, EB had me in her hands, her fingers curled around me, laced together, the thin strips of weak light from the window shining through the window.

10

Present Day

AROUND HER neck Elisa wore a silver pendant, shaped like a small tower, engraved with crosses and tiny indented lines. The pendant hung on a thick silver chain – she only wore it occasionally, its summit hanging upside down, lying into her cleavage. On the nights she'd stayed with me, she'd turn off the lights to undress, unclasp the necklace, pour it into the palm of her left hand and then place it carefully on the bedside table, push back the covers and slide into bed. I would laugh at the ritual, mock her, 'We should get a priest to bless you before you get into bed baby, but only if you promise to recite a few lines from the Koran when you come.'

'It'll get better,' she'd reply laughing at herself. 'Once I trust you I'll throw off my clothes in the lounge and do handstands.'

One morning she left early and forgot her necklace, I took it, tipping it into my hand, feeling the cold weight of the silver. I held up the pendant, lifted my glasses so I could see the marks on the column. The base of the pendant was a lid; I pinched the locket in my first finger and thumb and undid the top – undone, the small, hollowed column separated from the silver base. Inside there was a tiny scroll of paper. Taking a pair of tweezers from the bedside table I carefully removed the miniature roll of paper, which, like a spring, unfurled as soon as it left the barrel of the pendant. I placed the miniature scroll in my palm. Holding the paper open with my fingers, in writing barely legible, I could just make out the words.

Written in the form of a list, with short sentences and wishes, she'd penned:

B and I stay together forever.

The words were so disarming and naïve that I found it hard to believe that Elisa would have gone to such trouble to have written them on a twist of paper that almost didn't exist, then painstakingly inserted it into the locket.

* * *

We spoke in bed – a barrage of words that often made little sense, a web of intentions and promises that trapped us in consequences we didn't fully understand. Illogical, ridiculous, we behaved like teenagers drunk on our feelings for each other. Stumbling into absurd formulations – heated, panting, half contrived, we competed to express ourselves, the sheets threaded between our limbs. The windows open, the wind chime tinkering in the night breeze and from the street below the flat, the sound of conversations, whole words drifting up to the window. Exclamations, curses, declarations: 'Watch where you are going – cunt', 'Darling, can you hear me?' '*Limbisa ngai – nalingi yo*'. The sounds of London – random, colourful, abusive. It made us laugh as though there were other people in the room with us.

'Bianca, baby,' she said, 'I need you.' Her head resting on my chest.

I kissed her temple, muttered back, 'I prefer want. I *want* you. I *desire* you.'

She shifted slightly in the bed. I could feel her thinking, the air around her was agitated.

'*Want*?' she repeated, 'It's a need for me – involuntary and necessary.'

I laughed. 'My want is voluntary, not necessary. I can survive without you, but I *want* you beside me. Need is for food and shelter. Want is intended, it has agency.' Elisa stiffened. I continued slightly mocking, 'Maybe I can want, and you can need.'

'No,' she said, 'You need, and I will try to want.'

'Okay, then I will need if you want.'

She paused, 'I don't think I'm ready to want.'

'Then you need, and I'll want.'

'But I'm not sure I can need you any longer. I can only need you if you need me.'

'I am stuck on wanting, baby.'

'Then I can't want, I'm afraid.'

'How about if we both agree to want *and* need.'

'No, I don't think I can need or want you any more.'

We were laughing at each other, making fun of ourselves.

'Well,' I said suddenly, arranging the pillows behind me, 'Can we at least be clear about love? … We love each other. I love you and you love me.'

She looked up at me, one hand cradling my breast. 'No baby, I don't love, need or want you any more. You have ruined it all.'

'Good, at last we have some clarity!' I said.

PART 7

'Work the devil, 'til he's dead and gone'

1

Present Day

I WAS TAKING a night flight to Hong Kong and intended, with a sort of ruthlessness, not to let my day be destroyed. Tired, I didn't want to travel, not again, before the start of the new term, with chapters to write, a book to complete – I knew the inefficiency of a long journey, the days, no matter how I organised them, would be wasted; the readjustment when I returned, the general damn chaos.

I woke earlier than usual and, though the day had barely broken, it was already ashen, funereal. The steely, dark clouds low, sealing off the sky, so from horizon to horizon there was no break and the day was foretold. Stretching on the steps to my block before I started to run, I looked up and smiled, felt a flutter of excitement – soon, I thought, I'd pierce this English canopy, escape the island's tombstone dread.

I ran and ran, faster than normal, the day required speed. I tore through Bloomsbury, down Kingsway, the Strand and then the Embankment.

With my backpack on I found the small clearing, swung the bag off my shoulder and removed the gloves, fastening them tightly to my fists, and the shin guards to my legs. I then moved quickly, through a few katas, hitting harder than normal and pushing through the pain, my heart thundering; repeatedly I hit the trunk of a small tree, it quivered under the blows, the leaves dislodged, fluttering down – I grunted loudly. Nina sang stridently, loudly to me:

Birds flying high, you know how I feel
Sun in the sky, you know how I feel
Breeze driftin' on by, you know how I feel

The first commuters started to move through the park, the poor, who took buses across the city or walked – an army of casual workers, on zero hours, walking to work, cleaning car showrooms, portering at universities, in hospitals or in city banks; a regiment of dawn workers cleaning this apartheid metropolis, preparing the city for its daily frenzy.

Scattered across the park, walking with their heads down, men and woman exhausted, straggling, gave me a wide berth – barely daring to look, stealing glances into the clearing where I trained, a shadowy figure graceful and violent, cutting the air with my fists, sweeping my feet across the earth.

A woman huddled in her zipped-up coat, walking through the park, her head ringing with exhaustion, was caught in a swell of wind from a passing bus on the adjacent street, leaves on the path spun into the air. The smell of diesel from the bus, the surge of hot air, invaded the park and involuntarily the woman reeled, stood still to recover her balance. She passed me, muttered loudly, *hay tal locura en esta ciudad* (there's such madness in this city).

I showered at work and stood by the window, leaning on a makeshift lectern of books, looking out at the city, savouring the moment of calm.

* * *

The heat hit me hard; I knew the city, its embrace, this mighty global centre of capital. The buildings that reached out across the bays, huge tottering apartment blocks and offices, stretching into the sky like nerve endings, twitching and vibrating against the blue sky.

With my one bag, I left the airport, staff pointing the way through the giant halls to the exit, I found the queue of red double-decker buses and waited for the A11. Then, as I always did, I sat at the top, at the front of the bus, a pile of newspapers and magazines on my lap: *Hong Kong Economic Times*, *South China Morning Post*, *Oriental Daily News*. I didn't immediately read them, instead I sat, my phone still on flight mode, savouring the journey – the steep, twisting road through Lantau Island, across the bridge to the New Territories and then to Hong Kong Island, along the sea roads until the glittering skyline of the city comes into focus (subduing even the lush, green mountain range around Victoria Peak).

On the water, there were cargo ships piled high with containers and passenger ferries, which from my perch on the top deck of the A11 seemed to be perfectly still in the water. Then, as the bus approached the Western Harbour Crossing, I could see the great semicircle of mountains, High West, The Peak, Mount Cameron, and the dense, packed city skyscrapers along the harbour, from Sheung Wan, to Central and Wan Chai. Such beauty and contrasts in this city – a monument to capitalism, a boastful cry to the natural world that there is nothing that human society cannot do. No breathless escarpment, or rocky crescent of mountains rising out of the ocean, which human ingenuity cannot match in steel and concrete. Consequently, the city was doomed, its glory soon to be washed away.

I smiled, and felt my pulse quicken, my mouth dry in excitement. It was impossible not to love – and despise – this city.

A little beyond Sun Yat Sen Memorial Park, just before we entered the towering neon chaos of Hong Kong Island, I saw a crowd boarding an ancient tram opposite a tower block a hundred metres high that was crisscrossed with bamboo scaffolding; tenement life surged on the streets below next to offices and penthouses reaching to the heavens.

Hong Kong was my guilty pleasure; its frenetic pace was a match to my own.

My hand flat on the pile of papers, I thought that there was no place in this city for rest. As the bus shuddered towards the queue of traffic waiting to crawl along Des Voeux Road West, I felt completely calm. I knew that Hong Kong was mine – more than any place I'd visited; in it, I could breathe and hide.

I stayed in the usual apartment near the University of Hong Kong, and got off at Sai Ying Pun Station and walked the ten minutes to the main buildings of the university, stopping to eat at a pavement restaurant, ordering in my precise Cantonese – enjoying the minor spectacle this generated with the woman taking orders in the narrow restaurant, squeezed between the city's towers.

* * *

I had taught myself Cantonese twenty-two years ago. While travelling to Australia from Kenya, I had made a stop and fallen sick. After feverishly staggering out of the plane in Hong Kong, vomiting in an airport toilet, trying to explain that I had malaria and needed a hospital, I was placed in isolation and given intravenous quinine and quinidine. Two weeks later, the fever eventually ebbed and I slowly surfaced from the delusions and dreams.

As my strength began to return, a nurse came into my room and opened the curtain, speaking loudly and quickly in Cantonese. From the window of my hospital room, high up on the fortieth floor, was a view into another building, along with a sweep of adjacent glass, offices and apartments – behind this tower and in no particular order were further buildings, so the whole horizon was dotted, as far as I could see, with great glazed towers casting irregular shadows across the landscape. I was transfixed by the sight. Involuntarily, the words sprang forward and, almost despite myself, I started to recite, *My name is Ozymandias, King of Kings; Look on my Works, ye Mighty, and despair!* The nurse looked at me quickly, quizzically, silenced for a moment, and then continued her monologue.

Weak, and for weeks unable to move much beyond this private room, I lay still in bed as the same nurse, a small, wrinkled elderly woman, who was always laughing, arranged the room, adjusting pillows, changing sheets and the drip, and constantly nattering. A colleague from the university had been charged with visiting me and she came, on my orders, with books and CDs on learning Cantonese. Within a few days, I had acquired a smattering of greetings and a basic vocabulary and, by the time I was allowed to leave after six weeks, I understood simple Cantonese and could now respond to the nurse, Yu Yan. She expressed no surprise at all at my Cantonese, for there could be nothing more natural in the world, and though she corrected my pronunciation and would sit with me and noisily explain the nuances of Hong Kong Cantonese, she made no allowances for my status as a beginner.

When I left, Yu Yan brought me a flask of green tea, which she presented to me with a list of instructions. I nodded, agreed with her, thanked her, distinguishing correctly between *m-goi* and *doh-je* and said, finally, 'But Aunty Yu Yan you must know, my name is Bianca and not Mo Chou.'

I stayed for three more months in Hong Kong, abandoning my London life, the courses I'd promised to teach in Australia, taking the time to rest, build my strength slowly – sending messages to colleagues, comrades and lovers to explain the delays. It is so easy to step out of your own life.

I worked in the morning in a noisy pavement café, writing in yellow notebooks, moving into the shade when forced to by the sun, weaving through the maze of buildings and alleyways. Waves of euphoria coursed through me as I wrote in my neat tiny script. Drinking Vietnamese weasel coffee, black shots, one after the other, responding to the occasional comment I overheard with a phrase, a carefully pronounced sentence – soon I became a regular and chatted about politics, the papers piled around me, a dictionary of Modern Chinese always ajar on the table.

I would break to work my way through an article in the *Economic Times*, or to practise my Cantonese. My approach to learning Cantonese was no different from anything else I did: I went at it systematically. First, I would learn all the verbs (a relatively simple task in Chinese, as there is no conjugation); then I would learn all the adverbs and adjectives; learn all the grammar and rules of syntax and then keep practising everywhere and upon everyone. Occasionally standing, trying to enunciate the characters, asking a regular customer what a specific expression or idiom meant – enjoying the pleasure of mental strain, conquering a puzzle, my eyes sparkling, driving my words into the listener.

By the afternoon, I would have moved through the city to two or three different cafés and – with the sweet low buzz of adrenaline helping me to breathe, and the strange shuffle of smells, noises and sites never becoming entirely familiar – the experience always felt new. There were no London morning blues, no humdrum daily commute from my then flat in London's distant suburbia. My life was simpler and more streamlined. I relished the unfamiliarity, the joy in the most mundane tasks, ordering lunch or stretching in the sunshine. The simple thrill in not knowing exactly where I was each day.

In those months of voluntary exile in Hong Kong, each day felt like a new dawn; I wrote in the morning, improved my Cantonese in the afternoon, and every evening practised mixed martial arts in Causeway Bay.

These months, that time, those rich sensations – the joy of these simple routines in the city that had welcomed me with such polite indifference, were perhaps the happiest I'd ever spent.

I was back in Hong Kong only briefly this time.

2

Present Day

WHEN I RETURNED from Hong Kong, I phoned Jenny from Heathrow – unslept, drinking a coffee on the Heathrow Express into Paddington, looking out of the window. The morning was radiant, the sky vast, un-English, blue from horizon to horizon; it could lift the dead from their dust, stir love in the coldest heart.

In the distance over the roofs, on the fringes of the city, was a gulp of swallows – their flight looked desperate, the birds threadbare, flapping ridiculously against the sky. *How could they hope to achieve anything like that? How inadequate their organisation and strength to the task of crossing continents.*

I told Jenny to meet me at the office. She did not answer, so I left a message: 'Jenny, can we speak? I am back from Hong Kong. I have found something that will interest you. A pattern that draws in all the threads. I have something to tell you. I will be at the office in an hour.'

London is a hard place when summer has passed and the long months of the real winter stretch out. After decades of suffering abuse, racism and humiliation, the poor deserve the government they have, the system they accept – as long as they accept the blows of reaction and offer no resistance, let them suffer.

Yet, on 13 September, the same span of months ahead of us, there was a restlessness in London, an unhidden joy, the possibilities of life as open and expansive as the heavens; a vision of escape for everyone in the city.

When I arrived at the university Jenny was there. She was more dishevelled, tired, worn than me. 'I'll make you a coffee,' I said in place of a greeting.

'I've been told to cut down on caffeine,' she laughed nervously.

My bag slung over my shoulder, I turned the key and kneed the door open. I had dropped the blinds before I left, weeks before. I put my bag on the desk chair, indicated to Jenny to sit on one of the two leather recliners that faced each other across a small table stacked with books. I adjusted the slats on the window and the room burst apart with the light. I found the cartridges for the coffee and pressed the flashing green button. The machine screamed.

Jenny sat down, stood, sat again, put her head in her hands and rubbed her face. I placed the cup in front of her and turned back, repeated the action and put my coffee on the edge of the desk. I then walked to the whiteboard, wiped it clear with my forearm, picked up a marker, drew a map of the globe, continents recognizable blobs with arrows connecting cities and countries.

The whole activity took three minutes. I could feel Jenny's concentration burning behind me.

Over the blobs and arrows on the map I wrote names. When I stepped away, Jenny had stood once more and, holding her coffee, taken a step towards the board, her breath had quickened. Now she stood just behind me.

We had not exchanged more than a few words.

Over my flat, one dimensional planet there was a series of arrows clustered around the word Bangladesh. From where I had indicated Dhaka there were other arrows reaching out to Africa, the Middle East, Europe, America, India, Australia. From my sketch the entire world seemed to have emerged from the black web coming out of the Indian subcontinent.

I picked up the coffee from the desk, took a mouthful. 'There have been a series of recent murders in Hong Kong and Shanghai …,' I said pointing to the map with my marker.

3

Present Day

A FEW DAYS later Jenny called, 'Now you have my phone number, as well,' I joked when I answered the call.

'You gave it to me,' Jenny replied.

'I did?' I queried.

'Yes.'

I was in the direct line of the sun, so its full early autumnal force was on me; I felt warm. I was almost done anyway, and stopped running when the phone rang, sat down on the steps of a Georgian townhouse near Russell Square. I unhooked my backpack, weighted with gloves, shin guards, weights.

'Fire,' I said.

'Another murder.'

'I've heard. Citibank in Hong Kong, right?' Jenny didn't answer. I continued: 'And the link in this assassination is Rana Plaza … haven't we been through this, Jenny?' I felt my heart slow, the gentle caress of endorphins reaching into my body. 'Karl Lim was notorious, and we are no longer talking about the minnows, the rich nobodies Jenny – this is the 1 per cent, the 0.1 per cent. He was the crowned king.'

'I know, I know.' Jenny's voice was laced with panic. 'And my bosses are being leant on by Downing Street, the prime minister, who is being pressured by Interpol – who want to write a bloody report and behind them the CIA, China's Ministry of State Security. Its pande-fucking-monium.'

I got up, tucked the phone into my sports bra, adjusted the in-ear headphones, put a leg on the top step and stretched forward, gripping the arch of my foot with both hands.

Jenny continued: 'And have you seen the stock market, the Stock Exchange of Hong Kong? It has taken a big hit – panic selling. A run on the dollar. It's not a crash but it could become one.'

Not disguising my pleasure, I replied: 'I am beginning to like our assassin. He might have the right idea.'

'He is a bloody murderer and I need to find him.'

'Haven't we always?'

'What do you mean?'

'If we know what links these men then we can draw up a fairly reliable list of who is coming next. Right?'

'It's not that simple and I don't think its connected to Rana Plaza, its more general than that,' Jenny repeated. 'I need to see you.'

I stood on the pavement, then I stretched up, staring for a second at the faint, perfectly round sun – the image of it burning into my cornea, I squinted, shook my head, closed my eyes, the red flaming disk continued to throb.

4

1981 – Buguma, Nigeria

THE VILLAGE, the town – of a few shops, and stalls – with a run of low built bungalows on the main strip, and then further back huts built and placed, it seemed, in no particular order, curling around the riverbank. The place was a Garden of Eden – a paradise I had never seen or experienced before. Much of the first day we were silent, staring in awe at the thick impossibly green and verdant forest and riverbanks, every space, it seemed, had been taken over by life (as it should be, as it was meant to be). This was the cradle of life, and from the dense, lush green existence of Buguma had sprung the world – so outside, away from this centre, it started to thin out, to the north, the east and west, to the south (to those other parts of the continent that, as a ten-year-old, I already knew). We were in the womb of the earth – we all knew it and might even have said it to each other.

We helped to cook, kneeling on the soft sand, or sitting on small stools beside the family house – peeling, cutting, fetching. Kaarina was always put in charge – organising our days, conveying to other adults, in pidgin better than mine, that we wanted to explore or to swim. The boys – Fawari's two boys – were a little younger, a meaningless amount but it seemed to us a great gulf, and they were charged with taking us on a tour of the village.

The boy's names were Boma and Godfrey. Thin, tall and incomprehensibly able to do more than any child we had met – climb impossibly high trees, swim like the dolphins that were regularly seen in the area and take their turn at household labour. They urged us on – pushing us against our lifetime of tarmac, shops, caution and European rules.

In their own manner they also told us something of the area and devastation – or rather they pointed it out to us, without explicit explanation. We saw water with an oily sheen at the back of Fawari's home flowing slowly into the river, with its jumble of flying boats, engine boats and canoes filled with plantain, fish – dried and fresh, sea foods ready to be taken to Port Harcourt for sale.

A hundred metres from the waterside was the pipeline, a giant coiling snake, the Delta monster, twisting and turning through mangrove forests – Godfrey, the more fearless of the two boys, pointed at it and said loudly with a gummy grin, 'Shell … this is Shell. Big boss. Everything just died like that.' He snapped his fingers, and then ran off – the boys were a blur of movement; we ran everywhere, the embrace of the heat and humidity no obstacle us.

That night – the night of the second day – we had a clearer indication of the extent of the chaos from Fawari. Gathered around a single huge metal bowl, arranged on a bed of banana leaves, piled high with food, legs folded, were about eight of us. The woman and children, eating from the bowl with our right hands – as if we had always done this, as if we had not grown up on the alien colony in Port Harcourt. Kaarina laughing and joking – encouraging each of us to join her, a sparkle always in her eye. '*Na dis one we dey call food original*!'

Fawari spoke to us in pidgin over the bowl of food – '*Ona see the river?*' (Did you see the creek?) '*Na wetin dey make us vex an no hapi at all, we don dey poor like dat*' (You see how we are sad and angry, and we have been made poor) she kneaded a ball of fufu in the palm of her hand, then mopped it around the sauce in the bowl. '*Na Shell pipe bi dat*' (That's a Shell pipe') she nodded with her head, '*Dem no dey clean am, e no get anytin wey dem don change. Dem be* … (They do not clean up; they have changed absolutely nothing. They are …) she smiled at us, '*dirty pikin*' (dirty children).

5

Present Day

THE MURDERS and protests – the beautiful twins of 2014 – escalated through the year, each day the news reported fresh murders of the rich. In each of the cities and countries where people screamed in righteous anger – of their lives destroyed, lovers, friends, mothers, families lost to poverty and hunger it seemed that there was, at last, a riposte, in the killings. Like a divine intervention, the system operators were being picked off and killed one by one.

Almost every morning would start with the same ritual – sitting at my desk at the university, the computer on, I would read the reports, and excited, hopeful, I would, invariably, punch the air at the news. 'Millionaire heiress killed in swimming pool', 'Billionaire oil baron murdered on private island', 'Media mogul burnt alive in front of family'. Pulse racing, spirits soaring I would raise my head to the sky and celebrate the final arrival of justice, after all these centuries.

As more and more people were openly celebrating the murder of the 1 per cent, I noticed as I ran in the morning a slogan graffitied on empty shops, across department store windows, on bus stops, and next to it a stencilled fist, dripping in blood; and also, when I investigated, I saw the same words in cities across the world: *Qhubeka noma ufe – Sigue o muere – Endelea au ufe – Go on or die.*

www.firethistime.com

Blogpost #4 – 'The revenge of history'

There will be no more promises of climate reform, no more assurances that in the rich countries nothing will be disrupted, and that our lives of consumption will continue, uninterrupted, and that everyone has the right to hold on to what they claim is theirs. The rule of property, the sanctity of profit and possessions is over. Everything will change and your lives will be disrupted – for now, and forever more.

The power of the rich is being toppled. What will you do?

And the governments and the companies of the biggest polluters will be shunted into museums of capitalism. We are coming for all of you – each of the guilty – Australia, which continues to expand coal production, Canada's tar sands, the United States, with fracked gas and deep-water drilling (the country is now the world's largest oil exporter), and the UK's expansion of North Sea oil. The 1 per cent of these countries pioneered the modern world of environmental destruction, unleashing murderous pathogens on the planet.

Yet capitalism's fossil fuel frontier will be shut down – not in phased withdrawal, not in a gradual, timed slowdown, but immediately.

But let us not stop here. We declare an end to the entire economic system of unrestricted consumption and profit based on ecological depletion. The power of the 1 per cent began in the fifteenth century with the capture of millions of people from Africa, who were then shipped to the 'New World' to slave on land expropriated from its original inhabitants – a process that was so incredibly profitable that it provided the economic power to launch an era of fossil fuel-led industrial transformation and with it dramatic human-induced climate change.

The modern world started with the plunder of America and Africa, and now the catastrophe will end.

I felt that the Revealer's analysis was improving, it was clearer, sharper – more coherent. Still, I questioned whether I was onto something, if this was genuinely linked to the murders, or just a fellow traveller – a wordy mimic, a copycat in a growing movement.

There were other passages – more lyrical and colourful. Brighter, beautiful.

The *dead* will not be safe from our victory – there will be no resurrection, no late return to their throne. For too long we have seen our history as boundless, and irrefutable, a process in which humanity proceeds in a straight path to the future. But the murder of the 1 per cent shatters the myth of progress and explodes the human calendar, we are reaching for the emergency brake on the train of history. We are not taming, taxing, controlling, or curtailing the rich, but obliterating them.

The blogposts always proceeded with the same structure, minor, borrowed, philosophical flourishes (very minor, in my opinion), threats against the rich and then predictions about the future – with occasional laments about graduates living with their parents. The pattern was no different this time.

The global revolt has BEGUN. Attitudes have changed – fundamentally. A fightback has started. Unlike the thirty years of paralysed silent tsunamis of hunger that four or more billion have endured under the rule of the 1 per cent, THIS new offensive on our right to food, land and work has triggered the TOILERS of the world, to say, 'I want to beat – to kill – the politicians and the rich.' And this is happening.

It's too late now for any convincing 'solutions' from the rich. A risen mass of tens of millions has lost its equanimity, its tolerance, its acceptance and acquiescence – as Hegel put it, 'instead of submission, an atmosphere of hope and change is born.'

We have suffered generations of ruined poor farmers, then crushed urban and industrial jobs – now in miserable employment they take our very food from us: 'My children say: "Papa – we're hungry" and we're giving them a spoonful of rice – with no eggs any more. It's HUMILIATING.'

NEVER has there been a better time to launch the alternative – seize the land, the factories, occupy and take EVERYTHING – and NOW! The 99 per cent MUST act. We are full of ideas on what we must build anew. The rule book is already on the streets. Destroy governments, repair the planet – replant, requisition, redistribute. The 181 ruling-class representatives and politicians, including the pope who recently assembled in Rome with the UN, revealed the truth: they can't agree on ANY solution. Nothing! Let them eat mud pies!

Let the poor, the unemployed, the casually employed, out-of-work graduates – living with their parents, in an 'extended adolescence' – take control.

Across the world further murders of the rich will follow, watch carefully, near where you are reading this blogpost, in the neighbourhoods of the powerful, the dull, repetitive crash of the sea in the background, in the sun-drenched estates of the 1 per cent. We are coming.

Go on or die!

The Revealer

6

2012

THE END CAME in 2012 with a text message – Kaarina's parting soliloquy. I realised she was not a woman of regret; she did not dwell on things. There had always been both drama and control to her outbursts. There would be a great display, a show of emotion but then she'd regain control quickly and entirely – there'd be none of the exhaustion that comes from a real crisis.

'Baby,' I would say, 'Come here.' I would open my arms, come into the bathroom, the suds sliding off her shoulders into the water, condensation running down the window.

'No,' she would yell and snatch the towel I was handing her, 'It's too late. I've reached that point – you've pushed me too far and this time and there is no coming back.'

'Come on, baby, you know I love you.'

'I know that you probably hate me and that you are trying to kill me. How would you feel if I killed myself?'

'I would hate that, naturally.'

The light from the communal corridor, which ran outside the bathroom, crossed her breasts in a soft yellow glow. I tried not to smile. I was desperate to calm her down and return to our evening and the activities of our life together.

'Baby, come to me.'

* * *

When she finally left me, she sent a message from her phone: 'I'm sorry it's no one's fault. Just incompatibility. I think about you all the time. I just know it's not working. You are obsessed with your work, and politics. You should get some support. Maybe speak to the therapist we saw. It's not easy, be kind to yourself. I am so sorry.'

I remember the day, it felt like summer – all those false starts, those hopes that come with the sunshine. I had staggered out of my flat, tripping over paving stones, not looking at the traffic as I crossed the road. The sun beat down on me, people pulled off their jackets to let the day get to them.

The sun was scratching my skin, making me sweat. Suddenly I was done; I had to stop. I leant first against the railings along the road, held the black fencing. The early-summer frenzy, the swirl of traffic, the pedestrians veering past me – an old man rested an arm gently on my shoulder, 'Are you okay, love?' The rapids of the day hurtling through me, the urgency of the people and the vehicles blind to all of our pain – to the blows raining down on us.

The pavement was dirty, the air thick, the heat pressed against my coat. I typed into my phone a long text message, 'I'm so sorry for hurting you and feel terrible pain in your pain. I just desperately want us to work it out. I have heard you clearly. Please hear me now, you are so busy convincing yourself we are incompatible that you have stopped seeing us. One more chance, K.'

While I was still struggling to clear my vision and breath, crouching on the pavement, her answer came, 'If you need something from me I will respond if I can. B, you must know I love you and that won't go away, it will just change and grow if we let it go. But B you must know it's over.'

Suddenly I saw her standing in front of me, the soapy lather from the bath falling off her, holding the towel over her face and crying. I reached forward, put a hand on her shoulder – she jerked it off. 'Baby' I said again, before I left the room, 'come to me.'

* * *

I used to think that I was here to allow the divine purpose of the universe to unfold and that Kaarina and I were somehow *meant to be*. Yet the universe always finds a way to remind you that you are only splashing around in dirt.

I think I dreamt of Kaarina every night in 2012.

April had been hopeless; the winter had shown no signs of breaking and our hopes were now pinned on May. There is always such desire in England – for time to pass, for something else, something better to come.

I booked my ticket for the launch of the new book that Yusuf had organised in Johannesburg. The flight was in the day, so I travelled to the airport in the early morning commute, the clouds low and thick but in the distance on the horizon I could see a break, a sliver of blue light. The sign of life, of colour where the sun has begun to break, always lifts me. I was travelling on the tube through the warren of city tunnels, shunting between stations towards Heathrow.

There had been messages.

> *I am so sorry it's nobody's fault, just incompatibility. I think about u all the time too. I just know it's not working. You should get support. Our love Bianca will just change with new understanding and growth and letting go.*

I was speaking on 22 April, a day after I arrived, and afterwards at a series of seminars and public lectures, on the North African revolutions of 2011, on a new book and film I had made.

I had a window seat on the plane, shuffled my papers, read my notes. I felt suddenly restricted in the seat and needed to get up.

The bright cloudless firmament above the clouds, thousands of feet up, where I fancied grief would be starved of its oxygen, and in the glittering, white plane in the merciless universe I would be unable to locate my sorrow. The sun shone through the porthole windows; great shafts of light reached into the cabin – making the activities of the passengers seem sluggish somehow. In this direct, unfiltered light there was an intense, peculiar warmth. Unusually the plane was not full. I had a free seat next to me – the spacious airy cabin, quiet, almost meditative.

I was returning to Johannesburg and there would be no Kaarina. She would not be there, no matter what I did. I felt suddenly winded, and I couldn't breathe. I got up, clambered between seats and flight attendants and to the toilet. I sat on the toilet seat and sobbed. The fear rose and choked me. I could not escape. I wailed with my hands over my mouth. I stayed like that for a while, then stood and hit the mirror, my knuckles came up red. I wanted to pull open my chest, tear away my heart – remove the pain. I wanted to hit my head against the mirror, pull down these flimsy petitions and walls, rip open the plane. I clawed at my face and neck.

Finally, I crumpled onto the floor, wedged between the door and the toilet.

Eventually, I got up, splashed water on my face, tried to steady my breath. There was no relief, the tears, the panic, had not expunged the feelings – it felt like the breakdown involved passing into a new reality. That this time it was new. For once I was the target, exposed, stripped down – and there were no illusions in the path ahead of me. There was a sudden rush, an ambush of memories – the pleasure, the togetherness, the life lived. A clutter of thoughts that pounded on my temples, so I had to hold myself up in the tiny cubicle.

I looked at my distraught face in the lit mirror – patchy, red, clouded eyes, hair dishevelled, I pulled back the lock and the door, the light flickered to dim.

The plane tore through the sky with a shudder of movement, creaking like a sailing boat in the ocean. For a moment I was calm, thinking of the complete irrelevance of our concerns, our species' cosmic invisibility.

I could feel the gaze of passengers on my back as I moved along the cabin, but for now, I didn't mind: 'You too,' I muttered aloud to myself, 'are heading for the same oblivion, with your urgency, your rush to get somewhere – you too, within a blink of an eye, will be gone.'

I spoke to the other passengers, 'Can you feel the world turning? The spinning of the earth.' Standing in the aisle I looked to the screen at the front of the cabin, the speedometer recorded

900 kilometres an hour. 'The Earth,' I extolled to my audience, 'under our feet is rotating at one thousand six hundred kilometres an hour. And the planet revolves around the sun at one hundred and seven thousand kilometres an hour. Can you feel it? You see, everyone, what is the purpose of your worries, of your heartbreak, if we are crashing through space?' Then, with one final effort to detach the passengers from their lives, I murmured, 'we must release our grip on the thin membrane of the earth. Release. Fall. Get back to zero.'

This perspective had always been a comfort to me – a source of joy. It was the same desire I had as a child when I found a place to hide and could pretend for a few minutes that I would never be found. Aren't we such things in the universe? Unknown, invisible, forgotten yet also, somehow present – our tears and grief held in a measureless ocean.

I was standing in the middle of the cabin, holding on hard to the headrests of two seats on either side of the aisle – I don't know if I spoke this strange speech or only imagined doing it. I looked around the cabin, a few people had turned in their seats and a passenger was speaking to a flight attendant and pointing at me. People seemed uncomfortable; there were strange looks, and then an announcement was made that everyone had to return to their seats.

I dropped back into my seat and for a second, in reverie, felt a sort of escape.

An attendant came up to me, hobbling along on her heels, wearing a tight black skirt, her open sweet made-up face, 'Can I get you anything madam?'

'Thank you – a whisky.' I felt my heart and stomach shunt back to its usual tack, the swirl of emotion, the panic. I watched the attendant walk down the aisle to fetch my drink.

* * *

When we arrived, I shuffled along the plane – I felt stunned, the great gust of emotion, loss and pain conceded nothing to exhaustion, to the storm that had now blown around inside me, keeping me awake, unable to focus on my notes for the talk the next day.

The last time I was here with Kaarina, we stayed in the executive suite where I worked while Kaarina was in town; then, in the evening – over the meal – listening to her talk about her day and then back in our room, making love.

Right until the end, the sight of her naked body made me breathless, how she bent over as she unhooked her bra and then held her unsupported breasts, the tender modesty as she turned away from me and the anticipation of her body against mine. The effect was always the same – choked by a childish excitement, full of desire and love.

I was almost at the end of the line to passport control. I swung my rucksack onto my stomach, unzipped it, the contents, clothes, pills, books, papers, pushed against the zip. I found my passport, opened it as I was waved to a free counter – the lighting was dim. I pushed hard on the contents of my bag, forcing them back into place, struggled with the zip.

We had stayed on the seventh floor of the hotel and needed a special card to access the lift. The area around the hotel was flat, the night large, the sky clear – the blue winter skies arched over the industrial estates, the rundown Johannesburg suburbs, the road with queues of the poor, waiting for transport, buses and combis.

We came into the room in good humour, Kaarina was playful, I took a shower. I always preferred to shower before bed, Kaarina in the morning. We left the curtains open, there was a twinkle below the window of the lights ringing the concrete façade of the casino opposite and the sound of water – an oversized replica of the Trevi Fountain in Rome. Horses thirty foot tall rearing out of the water. Out of the shower, I dried myself in the large bathroom, dropped a towel to the floor. I opened the bedroom door, Kaarina immediately turned to me.

'How long are you in South Africa?' the immigration official asked.

I stared at him, then smiled quickly, rewound his words in my head and answered, 'About ten days.'

Standing, waiting for my passport to be stamped, I wondered if I were not visiting a recent death? A life gone. We are in constant mourning for life that has just passed, and life is the continual preparation for death.

The immigration officer flicked through my passport for a free page. I felt the past throb briefly and vividly in a hotel near this airport and it seemed more present and real than the vague and dreamlike present.

I slid close to Kaarina, our skin touched, I felt my chest open – the feel of her, the softness of her skin. I could feel the cool air from the room on my back and the lights from the courtyard fountain reflected onto the walls behind us.

We slept like the gods.

Once I had cleared passport control, I walked into the baggage hall with a dozen snaking conveyor belts. I travelled with a single cabin bag, which contained my computer, a change of clothes, my gym kit and a couple of books. I moved around the clusters of people, couples, families gathered around the coiling baggage carousels.

I felt my breathing tighten; I passed the bored officials at customs, chatting to themselves, barely looking up, and beyond them a short passage that led to giant glass doors that slide open to the arrival lobby – a hall, like a theatre, a stage, the glass doors like curtains, revealing a cast of arriving tourists and travellers received like celebrities by a crowd held behind a small railing.

I came out and scanned the faces. I felt dizzy. I couldn't see her anywhere – there was no call, no familiarity in any of the faces. I could see the exit and signs to the taxis, airport hotels and waning daylight spilling into the terminal. I tried to establish if the sun was shining – that would help. I would stand in the yellow light of the sun.

I decided that I would find the eye of the pain and occupy it, let it consume me – if there was a memory, an ache, a hurt, then that is where I would go.

* * *

The horror struck me in late November 2012. What if she is not dreaming of me, even occasionally, what if she is not stopped in her tracks, in her day, at night, in the arms of another person, by the thought of me? Our touch and our life. What if, after all this time, I am alone with my memories of us? The past so laden, so full, that it chokes me. I wanted some monument not to a false god, a fantasy deity of our relationship but to our broken love.

Strangely, in the bus that night, I started to cry as the rain hammered the road. I felt an ache and missing that drained the air from my lungs.

If I knew that she even occasionally dreamed of me, this would be enough.

How cruel I had been to Kaarina? I steadied myself with deep breaths. I tried to reason.

7

Present Day

THERE IS A common myth in these times of austerity and environmental emergency, that at a moment of great crisis, when we are on our hands and knees (a time like ours), a colossus will arise. Huge, almighty, brilliant, this superhero will stand faultless above all of us – it will not stutter over its words, struggle with its formulations; the sweat and dirt of life will not cling to its backs, as it clings to ours. This colossus of our age will not suffer from doubt, hesitate about the next step. The colossus will be a young black woman of 22, with low-level autism – or, even, the child who sits silently at the back of the class, wondering what is going on. The colossus is not a young man in his early thirties living with his parents, without a regular sex life.

The geniuses of our time, who will rise, are not colossi like this.

I was still battling to pin down the blogposts, to find behind the random, unstructured arguments, the person, the assassin. I had to keep ahead of the police, the agencies that, I knew, would be busy chasing the same leads. Trying to crack the constantly changing VPNs, the rapidly copied and translated posts, scanning the text for clues where the next murders would occur – now escalating wildly around the world.

www.firethistime.com

Blogpost #5 – 'Watch our loved ones rise again'

Hungry for ever-increasing profits, the fossil fuel-guzzling billionaires cannot be spoken to, provoked to reason; their dizzying, devastating power must be brought down by our efforts. The 1 per cent will not be stopped with a gun pointed at their backs, but with a bullet in the head.

Analysis is important, and it can be arduous. Yet, we must zealously seek the truth. Only those who do not dread the gruelling climb have a chance of gaining the dizzying summits. We must understand who the 1 per cent are and what they are doing to us, and Mother Earth.

The super-rich – Buffett, Gates, Branson – entrust their billions cash pile to hedge funds. ALL the big capitalists – banks, finance, industrial, oil, arms, food, textile, engineering – are RUNNING these huge multi-trillion dollar funds. The KNOWN quantities of accumulated capital deployed in these funds have doubled from $14 to $28 trillion; the 'unknown' quantities are yet to be counted. The whole capitalist class – since the crisis has lost all confidence and hope of a decent, reliable rate of return from banks/equities/shares/stocks, government bonds (a miserable 5 per cent or more) and from both residential AND commercial property. There are now ONLY commodities – oil, metals, 'softs' (food). In the face of the crisis, in fact, we witnessed trillions pour into oil. It shot up to an unprecedented high.

Do not believe in the 'solutions' of the liberals, NGOs and the UN.

All the NGO/UN 'solutions' to save the planet that involve small farmers exist in a parallel universe, one in which the multinationals already have a global monopoly over the commodities (such as fertilisers, equipment and seeds) that poor African, Asian and Latin American peasants need to buy in order to farm. After thirty years of economic adjustment, there is no irrigation, no natural fallow, not even neolithic tending, thanks to it all having been driven into 'cash crops' to cultivate fresh tulips/roses/asparagus for the tables of the Savoy and Dorchester hotels in London.

We declare an end to the UN and NGO solutions advocating 'environmental change through small farmers resorting to nice multinationals'. We say seize the land you peasants, seize all factories you workers! THEN we can devise a progressive and productive way forward. Until we do that, NOT a single problem for the 4.8 billion people hit by the food and environmental catastrophe can be solved.

The 99 per cent must seize all production, the peasants all the land! For all the myriad superficial changes we have seen – fundamentally – capitalism and imperialism remain the same! We CANNOT move forward until we TOTALLY EXPROPRIATE (and TOTALLY ANNIHILATE) the 1 per cent (in reality, the 0.001 per cent) and reclaim the earth, the common treasury for all and then REBUILD – cooperatively, with each other, our lives and planet.

We call for the immediate end of all fossil fuels and their death inducing side products like chemical fertiliser, in favour of a scientific, worker/poor/peasant-led natural, but scientific, urban-hatched revolution.

We reject the catastrophic 'Green Revolution' now being revived by the quasi feudal elements of the UN/NGOs and their ilk, which will yet again involve slaughtering whole continents of producers and land. We can and must start afresh. Look at the soil in Ethiopia or Brazil – destroyed. Instead, we must destroy *their* Maxwell House coffee prairies and ethanol plantations forever.

This must happen on a global basis, based on the reports and facts centralised by the arising, risen and growing wave of the 99 per cent. Because the 99 per cent include all kinds of workers and students who KNOW about agriscience, we will ban all GMO and sow on a globally free distribution basis, tried and tested seeds for the birth of not only food for all, but GOOD HEALTHY additive-free, garbage-free FOOD for all.

The argument being that, ONCE the workers/poor/peasants run everything – initially with guns in their hands – they, we, will of course, produce only for need, health, joy, strength and global contentment!

We will consign profit to a museum.

We KNOW food, shelter, drink, clothing can be SORTED! WE PRODUCE IT! It's no big problem! Humanity had it quite well organised 5,000 years ago before the rise of class!

Today, this is a doddle, as José Buenaventura Durruti said in the ruins of Barcelona in 1936! 'We built it in the first place. We will rebuild it again one day, as WE want.'

Yet, the ruins of the world are far greater today than they were in Durruti's time – the whole world, the very source of all wealth, the earth itself, is broken, yet we still stand on the dead, dissected land and declare, 'We will build it again – breathe life and love back into the planet, and into each other.'

The actual, physical annihilation of the rich is of the greatest importance.

WE HAVE STARTED SOMETHING that awakens, sharpens, recruits and wins!

Go on or die!

The Revealer

8

Present Day

THERE IS A tree outside the 'Deera Square' lecture theatre, where in the early autumn throughout the day, before the migration, hundreds, maybe thousands of swallows gather. Their piercing cry is not a song. On clear evenings in autumn, after I have been lecturing, I stand near the tree. The tree is alive, a foliage of birds, screeching, announcing, declaring; and, if the sky is still light, I imagine that they are looking at the sky and planning their escape, discussing the route they will take to Africa. I imagine them gloating about the adventures they will have in Cameroon, Zaire, Uganda and Kenya, and how beautiful the summers are in South Africa.

So, on this night, on this early evening, I was resting briefly on my short walk home – away from the pack of students who had just left me after my lecture – the collar of my jacket up and my beret pulled down flat over my hair.

My back to the road, I gazed up at the tree, which hummed noisily with the swallows, like a nest of wasps. I corralled my thoughts, stilled them so I could plot my evening. At 7 p.m. I was being interviewed by Democracy Now!; from 7.30 to 8.15 I needed to prepare an article for *Jacobin*; from 8.45 to 9.30 I had to read two draft chapters from a PhD. Then, until 10.30, I was going to work on my own project. Elisa was arriving at 10 and I would open the door, kiss her, and say, 'Baby, give me thirty minutes; I am finishing something.'

At some obscure, impossible to detect signal – perhaps a variation in tone of their peculiar song, one bird would decide to fly – and the entire flock, whole branches, would take to the air. The tree was suddenly naked as if winter had arrived in a single moment.

I felt a large, heavy hand on my shoulder – 'Bianca, where did you go? We were sitting at the back of the room and suddenly you were carried away in a cordon of fans.'

Mark was breathing heavily, standing so close to me I could smell him. I jerked my shoulder clear of his hand, 'I was watching the birds,' I replied. 'That cordon were my students.'

Jenny was standing behind him, trying to get a smile through to me.

It was strange seeing this man outside my office. I could measure him here, and get a proper sense of his bulk. He was big but sloppy – carrying his weight like a burden, like luggage. He looked vulnerable on the street.

Jenny pushed through, elbowed her colleague aside. Her top was loose, black, and she was wearing trousers and trainers. In all cerebral matters she towered over Mark, she could reason, she had read and she connected events – though she had no real capacity for abstract thought, no imagination. She was an empiricist.

'Bianca, can we come up to your office?' Jenny asked.

'No.'

'Oh – well, can we make an appointment to see you?'

'Does it require an appointment, can you speak here?' I indicated with my head the street, the pavement, the sprawl of London around of us.

'Why don't you let us buy you a drink Bianca?' Mark suggested.

'Please,' I said, letting the words come out thin, tired, exacerbated, 'No,' I repeated, 'Speak now – I mean now, because I have to leave.'

Mark started to speak, Jenny elbowed him; he was a man who needed elbowing and interruptions. 'Okay, sorry Bianca, basically …,' she cast a quick glance around her, commuters and tourist moved past us, the light faint, ebbing. We had squeezed ourselves into the inner part of the pavement away from the road, 'basically, we know, we think we know, that this is general not specific; that the killings, these happenings, don't have a specific theme, they are all over the place.'

Mark interrupted, 'Bloody random, here and there, without rhythm and reason. …'

Jenny shot out her elbow at him again, 'The pattern is too erratic, too general and the rest of the team, all of them, in the US, Interpol, ENISA, the bloody Chinese Ministry of State Security, agree. The killings are *not* linked.'

I played along, 'Which means that this is even more terrifying.'

'Exactly' Mark said, satisfied with my reasoning, 'fucking terrifying.'

Jenny continued, 'Though none of us know for sure, there is also the suspicion that this is not a crackpot assassin, but a team, a group, some sort of militant climate activists. …'

'Is this what they are saying?' I asked.

'It is what we are looking into,' Jenny answered.

'And the fires in Cape Town?' I queried.

'Who the hell knows if that was anything to do with it?' Mark spoke abruptly.

The birds, mostly martins and swallows, had decided that tonight was not the time for their departure – instead, behind Mark, I could see them swarming in the sky, in great pulsing black shapes, moving in one direction and then the next as if blown by the wind. The tree behind me was filling again, with a hundred feathered leaves.

Mark and Jenny continued to talk, I hardly listened.

A few minutes later, Jenny summarised, 'So, Bianca, we wanted to tell you the latest, that this is not about the Rana Plaza collapse, or events in Zimbabwe …'

'The Chiadzwa Diamond Fields,' I added.

Jenny nodded and smiled at my interruption, 'Yes, not specifically at least. It seems this is a general …,' she looked at me for the word.

'Attack,' I volunteered.

'A general attack on the rich,' Jenny continued, 'without any order in particular, but incorporating an entire range of the wealthy – factory owners, financiers, bankers, the idle rich, wealthy entrepreneurs, and even those further down the ladder, the wannabee rich – the salaried rich. Which means, if we include all these categories, then the potential list of those murdered number more than two hundred. An astonishing number and all over the place, in literally weeks. I mean everywhere. …' Jenny spoke quickly, trying to stall me from leaving with her words, as though building up a verbal barricade – nervous that I was about to flee, to migrate.

'This man must have accumulated a huge number of air miles,' Mark added with a smirk.

'So, this is basically what we wanted to tell you,' Jenny concluded.

'But why,' I asked, genuinely perplexed, 'did you come to see me just to say that there's no pattern?'

I left Jenny and Mark a few moments later in a swirl of international policing acronyms, primitive theories of revenge by dreadlocked environmentalists, or of a secret Ponzi murder pyramid, with each murderer promised money and high rates of return in exchange for another killing. I walked quickly, weaving through pedestrians, moving onto the road, then back to the pavement. I chuckled to myself, *if this was the best that global policing could manage then we were closer to the end of the world than I thought.*

9

1981 – Buguma, Nigeria

I REMEMBER the next morning in slow motion, however hard I try to speed it up, to make it run at normal speed I fail.

We slept in a room that had been specifically emptied for us – the dirt floor rubbed hard was smooth and dry. There were three foam mattresses, the sort that were normally sold at the side of the road, and after a single night hollowed out so you fell into a soft crater made by the weight of your body, an inch from the floor. They had been purchased specifically for us and cost half of Fawari's monthly salary. The foam became hard and hot so for the third night we had, on Kaarina's orders, piled the mattresses on top of each other and slept on the same single strip of foam. Impervious to our hot bodies, lying side by side, sticking together, sleepy hands swiping away mosquitos – despite the burning of orange peel and coconut husk to deter them.

The blast blew the door open and, in the distance but clearly visible, was a huge orange glow – a ball of light and heat that felt like the sun. I was the first up and rushed to the door; fire was coming from the river. I heard shouting and a stampede of people that seemed to pass around us from the town, and crashing down the bank of the creek.

The temperature was intense, and the roofs, the leaves and branches of the trees crackled and burned – whole trees further away, on the outer perimeter of the town burst into flame. The scene was dreamlike – I shook my head and turned back to the room. Maïmouna was sitting up, her back against the far wall, looking blankly at me; Kaarina knelt over her, and her face – the first sure sign that this was no dream – twisted in fear.

In the end, seconds later, Kaarina and I stumbled out of the hut; Kaarina ordered Maïmouna to stay where she was and not to move. As soon as we left the room we were carried along in a wave of humanity – it seemed as if the shouting, crying, screaming lifted us towards the heat and burning; towards the fallen sun.

About a kilometre from us, where the oil pipeline snaked through the mangrove forest, there had been a leak – for hours oil had been leaking, gushing out in a black fountain, coating everything, the mangroves, the water, the soil and the people. The land had turned ink black, with thick, deep pools of oil covering an area more than two hundred metres wide. This eruption of oil – pushed out by the pressure in the pipeline – had been uninterrupted for hours, before we went to bed and before we had eaten.

By the time we awoke to the blast, and Kaarina and I made our way to the creek, it was early morning – there was even, in my memory, the sound of cockerels. The horror was happening before us, but it was still not immediately clear what was going on. There was a mass of people, and a fire – a blaze, that seems now, in my mind's eye fictional, a scene being played out. The colour of the flames was black and where they lapped up and burnt the taller trees, blood orange.

Kaarina and I held on tightly to each other – the panic beating hard in our ears, but there was also a terrible excitement. With hundreds of others, we slid and rolled down the small embankment and came to a wall of people who were not moving, because they could not – they had gathered, or been stalled, by the fire on the edge of the water – which a little further off, had turned black and was burning. The heat, which we felt even though we were shielded by a crowd of bodies, prevented anyone from moving further in.

Kaarina – more practical than me – was holding on to me; she dragged us through the thicket of legs and bodies, villagers standing motionless on the bank; she pushed us on, even though the heat was immense, burning the air, making us choke on each breath. We weaved through the crowd, searching for Fawari, for uncle, and the boys.

Then, when we neared the water's edge, I saw two things, neither of which was entirely intelligible to me then. The water several meters from the shore of the swamp was bubbling, and beyond it, burning – a glistening, surface of flames raged on the water and then on to the other bank, and the forest behind it, as far as we could see, was a black fire that had turned the morning to night.

The second thing was initially stranger than the first – and it was this, I think, that prevented Kaarina and me (and the entire group of villagers) from moving: out of the oil, in the flames, on its edges, along the banks of the swamp, and deep into forest where it burned, were human beings. And they were not still, or silent as they burned – Kaarina looked, like me, strained to see, and then calmly, without horror, said, 'I think there are people in the oil.'

The harder we looked the more we saw – alongside the bodies that moved, that burned, were others that lay rigid on the ground, arms and legs thrust awkwardly in the air with their clothes and skin burned off.

When it became clear what was happening, we were immediately conscious of voices around us, men and women began trying to get those they thought could be saved – some dived into the water.

We overheard voices, snatched conversations: 'One friend knocked on our door and told my husband they were taking fuel. My husband ran out with two buckets and now he has gone. *Dis na curse from God*' (This is a curse from God), shouted a large woman to anyone who was listening.

Impotent to approach the flames – to do anything to get to the burning shapes – others started to shout their lament: 'There were mothers there, little children,' said a man, who saw us, small and cowed, and futilely put his arm out to protect us and spoke – into my face, he said, 'I was begging them to go back.'

A woman in a yellow T-shirt sobbed uncontrollably, slapping herself on the face and clawing her own arms in grief.

We did not need to speak; we knew that we had entered the inferno, for Fawari, and to the loud laments around us, we started our own: 'aunty, aunty'. I pushed away the large man's hand, and we burrowed again into the crowd, shouting as we went.

Only when we reached the verge again and started to climb it did we think, without speaking, that our Fawari would surely be with Maïmouna and the boys back in the compound. We slid on the mud, unaware that our clothes and hair were burnt; breathless, halfway up we turned and looked at the scene below. Our minds only now had fully adjusted to the incomprehensible spectacle; we saw it in front of us, for the first time.

I could make out the entire vast expanse of the fire, and the burning oil on the water, the raging red-orange flames in the forest, and the black smoke burning off the top of the fire. From this distance, we could also make out the human shapes in the water, and in the distant fires – by now they all seemed still and there were not ten or twenty, but hundreds. A whole legion of blackened and burnt souls.

Activity, breathing, sheer life energy had overtaken fear and we looked on amazed and stricken.

10

Present Day

I HAD NO technique for handling these interviews, no tried and tested pattern – no preparation that I needed to carry out. I was simply and always myself. In those cramped, shiny studios with the lights on me, or staring into my computer for a phone-in interview, I was direct, abrupt and honest. I was pure.

I moderated my responses by network – if it was the BBC, CNN, Sky, or any of the large state or corporate broadcasters I was uncompromising. These were institutions of state and commercial propaganda, with varying degrees of sophistication, but the same ambitions – support for the international order, and ridiculing dissent. All of their reporters I regarded as vermin, and careerist mediocrities. I was contemptuous.

As for the others, Al Jazeera or RT for example, I was normally polite. For the media that existed on the margins of the left I was civil – direct, forthright and good-mannered.

As a result, much of the mainstream media had a love/hate relationship with me. They loved the ratings I would secure for their news programmes, interviews or for savaging their studio guests, but news anchors and journalists frequently refused to subject themselves to my disdain for their careers and self-importance. So I had been informally barred from appearing on the main channels, chat shows or news programmes. My name had even appeared on a hidden list of proscribed guests on the BBC, uncovered by an investigation carried out years ago by the Glasgow Media Group.

I had been no-platformed but what did I care? There were now a thousand online platforms, with audiences every bit as lively and large as the corporate networks.

Tonight, was different. The BBC – like all the jackals in the international media circus – was starved of proper, uncompromising and clear-minded analysis into what was happening in the world. The circulation of its normal studio guests had always been lamentable, but now it just couldn't hold. The pace of murders had picked up; international attempts to solve the 'crime wave' had proved futile and the panic among the elite was almost hysterical.

Alarm gripped every newsroom, pressed hard against the hearts of liberal and conservative commentators alike, and taxed every feeble-brained journalist in the world.

To understand what was really going on, they were forced to turn to me.

To confront me they used one of their big guns, with whom I had clashed before. Robert Shirley was a large man, who wore striped shirts, had a reputation for drinking heavily and had achieved notoriety for his cufflinks and interview style. He was a man who could silence potentates and presidents, or so the guff went. In the age of digital media here was a one-man justification for the licence fee.

On a level horizon, molehills look like mountains; and the incessant flatness of the present era can be measured by the altitude of its greatest minds. Shirley was one of these great minds.

Shirley was loud and obnoxious – balding, with a fat neck and blotchy skin. He was a dreadful man who had made a fortune as the chief executive of an American news network, and now hired himself out to the BBC for an undisclosed figure – though widely reported – and wrote right-wing histories of the twentieth century, biographies of politicians (three on Winston Churchill) and airport novels. In his crimes against good writing, he single-handedly contributed to the deletion of a sizeable forest.

Robert was the kind of man – from the class I despised – who was unstoppable. A great sweating juggernaut of a man, with the pomposity and arrogance of an entire system that had ruled for too long – yet he was just a scribe, a court jester to the 1 per cent.

I had seen the promos for the interview with me and found the whole thing absurd. 'Robert Shirley in conversation with outspoken critic and left-wing firebrand Bianca Natsai Ndour'– the publicity, the spectacle, the clips of him in action, on location in a desert city, reporting from a war zone, wearing a flak jacket and helmet, and in a well-lit studio challenging a politician. Robert Shirley was like some grotesque overgrown boy scout from an English public school. I was there, too, in the clips, pulling out my microphone and walking out of an interview, speaking at a public meeting, and marching against the Iraq War.

I finished my work at the university and walked to Bush House at the southern end of Kingsway between Aldwych and the Strand. I enjoyed the walk, the soft, autumnal light, the sound of the birds, loud, declaratory, competing with the mechanical noise of the city – the shudder of buses, car horns and the echo of sirens.

I was counting. Every fifth shop, alleyway or building, I passed someone – normally a man – bundled up in a blanket, or with a sleeping bag draped across his hunched body and words written on cardboard appealing for money for shelter and food. As I continued down Kingsway and crossed Great Queen Street, I saw a woman, her black hair was parted in the middle, her eyes were bloodshot and tired; she had a child with her and, as she sat in an empty doorway, the child, aged about six, held out a cup to anyone passing.

Austerity raged through this country and turned the city once more into a place of naked poverty. The advertising hoardings normally erected around the system in the rich cities of the North had been torn away. Across the country, whole communities were being destroyed – the few services on which they had depended slashed, the poor turned out of shelters, prisoners released onto the streets and asylum seekers tortured in detention centres and then deported. Make no mistake, the future had already arrived.

I passed the chain cafés, the restaurants and the scrubbed limestone buildings of Kingsway and then turned right onto Aldwych. I saw Bush House, and felt a familiar warmth, the comfort as the boiler lit, the ignition to my rage automatically triggered.

Shirley was not just anyone, he was a faithful representative of the rich – its canary in the mine, its hired gun in the daily battle to maintain hegemony. Or more simply, to keep the lies hidden, so the murderous operation of the system could grind on and on. And I was going tell him what was happening to his class.

I entered the building and was immediately mobbed by a small crowd, a cameraman and researcher, and a young reporter, a woman, who tried to question me. 'Bianca, do you condemn the killings? Why have you repeatedly refused to distance yourself from the events that are taking place? Some would say that you have even spoken out in favour of them.'

Before I felt a hand on my shoulder, and was directed away, I laughed, then smiled sweetly and without a hint of irony asked, 'What question do you want to ask me? Do you mean the murder of the rich, the bankers, the corporate executives, and that posse of global criminals who are being killed around the world? Is this what you want me to condemn? I think I have been very clear – rarely in history can you say this, but we are living through a moment of extraordinary reckoning. The rats, forced out of their lair, are panicking – watch where they run, get ready for what they unleash on us.' Without pause, or hesitation, no gulp for air between sentences, I spoke fluently – did not stumble for words, or allow any space for interjection.

In the polished hallway of the BBC, among the brass handrails, the marble stairs, the parquet flooring, the crowd and bystanders fell completely silent, so all that could be heard was the click of still cameras, the static from two-way radios and my voice.

An assistant, a clean-shaven man, young, with his balding head shaved, dark-rimmed glasses and a grey top, nodded to me and said again, 'This way, please, Bianca.'

The journalist who asked the questions, recovered as I moved towards a door that was being held open for me, 'That is,' she started, as the noise picked up, 'an astonishing admission.'

Astonishing, really? It was what everyone was thinking. I was just being honest.

* * *

There were two of them. Shirley was in his normal place, the swivel armchair, the backdrop, and the desk, with an embedded computer screen and a notepad in front of him. Then – alongside Shirley – was a thin, coat stand of a man, narrow, a tendril of veins and ligaments, Andrew Osbourne, his face skewed from a stroke, so he spoke from the corner of his mouth. He ran chat shows with politicians and historians and wrote – like they all do these days – in fabulous prose about great wars and invasions (he had written yet another recent celebrated biography of Churchill). Officially, Andrew was another guest on the show, but in in reality he was Shirley's sidekick. A sign of weakness.

Sitting in the lights waiting for the interview to start, I stared hard at Shirley and recalled his justification in his every waking moment of each genocidal bully, each blood-soaked war for oil, land and prestige. The man deserved nothing except my disgust; unlike the rest of his guests, I did not pretend. There would be no locker-room friendship before the cameras started to roll.

I would scatter the two men to the wind.

Shirley's sidekick introduced me and the topic. With the bright, angry white lights on me, I sat on a bent leg in a cramped bucket seat, as shadow figures danced silently behind the cameras. 'Professor Bianca Ndour is a celebrated controversialist – taking positions that many of our viewers consider abhorrent. Never afraid to take on difficult topics, she has written – declaimed some would say – on Islamic fundamentalism, environmental change, corporate power *and* mindfulness. Today we interrogate Professor Ndour on her theories about the One Per Cent Murders, as they are being called. What is behind this global pandemic that is targeting the rich?'

The lights faded briefly, there was the muted, synthesized sound of the opening credits, a woman rushed onto the set and dabbed Shirley's nose and cheeks.

He tried to disarm me, 'Professor, what is going on? The outrageous wave of violence that we have seen, has killed dozens, and has been almost universally condemned except by you.' Osbourne tittered.

I could smell their fear in the studio. I responded, 'Do you need help today, Robert – can't cope without backup? I am flattered. Controversialist, taking positions your viewers would consider abhorrent. I know that standards have slipped at the BBC in recent years, but for a man with access to these viewers, you are astonishingly cavalier with any notion of truth. You know nothing of what you say, yet you traduce both your guest and the truth recklessly.'

Shirley sat back, raised his eyebrows indicating to Osbourne to take the lead. 'Are you denying, Bianca, that you have condoned the murders? Because I have here ...,' he lifted a pile of folded papers, 'a list of your public talks where you state categorically your support for the "pandemic", as Robert has called it.'

'Do I approve of the violence? What violence? Whose? The violence that you have – both of you,' I turned and pointed at Shirley, 'spent wealthy years celebrating, writing nauseating books salivating over imperial tyranny and the never-ending murder spree of the rich ... in their wars. How many died in Iraq and Afghanistan? In the wars you both supported? Six-hundred thousand at the most conservative estimate. ...' Shirley tried to intervene, I sped up. 'In the deaths in the factories that make your suits, ties and shirts in Bangladesh, Thailand, Vietnam, or the dead in the mines in southern Africa, each listed on the London Stock Exchange, swelling your share portfolios and your pension investments.'

'Bianca, Bianca ...,' Osbourne bleated, 'before we get carried away, you have to be cautious. The figures you mention are open to question.'

'To you I am "Professor" – not "Bianca", not "Prof. Ndour", just "Professor". Know your place. We are not debating politics at your club, in your Maida Vale mansion or over a glass of Château Lafite Rothschild. The figures I quoted are not figures at all, they are flesh and blood – my brothers and sisters. Do you know Faisal Rezgui?'

There was silence, blank faces.

Shirley intervened, leaning forward, adjusting his tie – one of his signature ticks. 'It is our prerogative, Professor, to ask the questions.'

I waved him away, 'You have no idea who he is, do you? Faisal Rezgui. Yet he was murdered in detention by a Group Four security guard near Gatwick – one of thousands of children being held illegally, in the UK. Do you know about Group Four?' I addressed this question to Shirley. There was no reply. 'You should because your friend, Andrew here, is a non-executive director on its board.' I turned in my seat, faced him, 'How much do you get for doing that? One day a month – £700,000 a year.'

Even the most refined and highly polished media intellectual or politician cracks at some point – I like to make these men crack, break them and then see them shatter, then collapse to the ground. Osbourne was making it easy for me – he was silent long enough for me to continue.

'Faisal had brothers and sisters, and a mother, and after being held for months in illegal detention – by a government and party you both support – he was murdered, his throat crushed, so you could curl a single hand around it. …' Television requires reality, demonstrations, vivid visual imagery, so I put my hand out, held it towards the camera, to indicate the size of Faisal's crushed neck.

'Answer the charge Professor … do you condemn the One Per Cent Murders?' Osbourne spluttered. At least he had recovered his power of speech.

'Now you lay charges, do you? I don't call it murder; I call it justice. And it has led to uprisings and rebellion everywhere, in Port of Spain in Trinidad, in Georgetown, rejoicing in Bangkok, Beirut, Berlin and that is the nature of the historical moment through which we are living. The game is up, the long global rule of the rich, its centuries of genocide and murder, is nearing an end. Murder, you say. This is a movement. A network. A web. Tied to groups and protests – uprisings of people – across the world.'

Shirley had edged forward in his chair, someone – off camera – had handed him a note, he seemed flustered; finally, at the end of his long illustrious career, he was choking on his own contempt, the script to his life was running dry.

He indicated to Osbourne and then spoke, 'You seem to know a lot about what is happening, Professor – do you want to elaborate in these networks? You are not a stranger to rioting and covert groups, are you?'

'What are you saying? I have not taken part in a single riot. I have been on a number of demonstrations that have ended up in conflict.' I stood suddenly, pushed the chair back with my foot, 'And have some respect,' I snarled, 'for an African woman, and don't accuse me of being a rioter; you won't provoke me into becoming abusive, you just sound idiotic. Show some respect.'

Osbourne seemed desperate, he was pulling at his tie, the collar popped open and the button flew off. I felt that if I carried on both men would implode, so I carried on. I sat down again, and continued, 'Your job for years, both of you,' I opened my arms, 'has been to divert attention from the crimes of the class, the 1 per cent you support. What about the $9 billion of Iraqi money that went missing under the first two years of American and British occupation, under your watch Robert, when you were the special reporter for the BBC and based in occupied Bagdad? Look at Halliburton, and the other corporations, that stole money from Iraq and Afghanistan – what was your kick-back for keeping silent? Then the banks ... should we start on the banks, first the crash of Lehman Brothers and your involvement, Robert. ...

'I don't want to bore your viewers, but the truth is – today – we are teetering on the edge of a recession in the world's largest economies, but today there are a few too many more banks for the Federal Reserve to hand half a trillion dollars to. And what are we seeing? The usual vicious circle of capitalist crisis, work-places closed, gigantic banks and corporations bankrupt, and millions sacked and with less spending, there are more bankruptcies, more mass sackings. The last crash was only the dress rehearsal to the coming storm.

'You see you are not doing your job as pro-capitalist spokespersons for the mega-rich, you are not even diagnosing the crisis correctly ... or at all. You are not monitoring the trends, but just seeing the headlines. The mega-rich – the 0.1 per cent – are a bit fed up with losing minor chunks here and there in collapsed bubbles like dot-com and subprime, and they have started to invest in something more reliable, "softs", agricultural products, crops – and the spike in prices has led to uprisings. ... This is not about the murder here and there of a few members of the super-rich but of a historical moment. The end of an era of fossil fuel-led capitalist devastation. It's over. Whatever the killers say, the website posts that keep popping up, we have to look elsewhere for the clues.'

Huffing and puffing, desperate to find a way in, to regain some order to his show, Shirley just shouted – trying vitriol, and indignation in place of analysis. '"The murder here and there", this is a shocking way to speak about vicious and targeted killings. Young and old, men and women, even children killed in a plot – carried out by a crazed group. You are a fool to think that chaos will be the handmaiden to a new society – it won't, Professor, and you are reckless to be advocating it.'

I let him vent and then spoke.

'At least your last comment has the merit of a certain analysis. It is impossible for you to conceive that without the class you work for and worship, society will fall apart. That this class holds at bay a state of nature and prevents us from ripping each other's throats out. Capitalism is a war of all against all – ending it ends the war. Secondly, there are popular movements ready and willing to take over, while the rich bunker down and dig trenches to launch their counteroffensive. The extent of their panic, their persecuted belief that the time has come, is leading to fantastical and dangerous behaviour.' I felt the full command of the audience in front of me in the studio in Bush House, and the millions watching beyond. What was this sensation? I was impenetrable, unstoppable – like the wave of popular uprisings about which I was speaking, or the historical moment into which we had been propelled.

I can't remember exactly how it finished, except that I said, somewhere near the end, 'The One Per Cent Murders – as you call them – is just the beginning of the end.' There were more wild denunciations from the pincer movement of these two men, sitting on my left and my right, trying to squeeze me with the puny weight of their thinking. They could do nothing to stop me.

An assistant came up to me at the end of the interview to remove my microphone, she whispered to me, 'Bianca, you are pure gold, you state the truth with words like bullets, they are warmongering liars, and hypocrites. I want you to know …,' she came closer to me, breathed on me, 'that I am with you.'

As I left the studio, ignoring Shirley's proffered hand, Osbourne's suggestion of a drink, the producer declared, loud enough for us all to hear, 'What a fucking clusterfuck.'

PART 8

'Open your heart to what I mean'

1

Present Day

AMONG THE PLACES I went to in London to disappear, was a Senegalese restaurant – Chez Fatou – in Deptford. The area was being developed, and slowly the Nigerian, Ghanaian, Cameroonian bars and restaurants were being forced out, to find new locations, to seek out the last corners of the city not being taken over by boutique Italian restaurants, tapas bars and chain cafés. Chez Fatou was rare – fighting hard to stay put, sandwiched between nail bars, opposite a double-fronted art café. The scrawled signage – painted above the entrance – had faded, so now it read Chez Fat.

Inside, the place was dark, bleak, the white walls smudged brown, curled posters of Youssou N'Dour, an image of Abdou Diouf, a former, former president of Senegal, in a broken frame, hanging over the door to the kitchen. The toilet was seatless, the sink broken – the place a calamity and the food magnificent. When I arrived, I received a perfunctory nod from Fatou, a few pleasantries in Wolof, and took my seat in the corner, and waited for the food – they knew who I was, but they also knew I needed to be enveloped in West African anonymity.

I was served grilled fish in an onion sauce, with rice and a salad. I drank one glass of bissap and water, and then sat and read. For all of this – my weekly, fortnightly or increasingly monthly visit – all I ever needed to say was, '*Na nga def* – how are you?' And occasionally – when I entered and the room had a few people eating – I would say, '*As-salāmu 'alaykum*'. These rituals of greetings drew a line around me, protected the space I needed in which to be alone, in company but to be free of speech and interaction.

For a woman so relentlessly in public, so observed, so seen – so constantly dragged away from herself – these places of peculiar freedom meant everything to me.

* * *

Pulling up my hood and drawing the pull cord tightly around my face, I zipped up my leather jacket, felt the collar tighten around my neck and walked from the bus stop along Deptford High Street. Dusk arrives at 5 p.m. in the winter in October, with the sky a dirty grey sheet pulled over the tops of the buildings. I hurried along the road, weaving my way between market stalls noisily packing away their produce – Chinese imports of bags, watches, pots – and food stalls selling yams, sweet potatoes, mangoes, sugar cane and coconuts.

There were several of these strange strips of life – vibrant, loud, declaratory – in the city, where people, ripped from their own continents by the history of empire and colonialism, had found themselves. The faces moving around me were mostly black. A large woman, her hands worn, was standing in the middle of the road, one leg resting on a large aluminium pot, a van was trying to pass and she was gesticulating, and arguing with it – refusing to move.

It was hard for me to see anything and not also to see everything – the whole story, the waves of people arriving, the poverty of their shared lives, the longing, the ache of missing, the racism and the resistance and then – as I neared Fatou's, lowering my head against the rain (it had rained every day since the start of October – with only the briefest, most pathetic interludes) – and then, I thought, it all starts again. The government had escalated the deportations, there were now regular raids, camps near each port of entry where these people, the people bustling around me now, my people, were bundled on planes and transported once more.

I pushed hard at the door – it sounded an electronic melody – I entered the restaurant, the door swung closed on me, the clutter of voices and music from the street muted. Without

Deptford, without this, what would the city, this country, be? A rancid white racist husk, hollow, foul, petrified. Even with the relentless rain, the grey that squeezes hard around the heart of every living creature in this country, there are still bands of light, of sunshine.

* * *

Huddled in the corner, the meal finished, I was sipping on a small glass of sweet tea, leafing through the newspapers I had brought, making notes in the margin – satisfied, complete, relaxed, pleased with what I was doing, and with what I had done.

The room contained a few early diners. One couple sat opposite each other, in amicable silence – the woman was young, her hair in tight, long narrow braids, the man with a goatee, his head shaved, wearing sunglasses. There were random, momentary explosions of conversation – something shouted in Wolof or French, with a word or two in English, from the kitchen, or from the restaurant to the kitchen. Then silence would return and we would eat or read, or nod at each other, without words.

I circled a story I was reading, made a note to add it to my file – to the board I had put up in the lounge. 'Hong Kong police are investigating what appears to be a crime linked to the One Per Cent Murders, after the decomposed body of a wealthy 62-year-old woman was found bundled into a large chest freezer at her home with her hands and legs bound and a plastic bag over her head. No money or valuables were taken.'

I laughed to myself – what those idiots who were investigating these murders could not do was contemplate the possibility of copycat acts, an expanding political upsurge, an inspiration to carry out similar actions in the name of the website, *The Fire This Time*, that was beginning to appear openly.

This act – the latest murder – was evidence of the widening of the action, irrepressible, unstoppable. I slapped the paper down on the table, so my glass jumped, I felt a shot of adrenaline. The clarity of clear and positive thought.

The door to the restaurant swung open, a burst of the street came in – the noise of the stalls being cleared away, the scrape of hard bristles on the road, jets of water from a council truck washing away the rubbish. I didn't look up, but I knew who it was and, in an instant, less than a second, I knew exactly what had happened.

Mark blustered in, louder even than the noise of the street that he carried with him, standing inside, broad, full, in comic triumph – he had an image of himself as a loud, robust, laughing man.

I realised suddenly that I was being followed – perhaps had been already for a few weeks.

Apart from my work at the university, I did not keep routines; there was no prescribed day or week when I would visit Chez Fatou, or Pavarotti's, and, though there were places to which I ran, parks in which I trained, even these I varied. I surveyed my weeks in the seconds before I looked up – listed in a few moments where I had been, what I might have betrayed. Nothing.

Drained of emotion, my tone flat, breathing in deeply though my nose, I sat up straight, and said, 'This doesn't seem likely, Mark.'

He lumbered over, smiling, making, as he did, a play of his weight and size. He hooked the chair opposite me with his foot and pulled it out and sat down. With legs splayed, back bent, Mark put his hands on the table, and took a newspaper from the pile in front of me that was decorated with my red scribbles and arrows.

The restaurant was still. Fatou had come out of the kitchen and stood in the threshold, her arms on her hips. She made eye contact with me, then returned to the kitchen.

For a man of such bluster, who played the part of the stupid policeman, the bully and clown, Mark was very direct as he launched himself at me.

Mark put the newspaper down and said, 'You see, Bianca, I have a problem. I want to explain it to you. We are doing the same work … you and me.' He waved his open hand over the pile of papers. 'Trying to work out what is going on. The way I see it, essentially, who did what and when. But I have begun to think that "Why?" is the most important question because it will get us to the "Who?" If we can work out why these murders are taking place, then our list of suspects narrows down ... massively.'

He was looking at me as he spoke – he paused and reached across the table to the glass of water, took a sip. I heard people speaking in the kitchen.

He continued, 'The website helps, *The Fire This Time*, the blogposts are helpful ... but they are not everything. I am not even sure they are directly connected. ... Then, there are supporters, those like you – though I suppose there are not many like you – who have been quite clear about what position you take in relation to the murders. As hard as I find it to believe – a woman who has spent her working life studying people, protest, society, suddenly throwing herself behind a criminal movement of murder. But I don't understand these things,' Mark shrugged, faintly smiled, 'It doesn't seem to make sense. You see what strikes me, Bianca, if you'll allow me. ...'

He allowed a momentary pause, a slight questioning in his eyes, a mock request to continue, I raised my eyebrows, nodded assent.

'Is that your support for these, these ... events, is because you genuinely believe in them, or you like the noise of publicity – he put on a voice, a reporter, a newsreader, "Outspoken professor defends the One Per Cent Murders" or ... and this is what has been really intriguing me in recent weeks ... you are – how should I put it – more directly engaged.'

The restaurant, the couple, the kitchen staff, had, with impeccable politeness, started to speak voluminously among themselves, without pause – keeping up a background noise.

I straightened myself in the chair, took my hands off the table, crossed my legs, pushed myself back, so the chair scrapped along the floor. Mark was waiting.

'Let's deal with each of your suggestions,' I said. 'The middle one first. I do not do things, show support, speak, or make noise, for the sake of publicity. I think you know this. Now the first point. Do I genuinely support these acts? I remember these kinds of questions and arguments – that are set up with a false premise, a type of syllogism. In the past I was accused of being a revolutionary. Or, more absurdly, I was often asked by students if I *believed* in revolution.'

Around his shirt collar, buttoned almost to the top, Mark was sweating. He was a man who always dressed in sizes slightly smaller than he needed, so his clothes would pull and stretch around his body.

'… "What sort of question is that?" I would ask. Whether I believed in revolution, or if I was even a revolutionary, was irrelevant. The fact of revolutions lies beyond my belief in them. They exist. They are. For me it was more interesting to ask how they could be driven forward, influenced, powered.'

Fatou had come out of the kitchen and stood with her arms on her hips, at the same time the door from the street opened and three men came in – large, strong, handsome. The first two had shaved heads and beards and wore tracksuits. The third, the tallest, wore a white T-shirt, silver chains and bracelets, and a large gold watch. I recognised them. The men made a drama of their entrance; they let the door crash shut and spoke loudly to Fatou – they then turned to the corner where I sat and shouted a loud greeting to me. 'Bianca, *na nga def, ça va?*' Then, the third man moved to the table near me, indicated to the others to follow, and said, '*Ma sœur, ça fait combien de temps? Comment vas-tu? Je suis heureux de te voir.*' Then, in an entirely different tone, '*Qui est cet homme? Nous allons rester assis ici … et ma sœur, s'il y a quelque chose dont tu as besoin, dites-nous simplement. Nous sommes là pour toi.*' Sister, how long has it been? Who is this man? We will sit here and my sister if you need something just tell us. We are here for you.

With a clutter of chairs, placing their phones on the table, adjusting their seats so they faced us, they started speaking to each other, while staring at us – one of the tracksuited men called for beer from Fatou – '*Ma sœur, Fatou, deux Gazelles s'il te plaît.*'

Despite Mark's about-turn, his sudden seriousness and commitment to proper policing – which had even surprised me – he could not disguise his nervousness. These were the men he normally arrested, or whom he regarded with instinctive suspicion. Within the boundaries of his narrow whiteness, these feelings were automatic, involuntary to him. The totality of existence was beyond his powers; everything had its place in the grid of life, black and white, small and large, adult and child, no matter what efforts he made, his entire vision had already been mapped.

Under his shirt his muscles twitched – he swallowed, his Adam's apple lifting and falling.

I continued, 'And your third point, Mark, is unclear ... you will have to elaborate.'

For the first time since he had come in, he leant forward. He ran his hands along his trousers, 'You see, Bianca ...,' he spoke calmly, 'there is a mystery that I would like you to help me with ... a coincidence.' He reached into his inside jacket pocket, and pulled out a piece of paper, unfolded it and started to read.

He read from a list: 'In August this year you travelled to Hong Kong, from 19 August to 10 September. You will recall during this period two businessmen were murdered – Raymond Ka-Shing and Michael Kwok – what could be called the high point of the One Per Cent Murders. At the start of the year, Charles King was murdered in his apartment in the Docklands. You were – if I am correct – teaching at the university. In other words, in London. Then, on 23 March you travelled to Senegal. On 28 March Daniel Couper was murdered. Quite a coincidence, no? You then travelled, on 25 April, to South Africa and, though we have not directly connected the destruction of wealthy neighbourhoods in Cape Town to the murder spree, we think there might be a link. You were in the city for the entire duration of the fires. My colleagues in the city even tell me you were arrested on suspicion of assault at a party.' Mark paused here and looked up, pleased with himself.

I laughed loudly, with surprising force, rubbed my eyes and then through the laughter, 'I am flattered, Mark. But you are forgetting something. ... I was also in Washington in March 1981, when Ronald Reagan was shot. ... I was also involved in that attempted murder. Although I was only thirteen. Then, there are a number of murders across Africa in the 1970s, still unsolved, I might be your woman.' This was easy – the propositions were clearly ridiculous, wild, the idea primitive, desperate. If only the world worked to such simple theories.

The couple got up, the woman put two notes down on the table, moved towards the kitchen, called out to Fatou and then left. There were five of us left in the restaurant.

Mark was undeterred, 'You see I had a few problems getting this information. It seems your passport – one of your passports – has another name, or rather your real name. So, I had to ask Andrew Ashley – your VC – and he confirmed each of your trips. All of your speaking engagements, and the time away from the university.'

Large men sweat, even if they are fit – under Mark's arms there were great crescents of sweat. His temples were perspiring.

I continued to mock him, 'You are forgetting the moon landings Mark. ... I was only a few months old, but I was intimately involved.'

Mark smiled weakly. 'I am struck Bianca by the coincidence, it is quite striking don't you think?'

The three men were getting bored, I could tell – there were explosions of conversation and laughter, then silence. They had nothing more to say, no more rustled-up chitchat. They turned their chairs turned towards us, and stared at Mark.

I took the glass of bissap, knocked back the last mouthful, 'Maybe it is, Mark. Though you need more than dates and travel itineraries. If this is all you have, I am sorry to disappoint you, but you don't have anything at all.' I pulled my hood up, called to Fatou to bring the bill. I then shuffled the newspapers together and, removing one from the pile, a large circle drawn around the article, 'A story from two days ago, billionaire Richard Sharp, the world's eleventh richest man, was found face-down in a pool of his own blood on the morning of 4 September in his LA home. He was 59 years old. Forensic evidence suggests he was killed the evening before by 45 sharp and blunt blows to the head, neck and limbs. He was still wearing his Rolex watch, but his mobile phone, as well as the murder weapon, disappeared. Nothing else was missing. Police refused to speculate whether this murder was linked to the One Per Cent Murders.'

I was tired – work, practice, study never tired me, but people did. People like Mark. The strain of having to keep going, to maintain my interest and curiosity. To pretend. This used up all of my energy – somehow, to corral my sprawling thoughts, the spider's web of thinking, into a discussion with a policeman. This exhausted me.

'And Mark, read the papers … another murder in Hong Kong yesterday. Others – apparently – today.' I tapped the pile of news in front of me, 'all of it listed, one after the other, here … you flatter me if you think I can be simultaneously present in Hong Kong and California … and then here, with you, a few hours later.'

I got up. Mark tried to interject, 'I don't think we are finished.'

'Yes, we are.'

Mark rose, looking lethargic, sodden. 'We will be in touch,' he said, reaching for his jacket on the back of the chair. 'We have more questions for you.'

The police are like the British royal family. They always use plural pronouns; it swells them, and creates a distance between them and us. It highlights the sense of an army behind them, the power and the institution.

As Mark moved towards the door, one of the men put out his foot, quickly enough for Mark not see it; it caught him and he stumbled; he fell forward, tried to catch himself on a table – his arms flailing, missing a step, trying to stabilise. He upended a table near the door, which crashed on its side, and Mark slid forward on his front foot – the impression was strange, grotesque, his legs akimbo, his jeans pulled tight around his crotch.

There was a snigger from the three men – I shouted '*arrêtez*' and they were silent. I stepped forward, approached Mark. 'Let me help you,' I said. Mark was already upright, straightening his jacket – he was comfortable with anger. I understood that. He turned abruptly to the three men, one of whom was standing, and under my silent instructions, holding out an arm to help him, his face twisted in fake concern.

Mark tensed and stepped towards the men, snarling.

To see two large men, standing chest to chest, sizing each other up, always amused me. In the old lexicon, in the words of *The Elation of Being*, I saw this behaviour not necessarily as primitive, but rather as confirmation of our deepest unconsciousness. Of the aeons we had spent scrambling around in the dirt. When men fought each other, muscle to muscle, hate to hate, they were only playing out their part in humanity's deep sleep. All violence was an unconscious act.

There was too much at stake for these men actually to fight. Fatou came out of the kitchen and ordered her man to stand down. I stepped between them, saving Mark from a final humiliation. He uttered loudly into the room before he left, 'You better get out of here before you're arrested,' and then, under his breath, 'fucking Africans'.

After he had gone and before I did, I turned to the room, the men all standing, collecting their wallets and phones from the table. Fatou in her position behind the counter.

'Thanks – *merci, mes amis*,' I said as I left.

2

Present Day

REREADING THE REVEALER'S last blogposts, I found what I was looking for, what had been staring me in the face, the hitlist: 'Once more, REVOLUTION has been put on the agenda of twenty-first-century humanity by the 1,635 billionaires. ...' Then, one night, I started putting names together – this is easy to do, there are online records – and, against these names, these individuals, I crossed off those who had already been killed. Between the list of murders of the rich, since the start of the year, and the list I had now put together, there were some anomalies. Some members of the rich in their low millions, lottery winners, the almost super-rich, even high net-worth individuals with tens of millions had been murdered. These I had to discount – they were, I decided, not part of the 'core group'; they were slightly peripheral to the 1 per cent killings. I had no proof, but I speculated that these were carried out by copycat killers, expressing an entirely healthy hatred for the rich – in all of their guises, those with a few million, ten million, even a few hundred million.

But the Revealer had been very precise – each of the 1,635 billionaires. They had been counted precisely. I came within a dozen of the figure. Discounting the peripheral murders my list revealed that fifty-seven billionaires from the original list had already been killed. There was a lot more killing to do, but the Revealer – I realised – was relying on the power of example. It wasn't necessary for her to kill each of the billionaires herself. She could, as my analysis showed, 'subcontract' the murders to the general public.

So when, at the end of November, the northern winter started its erratic on-and-off freeze, I was not surprised to see that the

Revealer had started to produce names, lists, addresses – offices, clubs, summer houses and penthouses. Revealing in astonishing detail, the movement, across cities, country clubs and continents, of the ultra-high-net-worth individuals.

One typical case. The Revealer detailed the movement of Thomas David Kadoorie, who owned an estate in the Caribbean: 'he wakes at 6 a.m. and squeezes two oranges, eats one banana and spends ten minutes on his exercise bicycle. He then changes into his swimming shorts and spends two hours kitesurfing on the private beach in front of his estate. Access to the beach is guarded, but there are two tracks from the north of the Blue Mountain range that – with a conventional GPS, set to Strawberry Hills – leads directly to Kadoorie's beach. The other easy access point is, naturally, by sea – a paddle board, canoe or small powerboat is sufficient to reach his estate.'

Whether these instructions were taken literally – providing as they did, a roadmap or guide to killing the rich – was not really the point. They provided the exact location of tycoons, industrialists and media moguls, their peculiarities and routines and even their bowel movements. The Revealer wrote in the middle of October, for example: 'Samuel Gates – after drinking a cup of green tea in bed, spends approximately five minutes on the toilet, reading the day's entry from a self-help manual (currently, he is reading *The Daily Stoic – 366 Meditations on Wisdom, Perseverance and the Art of Living*). After his first coffee, taken at his desk overlooking the Hudson River in Arcadia Hall, New York, he returns to the toilet for a longer period, taking with him the *Wall Street Journal*.'

There were so many details. And each week, more information – telephone numbers, registration plates, dog walks, shopping trips. Every activity catalogued. Apart from providing enough information to launch an attack, it showed, as many people were beginning to point out, that the lives of the 0.001 per cent were incredibly monotonous, bound by strict routine and lavish indolence.

Those billionaires who worked on growing their already obscene wealth from early morning to late at night were even more grotesque. Their downtime – between restructuring their businesses, firing workers and destroying the environment – they spent buying yachts, flying friends to champagne parties on Caribbean islands or for exclusive wine and cheese tastings in log cabins built on melting glaciers in the Alps and in back-country ski lodges in the Andes.

The information provided by the blog gave anyone with a modicum of anger and revenge in their hearts enough information to cross another name off the list of 1,635 billionaires. The panic it induced in the rich themselves – the real purpose of these lists – was enough to chase them into their bunkers, and onto their gated islands.

3

Present Day

IT WAS THE best thing that could have happened. That little, surprise visit from Mark in Deptford. Each of the subsequent events was, more or less, predictable on the basis of his appearance that night. The other questions to which he had alluded, his deeper suspicions, might as well have been written down for me – made entirely visible.

The first of two strange things that day happened in the morning. The city sky cleared, and the transparent, crystal blue opened on the city, in a moment of rare clarity – of forgiveness, I thought. The city streets were cold but bright, and commuters, rare in their late autumn shuffle to work, their quest for invisibility, stood still and looked up – almost daring to speak to each other.

The one point I shared with the VC were my early starts. When I had showered, and made my way to the office, along the corridors, knowing I would not see any of my colleagues, I often saw Andrew Ashley standing outside my office, his fat jowls, his pompous red face, ready for me.

He started to blubber before I had even got to him. I was so taken up by the sight of this man, his vibrating, blustering face, that I didn't hear anything he said. I was completely deaf to him.

A few steps from the door to my office I dropped my kit bag, and tried to concentrate on his monologue. As he spoke, I stretched, reached up to the ceiling tiles; turned my body left and then right, swivelling on my hips; cracked my knuckles; lifted each leg in turn, holding the foot into my hands; rolled my head on my shoulders, tilted it from side to side.

He spoke, rambled; 'most unusual to have the police contact us and you will understand, Bianca, that I had to provide them certain information about your work. Your comings and goings – contractual matters. I have never had a high regard for the police, not for years, and though I do not believe they are a simple instrument of the state … so not quite a Leninist in this regard, "special bodies of armed men", ha! ha!'

I was standing in the middle of the corridor, one arm on my hip, staring at Ashley. His jabbering, his constant obsequious efforts to curry favour, were revolting and amusing; his determination to be liked by me was impressive. This little round man in his expensive suit, dissatisfied with his fat salary, frustrated – now that he had given up research – that he had already reached the pathetic heights of his career, and had nowhere else to go. Except to my office.

'I come very close to distrusting them. The Marxists are right that they have an almost complete monopoly of violence.'

There was something about my presence that provoked people – minor middle managers, or senior academics, they felt that they needed to prove their left-wing credentials, assert their familiarity with a radical vocabulary. I found it tedious.

'Thanks Andrew for informing me, but I have already had my set piece with the police – who seemed to have been equipped with the irrelevant details of my travel itinerary for the year. They explained you had provided them with everything they needed.'

'Yes, well, they didn't really give me a choice. I was compelled,' Ashley bleated.

'No, Andrew. You have no statutory duty to inform the police, when asked, of any information. To put it in simple terms, you are not required to disclose confidential information about your staff. Unless you were arrested and questioned.' I was playing with him – I did not care what he had said in fawning compliance with the police, nor did I regard any of the information he had surrendered as confidential.

He continued to bluster and, as he did so, he seemed to swell, to push against his shirt so the buttons strained – 'Well I hope this won't,' he concluded, 'damage our close working relationship. Your work for the university, the reputation …'

There was one aspect of my character that frightened me, a single variant that could not be accounted for: I would occasionally behave in a way that was entirely unexpected. It would catch me off-guard, upend my planning and my habitual careful organisation. The surge of nervous energy would bubble up as I became overloaded with racing ideas – and then I would act.

I had diagnosed this phenomenon years ago as a condition of limited self-regulation rather than a deficit of attention – in fact, I had an ability, a state known as hyperfocus, a capacity to remain centred for hours. Unexpected, unpredictable, I still suffered from these random, spontaneous urges. I had one of these now.

I walked up to Ashley, put my hands on his face, cupping his fleshy cheeks – like one might a small child – and I said, 'Andrew, you must stop worrying … this exhausting desire to please me is going to kill you. You do not need to fret, leave the police to me. I have everything under my control.'

I could feel him trembling, in excitement or fear, I do not know. Then, lowering my face to his, staring hard into his eyes, 'Everything is changing, Andrew, here as well, nothing is going to be the same any more. Nothing. Are you ready?'

Still gripped by this peculiar rage, this frenzy of impulsive behaviour, growing in me, I kissed him hard on the lips. Then, I pushed him aside, so he stumbled, speechless, against the corridor wall.

As I closed the office door behind me, I felt for the first time a tightening of the noose – I knew it was coming. I gripped the windowsill, stared into the city, the other office blocks, the stick figures on the street and the strange, bright winter sky.

* * *

The second peculiar thing happened that night.

There are degrees of darkness in the winter – the sky starts turning dark at about 3 p.m. in midwinter, so that by 4 the streetlights are already on. Then, a few hours later, the night is absolute. And, even in the city, there are still streets, alleyways, parks and squares that hold the night, that remain unpolluted by the city's lights – pockets of deeper dark in side streets, in the middle of parks.

Leaving the university late, after my last student had left, the final emails sent, I took my normal route back. The streets are never completely empty – but there were only a few people out. I saw a pack of women – tottering on their heels, wearing tight blouses and short skirts – loud, drunk, zigzagging across the road.

I wore a black woollen hat, pulled low, over my ears, and jeans, trainers, and my leather jacket – my backpack drawn tight against my shoulders. I walked without thinking, along Chenies Street, right onto Tottenham Court Road, left onto Tottenham Street.

When I reached Scala Street, I knew there was someone behind me and that I was being followed. I passed Pavarotti's – the restaurant closed, the shutters down.

It was a sense more than the sound – it is always the sense. Most things can be taught, but not the ability to sense a presence.

They knew what they were doing – far enough behind me for me not to hear the slurp of their feet on the wet road, close enough to make up the distance quickly. I estimated the distance, no more than ten metres.

There was a sudden burst of movement, despite the darkness, a subtle shift in the shadows – the feet light on the ground. When I turned, the figure was almost on me, a man, tall, slender, quick, his face hidden in a twine of scarf, he lunged for me, tried to hook his arm around my neck, to lock me down.

I blocked his right arm with a quick movement of my left. He was then exposed, open, his right arm and fist wide, his face and head unprotected. Quickly, I moved forward and hit him hard in the neck.

The impact froze him, first shock, paralysis, breathlessness – and then pain. It was now simple. I had instinctively put a leg back to steady myself, to stand firm. I now swept my back foot hard and fast under his feet and, at the same time with my left arm, I pushed him to the ground. He fell stiffly like a rootless tree.

Taken up with trying to breathe, restless in his panic – he was harmless, writhing on the dirty street.

I went quickly to work, I searched his pockets, pulled away the scarf. He was dressed in an old tracksuit, which was tight on him, and clean white trainers. Before I even found his ID, his clean-shaven face, his prime white features told me what he was; but, this idiot had come out with his warrant card. Police Officer Paul Hughes. They might as well have sent a squad car.

I knew what had happened, and I recognised what trap I had walked into.

4

1981 – Fawari

FAWARI WAS GONE and so was one of her sons, Godfrey – the other, Boma, was sobbing, curled up in the corner of the room where we had been staying, his grandfather trying to console him.

Vehicles – two unmarked Shell Range Rovers – were sent in for us, arriving two days later.

The pipeline had been leaking for days before it blew. If Shell had turned off the oil well from the station, the pressure inside the pipeline would have reduced, causing the flame to burn out. They didn't and, although they had been alerted to the leaks, they did nothing.

A stolen jerrycan of petrol, sold on the informal market, can equal two weeks' wages for a poor Nigerian. When news spread of the oil leak, under cover of darkness hundreds rushed to the site with cans, bowls and buckets to collect as much fuel as possible for their vehicles, generators and kerosene cookers. After we had gone to bed, Fawari followed her boys, who had followed the crowds, calling after them to come home. Then, a spark from a passing motorcycle in the village ignited the ruptured pipeline.

Before we were taken from the village, piles of scorched bodies were dragged from near the pipeline and lined up along the main road of the village – Kaarina and I saw them, and wondered which was Godfrey, where was Fawari. Hours before we left, we joined villagers who hurriedly organised a mass burial for half of the charred victims.

Two hundred and sixty people had been killed.

* * *

With the keen sense of justice that only a child has, we knew – all of us, each girl – what had happened and who was to blame. For two years I did not speak to my father – Maïmouna's silence lasted for three months. The company, the industry and the oil were to blame, completely and categorically.

Shell did what it always did – it denied responsibility and explained in press releases I discovered years later that sabotage was the cause. The poor themselves – those thieving, bedraggled wretches – had brought it on, grabbing what they could, like their politicians, for free. The leak was vandalism and the state government, anyway, was responsible for maintaining the line – there was even a phrase used for the slaughter by journalists, 'you chop, I chop' and 'It's our time to chop.' Later, academics turned this into a theory: the poor, the company and the state each take their turn at the trough – homo africanus is trapped in a web of sensory and affective passions where we prefer to 'eat' than produce or think.

Howard decided to send us away at the end of the first month; Kaarina's family stayed and moved back to Cape Town in the late 1980s.

Fawari has never left me – not really. Though for months we did not speak of it, Maïmouna and I slept in the same bed, and held on to each other crying hard, trying – I imagined – with our tears to wash away the oil that clung to Fawari's body, the oil that had continued to burn even when Godfrey dived into the water, trying to wash off the flames. I thought our tears were pure and would wash life back into them.

Even then I knew that Shell simply sat at the apex of a pyramid of suffering and that stab by stab that pyramid had to be brought down – as confused, angry, inchoate as I then was, I had this clearness of vision; what other answer could there be for the dead, for Fawari?

5

Present Day

FOR ALL OF the world-conquering power of the ruling class – the 1 per cent – their total venality always surprised me. They were stupid – so obsessed with privatisation that they had even outsourced their thinking to a paid class of statisticians, bankers and ideologues. An entire machinery of thought to justify what they could not. And even those people not quite in control of the levers of economic power – not exactly the owners of the means of production – but nevertheless with some handle on financial transactions, investments, currency deals, speculation, their thinking, their reasoning was pitiful.

Since I first read the Manifesto, the phrase that has always stayed with me was, 'The bourgeoisie have played a most revolutionary part. They have constructed means of production so great that no one knew the like. . . . But, above all, they have created their own grave-diggers.' That fact, combined with the crystallisation of the fundamental idea that we cannot just lay hold of the existing state machinery, but we must smash it. Obliterate it was the central message I had always taken away.

Today, after the long sleep, the aeons of time that we have spent unconscious, at last humanity is seeing new ripples of resistance that will soon become an unprecedented wave, with no possibility of retreat. It is as if the 1 per cent itself is broken, fractured and unable to rule.

Amid this crisis, the escalation of the global murder spree, the deepening panic among the rich and the widening arch of protest and uprisings, I was invited to speak in the city – at a club of London bankers, The Venue. I was still surprised that they invited me – with my peculiar mix of political economy, loathing of the rich, dismantling of the free market and capitalism, and New Age titbits.

The Elation of Being was still the dominant element of my fame. I used it to get in and peppered my talks with economic criticism and spiritual self-help. I remember when I had first made the shift, one of my abrupt turns, from spiritual guru to socialist radical, I was applauded to the rooftops by a large, upper-middle-class audience at the Buxton Festival, talking about my anarcho-communist politics and my father's adherence to the same analysis. But it was just that, an intellectual's analysis, not a tool of an actual revolution.

Now it was my passport to the 1 per cent, though I had never realised how much they really wanted me.

Though bankers are dull, stupid for the most part, I enjoyed these gatherings. As usual, I could say what I wanted and so could they. I had also learnt something of their thinking, their manner of reasoning, their planning at these gatherings. I saw them as the weathervanes for the 1 per cent, for the 0.1 per cent.

The club was a hotel off Park Lane, too exclusive to be on the main drag; they had converted a Georgian townhouse, non-descript on the outside, palatial on the inside. A pool and leisure facility in the basement, a plush, idiosyncratic suite of rooms on the ground floor – thick pile carpets, heavy curtains, chandeliers – the walls a jigsaw of framed paintings of members, and nineteenth-century farm animals, cows, fowl and horses. Even their function rooms on the first floor were peculiar – leather sofas, blackout blinds and giant photos of the rich – in action. Warren Buffet in conversation on a boat. Larry Ellison running in the mountains.

Once more I had been invited to speak on *The Elation of Being*, though, from experience, I knew I could choose my subject and, as usual, I would extemporise. I made my way from Green Park, down the busy thoroughfare of Piccadilly, and right onto Down Street. The weather had resumed its death wish – and the sky, even at 2 p.m., was ashen grey. I was cold and, as I walked, I pulled up my collar, hugged my arms around my torso.

Larry Hines – broad, tanned, his teeth bleached – welcomed me, expansive and relaxed. He took me immediately upstairs. He was the club's frontman, a philanthropist, who had grown his family fortune running a firm of vulture capitalists; he would buy sovereign debts at massive discounts and then collect them from poor countries. Even an innumerate child could see the blood dripping from his hands. Inside the building, the large lobby, the mahogany bannisters and soft chamber music enveloped me.

There were a few faces I recognised and nods, cheery greetings, waves. Clusters of men and women, dressed informally, a crowd of bankers and financiers who did not keep regular office hours. There were about thirty. The lounge chairs and sofas had been chaotically arranged around a small, mahogany coffee table, with a swivel office chair behind it – on the table was a glass cafetière filled with coffee, a notepad and pen. I sat down.

Hines introduced me – briefly. He adopted the English private-school habit of referring to people by their surname. So, after referring to me as Bianca Ndour, I became simply Ndour, and everyone else was Alexander, Renton, Ly, De Witte, or Fancy.

I wanted to get my talk done and to hear what they had to say. I started to speak without any preamble, I threw myself in head first, standing up, launching into them.

'First, if you have been watching the markets carefully,' there was laughter among the group, 'You will see that there is what appears to be a $7.1 trillion shift of spare capital by the 1,000 billionaires and the various hedge, pension and, crucially, commodity investment funds. Even some of the funds that you manage. Some of this shift has been triggered by the One Per Cent Murders. Yet, we see a massive lie machine involving the global media and press repeating causes ranging from "bad weather", the greedy new middle classes in China and India, all in a desperate attempt to divert attention from the super-rich who caused the sub-prime crisis years ago, or even the pandemic a decade ago, now hurrying to get their massive capital out of sub-prime and to switch it to oil and food and to speculation in futures and derivatives, betting the price upwards in leaps.'

I paused in my analysis, the audience a bit stunned, even if they knew me – some always came along expecting New Age help, a solution to their life situations, a justification for the obscenity of their wealth in trite formulations about the 'soul of the world', and following your 'inner being'. I poured myself a fresh cup of coffee, then handed it to Hines, and muttered, 'Larry – be a darling and heat this up for me.' He looked confused, and then smiled, looked around for help, then took the cup out of the room.

I continued.

'I think it's important to understand the explosion of struggles in at least thirty-three countries against the price rises in rice, wheat, corn and cooking oil that is jeopardising the lives of well over three billion people. These events are linked, directly, to your speculation, the enormous movements of capital and the profits of the elite you serve.' There was more tittering. 'We have already seen the first wave in 2011 in North Africa and the Middle East, but new movements are developing. A further, deeper intifada, incorporating a far larger swathe of the planet. Intimations of the future, I think. …

'You are all fixated on the murders – as if this was the only story, the nub of all events. But what we are seeing is far more significant. They combine into a deadly cocktail, one feeding off the other. The new crisis facing the global poor – provoked by the lethal price rises in basic staples organised by the billionaires in Chicago, New York, London and Tokyo and the other principal futures exchanges – executed by you. You know them, you work for them, you kill for them – you skim the milk off the top.'

Hines came back in with my coffee, the cup and cafetière rattling slightly on its saucer.

'The fatal assumption is that the poor are quiescent and stupid and ill-informed – this is an even bigger miscalculation than your headless strategy of accumulation at all cost! And here, in this rotten cesspit of profit,' I opened my arms to indicate the room, the city, the rich, 'You must take account of the chasm that the super-rich are widening by heightening racism and developing fascism. It is into the apparently clean hands of these far-right, fascist and racist forces, if they are not stopped, who will fill the vacuum left by utterly corrupt politicians for whom voters across Europe and North America, are now refusing to vote.'

I went on like this for another twenty minutes, angry, adamant, and uncompromising as I neared my conclusion.

'It is the actions of the 1 per cent – your bosses – that are lighting the blue touch paper of revolution. If capitalism gave us all a guaranteed, secure, decent home, job, food, leisure, then revolution would then really become a remote possibility! It doesn't, can't, won't, never will. Today, we add to the crimes of capitalism the unleashing of viruses and the pulverisation of the planet – the one and only source of wealth. And its own principal fundamental dynamic of intercapitalist competition ensures the constant battle between the "hostile band of warring brothers". Capitalism survives by cutting costs to raise the rate of profit and accumulation one degree above that of its rivals and so "stay in the game" by jockeying for and securing "top-dog" position all the time.'

The words flowed now. I had the audience in my hands – its concentration and focus complete. This capacity I had was a variety of hypnotism. Even Hines, sitting on my right, the richest person in the room, was held by my spell.

'The permanent instability of capitalism is now more frenetic than ever – as Marx wrote, "The bourgeoisie cannot exist without constantly revolutionising the instruments of production, and thereby the relations of production and with them the whole relations of society. Constant revolutionising of production, uninterrupted disturbance of all social conditions, everlasting uncertainty and agitation, distinguish the bourgeois epoch from all earlier ones. All fixed, fast-frozen relations, with their train of ancient and venerable prejudices and opinions, are swept away, all new-formed ones become antiquated before they can ossify."

'You must listen to one of the most commonly heard complaints today, the utter INSECURITY of our material lives! This class that you serve has swept away all security in life – from incomes to rents, to health provision and educational progress. And each of these gigantic multi-trillion-dollar financial, speculative bubbles – dot-com, war, sub-prime, food and commodities – authored by some of you in this room, has catastrophic consequences in the everlasting uncertainty that plagues the lives of billions – from China's remotest villages to the heart of London, New York and Paris.'

There was a paralysis in the room – a complete stillness, the faces motionless, mouths open, eyes wide. Was I wasting my time? I thought if I had them like this, if I stripped them naked, then they would speak openly to me once I was done, let out the inner anguish – secrets from their masters that even I did not know.

I had paused, stretched, poured myself more coffee. 'You are all obsessed with the One Per Cent Murders. Not because you will be targeted, but because the entire global game that sends your children to their expensive schools, pays for your staff, for the houses you own in Italy, in Monaco, in the Caribbean, and satisfies your lust for ownership, is coming to an end. And these murders over which you weep, and beat your chests in anguish – signalling as they do, the start of the end – mean nothing compared with the millions your games and gambling have killed. At the last count, last year – 2013 – 42 million dead, as a direct result of the spike in prices, and the profits that have accrued to you and your children, from the speculations on the markets you play, for the rich, for the "ultra–wealthy" individuals – as they call themselves.'

I sometimes went too far, I couldn't help myself. That rage inside demanded a voice – thrashing, and turning within me, until I had to let it out. I paused, swallowed the last mouthful of coffee, breathed in deeply, then stared out at the group and said calmly, looking around me: 'If everyone in this room were to disappear, like this …,' I clicked my fingers, '… and you no longer existed – all of you – then the world would be marginally, but instantly, a slightly better place.' There was a nervous titter of laughter.

Even in their concentration, their focus, there was a percepti-ble change in the atmosphere – a shift, a slight movement in their seats, an uncrossed leg, a cleared throat. I lightened my tone, became the professor again and continued.

'And because of the degree of globalised uniformity – not only of production but also of ideological reproduction – on TV, internet, social media, and so forth – as well as the interconnectedness and interdependence of most of global production – components for one computer, from one phone. ...' From the pocket of my jeans I pulled out my phone, held it up, 'Being from dozens of different countries – any serious explosion of protest anywhere impacts palpably and relatively rapidly on everywhere, and so the interconnectedness of capital upon labour is just as intense as its obverse. The burden on the global poor is intensified as the 1 per cent heap greater and greater deprivations and austerity on them to make themselves richer.

'These murders that occupy your minds so much ... are just the start. The trigger to a wider revolt, once the path of retreat or advance for the 1 per cent, the ruling class, has finally been cut off.'

I breathed in through my nose, let out a long stream of air from mouth and said, 'Intimations of the near future, I think.' And sat down.

Hines was the first to surface, three or four seconds after I had sat down. He stood – for once breaking his cultivated informality, 'Ndour, thank you, thank you ... a breathless, brilliant, provocative analysis as usual.'

There was an enthusiastic round of applause – some leant forward in their chairs, a few even stood and clapped. I smiled demurely, put up my right hand to stop them, indicating for them to sit – waving modestly.

'Ndour has told me that she can stay for another hour and answer questions. Does someone want to get us started?'

A man in his forties, wearing a striped shirt with the top button undone, with short cropped hair, raised his hand. It was good to see them do this, to behave themselves like schoolchildren. A couple of other hands went up.

Hines knew them all by name, 'Klatten – Carlos, keep it short if you can.'

Klatten stood up, placed his hands on the back of his chair as he spoke, 'You are right, Bianca, in your analysis – as hard as it is for some of us to hear. Multinationals and speculation are responsible for grotesque structural violence and the monopolising and destruction of the Earth's riches.' He had an accent, I couldn't place it – German, French, American, it was all in there. Educated in the rarefied atmosphere of elite international schools, here was a man, a representative of a class, who was genuinely a product of several of the world's richest countries rolled into a single body. 'It is us,' he continued, 'market speculators and financial bandits who have constructed this world of horror.'

They did this sometimes in front of me, expressed regret – whether it was sincere mea culpa, or an attempt to ingratiate themselves with me, I did not care. I accepted it as the force of my analysis, the power of my oratory.

He stopped. 'Carlos, continue, please ...' I said.

'Well the way I see it, hunger has not been down to fate for a long time – just as Karl Marx thought. Murder is behind every victim – silent mass murder. Right?' He looked at me nervously.

Even I was taken in briefly by this, the room silent, everyone listening. The best part he had saved for last.

'I believe that one day the starving people will rise up against their persecutors – it's just as possible as the French Revolution was. Maybe that is what is happening now, as Bianca explained.'

Then, most surprising of all, there was a murmur of agreement around the room. I now felt I had to shake them out of their self-satisfied, back-slapping group therapy– so I congratulated him.

'Very good, Carlos – say, six out of ten. Wrong revolution, the French Revolution was how your lot came to power, what you need to read about is the Russian and Spanish revolutions – how *we* once seized power ... but good, good – right theme: revolution!'

Carlos shrugged, dropped back into his chair.

Other hands were raised. 'Come on,' I said, 'isn't someone going to challenge me? I am told you are the prizefighters for the 1 per cent. ... Don't you have something to defend?'

A woman sitting in front of me – in tight jeans, a loose blouse, with shoulder-length sandy-coloured hair tucked behind her ears – raised her hand. Hines, desperate for a role, introduced her, 'Françoise Byrne ...' pronouncing her name slowly, for my benefit – despite everything he couldn't help himself. I knew who she was, an heiress, well-known for funding Buddhist retreats for the super-rich on an island she owned in the South Pacific.

Françoise was unrattled and spoke in a high nasal pitch that grated and scratched on the ear. She wore oversized square black glasses. Nothing can truly dislodge the super-rich except a gun, I thought as she spoke.

'Bianca,' she whined, 'I was hoping to get something else from you – not this, this, sociology. We have all read your brilliant *The Elation of Being*.' Like obedient sheep, the room sounded in agreement. 'Could you perhaps say something about the book, for those of us who are less equipped to understand your political economy?' She turned to Carlos, and smiled: 'Maybe you can translate what you are saying into the language of *The Elation*?' There was more murmuring of agreement.

Ridiculous, infuriating – this room would agree with anything that was said, anything that I said. Nevertheless, I complied.

'In the language of *The Elation*,' I said, 'the earth under your feet is beginning to tremble Françoise – the oceans of the world are overflowing the coastlines. For years you thought this was something that only happened to others and you could always find higher ground. Now all of your friends and your family fear the coming loss of everything they own. Their possessions and their loved ones risk being destroyed.'

The same stunned calm had returned to the room.

'Your life – its projects, it hopes – will be ruined. So now, Françoise ...' I was sitting down again; I stared directly at her. 'You must face the disaster confronting you and truly understand the Universal Soul. The One Soul. Only when you are released from this fear of loss, when you let go of what you own, the horror at the unknown will evaporate and you will understand that the single story of the world is also yours.

'Our lives are short and it is important for us to see that what is happening today is only part of the endless transformation of the earth and the development of its Universal Soul and One Consciousness. As part of that soul you need to prepare for the approaching transformation – you must begin to ready yourself. It is coming. Recognise it, surrender.'

The more obtuse I became, the more they caved in and lauded me. The applause for this little, ridiculous act was rigorous.

Several questions later I was done and Hines stood and thanked me again. A small crowd gathered around me. Françoise was the first – whinnying loudly, with no shame, no humility, 'Thank you Bianca, for your wise, wise counsel.' She said something else about being in touch, and a trip to her island, and handed me a card.

Then I got what I wanted.

* * *

The room was empty except for a small group, a huddle of three men and two women. Hines conducted them towards me. 'We want to speak to you Bianca' – his tone was conspiratorial, low – 'as someone – like us – who understands what's happening.' There were nods of agreement from the circle of men and woman. 'What we are going to tell you is known only by a very small group, and we need to know that we have your word that you will keep this to yourself.'

I reached for his arm: 'Of course, Hines,' I said.

I had heard rumours and took these as a good sign, like the beauty of sunrise in a cloudless sky after weeks of rain. There had even been discussion on various hidden forums on the internet, but there was such shit online it was impossible to distinguish between what was true and what was fantastical. But now, in this club, I had confirmation – direct, categorical, hard to believe. I held on tight as Hines spoke, tried not to betray the pleasure I began to feel as I heard the news.

'We need thinkers like you, Ndour, those who can really think, and are not afraid to confront the facts, the brutal reality. You would have everything you needed, facilities, time, researchers … anything.'

The group nodded together – steering Hines with approval. The doors to the room were closed.

'Whatever we build – what we rebuild – must be based on a more just future. For this future we need you, your uncompromising, critical view of the world … and, if I may say this, your willingness to keep us on our toes.'

By this point, I knew what he was speaking about, but I wanted to hear him state it more categorically, it needed to be said openly, fully. 'Excuse my stupidity, Larry, but can you be clearer – what precisely are you speaking about?'

'Of course, of course, Bianca, you are right …,' he responded quickly, 'you need the full picture. Doby …,' he indicated a dark-haired woman in the circle, 'Julianna,' he corrected himself, 'will explain the project.'

Julianna was narrow, slim, her face pointed, with a mole on her chin – like all of them she spoke with the accent of the rich. 'We are calling it Meridian. It's an island archipelago in the Pacific, about 1,000 kilometres south-east of French Polynesia with a surface area of about 4,500 square kilometres. Do you know Cape Verde?'

'We are on good terms,' I replied.

She smiled. 'Well, it's about the same size, across more than fourteen islands. The landscape is incredibly varied from dry plains to high, active volcanoes, tropical jungle with Jurassic cliffs rising sharply from the ocean. It has everything in abundance, water, more than 300 days of sunshine a year, an average temperature of 25 degrees C – perfect for solar power. Ideal also for wind power,' she paused, looked around, 'as an energy source and for those who like to kite surf.' The group chuckled; Julianna smiled at the man next to her. 'It is already being built.'

Hines interrupted: 'And the simple beauty of it is that it is unknown. It was once a secret base used for a brief period in the Second World War, but it was too remote. It is not on any shipping lanes, and … and …,' he turned so he could address me directly, 'it does not even appear on any maps – that was hard, I understand, and involves the continual scrambling of satellite surveillance.'

He returned the baton to Julianna, indicated for her to continue: 'Invitations are going out … to an extremely select group, a few thousand at the most. People like us, those who have something to contribute, resources, capital, unique intellectual and artist skills. …'

A short, stocky man in a polo shirt added: 'But the idea is to build a meritocracy … this is not just about buying your way in, but showing that you have earned it.'

'Yes,' Julianna declared, more animated, 'those who can help design the new world.'

I spoke, 'So what you are describing, my friends. …' I tried to match their camaraderie, looking at each of the smooth faces in the circle in turn, none ragged from life, each cared for, pampered, 'is a gated island. I suppose this is the logical next step from a gated community.'

Hines sounded a little disappointed. 'Bianca,' he pleaded, 'what you talked about today is true, as you know, but it's worse than even you have described. On every front – environmental destruction, climate breakdown is already here, as all the evidence shows, and it is beyond repair, it has started to spiral and nothing we can do now will help. The treaties, the commitments, the international signatories, it's all bluff, noise, nonsense. Then the political and economic breakdown everywhere – in the north and the south. And the global elite is giving up, the exodus is already happening … this, this, Meridian, is a chance to hold on to what we have, to give humanity another chance. Everything shored in mountain vaults, seeds, medicines, discoveries, and we will have laboratories, centres for thought, a great library, and we are creating an ecosystem that will mitigate the worst of the changes in climate, avert the catastrophe for us.' He stopped, then added, 'All so humanity can start again. …'

'But it costs …' I said.

Julianna spoke, 'It does, but not for everyone. A number of us – a large number – have repeatedly mentioned your name. This is the invitation, Bianca. Will you join us?'

6

Present Day

THE SPLIT HAD shattered my confidence. Despite my efforts at enlightenment, to let go – to *release* as I had told my followers years ago – I, too, was trapped. For years I had preached stepping out of unconsciousness and into conscious being. I had written, 'Use the despair, fear and depression of your everyday lives, the morning dread as the light seeps through the curtains that makes it a struggle to get out of bed. Use the horror. The wish to go back to sleep, to be taken back to oblivion and deep unconsciousness. Take on the waking wish not to be alive or, when you get up, the dread of the day, the sickness stretching deep into the past, casting a black cloud over the future – the unconstrained existential misery that clouds the reality of our beings. Break this pattern, clean yourself down, move into the present.'

My reaction to Kaarina, to loving her, had been infused by everything I had once rejected – passivity, control, abuse. I had spent my entire adult life in formal opposition to capitalist society, to the imposition of its wants. I thought that these values could be conquered and overturned, by sheer force of will, by a rising consciousness and a new dawn of *being*. Heartbroken, raging, pathetic, I found myself enslaved, caught in the same habits of thinking as everyone else, the same obstructions of thought. For a time, nothing could be done – in the face of life's reckoning with me, my political training, my own spiritual perspectives dissolved into the air.

There is no immunity in life, no inoculation.

I ordered my second coffee of the day. I sat back on the wooden chair, the table where I had been leaning to write rocked. I took the cardboard placemat from the table, folded it, bent down and wedged it under the table leg. The corner where

I sat was by the door, near the counter. I had the window behind me. The street, the shops across the road, were strangely captivating – a Chinese herbal clinic, a Thai massage parlour, two Turkish restaurants.

The sun tried to break through. The clouds, which scattered and stretched, broke in the sky. I felt the light on my face and where it fell there were large, deep, glittering pools of sunlight. I could hear the birds, the city flocks of starlings, even parakeets – what a strange city. I thought that perhaps the day would shine after all.

I had so much still to do, how could I be wasting time on the useless dead and spent past?

7

Present Day

THE NIGHT HAD already fallen. It was still, dark, outside. A thick shroud of night covered the building, muffled our conversations so everything we said came back to us again and again, over and over.

I had my legs up, crossed on the sofa – the burning restlessness in my stomach gone, my internal dynamo, urging me on, forbidding rest. I released, let myself sink into the sofa, put my hands behind my neck, pulled my braids free of my T-shirt, so they spilled over the arm of the sofa. I cracked my knuckles, let gravity pull me into the cushions.

My sister used to call me the 'Lost Girl'. I would play for hours by myself as a child or read, and constantly test myself – when there was no one left to beat, to out-think, race or fight, I would challenge myself.

'Lie still,' I would shout to my sister from under the bed, then only nine. I would grip the frame and lift the bed and my sister into the air. Levering the bed up with my arms, then down again, and repeating the exercise until the muscles in my arms burned and Maïmouna screamed for me to stop.

'Down, down Bianca – let me down,' she would shout.

I felt myself sink further into the sofa, and I gave myself a few more minutes of immobility until the familiar urge to work surfaced again – I had papers to read, and emails and calls to make. Considering what was happening around me, it was amazing even to have this time to ponder, to let my thoughts wander.

* * *

Lying on the floor our clothes around us, Elisa on her side, her head resting on a pillow, we spoke – told stories, it was always after we had made love that we did most of our talking. We needed to be naked to speak properly, for the charade of life to be stripped from our bodies; to clear the day from our skin.

I buried my face in her hair and breathed in. She smelt most like herself in the nape of her neck, in that smooth angle of her body was her private scent.

I reached for the remote, pressed play – Nina came on:

So I remember every face
Of every man who put me here ...
Any day now, any day now
I shall be released

I sat down, let my head fall back on the pillow.

I had the power of a rage that did not diminish or fade with time, but which continued to throb – as raw and innocent as it had been when I was a child.

I started speaking: 'I was about fifteen. We were living in Kenya, near a park in a middle-class area of Nairobi. I would train in the park.'

'Nothing changes,' Elisa said, laughing.

'... and with the little pocket money I had I paid for lessons in a gym in the city. Every day, in this wealthy subtropical park with palm trees, English oaks and conifers and even a duck pond, I would practise my katas and train. There was a man, a great white meat cleaver of a man, well-dressed, and he would sometimes walk in the park in the evenings, before the sun was down. He would smile at me and I would smile back.' I paused, breathed in, steeled myself for the rest of the story.

'Then one night, I was sitting by the gate inside the park, leaning against the perimeter wall, breathing hard. The residents of the large houses around the gardens paid for a ranger, a whole team, who would drive around the entire wooded enclosure as the sun set, in a green pick-up, locking the gates. I knew I had a few minutes before they turned up and I would have to leave. I remember the frenzy of noise, not sweet and harmonious English birdsong, but howls – the tree would be perfectly still, but the vultures, flamingos and monkeys, or whatever they were, would be screaming invisibly. And the noise would always start as the red and orange sunset spread across the sky, changing the colours of the park, signalling sleep or death, or both, to the animals. That howling like hyenas. I found the whole insane orchestra terribly funny – each time. The sweet, innocent stupidity of the animals and the blind beauty of the sky.'

Elisa grabbed a jumper strewn on the floor, pulled it on and sat facing me, her feet pressed against my legs.

'Then the giant, broad ox of a man who'd been walking in the park with his little dog appeared and he started talking to me. Immediately I could see he was excited to encounter a teenage girl, in shorts and a T-shirt, and from the way he talked, two hundred words a minute, tripping over sentences, slurring his speech, the way men get, blinded by their lust, "Where do you live? What work do you do? Oh, you're still at school. I'm surprised, I would have thought you were older – at least eighteen. What school? What do you want to do?" I was abrupt.' I paused, swallowed, took in some air. 'I remember his eyes over me, on my chest, between my legs.

'I stood but he was beside me, asking if he could walk me home. "No – I'm not going to be walking," I said, then before I started running, he put his hands on my lower back, a finger between my buttocks.' Elisa stared at me, unblinking.

'Then it all happened quickly. I turned so he couldn't touch me, couldn't get closer. I faced him and then with my right leg back I punched him hard in the throat. I can't remember if I'd been aiming for his face, but I got his throat and he choked, stumbled back, folded and fell, clutching his collar as though I had cut his neck.' I'd been looking at the floor and now raised my eyes, found Elisa's. 'Just before I hit him, I could see his smile – there was a flicker, a thought that he was going to get what he wanted, that stoned gaze of male longing. Somehow, I was going to give him what he wanted – like all black girls in Africa eventually did ... I knew in that split second, before I threw the punch, that men are at their most dangerous when they start to believe their erotic fantasies. That night I couldn't get his smile out of my head.'

Elisa reached for my hand, laced her fingers through mine and squeezed, 'What happened next?'

Nina continued to sing loudly into the room:

And now we got a revolution ...
I'm here to tell you about destruction
Of all the evil that will have to end.

'There was no next, not really. He sat squealing on the ground, then shouted that he knew where I lived and that he would call the police. I laughed, turned my back on him and ran home. I never saw him again.'

'He was too scared to come to the park again?' Elisa asked.

'I think he'd been exposed and that he was too stupid and fat to do much damage. He probably found another middle-class Nairobi park, or slum, or shopping centre, to have his little perv at black girls. I also learnt something important about fighting, something I had known theoretically from studying Wing Chun – there was no opponent too large or too strong. It is all about an economy of movement, leverage and deflecting and using the greater strength of an opponent as an advantage. For example, I knew I could have easily kicked him with a hundred pounds of force and broken his knee which would have crippled him for the rest of his life! But I only learnt this technique later, in practice. This is another story, though. As I was running home all I could think was that I should have done something to him so he couldn't do this to anyone else.'

Elisa laughed, a quick short laugh, 'You mean you should have blinded him?'

'Yes – exactly. Or something like that.'

After these revelations, these stories, I thought I could tell Elisa everything and that maybe she'd understand.

8

Present Day

I COULDN'T always hold it in, the anger, the rage, the instinct to act – this was my principal fault, this was how I almost failed. They intended to make it public, to inflict maximum humiliation and to do this while I was teaching – my last class of the year.

My students – those I had chosen to teach, hand-picked to attend a special class on contemporary social theory, which was really an opportunity to say and teach what I wanted and to discuss weekly, monthly events, to write my global updates – free-wheeling, pacing backwards and forwards in the classroom, my phone recording my thoughts.

This was how I wrote – by lecturing, in effect my entire *oeuvre* was an oral text. All my books, most of my long articles, had been narrated to my students and my lectures were copied initially – two decades ago – by a typist and then recorded with tapes, Dictaphones and now my mobile phone. I would walk the entire length and width of the lecture theatre, hardly ever hesitate, almost never return to a phrase. Like this I could finish a book in two or three months – all of it, preface, introduction, chapters, conclusions, narrated in front of my students. My writing process, the dictation of all my books, was my preferred method for writing.

I had my students – almost forty of them – sitting informally, with their computers and notepads, in a small lecture theatre, rows of desks, some dragged forward. The table at the front was where I sat, the place to which I returned after pacing around the class.

It was 7 December, but there were still some leaves on the trees: for a few days it had been bright. The last of the autumn light, and the pale sun shone through the auburn, rust-coloured leaves, and gave London a faint reddish glow. Night came early now, already by 3 p.m. the day had begun to fade, so I had to turn on the classroom lights.

There was a peculiar panic in the air. This was not a London thing; it was wider, broader than that. If I said that there was a sense of the end of days, I'd be exaggerating, but not completely. There was a generalised, chaotic mood that infected everyone.

The prolonged, sick frenzy of shopping that lasted all year, but intensified like a seasonal fever in December was a period when the great lies of society are revealed. December is a terrible month, the illusions of the family, liberation through buying, the immense misery of debt, ripples through households and communities, as people scramble for their allotment of happiness.

Though this consumer frenzy was not completely gone, it was now mixed up with something else, something far more potent and powerful. In the sea of people among whom we live we are each no more than a drop in the ocean, and we can only feel the great contours of history when there is a general change among the whole of society – a crisis, a war, a breakdown, an emergency or a revolution. In the UK, we were now entering one of those periods that in other parts of the world had been tearing up societies and destroying governments; now, the global moment had begun to infiltrate one of the oldest citadels of capital.

London was a strange place –the hold of the old world was finally beginning to loosen.

Everyone knew there was something in the air.

* * *

Five minutes before the class ended, a few minutes before 5 p.m., I was arrested. Outside the building, there was a loud clamour, raised voices, shouts and screech of tyres, and then the irrefutable blue pulse of light. Some of my students had gathered outside the room, about twenty, waiting to see me, to request last-minute assistance before the end of term – I heard their voices, a few of the brave ones, I knew, trying to prevent the officers from entering the room.

I stopped speaking, leant on the desk, and waited; two students came up to me, one spoke softly in Cantonese, 'Do you want us to do anything Bianca?'

I smiled, 'Thank you – May Ying ... but for once I don't think there is anything we can do.'

Students don't understand defeat; there is no weight of loss on them and they fight accordingly; victory is only ever a question of tactics and determination. They have in their best moments an irresistible power and voluntarism. Their idealism – what I want I get – makes them the best recruits to a cause, but I also knew that while they rise like rockets, they fall like stones. I supplied their rockets with fuel, kept them airborne. And now, as the noise outside the class intensified and the police tried to enter the room, I marvelled at their hope, their willingness to fight and the refusal to be constrained by history.

One of the students who had spoken to me, Ying, turned to the class, shouted for everyone to stand quickly, and come forward, and for about fifteen students to throw the tables and chairs to the back of the class, the rest to form a protective circle around me – 'kettle Bianca' she shouted, *how I love my students*. All of this took a few seconds. When it was done, by the double doors at the back of the class, and along the entire width of the room, was a jumble of overturned tables and chairs – a mass of entwined metal legs – that reached almost to the ceiling.

It was an act of beautiful, primordial lunacy. A small-scale revolt that made me laugh – I said nothing, I did not reprimand them or, for once, direct them.

I sat on the table at the back of the class; the students, all of them, in a semicircle, a cordon around me. I was kettled. The students pulled their hoods up, wrapped scarves around their faces; they put their backpacks on, and the stronger ones took the front, so when the police finally entered the room, pushing away a few of the chairs and tables so they could see over the barricade, they encountered a mass of people, their arms bent, their fists clenched. And buried at the back, just visible, was their teacher.

I immediately recognised two faces – Mark and the man who had attacked me in the street. Both were in uniform and stood at the front of the group. That arrogant, cocksure composure of uniformed policemen.

Mark spoke – but couldn't be heard, so I told the students to let him speak. He repeated, shouting: 'I see that the Chieftain of the People has her Amazonian Guard to protect her.' His officers were picking their way through the mesh of furniture.

As the barricade was slowly dismantled, students came forward and threw chairs in their path – shields went up. Seen from above, the room was split between the police, about twenty of them, and a retreating tide of tables and chairs, and then a small army of students, in jeans, sweatshirts and trainers.

I stood up on the desk, so I was raised above the group and shouted back to Mark, 'The Queen of the Amazons is protected by Revolutionary Nuns and this group is made up of women and men. …'

As the barricade was pushed towards us, penning *us* in, I saw that behind the police, several photographers, and two camera teams had entered the room and, within a few seconds, we were flooded with white light and the pulsing of the flashes of the still cameras.

I would wait another minute before I called off the students – let them fight a bit, I thought, let them see the reality of this democracy, the brutality of the police. Let them taste their first blood. There was only so much teaching I could do – the state, armed bodies of men, the protection of property, the violence of the 1 per cent, were lessons that could only be learnt at the end of a baton.

Four of the students were already down – their head in their arms, choking on pepper spray. Another – tall, thin, courageous one – had picked up a chair and brought it down repeatedly on the helmet of an officer who had managed to clamber over the barricade. This student, too, had now been brought down – tasered. He stood for a second, shook, then fell, his fall broken by his backpack, his head hitting the floor hard. The officer dropped his taser and stood over him, kicking, another joined him – the dam of furniture had been completely breached. The student's head was kicked so it jerked to the side, blood started to trickle out of his ear.

The students surrounding me were scared and angry. A few burst forward to defend their comrade, one woman – women always fought with more wild determination than men – screamed, howled, and started to swing her bag wildly at the police, in her rage she even forced them to retreat for a second.

I now crouched on the desk, whispered to the group then, parting them with my arms, jumped down. The group moved back, apart from the woman who still screamed as she swung her bag. I faced the police.

Stunned, the room was momentarily silent – I had the floor.

'Let my students go, Mark, and I will come with you.'

'We don't want them ... your fan club can stay.' He was breathless, sheltering behind his men at the back of the class, speaking into a loudhailer.

One of the officers, fending off the woman, had grabbed her bag – his body strapped together with armour, a breastplate, shin guards, shoulder pads. His face, and the face of his colleague, were twisted in a concentrated snarl – salivating. The student held on to the bag as the officer pulled it quickly, yanking it violently from her grip. She tottered, then fell. As she hit the ground the second officer, a larger man, bearded, broad shouldered, kicked her hard in the chest.

All witnessed, all filmed – my pulse hardly quickening, with two steps I was in front of the two policemen, my right leg forward, the left one back. I swung my back leg up, kicked high and hard into the temple of the bearded officer. He clutched his head, and then fell – loudly, dazed. Before his partner even realised what had happened, I was crouching on the floor, at his feet swiftly I grabbed his two ankles, and pulled them towards me. He fell like a plank of wood – falling back, too surprised even to break his fall. There was a crash as he landed, winded, on the metal legs of the upturned chairs. He groaned and tried to get up.

As a group of officers came towards me, Mark shouted at them. They dispersed, and he came forward, handcuffed me and then with one hand on my back and the other holding my arm, he led me out of the room, through the corridor and to the main doors of the university. Along the corridors, pressed to the walls, were students and lecturers, cleaning staff, they all shouted, and cheered as I passed, calling for me to be strong and that they were with me. They jostled with the police, who were scared, unsure, their bodies pressed tightly against me.

Once outside and to the waiting vans and police cars, the sirens sounding – camera crews stood on benches and step-ladders. There was a bigger crowd, maybe two thousand, word had quickly spread. The path to the van – its doors open, officers waiting on each side – was blocked, by students, workers, cleaners, even a few colleagues. They had started to push against the scrum of officers who held me.

The blades of a police helicopter beat a steady rhythm above us.

'What do you want us to do, Bianca?' someone from the crowd shouted in Wolof. 'Tell us what you want ... we can free you sister,' someone else shouted.

In the crowd – huddled tightly together – I saw, a few metres from me, Elisa. Our eyes met. Hers were wet, she raised a fist. Others copied her, until the whole crowd, as far as I could see had raised their fists – first one and then the other.

'Let them take me,' I shouted in English and then repeated in Wolof, Cantonese and Spanish.

The message spread like an echo across the crowd, and a path was opened to the van – I was bundled in and, as we slowly moved away, the group filling the entire, pedestrianised forecourt in front of the university, stood silently, with fists raised in the air.

9

Present Day

WINDOWLESS, brightly lit, containing a table with a digital recorder, with a semi-transparent mirror, the interrogation room was like every other one in which I had been. Soulless and brutal. I was held for twelve days in a police cell in a station in Lewisham.

Lewisham is a strange part of London. Like all areas of this ever-growing megacity it was once a village, then a suburb and is now just another thoroughfare of penthouse flats and offices. The street market – a rough gathering of the city's working class, South East Asian and African populations – had somehow managed to resist the power of the rich.

The main peculiarity of this hideously refigured suburb was a giant police station – built twenty years ago and equipped with tunnels, vaults, holding pens, stables for horses, sleeping quarters for a hundred officers and interrogation rooms.

* * *

Jenny and Mark sat opposite me, reversing the roles they had played in my office, when I had advised them.

Jenny played dumb, and Mark tried to shine.

A few hours after I had been arrested, the accusations read out, the bumbling of the arrest, there was the panic and excitement of a high-profile detainee in the station. Mark repeated the original allegations, 'You are being held, Bianca, without charge under the Terrorism Act – we are holding you for questioning. We want to ask you about a conspiracy to murder after what we believe to be coordinated attacks that has led to the destruction of individuals and property around the world. We believe you are involved in this conspiracy, but the extent of your involvement we still do not know.'

'You are surprisingly coherent, Mark – I am pleased.' I sat with my legs crossed, in my jeans, trainers, a long-sleeved T-shirt and, over it, a hoodie. I was concentrating on my breathing; in through the nose, to the count of three, then slowly out through my mouth.

Jenny was avoiding my gaze and had turned her chair towards her colleague. 'I thought you were the smart one,' I said, addressing her.

Mark ignored me and carried on: 'We have a lot on you … your travel schedule, and your …,' he looked at Jenny, 'assault on our officer.'

Jenny spoke, 'Listen, Bianca …,' she said, looking at the table, to Mark and then nervously up at me, 'we really just want to question you. I wanted to ask you in for questioning in a more diplomatic way, but we don't always get what we want.'

'Are you trying to apologise?' I asked.

'No,' said Mark adamantly, 'she's not.'

Jenny resumed. 'To add to what Mark has said, we have heard that you have been working with a group – that you *have a group* – and that you swear then to silence and teach them.'

'Well done, Jenny, you have found out that I am a teacher. Top marks for policing.'

She ignored me. 'And this group is preparing for "events". It is being trained for them. It is planning to act.' Jenny looked down to a pad in front of her, folded over several pages and read, '"We built it in the first place, and we will rebuild it again tomorrow – as we want. This vision will give hope and inspiration for the fight to come. For we will have to fight! The more we can recruit before the full confrontation begins – the better."' She stopped reading and looked up at me, stared at me.

These were my words. My exact words – but how did she have them? I concentrated on keeping my breathing steady, my pulse regular.

Mark continued: 'You see, Bianca, your walls are not unbreachable … one of your inner circle has spoken.'

Fools, these people, always too eager, like hungry children with no control over their appetite. Jenny frowned, hit Mark's thigh with the back of her hand. Mark resumed after a slight pause: 'Blabbed to us, she did. She got it all out – the whole pact of silence, the conspiracy. Who you really are.'

Then I realised exactly what they knew.

Lydia had spoken to them.

* * *

It came out in a stream, a confession, Jenny joining in, Mark taking the lead. They told me what had been said, the whole revelation. Energetic, excitable, they couldn't help themselves.

No clear dates were provided but that didn't matter – from the fragments I heard that day Lydia had spoken to them. Sometime after I had threatened her, terrified, she had gone to the police – hysterical, in tears, insisting on speaking to the officers in charge of the case.

'When we finally got to her she was barely coherent, and the case has thrown up so many wannabes, fringe freaks who want to be part of the events … so much police time, and each lunatic has to be questioned.'

Mark was speaking, boasting, he couldn't help himself.

'Her fear convinced us,' he said after a pause.

Once her tears had subsided, and they had assured her she would be protected – easy promises to make – she spoke, a gush of revelations. She had been my student, then my lover, and when I broke it off, I had threated to kill her – to blind her, she'd said – if she spoke.

Mark's breathing was short; he kept swallowing, playing with the disposable coffee cup in front of him. 'She said that you were forming a group among students and followers, and that this group was sworn to secrecy.'

Though they didn't name her, Lydia was now being held in a witness protection programme. Jenny explained: 'She has been relocated because of the level of threat to her and the circumstances of the case. We are taking this very seriously, Bianca.'

Lydia was their witness – their evidence. The group – the witness had said – was being prepared, trained; and it had violent activism at its core. 'Saving life and the planet by murdering the 1 per cent – essentially that is it, and you have been at the centre of the planning.

'The witness says you are doing this with others, and that you have contacts – other groups, other networks – working together, internationally.'

* * *

Jenny and Mark had pinned their hopes on me. They were still depending on me for so much. I felt guilty letting them down – these two people, hopeless, incompetent, unable to keep up, but whom I had nevertheless got to know. And now they were dependent on me for their promotions and their reputations.

What was my emotion? Disappointment? No, I felt compassion.

Their investigation had yielded nothing, and within days of being held, we all had begun to realise this. Pressure on the police had been hysterical. Politicians, the rich and the media wanted charges to be brought, progress in the case and they needed a confession, a quantum leap – for the dam to break.

After three days they resorted to pleading: 'Listen, Bianca, we know you are involved, but we think you are just a minor part of the puzzle. Maybe just a propagandist for the cause. And it would be better for you to come clean and to let us have what you know – perhaps all you'll get is a warning, not even a sentence.'

When their soft pleadings failed, senior officers came in and hammered the table, questioned me through the night. Threatened me. Lawyers were offered, promising rigorous defence. Other officers from other police units around the world arrived and more questioning took place, and I insisted on being questioned in French, Spanish, German, even in Zulu by the South African team that arrived one night.

Through it all the panic kept rising.

The key to survival is to rise above yourself, to look down and see the curve of the planet, to hear the discord, the noise, and find the pattern, to pick out the keywords, to identify the common theme from the thousands of words and movements that reach you. From my imagined perch high above the skyline, I could see it all unfolding.

Outside the station, from the first day of the arrest, there was a constant vigil, thousands strong, which the police no longer even tried to move on – a strange midwinter occupation of this still bedraggled suburb, the beat of drums through the night, the glow of fires that flickered against my cell walls. The protests, this street carnival, grew by the day. We were all beginning to draw the lessons.

In the winter days I was held in Lewisham police station, cities, countries, continents were gripped by a fever – sitting cross legged in my cell I could see from horizon to horizon, turmoil spreading over the entire planet. I even heard it in the police station, the high frequency of panic – the short tempers, the slammed doors, the general quickening of the pulse.

Meridian had now been exposed – an armed and protected hideout for the rich, their last place of retreat on earth. The coordinates of the island archipelago had been leaked and published on every website and news outlet. Scale drawings, artists' impressions of the archipelago appeared on every front page, even photographs of building work – the details provided from a secret source. I floated above the narrow cell bed, my back straight, my legs crossed, my head erect – savouring the moment.

Had the police expected me to be surprised, and plead guilty in a gush of fear? Impressed with their policing. Grateful, even? I laughed to myself.

Days later I was released.

10

Present Day

BEHIND THE façade of our democracies is an immoveable, brutal force that cannot be dislodged with polite words or thanks. The period of open brutality – of pure class rule – was about to begin. I knew that I needed to get out of the station before the full realisation of the crisis had reached all countries, each country club, boardroom, secret service, and government. When parliament, elections, and the law, fail to protect the interests of the 1 per cent, the true nature of the global order is revealed.

Fascism is the executive tool of the 1 per cent when parliament no longer works for them. Crude? Simplistic? Yet this is exactly what was happening and those who had not studied our modern history would face its death squads once again – and the piddling One Percent Murders, the Red Terror – as it was already being called – would be seen for what it was, a breeze through a summer meadow.

* * *

Twelve days after I had been arrested, I was released. The police wanted to do everything in their power to mitigate the humiliation, to release me by a secret door or to drop me in a field – to avoid the cameras, the crowds, the jubilation.

I needed to get out while I could – publicly, in the glare of the cameras and publicity. Behind Mark's rosy face, Jenny's naivety, other forces were mobilizing.

The police had no alternative but to release me to the crowds – through the front door of the station. Trying to mitigate the disaster they let me go at 6 a.m. The mass encampment around the station was quiet, there was still a darkness like the dead of night, a frost in the air, and only the distant roar of the first aeroplanes, coming into the city's airports.

When the doors were opened, I stood for a second, felt the coldness of the morning envelop me, heard the first notes of the dawn chorus, and saw, spread out on the far pavements, on the embankments, and adjoining roads, hundreds of tents, some illuminated by torchlight. Against the side of the tents, placards, scribbled in coloured pen with hurried slogans: I Want You to Panic, This is What Democracy Looks Like, Occupy Meridian, Eliminate the One Percent and, between two lamp posts on the opposite side of the road, was a large banner, Free Bianca – Go on or Die!

Below the steps to the station, huddled around cameras on tripods, were the press – they were the first to see me, a cry went up and the bright glare of artificial lights quickly flooded the pavement. There was then a small stampede of journalists and then, behind them, demonstrators pushing their way towards me.

The night began to break, the light spreading across the sky as the city stirred. Jostling, trying to push through, I saw children, their faces flushed, holding placards – squeezing between the media scrum, elbowing themselves through.

One demonstrator – a face I recognised, a student of mine – had a megaphone over his shoulder and, around him, clearing a space, were a group of about thirty others, most dressed in black hoodies, florescent bands on their left arms. He shoved himself through, reached me, then indicated to the others to create a cordon, so I could move forward.

Three metres from the station, on the side of the road, was a small wall, the group moved towards it – chants had started, cheers as I stood on the wall, the group circled me, keeping the pack of journalists, and cameras away in their place. I was handed the megaphone.

I strung the megaphone around my shoulder and reached my arms into the air, my fists clenched – the cheering grew louder, then came together into a single chant, 'Go on or die!' I opened my hands, spread my fingers, widened my arms – slowly the noise faded, so all that could be heard was the clicking of cameras. For a moment I remained still, my arms raised, listening.

From deep in the crowd, I saw Elisa pushing herself forward, shouting to be let through. I called for a passage to be opened. When she reached me, I dropped down from the wall and cupped my hands around her face and kissed her. Her cheeks wet, her breath warm – I felt her life enter me. I kept hold of her hand as I climbed back onto the wall and lifted the megaphone to my lips. In the silence before I spoke all I could hear were the birds.

Already there were inroads into the winter, I thought, yet early signs of the transition are difficult to see among birds. Standing on the wall I tried to distinguish the birdsong – the percussive click of the robin, the rebuke of the blue tit, the squeal of the blackbird. I could now hear them all, like I had heard their songs in the city during the lockdown ten years before.

I felt the cold against my cheeks but sensed already the end of the winter. Still not speaking I lowered my arms; I let the birds sing undisturbed. For some months longer, these birds would still be fully occupied with nothing more than pure survival, squabbling for scraps of food, but already spring was being born. New life was now unmistakeably growing in the hard December soil – looking around me, to the hundreds of upturned faces, I saw the end of the long winter.

Acknowledgements

This peculiar story would never have seen the light of day if it wasn't for the help of comrades and friends: Ruby Abercrombie, Femi Aborisade, Fabiawari Batubo, Ray Bush, Selina Cohen, Jason Cohen, Gacheke Gachihi, May Lui, Yen Ly, Danny Millum, Abiodun Olamosu, Kristy Siegfried, Colin Stoneman, Mette Wiggen, Jörg Wiegratz, Andy Wynne. The encouragement and enthusiasm of Abiodun Olamosu and his publishing company, Books Farm House & Publishers, has been a source of pride and joy to me. Olamosu is a long-standing socialist and revolutionary and he has provided the prefect home for Bianca in our upside-down world.